War of the Unde
Book 2

Heartsong

A Gargoyle Monster Romance

S. E. Wendel

S. E. Wendel
se.wendel.author@gmail.com

Cover illustration by Bethany Gilbert Art
Interior graphics provided by Adobe Stock
ISBN: 9798988482840
ASIN: B0CC34M69T

This story is for everyone who struggles with chronic pain. I see you, and I know it sucks. Continue to advocate for yourself because no one deserves to live with it.

And if you're a migraine sufferer like me, you have my permission to flick anyone's nose the next time they ask if you've drunk enough water today.

Before You Begin...

I hope you're ready and excited for *Heartsong!* A few quick notes before you begin:

This is book 2 of the War of the Underhill series. You don't have to, but the best place to begin this series is with the prequel novella *Stone Hearts. Heartsong* can stand on its own, but you'll definitely get the best reading experience if you start with *Stone Hearts.*

As with *Stone Hearts,* this book includes a glossary of (mostly Welsh) phrases, places, and people in the back. There are also some chapter notes at the back to help explain a few historical aspects or just some facts I find fascinating. So don't be afraid to flip to the back.

Okay, enough of that! On with the show!

Prologue

Long ago, in a time when time was kept through song and stone and crown, a desperate people did a desperate thing. When Julius Caesar stepped onto the shores of Albion, with five legions at his back, the Pritani, the Celts of the Green Isle, turned to magick to save themselves.

Their magick-weavers, the druids, called upon the magicks of Albion using a language older than man. From the earth the druids pulled great stones, carving them into mighty warriors. To give them warmth, the druids offered their own blood—and to give them life, they used ancient magick. From the stones sprang terrible creatures with wings and claws and fangs.

Fiercer than a pack of wolves and stronger than the bears that once roamed Albion, the guardians fought alongside the Pritani against Romans, Angles, and Saxons for six hundred years.

But the magick that gave life to the guardians had been stolen, ripped from the earth and the fae who imbued it there so long ago, when they were the lords of Albion. And the fae did not suffer thieves. In one terrible blow, the vicious Faerie Queen Titania attacked, stripping away the magick that gave the guardians life and rendering them stone once again.

Killed or cursed, the guardians were no more.

For over a thousand years, what remained of their kind slept in stone slumber, time passing and the human world turning around them. Relegated to the mists of myth and legend, hope faded for the guardians.

But one escaped her kin's fate. One lived on to keep their stories and their memories alive.

Now, it is time for their story to begin again.

1

San Francisco, Present Day

With a puff of relief over her large knit scarf, Anna Kincaid hustled into the lobby of the newly renovated Milton Building. Sleek stone and an immaculate water feature with cascading ferns were the backdrop of her wide desk that faced the front doors.

Slipping behind it with her cup of piping hot macchiato—a little habit she'd picked up now that a cup of coffee wasn't an unaffordable luxury—Anna went about her morning routine, getting ready for the day's visitors to the new Gwyneth Collection. There was something soothing about the routine, something that helped her make baby steps every day in accepting that for once, something had gone right in her life.

If anyone had told Anna a year ago that she'd be happily sitting in a quiet museum, a genuine smile on her face for the visitors trickling in, she'd have called bullshit. With a degree in history with a focus on early-medieval England, Anna thought for sure she'd be bound for some crappy-paying admin job that slowly sucked the soul out of her. She'd resigned herself to that fate—if it paid and had benefits, she wouldn't complain. Aloud.

Instead, Anna found herself twirling in her ergonomic chair, looking forward to the day. Just over two months ago, after years of working in minimum wage and temp positions while performing financial acrobatics to make ends meet, Anna had applied to this position on a whim. A rich, eccentric couple had spent their lives collecting statues—mostly grotesques from around the world—and had decided to share their collection with the public. Anna's eyebrows had nearly hit her hairline in surprise while reading the job posting; it seemed too good to be true. Decent pay, not high but it had benefits and enough to pay the rent and fill the fridge. Mostly admin and front desk work mixed with docent duties. Yet the chance to work with actual history was too much temptation. That and the healthcare.

She'd promised herself she wouldn't go another year without it. Not with how bad her migraines were getting.

So Anna had pasted on the fake smile she'd worked her life to perfect, the one she threw at family court judges and skeptical welfare agents and unyielding debt collectors, and nailed the interview. Just a few minutes in the collection made her desperate for the job, if only to stay with the amazing pieces. She swore she could feel the weight falling off her shoulders when one of the co-owners of the collection, Carrie Gwyneth, called to offer her the job the next day.

Wednesday through Sunday, she sat in her cushy chair, waiting to greet visitors to the museum. Though not affiliated with other big museums in the California Bay Area, like the MOMA or de Young, the museum still pulled in regular traffic thanks to its prime location in the Presidio. Anna was proud to help show this place off to the public—and thrilled with the steady paycheck that paid the bills, bought occasional meals out, and provided her cat Captain all the wet food he could want.

The icing on the cake was that the Gwyneth Collection was, in a word, exquisite. During her first tour of the museum with Carrie after being hired, she'd openly gawped at the exhibits. The statues transfixed her in a way nothing, not even classical statues, ever had before.

Which was a little odd. There was nothing overtly beautiful about the Gwyneth statues. Most of the collection consisted of grotesques.

People mistakenly called them gargoyles—though the Gwyneths had some of those, too—but the grotesques weren't used to divert rainwater. Instead, they were free-standing statues that had adorned this cathedral and that capitol building. Many of them were monstrous, with flashing fangs and bat-like wings. They looked like demons, or what medieval Christians must have construed demons from. Some had horns like a ram, others like an ibex. All had claws on their hands and talons on their feet. But perhaps the most remarkable thing about them was the very stone they were carved from.

Like many of the patrons who visited the Gwyneth Collection, when Anna had originally thought of gargoyles, she'd imagined dreary gray monstrosities, carved from the gray or blonde stone used for the buildings they perched on. But the Gwyneths' came in all varieties of colors, from gray to white to a few pinks. Many looked to be cut from various shades of marble, others limestone or granite, and she swore one was hewn from an enormous block of obsidian.

Her favorite piece of the collection, however, wasn't one of the marble statues, not even the obsidian behemoth. No, her grotesque was a dark slate gray with veins of white and gold running through him, and sometimes Anna wondered if it was real gold striating his chest and arms. The statue had been rendered as a creature readying to attack. So many of the pieces crouched or had their wings unfurled, as if already in the heat of battle. Hers stood with knees slightly bent, wings just starting to unfurl. His arms flexed, claws extended. Ready for whatever came.

A familiar blush crept over Anna's face at the thought of calling the statue *him* and *her statue*. It felt wrong to be so proprietary over a hunk of rock, especially one she didn't and would never own. Still, whenever people gathered around her gray warrior, ogling and taking pictures and tittering over him, Anna felt an inexplicable wave of jealousy. Which was silly. Absolutely nuts.

"Good morning, Anna."

Anna smiled up at her boss and co-owner of the exhibit, Carrie

Gwyneth. Carrie was one of those women who could've been a mature thirty or a young fifty; she had that ethereal quality to her, skin luminous and blonde hair always in place. She didn't wear any makeup aside from a swipe of lipstick and mascara that Anna could see, and her nails were always perfectly manicured points. She was curvy, almost plump, and a little taller than average height, but the way she carried herself, she could've been one of those tall leggy early Hollywood stars, flouncing across a movie set.

With her regal air and color-coordinated pantsuits, Carrie could've come across as intimidating and cold; instead, she was one of the warmest, kindest people Anna had ever met. If a little odd.

"Morning. The new brochures arrived last night and they look great. I think the new graphic designer is going to work out," she chirped, still not totally used to this peppy person who now inhabited her body. She was used to quips and sarcasm and giving the world the middle finger because that's all it'd ever given her. Was this who she was when she was content? It was a strange feeling.

Carrie smiled, the hazel-gold of her eyes glimmering. She took the offered brochure, unfolding the paper to look at the high-res pictures they'd had a freelance designer come and take last month. Anna thought they showed all the photographed statues to the best effect, especially her gray warrior. She might be biased, though.

Carrie hummed in pleasure. "These are wonderful," she said, letting loose a trace of the lyrical accent Anna just couldn't place. The best she could determine was British but that didn't quite fit. It wasn't the posh accent of period dramas, nor the thicker northern accents. The Gwyneths said they came from Wales, but Anna didn't think that fit, either.

"Very good lighting and angles," Anna agreed.

Carrie hummed again. "They almost look as though they . . ." She smiled sadly, her gaze searching Anna's for a moment that stretched into awkward. "Were alive."

Anna swallowed hard. She liked Carrie, the woman was a great boss, all the other docents and staff loved her, but there were times like these when she made a shiver run up Anna's back.

"They're beautiful statues," Anna croaked.

"Yes. I'm pleased we found you, Anna. It means so much to Gavin and me, to have the statues surrounded by people who admire them as much as we do."

Anna bit the inside of her cheek to stop herself from saying something inane. She'd had more than one long conversation with her boss about her appreciation of them, what she liked and admired about the pieces, her interest in their history. Carrie or her husband Gavin always had some new, interesting tidbit to tell her, where they had acquired a piece, the lengths they went to gather them. But there was always something, just out of Anna's understanding; Carrie would look at her much as she was now, still serene but inexplicably sad, a look of longing carving deep shadows under her golden eyes. It made her seem older.

When Anna said nothing, Carrie cleared her throat. "I hate to ask, but would you be available to stay late tonight? The specialist we've been waiting on will be flying into San Francisco tonight and wanted to pop in around seven for an initial look."

"Oh, June Parkhurst?"

"Yes, we've been anxious to get Miss Parkhurst in and see what she thinks of the clan." Another of her oddities—Carrie had a way of saying *the clan* instead of *the collection.* As if they were more than statues and codices and art.

"Then yeah, I can stay to meet her."

"Wonderful!" Carrie smiled warmly. "She just wants to poke about and see what she's in for—shouldn't take more than an hour. To make up for it, take a long lunch and dinner is on the museum."

"Oh, you don't have—"

Carrie waved her hand in a sort of flourish, nixing Anna's polite refusal. She always did when Anna tried to decline their kindness. It wasn't that she was ungrateful, far from it, but she worried too much kindness and she'd come to rely on them. Anna hadn't relied on anyone in a very long time. She wasn't used to it, had spent her first few weeks wondering what Carrie and Gavin would *really* expect of her. Finally, after a month, Anna had started to realize that's just who Carrie was, always generous, always apologetic if she needed something extra from Anna.

"We take care of our people," she vividly remembered Gavin Gwyneth telling her on her second day, after she'd double and triple checked that the health plan was as robust as it looked. Specialists *and* dental *and* vision? *Swoon.*

At eight o'clock, the security doors unlocked themselves and a few patrons came in, shaking dew and clinging mist off their overcoats. Some were regulars, like the art grad student, loaded down with sketchbook and easel, who swore the statues were going to be her thesis; the older man, perpetually hefting around some Dostoevsky tragedy, who liked to sit and read under the obsidian behemoth because the creature "kept things quiet," as he liked to say; and the slick businessman who looked straight out of the 80s with his nice suits and silk scarves and coiffed hair.

Carrie gave her another smile and rapped her knuckles on Anna's desk before going to collect the new guests and give them a personal tour.

Anna grinned, getting comfortable in her big chair. She was happy for the day to start, and even though she had to stay late, she knew how to make the day better. She knew just where she'd take her long lunch.

Madness felt like a skipping record, crackling from one track to the next, never to hear the end or beginning of a song.

At least, that's what it'd felt like to Frey since records were invented.

Before then, it'd been swirling gray fog that sometimes revealed a face, a memory, a sound. If he focused, he could see through it, could peer past the madness with unseeing stone eyes into a world that thought him myth.

But now, everything was silent. Clear. The fog lifted, the song of his mind played in full.

And it was because his mate was near.

My heartsong.

A phantom growl, the memory of the sound, reverberated through Frey's mind, and he could almost feel it strumming in his throat. His body hadn't moved in almost fifteen-hundred years, and it hadn't been long after being turned to stone that he'd forgotten the sensation of movement. But now, now his mate was near, and he could remember growling; he could remember roaring and shouting and purring and speaking. He wanted to do all these things, especially for *her.*

He knew she was near because his senses had come more alive than they'd been in centuries. It was a maddening pattern with her, she would come and go, giving him precious hours of phantom sensation. Then she would leave again, taking his sanity with her.

He didn't even know what she looked like, not really. True, he shared a sort of consciousness with his fellow guardians. Since succumbing to the curse, Frey had felt his people in their stone prisons, had heard their whispers and whimpers. Sometimes he'd spoken with them, the fog clearing enough to peek out at another trapped soul. They had learned many things from each other, the stone sleep allowing for just enough awareness to hear and snatch images from the world that flowed around them. Many had retreated deep into this collective consciousness, the only comfort they had against the relentless tide of time.

Frey hadn't told his kin, but he had a second comfort now, waiting anxiously for when his mate would draw close. All he had was an impression of her, as even with his senses restored somewhat by her presence, the curse ensured that he couldn't quite *see*, couldn't quite *discern.* Dark hair. Eyes the color of rich earth. Tall for a human woman. That was all he knew, but it was enough for Frey. For now.

He didn't know what she looked like nor how she sounded, smelled, or tasted. But he would know. Soon. He had to believe it, had to hold onto this shred of hope with all his claws or else he would drift away, like so many had.

He had a mate, *his* mate, and it had to be enough.

Frey sensed her nearing, felt his stone flesh warm as she drew closer. He had no sense of day or night as a statue, but he'd come to realize that his woman took a meal near him. It was the clearest image he had of her, the back of her head, with those slight waves in her rich brown hair. He wanted to run his claws through that hair, use it to pull her close, into his body, where she could never leave him again.

Like most of his kind, Frey had always hoped to find his mate, his heartsong. Since their creation, over two thousand years ago, by a desperate clan of druids in the hills of what was now southern Wales, the guardians had only ever been able to sire younglings with their mates. Created to help the native Celts fight off the invading Romans, the druids had turned to magicks that were not their own, stealing from the fae themselves. From all manner of stone, the druids carved great statues, consummate warriors with bodies made for battle. Into the stone they poured blood and magick. The original spell had birthed them, but after the rock-born, the guardians had found their mates and become their own clans. Perhaps it was for fear of the creatures they had created that the druids ensured their numbers would always be low, but it wasn't the guardians they should have feared.

It had been like any other Gorsedd, the bonfires big and bright, and the dancing had gone on long into the night. All the guardian clans from across Albion had gathered at the Gorsedd, that night on Beltane, to celebrate the end of winter, the coming of spring, and, most importantly, for unmated guardians to find their mate.

Frey had had such hope, had felt it in his wing bases that this time it would happen for him. Just because the clans came together every few months for the Gorsedd didn't guarantee that a mate would be found. Not all attended and some didn't want to be mated until much later. The goddesses could be tricky like that, but Frey had been sure, so *sure*, that they would smile on him.

Instead, that night, there was only ruin.

He remembered the eerie light that had burst from the forest, blue and ghoulish. It sucked the very warmth from the bonfires, snuffing them like candles. The moon had been full and high, and guardians saw well in the dark—everyone beheld the fae on their fire-spitting mounts.

Frey had entered the battle with only his claws and his wits, weapons surrendered for the night of thanksgiving and celebration. He'd ripped through fae and beasts, all feeling the same under his claws. So many had been struck down in the first wave of attack, blood soaking the Gorsedd glen.

The second attack had been worse, so much worse. For centuries, Frey often wished that he'd been taken in the first wave. To go to the afterlife with honor and his kin.

Instead, he was caught in this stone hell with so many others.

The Faerie Queen had ridden her snapping, scaled mount through the crowd of them, casting a shimmering light across the glen that looked like the gray of dawn, but somehow without the promise of sun. She'd opened those perfect lips, stained with berries and blood, and cursed his kind, sucking their magick away.

Without it, they were mere blood and stone. Not enough to sustain life.

The fate of those frozen into their stone prisons had been much worse than dying. The centuries loomed across their scattered consciousness, a never-ending torment. From what Frey could remember, he was separated from his kin for a time, and those had been the hardest years of all, the silence overwhelming.

Slowly, as the years passed, he was rejoined with other stone captives, and it was a small comfort. There were dozens of them now, he thought. Why they were all gathered after being separated, he didn't know. Why they had been moved recently from the quiet room they'd shared for centuries, he didn't know.

At first, the new sounds and glimpses of many humans had overwhelmed his deadened senses. But then—

She stood before him.

Just out of reach.

Frey came alive, sensation and feeling exploding through him in a meteoric strike. It'd taken days to determine the reason for his sudden change, but it always came with glimpses of *her*.

He knew then that the centuries of emptiness and quiet torment were over.

Now, his existence had expanded and yet narrowed. It was all ever *her,* and he raged behind his stone prison, his blood just beyond flowing, his heart just beyond beating. Although she was human, Frey knew that she would be his. She was living hope for him. For all of the guardians.

He didn't know how or why, only that the goddesses wouldn't have sent him his mate now for no reason.

He had to believe it.

He had to get to her.

But how?

She didn't mind, she really didn't, but Anna was starting to regret agreeing to stay late that night to meet the art specialist. Sure, she'd be doing the same thing at home that she was here—eating takeout while watching sitcom reruns—but she'd be doing it on her couch in *pajamas*. Her truest form came with stretchy lounge pants and a cozy fleece hoodie with deep pockets. But she'd told Carrie she could and would, and dammit, Anna was determined to be a gold star employee.

Luckily, June Parkhurst (whom Anna totally hadn't stalked on social media off and on all evening, nope, not at all) arrived promptly at seven. She waved at Anna through the security doors, and Anna buzzed her in, knowing it was her thanks to all the internet stalking she definitely didn't do.

Wearing a modest but sleek green sheath dress underneath a light trench, Dr. Parkhurst walked inside from the late-autumn darkness exuding chic academia. Lithe and graceful, her long, slim limbs moved seamlessly under the sharp lines of her clothes. Her fiery red hair was pulled up into a perfectly messy bun, and large square-framed glasses accentuated the curves of her face and gray of her eyes. In a word, she was lovely.

Anna had that awful first moment of feeling entirely inferior; she was tallish for a woman, but Dr. Parkhurst, even in her low heels, was an amazon. Anna carried her weight well, but she certainly struggled with it, especially after college. Working desk jobs and having little free time or inclination to take care of herself between migraines had meant that she'd put on a few sizes. She didn't usually think much about her body beyond being an unlucky attachment to her often-aching head, but when faced with women who looked like actual fairy princesses, any mortal woman would feel a smidge inadequate.

That was, until Dr. Parkhurst gave her a small, shy smile, her long strides slowing as she cautiously approached Anna at her desk. There was something disarming about that smile, and it made Anna realize that, with her hands now wringing her purse strap, Dr. Parkhurst might actually be a little uncomfortable.

"Hi, I'm June Parkhurst from the—"

"Yes, hi! Nice to meet you!" Anna stuck her hand over the desk, and Dr. Parkhurst took it, giving her a limp, clammy handshake.

"Thank you for meeting me. I know it's after hours."

"That's perfectly fine. I love it here and don't mind showing off the clan—collection, I mean." Great, now Carrie had her personifying the statues, too.

But Dr. Parkhurst just smiled, and Anna went about collecting the few things she always carried with her on tours; key card, small flashlight, brochure, exhibit map, all the good stuff. It paid to be prepared for both the mundane and oddball questions.

"Anyway, off we go. I'm Anna by the way," she said, flourishing a hand in front of her nametag.

Dr. Parkhurst smiled, no laugh like she sometimes got, but she'd take it. The other woman's posture was ramrod straight, but Anna didn't think it was just because she came from old money.

"We really appreciate you looking at the collection, Dr. Parkhurst."

"Please, call me June. And it's me who's grateful. The art world is all abuzz with this exhibit, there's nothing really like it. I know a few people who'd kill to have this access." She cleared her throat and blushed, as if those handful of sentences were too much.

Anna smiled through the awkwardness, hoping she wasn't putting out some kind of vibe herself. Her internet snooping had revealed that June was somewhat of a genius recluse, had graduated with PhDs in art history *and* architecture by the time she was nineteen. After seven years in the field, she could have any position she wanted, prestigious fellowships at any Ivy League back East or Oxford or Cambridge across the pond. But she opted to stay on the West Coast instead, often working out of her family's estate in the ritzy Belvedere Tiburon area. The news media coverage on her was fairly old, around when she graduated, but since then, June had stuck to her work and her estate, meaning the media eventually got bored of her.

Anna supposed the museum should take it as a compliment that such a woman was willing to come out of her castle to look at them in person.

"So, would you like the general spiel we give visitors?"

June smiled politely. "I've done my homework, Anna."

Anna shifted the brochure against her chest to make sure the clipboard hid it.

The other woman cleared her throat. "Besides, I'm sure you're tired of giving the same speech today."

Anna noted the strained lines around June's eyes and decided to let the woman off the hook. She wasn't being rude, it was just painfully obvious she found the whole situation awkward.

"That's true. Sometimes I think I know what a parrot must feel like."

That got a real laugh out of June, and then there wasn't any reason to speak again because they'd entered the main gallery. The museum was a sprawl of smaller corridors with a statue at the end and sometimes small alcoves in the wall with others. They all branched off of a main corridor that essentially did a rectangular circuit back to the front lobby area, displaying the statues as well as other artifacts and information about early-medieval Europe. But there was one area, the gallery, where the main corridor expanded into a cathedral of history.

It always took Anna's breath away.

Easily three stories tall, the gallery had frosted skylights to let in natural light, which filtered down into the space to create a sort of glow against the whitewashed walls. The floors were a warm oak, a stunning contrast to the columns and pedestals. A second-floor gallery ringed by an elaborate banister hinted at more treasures above, but the main spectacle was on the ground floor. Arranged like Greek gods, with a faint blue alcove behind them for a splash of color, were the grotesques. They stood evenly spaced, in different lifelike poses. Some crouched or knelt, others stood or looked as though they prepared to jump. Many snarled or had their hands raised, sharp claws poised to attack.

No enigmatic smiling Italian merchant wives here.

Anna didn't know how the artists had captured such life and movement in the pieces, especially as the majority were supposedly from early-medieval Celtic sites, far away from any classical Greek influence. Some didn't seem sturdy enough to be balanced on the rooves of cathedrals, posed as they were on one foot. Carrie and Gavin had had stints put in to reinforce them and the whole museum was a climate-controlled environment. Anna shuddered to think about any of the statues plummeting to their demise.

She looked down the length of the gallery to assure herself, relieved to see her statue standing at the far side. She knew it was silly to worry about a statue, especially when this one was planted on two feet and looked sturdy as an oak, but she couldn't help it. She found his strong stance reassuring, the grim, determined lines of him always catching her eye. The artist had rendered him with a type of old pants that laced closed and ended at his calf, just above his elongated, taloned feet. It left that wide, heavily muscled chest bare—something Anna definitely didn't trace with her eyes every chance she got.

He was placed with several of the other largest pieces at the head of the gallery, but to her, he always stood out. The others were just as fierce, just as terrifying and strong, but there was something about her statue's face, the solid set of his jaw, that made Anna think he was looking out at the world, ready to meet it.

She glanced over at June, expecting to see her mouth open in wonder.

Instead, June was frowning. She did have a bit of awe about her, her eyes wide as she slowly turned her head one way then the other, trying to take everything in. But something seemed to trouble her, a line forming between her brows.

Anna started to ask if something was wrong, but June drifted toward one of the bigger pieces.

It was a male, tall and broad, hewn from what looked like granite. Not one of the flashier pieces, but many were drawn to him for his looks nonetheless. He too was in a battle pose, knees bent, claws and fangs flashing, but time hadn't been kind. One of his arms had been broken off at the elbow and on the same side, his horn was missing.

June looked up at him as many did, with pity.

But then she reached out, gently touching the base of his pedestal and sliding a finger along one of his time-worn talons.

"Oh, no," she murmured.

Anna watched, fascinated, as June continued to murmur to the statue as if she could console him. She'd heard about taking your work seriously, how sometimes inanimate objects could take on a life of their own, especially to artists, but this was a little extreme.

Still, she didn't judge. She called one of these statues *hers* in her head, after all.

"How long has he been like this?" asked June quietly without turning around.

"I believe the Gwyneths acquired him like that. They've done a lot of restoration to try and make sure nothing else happens, but no one knows where his arm or horn are."

June made a sad noise in her throat, and Anna decided to leave her to it. She was really only here to chaperone, after all. June was already an expert.

She meandered slowly, liking the new perspective of the pieces at night. There were recessed lights in the walls, and some light from the city outside filtered in from the peaked skylight, but the room was still much dimmer than during the day, bathed in a soft blue. Anna liked the shadows that played across the statues' stone faces. It made them look all the fiercer.

Twenty minutes must have passed as June and Anna slowly made their own ways down opposite sides of the gallery, June murmuring to herself or the statues and Anna pretending like she wasn't itching to get to her statue.

It was only because she'd looked down at her wrist watch to check the time that she noticed the mist curling around her ankles.

Anna yelped, thinking at first it was smoke, but it didn't burn the back of her throat like smoke. Looking around, she realized the mist billowed along the ground, about a foot tall. She took another breath but couldn't smell anything.

Heart racing, she called out to June.

"I think something's wrong," she said, striding across the gallery.

The fact that her heels didn't seem to make any noise along the hardwood made her breath quicken into a panicked staccato.

June blinked at her and then looked around, her brows shooting up her forehead.

"What—?"

The unzipping of nylon rope echoed across the gallery, and as if from nowhere, thick coils, like vines hanging from invisible trees, fell from the skylights above. Booted feet followed, and Anna watched in shock as a dozen men in black tactical gear slid down the ropes into the gallery.

There were shouts, men calling out to them, to one another.

Anna reached for June, but her hand was sluggish. She wobbled in her heels and felt her brain slosh against her skull when she turned too fast.

June stumbled nearby, hands out to keep her balance. She caught Anna's gaze and blinked slowly. "Mist," she said.

There was something in the mist.

Of course there's something in the mist! Mist doesn't happen in a museum gallery!

But Anna's mind wasn't working fast enough to register that. All she knew was that those dark figures were coming for them now, some with hands out, some with weapons already in their hands. She gulped at the *click* of a gun's safety being taken off.

"Run!" she cried to June and pushed her toward the nearest doorway. It led deeper into the museum, but there was no going the way they'd come with so many men and guns in the way.

June stumbled and clawed at the wall for support before disappearing into the next corridor. Anna followed, vision swimming, her limbs loose and wobbly like Jell-O left out at a barbeque. Her right heel caught on a chink in the floor, and it was enough to bring her down.

She hit the floor with a *thud* she heard but didn't feel, the clipboard and papers disappearing in the thickening mist. She choked and coughed, the coolness of it slipping like fingers into her nostrils.

Anna scrabbled along the ground, feeling the vibrations of all those boots hitting the wood floor. There were so many, coming closer.

Heart pounding, her desperate fingers found the corner of something. She crawled closer, ducking behind one of the statue pedestals. Holding her breath, she reached up and grabbed the solid stone and hauled herself onto her knees, just out of the worst of the mist.

Gasping for breath, eyes watering, the room churned and blurred. In the back of her mind, she knew she needed to get up, follow June, call Carrie, call the cops, and most important, get the fuck outta here, but her legs didn't want to move and her fingers didn't want to unclench from the stone.

She looked up at the statue hiding her, the mist leaving her dazed rather than panicked.

Anna realized she hid behind her statue, the gray warrior. He loomed above the room, body angled and ready to deal with whoever the hell had just broken into the museum.

She grasped the thick curve of his calf to pull herself upright.

Something rent through the world—she wasn't sure how or what, an invisible strike of lighting, potent and electric, that knocked her world on a new axis. The room crackled and shimmered with pinpoints of white light, and for a moment, Anna thought she was passing out.

The hard calf clutched in her hand grew warm.

In her haze, it took a moment to register a great gust hitting the top of her head. Something soft and warm slipped around her, blocking out the meager light.

A roar filled the gallery, making the windows and Anna shudder.

Then, silence.

No boots, no shouts, no safeties clicking off.

Until, somewhere in the room, someone hissed, "Well, shit."

A shriek like nothing she'd ever heard before crashed around her, and suddenly her hands were free to clap over her ears. The calf and the leg attached bunched and sprung up, off the pedestal, toward the boots and their guns.

A chorus of human cries went up as great bat-like wings extended almost from one side of the room to the other. Two huge flaps scattered the mist and the boots, sending everything back, away from where she crouched behind the pedestal.

She was grateful for a breath of clearer air but didn't know how much good it did her. She was seeing things. The statue, *her statue,* had come to life!

He cut a brutal figure, looming over six and half feet tall, each wing extending over twice as long. Those horns she'd thought noble arched from his head in wicked points, and the hands that had been poised for movement now had wicked claws bared, ready to strike. His back was wide and bulky with heaps of muscle to support the wings. A thin tail lashed the ground behind him, smacking the floor with angry snaps.

A distressed noise leaked out of her, a whimper of mourning for her sanity. Whatever was in the mist had her thinking statues came to life. Those sparks of white really had been her passing out, and now she was at the mercy of whoever these intruders were.

The monster rounded at her noise, and her throat clenched shut in terror. Blue-gray eyes burned in his hard, inhuman face. His snarl displayed a set of wicked fangs and flattened his sharp nose like a cat's.

Those eyes took her in, and something about him changed. His stance eased, his wings dropped infinitesimally.

A pair of boots inched forward, gun coming up.

With a roar, the monster whipped around, wings and tail smacking the boots across the room. Shouts rang out again, and then Anna's vision was taken up with the monster.

He came at her so fast, she couldn't react. He was there in a moment, crowding her, huge hands tipped in claws closing around her, trapping her against a muscled chest that was hard as stone but so, so warm.

He heaved a great breath, ruffling her hair, and then his wings snapped open.

The bottom of Anna's stomach dropped out of her.

With a crouch, a leap, and four great heaves of his wings, the monster took flight, crashing through the skylights and out into the cool night air. She screamed as glass tangled in her hair. Her legs dangled, and she felt herself slipping from his hold.

She wouldn't survive a four-story fall.

A grumbling noise vibrated from his chest, sinking into her own. His arms adjusted her, holding her more securely to the hard planes of his body as they gained height.

Cold air ripped through her clothes, but it was nothing to the burning heat of him.

He hiked her higher up his massive chest, his face falling into her hair.

With another grumbling sound, he growled, "*Mate.*"

3

Frey's body buzzed, pinpricks fizzling through him like blood rushing through a limb that'd gone to sleep. His heart beat an unsteady rhythm, unsure still quite what it was supposed to do. Everything took an effort, a moment to remember how it was supposed to work—all except flying.

He cut through the air, away from that strange place full of strange warriors and fae magick.

Ffyc, is there no escaping them?

A growl worked up his throat at how thickly the fae magick had hung in the air, nearly clogging his nostrils. And when it wasn't the cold, metallic tang of that entering his lungs, it was the hot, salty smell of a dozen human men.

He'd turned to stone under attack and came awake to much the same. Had the world truly changed so little?

Another small sound emanated below him, and Frey tightened his hold on his mate, clutched tight to his chest.

Where she belongs.

He rumbled happily, spiraling higher to try spotting somewhere safe to land.

His heartsong smelled of vanilla and flowers and something rich, like amber or freshly turned earth or petrichor right after a soaking rain. Frey filled his lungs with her scent, so much better than fae magick or human male, head swirling with all the sensations that beat at him. Hardest to ignore—

His mate screeched into his sensitive ears, making them twitch and an annoyed rumble work up his throat.

"Calm yourself, mate," he soothed. "I have you."

"Ohmigod you *talk!*" she yelped, and then screamed yet again.

Frey grumbled through a grimace. "Yes, I can speak your human tongue. My kin and I have learned many of your new words through our stone sleep."

His perfectly rational explanation, one he himself considered highly admirable given the challenges he and his kin faced in learning anything at all, was met with another screech and resumption of wriggling.

Frustration sat heavy on his tongue, but he swallowed it down. It was merely due to all the new sensations, the suddenness of finally, *finally* being free. He just needed a moment to get his bearings, assure their safety, and then purr sweet things for his mate.

That roiling frustration bled into a sharp anticipation when he realized—he could finally look his fill of her. It was night and she'd tucked her face away against his chest and arm, but soon he'd truly see her. The glimpse back in that strange hall hadn't been nearly enough.

Beating his great wings, Frey gained height, flying past tall buildings of stone and glass that spilled light from thousands of windows. It was unnerving how bright the night was in this world, most of the stars obscured in a colorless sky. He spiraled higher, seeking a safe place to take her.

Finally, a dark patch stood stark against the bright grid of the city, and Frey turned his head in that direction. The silhouette of trees and bright reflection of the moon in a small lake beckoned him, and he was mildly content when they landed in a quiet, wooded place.

He was proud that his legs knew what to do in landing, talons digging into good fresh earth. Though reluctantly, he set his mate on her feet—but didn't let her go.

Holding her by the shoulders, he did indeed look his fill of her.

Wide eyes were luminous in the moonlight, looking up at him with blatant surprise from a face gone pale. Plush lips had parted slightly, drawing his mind immediately to the human custom of kissing. Guardians sometimes did so, too, though he'd never taken to it. He was more than willing to let his mate's lips convince him, though.

She was tall for a human female, her dark hair falling in a thick, windswept cascade down her back. Heavy breasts and thick thighs, perfect to fill his hands, hid beneath some sort of knitted tunic and dark braies.

His heart thumped heavily in his chest, and the *knowing* the elders spoke of, the perfect ring one heard in their ear when finding their heartsong, crescendoed in his very soul.

She was here. He was alive, breathing, and *hers.*

She swayed forward, and Frey purred for her, enticing her closer. He bent his head, closing some of the distance between their heights, desperate to smell and taste and touch—

Another screech, and a bony knee smacked into his upper thigh.

Frey grunted, more out of surprise than hurt.

His mate twisted in his arms with a practiced yet still unwieldy swirl of her elbows, and he let her break free of his hold, a little stunned.

Was she aiming for my cock?

Goddesses, she was!

He let her get only a few steps before, with a leaping bound aided by his wings, he swept her up in his arms under her back and legs. He held her high on his chest, frowning down at her with displeasure.

Attacked by warriors and now his mate—what had the goddesses done?

"Be calm," he told her again.

"I will *not be calm!*" she yelped, wriggling harder than a fish on a hook.

Frey held tighter, trying not to hurt her but determined to keep her.

"I will not harm you. I swear it, on my honor." He narrowed his eyes at her flailing legs. "So there's no need to further assault me."

"Assault you? Assault *you?*" Her voice had gone high-pitched, a cadence even Frey, whose mother and sister had passed when he was young, knew was dangerous when it came to women.

"Yes, assault me. I assume you were aiming for my cock just then. The angle was wrong and I am likely too tall for that maneuver." Not that he intended to give her any reason to strike at him again.

She screeched again, a horrid sound he was growing to hate.

"Let me go!"

"I cannot," he said. "Not when I've waited so long for you, *cân fy nghalon.*"

Her movements ceased so suddenly that Frey had to catch his balance. Widening his stance, he peered down at his mate, curious what she'd do next. Those luminous, dark eyes were scowling at him. Also something he was coming to dislike.

"What *are you?*" she demanded. "You have wings! And horns!"

"And claws and fangs," he agreed, flashing his at her in a smirk. If possible, her face paled even further, and she seemed to ball up in his arms, as if to get away from him.

Stop frightening her, dolt.

"I am a guardian. My kind, we were made to protect. You have no need to fear me. *Especially* not you, my heartsong."

"I don't . . . you were a statue ten minutes ago!"

A dark growl worked up his chest, one he couldn't bite back even as he felt her shudder in fear at the sound.

"Yes. My kind was cursed over a thousand years ago. We've rotted in our stone prisons ever since. I do not know how or why I have come to be here, but I can only think it the work of the goddesses. They have brought me to you."

"W-what?" She started wriggling again.

"You awoke me, my heartsong. Your touch . . . when I felt it on my leg, the curse released me. I *woke*."

She shook her head, more vehemently than Frey thought necessary, and to his horror, her eyes began to glitter with tears.

"No," she groaned, "no no no no—that's not possible. Statues don't come to life!"

"My kind aren't statues. We are guardians, first made by the Pritani Celts of Albion and cursed by the Faerie Queen."

A hysterical sound, not quite a laugh, burst from her mouth. "Celts. Faerie Queen. With magick, I suppose."

"Rock, blood, and magick made us, yes. The Faerie Queen stole ours, those of us she did not slay, rendering us stone. None of us knew how to break our curse, but we have solved it tonight, you and I."

She blinked up at him, her head lolling from side to side in denial. "No . . ."

"You are my mate, my heartsong."

"No . . ."

"Your touch woke me from the stone sleep."

"No no no—"

"I am Frey," he said over her rambling, "of the Clawtip clan. Proud son of Uther and Angharad, descendant of Cadfan the Rock-Born, and your mate."

Another odd sound, a sort of long, low whine, came out of his mate's chest. Frey tried not to be too offended—he understood what a story he told and honestly couldn't quite believe this was happening himself. Any moment now, he expected to wake up from this dream of holding his mate close to his beating heart. Soon, he'd be back in that quiet room he'd spent centuries in, the silence of the curse deafening.

He held her a little tighter, desperate for that not to be so.

He needed this to be real, for her to be real. He couldn't go back.

"I-I don't . . ." She buried her face in her hands, fingers working at her temples. "I don't know what any of that means."

He purred for her again, trying to soothe her obvious discomfit. "What is your name?" he asked, trying to distract her, trying not to sound as eager as he was.

Reluctantly, quietly, she said, "Anna."

"Anna." A fine human name. "I have longed to find you and look upon you, my Anna. It may have taken centuries, but I regret none of the many years it took to bring me to you."

Through her hands, he heard a groan and something like, "Who says things like that?"

He gave her her peace, content to hold her and take in the smells of the trees and night air. There were few animal sounds, but then, all the wise animals would have hidden away at the arrival of such a deadly predator as him. Though it was disconcerting not to see many stars, the moon at least was familiar, the pearly orb ringed in blue as it shone upon them.

Frey waited as she continued her little circles—but she went on so long and with her brows drawn so low, he began to worry.

"Anna? Are you all right?"

"I need to go home," she said, "*now.* It's too much—I feel the migraine coming on." She groaned, body folding in on itself.

"You are ill?" The bottom fell out of his stomach.

No. Impossible. He wouldn't allow it.

"Bad headache," she said. "I get them. I need to go home and take my meds."

"We will get you anything you need, my Anna," he assured her. "Just direct me to your dwelling."

"Oh, no, you don't—wait wait wait—aah!"

With a bounding leap, Frey threw them back into the sky, his wings flapping mightily, his resolve hardening. They would get his mate her medicine, they would talk, he would explain things, and then, perhaps, she would let him kiss those pretty lips of hers.

He always did like a plan.

4

Anna clapped a hand over her mouth, muffling her scream as the city whizzed by in streaks of light. It was also to keep down the dinner sloshing in her rebelling stomach as she flew toward home in the arms of a fucking monster.

Guardian. Gargoyle. Grotesque. *Whatever!*

She was hallucinating. Or she really had passed out back in the gallery. Neither option seemed great, but it beat whatever this insanity was.

A groan escaped her as they banked hard, but when she was finally able to peel open an eye, she recognized the distinctive silhouette of Grace Cathedral's pair of towers. With a shaky hand, she patted the gargoyle, pointing him westward.

With a few tiny moves of his massive wings, he adjusted their course, and soon they were soaring over the Presidio.

As they drew closer to her building, Anna couldn't help the panic knotting her throat, threatening to cut off her airway. What was she thinking, showing a gargoyle where she lived?

It's either that or stay airborne.

Not an option. She'd do just about anything to get to her meds in time to avoid a full-blown migraine. Those began when she was fifteen, growing in number and severity as she moved out, scraped her way through college, then ingloriously entered the job market. Her new neurologist, whom she could see now thanks to the museum's health plan, emphasized that stress was likely a large factor in her headaches.

No surprise. Anna's life had been one big stressor after another. Between the unstable home life and parade of sketchy boyfriends her mother provided, Anna had left the moment she could. Nothing had ever been handed to her. She'd earned her place in college, earned every scholarship and grant and student job. She'd tried hard to make other degrees work, things high paying like accounting or coding, but her brain just didn't work that way. So she made do. She always made do.

The headaches had unfortunately been the only constant in her life for over ten years. Her mother never took much interest in her, and once she was out of sight, she was out of mind. Unless of course Shannon needed something like a few bucks to get her through the month.

Anna had gotten through college and her first handful of jobs barely managing the headaches. She'd lost jobs over not being able to work. She'd lost friendships not being able to go out. Last year, as she sat alone in her dark apartment on her birthday, she'd vowed to stop letting it rule her life. The night after her first shift at the museum, Anna had made every medical appointment she could.

She would get this under control and her life back.

That promise to herself beat desperately at her temples, the muscles of her forehead tight, making her a bit more amenable then she normally would've been to flying around the city at night in the arms of a mythical creature.

Amid a neighborhood of old Victorian homes and Art Deco shops, Anna pointed out her four-story brick apartment building with its artistic corbels and antique leaded windows. She may have cursed having an apartment on the top floor every time she came home from grocery shopping, but tonight it was a small favor.

She loved her little place. The rent, for San Francisco and the Presidio especially, was an absolute steal. Mostly because it was a one-bedroom on the fourth floor and the landlord had been in a pinch. Anna moved in five years ago and hadn't looked back. It was her home, her sanctuary, one she'd worked hard to build.

And now she was bringing a mythical creature inside.

The gargoyle brought them down in an elegant spiral, his landing gentle and graceful. Anna jumped out of his arms the moment she was close enough to the roof. A huge hand, tipped in claws, reached out to steady her when she stumbled.

Hurrying to the small door leading down into the building, Anna grasped the handle in both hands and yanked. Nothing.

"No no no." Tears welled in her eyes, the pressure at her temples pulling taut.

"Anna . . ."

"I don't have my keys," she mumbled. A frustrated tear escaped her lashes.

Good god a statue had come to life and she was freaking out about not having her keys to get into her apartment! Part of her realized how insane this was, and how incongruent her reaction, but she didn't want to fight the heavy blanket of denial muffling her reason. Focusing on getting home to treat the coming headache seemed easier than facing whatever break from reality tonight was.

The gargoyle—Frey—made a considering noise, looking about the rooftop and the trees ringing the building.

"Does your dwelling have a window?"

"Yeah," she sniffed. She took a step back, regarding him. "Yeah, and I don't lock the bathroom one."

He nodded and without preamble scooped her back up into his arms. Bolstered by the plan and desperate to get inside, Anna didn't even care, just pointed him in the right direction when he asked, "Where?"

With another great flap, he had them airborne again. They found her bathroom window, and by the meager glow of her little night-light mounted by the mirror inside, Anna got the sash open. Frey held her steady as she clambered through the narrow window, shoving her shoulders through and then wriggling to get her ample hips and backside in.

Catching herself on the lip of the ancient bathtub, she got her feet under her just in time to bound over to the vanity and throw open the top drawer. Her hands trembled as she ripped open a new box, hunting for the auto-injector, and lifted her shirt to dispense into the soft flesh of her middle.

"Anna, what do you do?" growled Frey from outside, drowning out the soft *click* of the injector needle.

"Medicine," she muttered.

She sighed when the second *click* came and threw the auto-injector into the wastebin. Placing her hand on the counter to steady herself, she closed her eyes as she felt the medicine crackle through her. It felt a bit like how all the old animations of nerves firing looked, blue bursts that went off in a series.

When it was over, she cracked open her eyes, tongue stuck to the roof of her mouth.

The gargoyle was still there, hovering just beyond the narrow bathroom window.

What did she do now?

She was inside and he was out—and he certainly wasn't fitting through that window. She could slam it shut and run into her room, dive under the covers, and pretend like none of this had happened. The gargoyle would be someone else's problem.

The temptation was there, an ugly sort of curiosity overcoming her as her head fizzed with the effects of the drug. Could she make it back to the window and slam it closed before he got a hand inside?

"Anna?"

Those blue-gray eyes never wavered from her, telling her he probably saw in the dark a lot better than her. He probably saw the way her thoughts were turning as she stood in the middle of her bathroom, chewing her cheek in indecision.

For some reason, the sound of her name, said so gently, with such . . . *longing* softened her. She looked, really looked at him, and she thought he seemed a little . . . frightened.

He was big and bad and twice her size, but he was also a mythical creature hovering outside her window. With just one phone call, she could have the cops here in a few minutes.

And then he'd probably get sent to some lab somewhere, kept in a different kind of prison.

Crap.

I'm gonna regret this—and blame it on the meds. Anna sighed.

Waving her hand, she told him, "Go around to the other side, I'll open the bigger window."

Anna heard him grumble something but didn't stay to listen. In a haze, she entered her dark apartment, wondering if she was crazy to let him in.

She stood in the dark of her living room, her cat Captain chirping happily and rubbing all over her feet once he realized she was home.

"I know, bud," she said numbly. "It's been a weird night."

Her feet didn't want to move, gripped with indecision. Her phone felt heavy in her back pocket as her heart began to beat fast and reedy. The worst of the pain was fading from her head, though she could count on getting woozy any minute now. Woozy often meant sleepy, and the best thing to do would be to just go to bed.

She watched as Frey landed without a sound on the fire escape through the main living room windows. He cut a dark, hulking figure, like something out of nightmares and fairy tales. The sharp tips of his wings and horns were distinctly inhuman, and she knew the moment those gray eyes found her through the darkness, a slight green glow to the pupil like a cat's. Those pinpricks of reflective green made her shiver.

He did nothing but stand there, waiting. For her.

Anna sucked in a breath, stomach clenched with dread.

"If he does anything sketchy, scratch the shit out of him," she told Captain before creeping over to the large window.

It took a bit of work getting the old thing open, but she only needed an inch. Big, claw-tipped fingers wrapped around the sash from the outside, and Anna gulped as he easily opened the creaky window. She retreated into the dark apartment, giving him room to maneuver his big body inside.

Feeling Captain at her feet, she knelt to pick him up and give her hands something to do.

She didn't know how he'd manage with those big wings of his, but she watched in amazement as they slipped under his arms to wrap around his chest, the curves of the wing claws hooking together like a clasp. He ducked inside with far more grace than she'd managed, fitting his body through the opening without hardly touching the frame. He shut the window again behind him, the small *snitch* of it closing quiet but resounding.

Alone inside with a gargoyle.

She buried her face in Captain's fuzzy belly.

"Where are your lights, Anna?" Frey asked, padding further into the room. "I know humans no longer use candles, but I do not know how you make the light."

His not knowing how to use lights somehow both baffled and calmed her somewhat. "Here," she said, walking over to the main switch and turning on the overhead light.

Frey winced at the sudden brightness, scowling up at the fixture. "Interesting. It is what you call electricity?"

"Yeah."

He turned a look on her, but she just shrugged, carrying Captain into her small kitchen. She didn't have the wherewithal to explain modern inventions to an ancient statue-come-to-life right now. In fact, if she thought about it any harder, she'd start laughing hysterically.

She went through the motions of feeding Captain, who didn't seem fazed by their houseguest. Anna focused on her movements, trying to keep the wooziness at bay.

The gargoyle didn't help by announcing, "I will check your dwelling for dangers."

"There's not—" But he was already gone, straight into her bedroom, tail lashing behind him.

Her apartment was small, one of a handful of one-bedroom units on the top floor of her building. A living room, kitchen with dining alcove and banquette, bedroom, and bathroom were the only rooms, yet he took his time doing a full security sweep.

Anna watched him from the corner of her eye, unsure what to do.

She'd just pulled out her phone to check the time when he appeared before her, an unhappy frown on his craggy face. She jumped at his sudden appearance, and his mouth drew even further downward.

"You scared me."

His nostrils flared and flattened, not unlike a cat's.

"You are sure this dwelling is secure."

"I mean, yes? I've never had a break-in before."

He looked down at her, unimpressed. "It is not an ideal location."

Anna blinked up at him. "Well, I like it and it's pretty close to work."

"I meant it is not very defensible. It is high, yes, but the trees obscure the best viewpoints. You cannot even see the front entrance. Is there not somewhere better, safer I can take you?"

"This is my apartment. My home." Anna shook her head and crossed her arms over her chest, the weight of the day starting to pull on her shoulders. "Look, there are security cameras on the front door. We're safe."

"Cameras . . .?"

Anna sighed. "A surveillance device. It records things."

She could tell from his blink that she'd only brought up more questions with her answer, so instead beat a hasty retreat to the fridge.

"You hungry?"

That stony face softened a little, the corners of his lips tipping up in a fond grin that made Anna's stomach swoop. For the first time, she remembered that this was *her* statue. The one she'd gawked over and ate lunch next to like a girl with a crush. All the inherent dynamism and charm was still there, but infinitely more dangerous now that he was flush with life. She'd never have guessed the quick cunning of those eyes that cut to her nor those oddly soft-looking lips that curled in a smile.

That showed off fangs.

Shudder.

"I do not require food as of yet, my Anna, but thank you."

Anna swallowed hard. "Okay." She grabbed a yogurt out of the fridge to give her stomach something to work on other than her nerves.

As she walked to the couch, she finally stole a glance at her phone. She put down the yogurt, regretting it as her stomach swirled seeing all the messages from Carrie.

Anna, the alarm tripped at the museum, are you all right?

Anna, there are intruders in the building GET OUT

Are you there? Anna, please respond, please say you're all right

Anna, please tell me you're safe. Authorities have been contacted.

Anna, museum is secured, please let me know you're safe

And the alarming last message:

> Anna, if I don't hear from you in an hour, Gavin and I will be at your apartment. We need to know you're safe.

"Shit shit shit . . ."

With a few quick taps, Anna held her phone up to her ear. The last thing she needed was her bosses here.

Frey watched on curiously as she chewed her bottom lip, listening to Carrie's phone ring. He jumped almost as much as Anna did when, on the second ring, Carrie picked up and screeched down the line, "ANNA!"

"Carrie, oh my god, I'm so sorry!"

"Anna, oh Anna, I'm so relieved to hear your voice! Please tell me you're safe."

"Yes, I'm at home right now."

The phone crackled as Carrie puffed with relief. "When we saw the security feed cut off—we were so worried! Are you all right? Are you hurt?"

Anna considered lying, saying the thieves must have come after she left, but—*June.*

"No, I'm fine. Is June okay? We got separated and I . . ." God, she'd just left the other woman there. True, she hadn't really had a choice, but she hadn't even thought of the art historian until now.

"Miss Parkhurst is safe. She was the one who called authorities. They arrived just after Gavin and I did."

Anna sighed in relief. "That's good. I'm so sorry, I don't know what happened. There was smoke, a gas or something. It had something in it, we were moving so slowly and we got separated. I got outside and just . . . stumbled home."

Her gaze couldn't help flicking to the very big part she was leaving out of the story. Frey looked on with a frown, obviously able to hear Carrie on the other end. His mouth had gone downturned again, this time with suspicion.

"I'm relieved to hear it. We were so worried about you. We never thought anything like this could happen."

Art theft was always a real possibility, but that it happened so soon after the museum opened was disconcerting. Given all the tactical gear, Anna had to assume the raid was well planned. How had they managed it in the ten weeks the museum had been open? Especially with all the high-tech, advanced security Gavin Gwyneth had embedded throughout.

"I'm so sorry this happened, Anna. Please let me know if you need anything. We found your things and have them safely with us. I hate to ask this, but can you come tomorrow to give a statement to the police?"

"Oh, sure, of course I can!"

"We'll be closed tomorrow, so don't worry about coming in as early as you usually do. Rest as much as you can. Gavin and I will handle everything. Oh, Anna, I'm so sorry!"

Again, she assured Carrie that she was all right, then a few more times, trying to convince herself as much as her boss. It took a while to get Carrie off the phone, and by the time Anna hung up, she felt wrung out and left to dry.

"I'll need to go in tomorrow," she told Frey as she rubbed her tired eyes. "Give a statement."

"Absolutely not."

"I have to. It's my job. And I have to tell them what happened. It'll look hella suspicious if I don't, and the last thing we need is someone coming to look around here."

Frey advanced on her, fangs flashing. Not in a smile. Anna reared back further into the couch, throwing her hands up to protect her face. Frey stopped at her flinch, but the snarl stayed on his lips.

"You cannot go back to that place. It isn't safe. It's been attacked once already. And it's soaking in *fae magick*." He spat the words like the deepest insult.

Anna shook her head. "They'd be crazy to come back, especially in broad daylight. I'll be fine. Besides, I need to get my things."

"Things are meaningless compared to your safety," he insisted, looming above her. His wings had unclipped from his chest and now hung above him, making him seem ten feet tall.

Sighing, Anna sat back on the couch, arms and legs crossed. She didn't feel like arguing now, especially when she already knew she'd be going in. Despite her tiredness and denial, she wanted answers.

What the hell happened tonight?

"Why don't you tell me again what happened to you," she told him. "I need to know everything because I don't . . . this is all craziness."

His mouth pinched into a displeased line, telling her without words he hadn't missed her redirect. Anna didn't care. She was tired, absolutely drained, and the echoes of a dissipated migraine teased at the circumference of her head. She'd get her answers from a man that should be myth, and then she'd see about the museum.

And then she was going to take the mother of all naps.

Frey silently unfolded a blanket from a nearby basket and laid it gently atop his sleeping mate. They had found the end of her strength, and she'd faded into slumber some time ago. Shamefully, perhaps sooner than he'd realized, so caught up he'd been in his story of what had befallen his kin.

She looked peaceful in sleep, the lines of worry and pain smoothed from her beautiful face.

A grumble worked up his throat. He wouldn't soon forget the sight of her stabbing herself in the stomach. *Medicine,* she'd said. What kind of medicine could possibly require that? He wouldn't allow any harm to come to his heartsong, even by her own hand.

He'd decided to brood on her strange medicine rather than the times she'd jumped back from him. His head already swirled with disbelief and sensations threatened to overwhelm him—he couldn't bear the thought that he scared his mate.

Curled up under the blanket, a hand tucked under her cheek, he could be content that she was comfortable and safe for now. A possessive need to care and protect curled around Frey's heart, stronger than anything he'd felt before.

He considered himself a proud male, independent and strong. He'd chased his share of women before but had never let his head be utterly turned. Yes, he'd longed for a mate, searched for her at every Gorsedd, yet he hadn't been prepared for the way the knowing shifted his whole world. He could feel it already, his aligning with her.

And she's my only connection to this world. Her world.

The one he knew was dead and gone, swallowed by the merciless mouth of time. He didn't understand why he'd awoken, only that it was because of Anna and her touch. But why him and why now—he had no answers.

Outside his mate's dwelling were even more unknowns. Flying tonight, he'd seen a city so large, so full of humans that it defied belief. The world had changed; he knew little of its rules or dangers.

How am I to protect a heartsong when hobbled from the start?

A tide of grief threatened to overwhelm him. Why now? In the quiet left by his mate asleep, leaving him to his thoughts, it all seemed . . . insurmountable.

Through the centuries, thanks to the link shared by the guardians who remained, they shared what information they could. They listened with stone ears to languages changing around them, blaring from records and radios and televisions. He knew something of this modern world, knew many of its words—but tonight, getting to interact with this new world, had shown him that he didn't *understand* it.

And because he didn't know or understand, until he did, he had to remain vigilant.

Frey prowled toward the windows with their poor view of the

street below. Guardians slept as humans did, but he doubted he'd sleep for days yet after being imprisoned so long. All the better to make safe his mate.

It wasn't long before her black feline joined him at the window. Rather rotund, the cat jumped onto the back of a plush chair beside him and began kneading the upholstery. It blinked up at him, a light purr vibrating from its chest.

"We shall both keep watch tonight," Frey told it, not unhappy for the company.

And so it was, the two of them watching over Anna and her dwelling. In the quiet, Frey watched—and listened.

5

Anna awoke to a medicine hangover and two paws concentrating roughly a million pounds of weight on her left cheek. Groaning, she put up a hand in self-defense as Captain's purr vibrated in her ear.

"Good morning, *cân fy nghalon.*"

"FUCK!"

With a gasp, Anna lurched upright, sending Captain springing away in a huff.

Anna's mouth fell open to see the gargoyle, Frey, standing close by, almost blending into the colorless light of predawn. The weak light caught on the sharp angles and contours of his face, the pointed curves of his horns, and the meaty thickness of his shoulders. His wings were laid almost delicately across his back in something of a cape, fastened below his throat by his hooked wing claws.

He wasn't a dream. Or a nightmare.

Her head fell into her hands and she groaned.

Why? Why why whywhywhywhy?

Things were just going too smoothly.

After scrubbing her palms across her eyes, she looked up to find him still there, still staring at her with those fathomless gray eyes, bright and glittering like polished steel.

"You're real," she finally croaked.

"Most assuredly, yes, I am. It is early yet. You may go back to sleep if you wish, I will continue to keep watch."

"Oh, ah . . . no, I should get up." She went to stand but realized she'd gotten herself tangled up in a blanket—one she didn't remember pulling out of the basket. Anna had vague memories of dozing off while sitting listening to him recount his story.

"Did you . . .?" She held the blanket up.

He nodded. "Your comfort is second only to your safety."

Blinking and blushing, Anna occupied her hands with folding up the blanket. "Thank you," she said, not quite able to keep his gaze. "Sorry I fell asleep on you."

"It was a full night," Frey said with what she thought must be a rueful smirk. It eased some of the hardness of his face, though she couldn't say it softened him. He was all hard angles and planes.

Anna stood and stretched, keenly aware that he watched every movement rapturously. It was kind of unnerving how his eyes followed her to the kitchen. It was as if he was just waiting for her to ask or say something, but she didn't know what.

His stare wasn't threatening, but it still felt better to put a bit of space between them.

"I have to go back to work this morning," she told him as she poured milk over some cereal. "I can leave the TV on or—"

"You will *not* go back there, today or ever."

This again.

"Yes, I am. It'd look suspicious as fuck if I didn't come in. I could lose my job."

"Then you shall find another one. Somewhere that is safer," he insisted, marching into the kitchen to press his point. Although, unlike last night, he was careful to leave his arms folded behind his back, tucked under his wings, which she was grateful for.

"It's not that simple, and it's not your call. I love this job. It was perfectly safe until . . ." She cleared her throat.

"I won't allow you to risk yourself."

"Again, not your call. And the other statues are there. They're . . ." The few bites of cereal she'd managed sunk like a weight in her stomach. "They're all like you, aren't they? Cursed, frozen in stone?"

Frey's mouth turned down in a grim line, face gone stony as a mountainside. "Yes. There were many of my kin in that place, I sensed them. Which is why you cannot go back—it is saturated in fae magick."

"You keep saying that, but I don't understand."

"The fae are who cursed us. They are cruel and devious. You cannot be anywhere near them."

Anna shook her head. She remembered him talking of them before, but in the whirlwind of last night, in the face of a gargoyle statue coming to life, it just hadn't sunk in. Between gargoyles and now fae apparently being real, it was a large coffee kind of morning.

"If they're the ones who cursed you," she reasoned, "then it would make sense their magick would be all around you, wouldn't it?"

Sense and magick don't belong in the same sentence.

Frey frowned, considering, but just as quickly shook his head, making his fall of dark hair shine in the burgeoning morning light.

"It felt different. Not the same."

Anna threw up her hands. "I don't want to argue about semantics. I need to get ready."

She pushed past him to scoop out Captain's breakfast as the little void monster made figure-eights between her legs and then hurried to her bathroom. Frey followed a step behind, that thunderous frown carved onto his brow.

"You will *not,* my Anna. I forbid it."

She pointed her toothbrush in warning. "Tone it down, buddy. You don't get to boss me around." She was barely accepting he was real at all; she certainly wasn't going to accept him giving her orders.

"I am not, I am simply concerned over your safety. You cannot—"

An odd sound escaped his throat, making Anna jerk in his direction—something like a gurgle or a groan, it was followed by a vicious hiss as Frey's gaze whipped to the windows. A rare clear San Francisco morning, Anna watched as dawn light spilled into the room, the sun climbing over the Coastal Range to the east.

Frey's great body shuddered, and he staggered forward, reaching out to her as if through water. His wings stiffened, his hands froze, and his eyes—

Anna shrieked in horror as his eyes bled of all light and life, going cold and dark as stone.

In a few mere moments, the apartment was bright with morning sun, illuminating the gargoyle statue in the middle of her apartment.

"Oh my god!" She lurched toward him, reaching out with trembling fingers to gently touch his cheek—and immediately recoiled when she only felt cool stone.

"Oh, no." Anna gazed up at him, desperate to see any signs of life, but he remained motionless. "Are . . . are you there? Frey?" she whispered, heart clenched with dread.

He didn't answer, as imposingly silent as he'd been in the museum.

That silence echoed through the apartment, as loud as a thunderstorm and just as devastating.

Anna's face scrunched with tears, sadness sudden and crushing bearing down on her. She couldn't explain it, she barely knew this mythic monster, but seeing him returned to stone . . .

Would he wake up again?

When it became clear he wouldn't, Anna finally backed away, catching herself on the bathroom doorframe. Splashing cold water and scrubbing her face barely did anything to the shock gripping her tighter than a fist.

She numbly went through changing her clothes and gathering the few things she had. Every few seconds, she looked at Frey, hoping to see that stone crumble away to reveal him again. But he was always where she'd left him, frozen and lifeless.

Shaken, Anna scooped Captain into her arms and hugged him tight. His warm little body and purr gave her some comfort.

Kissing his soft black forehead, she whispered, "Watch over him today, okay? I'll be back as soon as I can."

The Milton Building wasn't the hive of activity Anna thought it'd be. It wasn't that she wanted to navigate police tape and journalists to get into work, but the sight of the quiet street front was nearly as unnerving as the statue in her apartment.

A pair of squad cars were parked outside the building, but otherwise, it was the usual fare of people on their way to work. Anna wove through them across the sidewalk and hurried down the little alleyway between the Milton and its neighbor, using her fob to unlock the supply door.

Inside, the museum was eerily quiet. The wide heels of her boots clacked overloud on the stone tile as she made her way to the lobby. No other staff or docents loitered in the breakroom. No visitors shuffled toward the bathroom or side stairs up to the second level. It wasn't until she made the lobby that she finally spotted anyone.

Carrie and Gavin Gwyneth stood with two uniformed police officers as well as a suited detective near Anna's usual front desk.

Swallowing hard, Anna schooled her face into vague concern. She'd perfected the *No, I don't know anything, officer* routine after years of her mom refusing to press charges against her sometimes thieving, sometimes abusive, always crappy boyfriends.

Keep it brief, keep it simple.

And keep your job, she added. Because, as her mom had so helpfully pointed out when she was eighteen, Anna was too chubby to be a stripper. And now likely too old.

Her footsteps were deafening as she crossed to the small group, and she realized why only when she stopped at the side of her desk. The soothing cadence of the water feature was missing, the rippling flow having been turned off. In fact, all the lights were off, giving the slate-gray stone of the museum lobby a distinctly cavernous feel.

"Oh, Anna, I'm so relieved to see you." Carrie broke the circle she and the others had made to approach her, reaching out to grasp and squeeze her hands.

"I'm so sorry this happened," Anna said.

"No, we're sorry."

"We thought this building was secure," said Gavin.

Anna tried not to gulp at the forbidding set of his hauntingly beautiful face. Tall and muscled, Gavin Gwyneth had a refined male beauty that felt more suited to bygone eras. Anna had nearly choked on her coffee when she heard he'd had a career as a historian and archaeologist rather than an Armani model. Just like his wife, he could have been thirty or fifty, with severe cheekbones and a pin-straight nose. At first she'd thought his hair, cropped close at the bottom but longer and pushed away from his handsome face in an elegant sweep, prematurely gray, but it was actually the palest blonde.

She knew the luck, wealth, and beauty distribution system wasn't fair, but damn.

Still, he was the kind of handsome that seemed to repel rather than attract. She'd never seen an employee or patron fawn over him, even though all the staff agreed he was the prettiest man they'd ever seen in real life. He'd never shown up with a pretty young thing hanging on his arm, only ever alone or with his wife. He was more often in immaculately tailored tweed or sweaters than flashy suits, and he drove a luxury but otherwise nondescript sedan. So much about him just seemed unreal.

Like a lightning bolt, sudden and sizzling, Frey's words zinged through her.

Fae magick.

Fae.

No no no, she wouldn't let the mythical monster in her apartment get to her—even if her heart gave a suspicious lurch remembering the sight of him turning back to stone.

Don't think about it. Don't ask questions.

Asking questions just brought trouble. Poking around where she wasn't wanted and wasn't supposed to be only ever brought *consequences*.

Still, the only reason she didn't quake in fear under the intense stare of Gavin Gwyneth was that his anger didn't seem to be for her. The policemen shuffled their feet, as if the breach in the museum's security was somehow their fault.

"Like I said, Mr. Gwyneth," said the detective, "unfortunately thieves are getting high tech. For every advance in security, there's always someone on the back end making double selling a way in."

Gavin's nostrils flared slightly with an unhappy huff, and if possible, his brows lowered even more.

Carrie patted Anna's hand, drawing her into the loose circle the group made.

"This is Miss Anna Kincaid, she was on duty last night." Carrie's eyes were full of guilt when she looked at Anna, saying, "I'm so sorry. Never again, Anna."

All she could do was shake her head, unprepared for the devastation Carrie seemed to feel.

"I'll do everything I can to help."

"I'm Detective Ramirez. I'll be leading this case."

She met and held the gaze of the detective, who gave her an assessing look before diving into initial questions. Anna went through her night, from eating takeout to June arriving exactly at seven. She walked them through the gallery tour, then how the room had filled with gas.

Here goes.

"There was something in it. I felt woozy almost immediately, like I was swimming through the air. I pushed June toward the next hallway. I fell and lost my things. I don't remember much after that—I think I stumbled outside and I . . . I must have gone into autopilot and walked home."

"You made it home last night?"

"Yes."

"Into your apartment?"

"Yes."

"Without your keys."

"A neighbor let me in and I'd forgotten to lock my front door," she said, careful not to make it too quick or too late. "I must have passed out once I got home. I finally woke up to answer Carrie's texts."

"Miss Parkhurst was able to get outside and call for help. But you went home."

There wasn't a question in there, but Anna answered, "I think I inhaled more than her. Because I fell. I can show you the bruises on my knees."

The detective made a few more notes in a little book, giving nothing away. With a swish, he closed the leather flap, looking her, Carrie, and Gavin over before saying, "We'll need to talk with Miss Parkhurst."

"She'll be here in a few minutes," Carrie said.

Anna's stomach clenched. *How much did she see?*

She worked to keep the anxiety from her face as the detective made a few more comments. Finally, he asked to see the gallery once again.

"I'll take you," agreed Gavin, extending his arm to indicate the men should proceed. Over their heads, he and his wife exchanged serious looks.

Anna didn't know what passed between them, but it was something to witness seeing a couple on the same wavelength communicate so much with just a few facial expressions. It was almost unnerving how keyed into each other the Gwyneths were.

Soon enough, it was just Anna and Carrie left at the desk—and one of the uniformed officers to keep an eye on the front door. And them.

Carrie waved her around the desk, and from the footwell pulled a beautifully woven basket. All of Anna's things—purse, keys, lanyard, clipboard—were collected neatly inside.

"I'm glad at least your things were easy to find, and nothing seemed broken." Carrie slid the basket to her, and Anna allowed a smidge of relief just to see and hold her things again. She'd felt vulnerable making even the well-known walk from home to work with just her phone.

"Thank you."

"How are you feeling?" Carrie asked. "Did the gas have any lingering side effects? Should we take you to hospital?"

"No no," Anna insisted, waving away Carrie's concern. "I'm fine. Slept it off."

"No headaches?"

Anna winced. She wasn't usually one to share details with her boss, but she'd had to take two sick days already in her short stint at the museum due to her migraines. That and Carrie had a kind way about her that just had truths spilling out of Anna.

Carrie made an unhappy noise in her throat. "Sit, please."

Plopping down in her chair, Anna watched in surprise as Carrie leaned over her to check her pupils. After a murmured, "May I?" and nod from Anna, she then gently probed her hairline and temples. With a considering hum, Carrie leaned back with a final touch to the center of Anna's forehead.

It was strange, but just the little contact had the lingering ache of last night's migraine seeping away.

Probably just a placebo from being touched gently by a maternal figure.

Not that she was desperate for such a thing.

Not at all.

Carrie didn't miss Anna's uncontrollable sigh of relief. One golden brow arched and she asked, "You've made appointments with a specialist?"

"Yes, I'm seeing the neurologist in a few weeks."

"Excellent. I'm glad to hear it." Carrie cleared her throat and a sheepish grin spread across her face, tipping the scales again toward her being closer to thirty. "I'm sorry to be so nosy. I just want to make sure you get the care you need. I was a doctor in the war. I take these things to heart."

Anna stopped her jaw from falling to the floor but only just.

Move over Most Interesting Man Alive.

Who were her bosses? Seriously.

"That's . . . I didn't know you were a doctor."

Carrie blinked, color rising in her cheeks. "It was a long time ago."

She was spared Anna's questions when a light tap at the door drew their attention.

June Parkhurst was even lovelier in the daylight, all warm reds and golds and browns, her tall frame swathed in a soft, emerald-green sweater dress. She would have looked like a princess if it weren't for the obvious concern marring her expression as the officer opened the door for her. He ushered her inside and pointed toward Anna and Carrie at the front desk.

"Wait over there please, Miss Parkhurst," he said, then turned to speak into his radio.

June approached cautiously, gaze bouncing between Anna and Carrie, her long fingers clenched in the knit cuffs of her dress.

"Hello again," Anna said with an awkward smile.

"Thank you so much for coming." Carrie hurried around the desk to squeeze June's hands, too. "I'm so sorry this happened, Miss Parkhurst."

"Please, call me June." Gently pulling her hands away, June said, "I'm sorry about the pieces. I only got a brief look at them, but they're amazing. I can't believe someone would do this."

Carrie shook her head sadly. "We never imagined something like this would happen."

"Do you know what was taken?"

Everything in Anna, from throat to stomach to toes, clenched.

"Two of the clan statues," Carrie answered with a genuine mournfulness, as if it were family members kidnapped. "The large obsidian male and . . ." She turned her sad gaze on Anna, "the big gray male at the head of the gallery."

"Oh no!" Anna gasped. And it wasn't for show.

Carrie reached out to pat her hand in sympathy. "I know you liked him. He was my . . . one of my favorites, too."

"It's unbelievable that they made off with two huge statues like that," said June, a slight frown disrupting the freckles on her forehead. "They didn't go for anything smaller?"

"A few other small things were taken, but nothing of much importance. Not like the statues."

"What kind of thieves would do that? It's hard enough selling a small stolen Matisse let alone a giant statue."

"Did the cameras get anything?" Anna asked through numb lips. *Should have thought of that sooner!* She blamed it on shock.

"No, they were disabled. They shouldn't have been able to." Carrie's face went stony, an anger simmering under the surface Anna had never seen before and that tipped the scales again towards her being fifty.

Static crackled through the air, the other officers confirming through the radio that they were on their way back to the lobby.

Looking between them again, June turned suddenly to Anna and said, "Can you show me the bathrooms?"

"Oh, um, they're down the hall to your—"

"Can you *show me.* Please."

Anna nodded slowly. "Sure. Of course."

She managed to give Carrie a *what can you do* grin before leading June from the lobby to the bathrooms.

They walked in silence, and Anna could feel both the officer and Carrie's gazes on their backs as they went. With every step, it felt as though June's anxiety bled into her, so that when they finally made the bathrooms and the door swished shut behind them, Anna's breathing had gone labored and her heartbeat rapid.

"I didn't want to say too much out there."

Anna stared at June in one of the mirrors. The other woman had wrapped her arms around herself, and her shoulders hunched as if to make herself smaller.

"There was something . . ." June's jaw worked, and it took her another moment to say, "I saw something last night. You got me into the next hallway, and I ran out the emergency exit. I turned around in the alley but you weren't there. And then there was this huge crash and I looked up and . . ."

June met her gaze in the mirror, those big gray eyes wide and beseeching.

"There must have been something in the gas," Anna forced herself to say through her dry throat.

"Of course there was. It was some sort of sedative, to knock us out. But I . . . I got out. I wasn't breathing it anymore. And I saw . . ." June took a sharp breath. "I thought I saw something fly away. Carrying somebody else."

Anna swallowed hard. "Like a helicopter?"

"Like a statue come to life."

The blood drained from her face. "One of the statues . . .?"

June nodded gravely, those eyes trained on her.

Careful careful careful.

Anna's guts clenched and knotted with a sick sort of anxiety. She'd already done so much lying today. She wasn't a righteous person, knew the world was a complex tapestry of grays, and had lied her way out of plenty of situations growing up. But she'd made a promise to herself when she was finally on her own that things would be different. She would try not to lie or obfuscate to get out of things.

That was the plan before the world threw so many fucking curveballs my way.

Should it worry her that she lied to the police and her bosses with such ease? What did it say about her that she was going to lie to June, who looked so vulnerable, like what she needed the most in this world was a friend and ally?

Anna wished it could be different. She was all for female solidarity, and it would be amazing to just spill her guts to the one person who maybe would understand.

But she had a guy in her apartment who needed her help—one who was currently a statue that the Gwyneths and police considered stolen property. The universe was a bitch sometimes, and Anna knew better than most that she had to protect herself first.

Wishes don't do shit.

So Anna did what she had to do. She gaslit. She lied.

"I don't remember much. It was mostly shapes. Whatever was in that gas, it had me seeing things. I barely remember getting home last night."

June stood silently with her answer for a long, horrible moment.

"I remember getting out," said June slowly.

Anna shook her head. "I don't."

She broke their contact by running a faucet and going through the motions of washing her hands. A skitter went up her spine when June came alongside her, the other woman's coiled nerves and suspicions pressing against her like a physical touch.

"What happened last night wasn't normal, even for art theft. This place . . . it isn't a normal museum."

Anna bit back her humorless laugh. *Oh, what an understatement.*

6

Anna didn't get back to her apartment until late that afternoon, two grocery bags and a heaping dollop of anxiety weighing her down.

The rest of the day had been painfully slow, going over her story again and again, answering the same question just phrased differently over and over. They interviewed Anna with June, separately from everyone else, in front of Carrie, in front of Gavin. Every combination. Her jaw and throat ached from all the talking, and she couldn't wait to crack open the new jar of honey and stir it into some hot lemon water.

She heard Captain hit the floor and pad into the kitchen to inspect what she'd brought. He chirped and meowed in greeting, weaving between her legs.

"Yes, I got you stuff," she assured him. Leaning down, she picked him up to hold like a baby and bury her face in his soft tummy. "How's our guest?"

Captain only chirruped again and smacked her with his paw for touching the tummy.

She put him back down and followed him into the living room.

The knot of her stomach only twisted tighter when she beheld Frey exactly as she'd left him. The saturated light of late afternoon cast deep shadows across his sharp angles, catching in the textures and undulations in his stone skin.

Hugging herself, Anna rounded the couch so she could see the side of his face.

That same anguished howl was frozen on his lips, and Anna hated to see it. Although stone, the despair was real in his unseeing eyes.

Captain's purr cut through the sad silence of the apartment, and Anna watched in surprise as her cat wove around the gargoyle's stone legs before folding himself into a loaf between Frey's feet.

Despite being a street cat for years, Captain loved everyone. Even non-human houseguests, apparently.

"Kept him company, huh?" Something about that gave her a little comfort.

Her cat purred harder and began rolling around between the stone legs and rubbing his big cheeks against the gargoyle's thick calves.

Mollified, Anna returned to the kitchen to deal with the groceries.

She hadn't known what to get, unsure if she'd have a houseguest or statue when she got home, but had opted for some meal options. She had to hope he'd wake up, and therefore needed to be prepared.

The guy hasn't eaten in over a thousand years.

Maybe it was crazy to hope he woke up again—things would be easier if he just remained a statue. If last night was just a fluke.

But Anna knew what it felt like to be trapped. To want out.

Her whole childhood had been a string of rundown apartments and crappy boyfriends, her mother unable to be alone for more than a few weeks. Shannon Kincaid was someone who needed to be taken care of, provided for, even if what a man could give came with fists and shouting. By the time she was eight, Anna was counting down the days until she was eighteen and could leave.

Her mother had rarely shown interest in her, and in the last weeks of living together, hadn't been quiet about what a burden having Anna was. How it limited her options. How it tied her down. Anna had borne it silently, then at the first opportunity, left. She rarely spoke to her mother; just obligatory holiday and birthday greetings, most of which were done via text message.

It wasn't some magical curse, no, but Anna knew what it was to be desperate. To want to escape. To look fate in the eye and shout *fuck you.*

So yeah, she hoped the gargoyle woke up.

She also hoped he liked chicken alfredo.

The noodles were almost al dente and the sauce just starting to simmer when it happened.

Anna was at the stove, ruminating on the continued lack of news about the heist. She'd remarked to Carrie that she was surprised none of the local news channels or papers had caught wind and turned up to poke around. Her boss had smiled wanly. *"We're going to keep it quiet."*

Sure, she could get behind that. In Anna's experience, you never invited trouble—and that meant keeping away from cops and reporters, among others. However, Anna didn't think things like this could necessarily be kept quiet. They had a way of getting out, of creating buzz. Everyone loved a juicy theft story.

Still, there were no reporters around the museum when she left after the interviews were finally over. Detective Ramirez had gotten promises from all of them to stay in town and stay in touch as he investigated.

Carrie had assured her everything would be fine.

"We'll need a few days to get things in order," Gavin had added. *"Everyone has the rest of the week off."*

The idea of having two paid days off, followed by the false weekend she and the others had on Monday and Tuesday, was almost as strange as the keeping the theft quiet.

By the time the sun had gone down, the pots were all beginning to boil and she was busy thinking over why exactly it was a bad idea to go to the news. A crackling sound reached her from the living room, like gravel spilling from a truck.

Captain came tearing into the kitchen, paws smacking on the linoleum.

A great whoosh of air, then the sound of something buffeting the couch.

"ANNA!"

Heart in her throat, Anna jumped away from the stove and ran into the living room.

Frey stood where a statue had once been, thick black hair whipping about his head as he looked frantically around the room.

When those gray eyes caught her, they held.

"You're awake!" she gasped.

A forlorn sound, like a groan and a growl all in one, emanated from his throat. Then he was stalking toward her, all burning eyes and arching wings.

Anna could only watch him come, stunned by the fearsome sight he made. She didn't know whether to be terrified or awed. Didn't matter—in a moment, he caught her in his arms, crushing her to his chest and wrapping his arms and wings around her, cocooning them in velvety darkness.

Too shocked to do anything else, Anna let herself be hugged tight to his hard body, cheek squished into his pectoral. The claws of one hand fisted in the material of her shirt while the other bore into her hair to hold her still.

Pulled to her tiptoes, Frey took most of her weight, holding her up as a purr rumbled from his chest and throat. With her ear mashed into his pec, Anna heard the wild cadence of his racing heart. And held so tightly, she felt how he trembled, ever so slightly.

With a light tug on her hair, Frey drew her head back.

Anna held her breath as, with the utmost gentleness, he touched his forehead to hers, careful of his horns.

"My Anna," he whispered, "*cân fy nghalon. Fy nghariad.*"

Swallowing the inexplicable tears welling along her lashes, Anna dared to touch the tense line of his jaw.

"Are you okay?"

A shuddering breath rushed out of him, puffing against her lips.

"I didn't realize . . . I never imagined I would return to stone. I thought the curse was broken."

When he leaned back, a chill rushed in where their skin had touched—but then his big hands cupped her face, as if he needed to hold onto her with both hands. It forced her to keep that gray gaze of his, sunken now with a deep despair that tugged at her heart.

She probably should have been terrified, having this huge gargoyle pressed to her from knee to chest, those wicked claws precariously close to her eyes. But even in the face of his devastation, his touch was achingly gentle, and Anna didn't feel the same trepidation as last night.

Perhaps the shock had worn off.

Perhaps, like always, life had decided to throw her another curveball and she just had to stand at bat.

And . . . perhaps she was desperately lonely herself.

"You don't normally turn to stone in the day? Or at least sleep?"

His lips pulled thin around his sharp fangs, and the sight of them did finally spark a hint of trepidation, though she made herself stare at them until her stomach untwisted. "No, never. My kind were made by humans; we follow the daylight like them and take our rest at night. It is the curse. It is not fully broken." He spat the words, nose wrinkling like Captain's did when he spotted the rival tabby one building over.

"Hey." Anna gripped his wrists, her fingers not quite meeting. Under her gentle but firm hold, she felt how he trembled. "It's going to be okay. You're awake now. That's something."

Her mantra may not have been the most inspirational, but *that's something* had gotten her through more than one rock bottom. There was always something to be grateful for, always a silver lining to find.

It could be exhausting trying to find anything positive, but the alternative was to buckle, even break.

She'd seen her fair share of broken people—broken hearts unable to empathize, broken minds unable to communicate, broken souls unable to do anything but harm. Anna had promised herself a long time ago that life wouldn't break her.

Drawing another long breath into his great chest, Frey seemed to steady. Somehow, he became bigger, sturdier. His shoulders squared just a little, his wings arched just a little higher. And something about that pleased Anna.

"Thank you," he murmured a moment before drawing her into another crushing embrace.

Anna had never been a hugger, nor one for a lot of physical contact—but maybe that was because it hadn't been given much before. She liked the solid weight of his arms, the unrelenting warmth of his chest. She just stopped herself from sighing in pleasure.

Okay, this medieval gargoyle was a good hugger. No need to get sentimental over it.

It was another long moment before Frey finally released her, though his hands stayed on her shoulders. He smiled down at her, some of that confidence from the night before returning.

He looked her over, and slowly that smile faded.

"You are in different clothing."

"Well, yeah. I changed this morning." Where was he going with this?

"You left."

Oh. This.

Anna stepped out of his grip, all the warm fuzzies leaking out of her, and turned back into the kitchen.

"I went to work, yes."

"My mate," he said, voice gone to a growl, "I *told you,* you cannot."

7

He'd displeased his mate, that was abundantly clear. The clang of their cutlery on her fine white ceramic dishes were overloud in the sucking silence of the meal.

Normally, Frey would've been humbled and effusive in his praise to eat a meal prepared by his own heartsong. Feeding a mate, a partner, the one with whom you raised younglings, was sacred amongst his kind; it was protection, caring, sustenance. It was a basic principle of being a mate worth a damn.

He recognized the chicken and the taste of heavy cream, though the noodles and types of vegetables and spices she'd added were new to him. Frey didn't care for the way the vegetables went slippery as he chewed, sliding down his throat in a mushy glide, but he said nothing. He was alive and awake, his belly full of warm, real food, and he sat across from his heartsong.

If only she'd stop scowling at him.

And if only he knew what to do with the cutlery she'd given him. The blunted knife was useless and the spoon was far too small for much. He mastered the fork quickly enough, though it was inadequately sized for his hand.

Still, he made do, as well as many appreciative sounds. It wasn't the finest meal he'd ever had, but it was the best because his mate presented it to him. The vegetables notwithstanding.

Soon, he would prepare her a proper meal. He'd prove to her what a good mate he could be. He may not yet understand this modern world of hers, but cooking, feeding one's partner, was essential, elemental. He didn't need the intricate machines littering her kitchen; just a fire and a will to please.

Maybe that will soften her scowl.

Not that he disliked her scowl—far from it, he found her spark of ferociousness mightily attractive. What he didn't appreciate was that he hardly deserved it for being right. She shouldn't have left and put herself in danger.

Tonight, he had to endeavor to convince her to stay within the safety of the dwelling where he could . . .

He had to persuade her now, so that if he was again confined to his stone prison, he could at least be at ease knowing she was safe.

The memory of being ripped away from his mate and the living world again soured his stomach, and he pushed his plate away.

"Done?" she asked, not waiting for an answer to whisk his plate away into the kitchen.

Frey turned in his seat to keep her in his sights. The chair gave an ominous creak under his bulk, and he dared not even twitch his wings for fear of splitting the wood in two.

Finding adequate furnishings and cutlery would be their first task when they made a nest of their own.

He couldn't help a pleased rumble at the thought of making a nest for his mate. Back within the clanhome he shared with his kin, he had a large dwelling, full of caves ready to be filled with a heartsong and everything she could need. It'd been lonely living in such a place after the deaths of his mother and sister, so Frey had spent much of his manhood collecting everything a mate could need. Since he didn't know what she'd like, he'd gathered a bit of everything.

There was so much lost to him and his kind, but he felt the loss of his dwelling most keenly then. Frey had to hope she wouldn't hold his lack of preparation against him. He had nothing to offer but himself now, and it would have to be enough. He would strive to be enough.

Frey didn't yet know her well, but Anna pleased him greatly. A meek mate would never have been for him. She was quick with her words and wit, as well as a sharp cut of her gaze from the corner of her eye. Her brows were always moving, a tell to her moods. And although they were often downturned at him, he enjoyed her fire.

He watched her in the kitchen, admiring her lovely form. She was all lush curves and rich brown hair. Round, plush lips tempted him to nip with his fangs, and the luscious flesh of her backside would fill his palms perfectly. Yes, he couldn't wait for the time when she would come to him happily; rather than attacking the plates under a stream of hot water, she'd round the table to him and lower herself into his lap to receive his kisses and nips and lascivious promises whispered into her—

"My bosses, the ones who own the museum, they think two statues were stolen," said Anna from the sink. "You and another one. So those guys did make off with one of . . . your people."

Her words sobered him. "Why would they have stolen one of us?"

"I don't know. Art theft happens. But a big statue is . . . gutsy, to say the least. Everyone is pretty baffled. The security system was tampered with, so there don't seem to be any leads on who did this."

"Even more reason not to go back."

She hit him with another dangerous look from under her lashes. "They'd be stupid to come back. And the owners are putting in better security."

Frey stood, tail lashing behind him. No mate worth a damn handed over the safety of his woman to someone else. Certainly not someone who'd *failed* before.

"That doesn't matter, my mate. The museum is unsafe. I won't allow you to put yourself in danger."

Anna snapped a small cloth off one of the machines to dry her hands with all the effectiveness of throwing down a gauntlet.

"I don't want to talk about that," she declared. "I want to discuss this mate thing you keep bringing up."

Frey couldn't help an irritated huff flaring his nostrils. "What is there to discuss?"

"You seem to think it's important. And you keep calling me 'mate.' I want to know what you mean."

"I mean you are my mate. My heartsong. My fated one, chosen by the goddesses."

She blinked at him, silent for long enough that unease tugged at his gut.

"You mean like a soulmate."

"Is that the human word for it? Then yes. My kind were made to have one. We may lay with others, love others, but there is only one heartsong for all our life. It is the only soul we may have younglings with."

The color drained from Anna's face, and she held the cloth out as if to shield herself.

"Whoa, *no*. That's not—kids aren't happening."

"It is too early for younglings, I agree. I want you to myself for a long while yet." He hoped his grin might soften her, even seduce her a little, but if anything, it only alarmed her further.

"I'm human," she squeaked. "I can't—we can't *reproduce*."

He did not like how she said that last word. "Guardians have found their heartsongs in humans before. It is not common, but it has happened. Even one of the First, the rock-born, had his soul claimed by a human maiden. We were made by human druids, with human blood. I assure you, my Anna, we are compatible."

A choked sound left her throat that he found difficult not to be offended by.

"It's just—it's not possible. I can't be your soulmate!"

"Of course, you are, *cân fy nghalon*. Even before last night, I stirred whenever you were near. My kind, even imprisoned, were aware of the world around us. At least in glimpses. But when you came to me, it was like I could finally see. It was your touch that woke me."

Abandoning the cloth, Anna walked past him into the main room of the dwelling, wringing her hands as she sat on the large cushioned bench.

Frey followed carefully, and when she didn't say anything, knelt on a knee before her. She looked up, startled, taking in his stance, and he watched her pulse beat rapidly at her throat.

"I know it is much to accept," he said, gentling himself for her, "but the goddesses surely know why they brought you to me. You are my hope, Anna. For myself and my kin."

She let out a pained sound, and Anna buried her face in her hands. "That's . . . no, you can't put that all on me. I'm no one, okay? I'm not special."

His throat rumbled with a displeased growl, and he covered her knees in one of his hands. "I won't hear you speak of yourself so. You are the most special human I've ever met. The goddesses may have chosen for us, but I am well pleased by their choice. You are everything I could want, my Anna."

She shook her head vehemently, making Frey's chest go tight. His hand slipped from her as she jumped up, turning her back to him.

"You don't even know me. You don't . . ." Something in her voice made Frey think it wasn't just to him she spoke.

When she turned back to him, it was with her arms crossed over her chest. It pained him to see her shielding herself from him in every way.

"I just don't believe what happened can be because of this mate bond. If you turn back to stone in the day, then the curse isn't really broken. And if it's not broken, then I'm not really your mate."

It was his turn to shake his head vehemently. She laid out her argument so logically, as if it was the only conclusion to make, and Frey rebelled against such a thing with his whole being. He leapt to his feet and took one of her hands in his. Drawing her gently forward, he placed her palm on his chest, above his racing heart.

"This is because of you," he growled. "I am here because of you, my mate. I *know* it. My kind feel it when we have found our heart-songs, deep inside. It is a knowing we only feel once. I knew you were for me even when I was stone."

"Then why did you turn back?" she demanded.

"I don't know," he admitted. "It was the fae and their magick that did this. The answer will not be simple. But that does not change that we are bound together. I may not know you yet, but I will learn. I look forward to it." He leaned down to fill her vision, to block out anything that wasn't him so she'd understand when he said, "I will cherish you and all that you are because that is the way of mates."

Anna's lashes fluttered, her eyes searching his, and for one glorious moment, Frey thought she softened, finally, to him. Just a little.

But when she opened her mouth to speak, it was to say, "You're wrong," with such finality it almost broke his heart. She pulled her hand away and retreated from the room, closing herself inside her bedchamber with the soft but resounding *click* of the door shutting.

Frey stood stunned in her wake, more cut down by two words from his mate than any axe or sword or fae magick had ever managed. But from that despair sparked an enraged determination that burned hot inside him, a molten core that he would not be denied.

He hadn't waited this long, hadn't come this far to give up now.

Standing before her door, he placed his hand on the painted wood. He could break it down with ease, could shred the thin wood with little effort; nothing truly separated him from her now—but he would give her time and space. At least a little. He wouldn't promise to always be so generous.

But she had to know, to understand, "I'm not wrong." He knew it with everything he was, and said it loud enough that he knew she heard, even behind the door.

Anna was his heartsong, and Frey would do whatever it took to prove it. He would have her, and they would free his kin. There was no other choice.

The rest of the night was an uneventful haze of passing lights and drizzling rain. The dwelling went quiet with the retreat of his mate, and from behind her door, he eventually heard the soft sounds of her sleeping.

He was once again joined in his vigil by the black cat, whom Anna called Captain. The cat was a pleasant creature, and Frey took small comfort in extending his hand for Captain to rub against. "If only you could speak," he lamented. "You surely know the secrets of your mistress's heart."

Two nights with his mate and he despaired of ever knowing those secrets.

This wasn't the way of mates. They were supposed to *know* each other. The pull of knowing brought them together, then nature, lust, and then love would do the rest. She would understand this if she were a guardian.

She'd be stone if she was a guardian.

Frey's lip curled in frustration. He never backed down from a challenge—he was the fiercest warrior in his clan, had had aspirations to challenge for chieftain one day. He would have position, power, respect to offer his mate. He was a lone warrior, skilled in battle and strategy, and earned his place in the world by the strength of his arm and wing. These were the strengths given to him by the goddesses, and it was up to him to use them to his advantage.

He couldn't offer family; his had perished years before in battle against the Saxons. He couldn't offer wealth, but he'd worked to fill his dwelling with fine things for his heartsong.

But that was before the fae had cut a bloody swathe across their world.

Now, Frey truly had nothing. Gone was his dwelling, with everything he'd collected for a mate. No home, no clan. He still had his strength, but what good was it when he couldn't protect his mate nor had access to any weapons he recognized to impress her with his skill?

As the moon arched across the sky, the despondency inside him grew. He was awake, he had a heartsong, but what good were they?

He didn't know how to soften or woo a human mate.

He didn't understand this modern world of hers.

He didn't know why he returned to stone with the sun, nor how to stop it from happening again.

A pit of dread sucked at his guts. Only a few more hours, then he might be pulled back into his stone prison. Frey shuddered, remembering the horrible stiffening of his joints, how his body had felt weighed down as if he sank beneath the waves of the sea. The pressure had nearly crushed him as his skin hardened and his vision faded. The world had closed in around him, denying him a glimpse of the day, of feeling sunlight on his face for the first time in over a thousand years.

The pain and shock of returning to stone had kept him silent when he felt the connection of the others pressing on his mind. Although muted by distance now, he was aware of his imprisoned kin, of their collective consciousness stirring at his sudden absence. He thought some of them, the stronger ones who refused like him to fade away, sensed his return, but he kept his silence.

What could he tell them?

Two nights and all he could offer was false hope. He was free, but not truly. He had a mate, but one who denied the bond.

Frey couldn't stomach delivering such a blow to his dying kin.

He would keep his silence, for their sake, now alone where he'd once had the comfort of his kind's collective consciousness at least.

Soft fur whispered against his claws, and Frey turned away from the window and his foul mood to pet the cat in the way he wished. Careful with his claws, he scratched Captain from head to rump and back again, earning a rumbling purr that filled the dark main room of the dwelling.

"I'm not completely alone, I suppose." He'd had the phantom sense of a weight on his shoulders throughout the day in his stone form and supposed he'd served as a feline perch for a time. He didn't mind.

Frey spent a long while petting the cat and drawing what comfort he could. He was no closer to any solution as the moon faded behind the gathering fog.

Anna's presence and touch had woken him—of that he was sure. That she was his mate meant their bond must have something to do with breaking the curse. But how?

Frey feared the answer rested in a completed mate bond.

The goddesses only nudged. The knowing brought guardians together, but it was the couple themselves who had to forge a bond that would last. Not all matings were a success. Every clan had a handful of ill-suited pairings. For as many reasons as there were guardians, not every mating was perfect.

His elder sister Seren had entered into such a turbulent matehood not long before her death with their mother in battle. Perhaps, in time, she and her mate would have come to love each other. Perhaps all Seren would have gained from such a pairing were offspring. Perhaps if she'd been happy in her matehood, she wouldn't have been in the battle that took her life.

Frey had vowed his own mating wouldn't fail. *He* wouldn't fail.

You're wrong.

Anna's words haunted him, no matter how he railed against them.

He would find a way. Somehow, he would complete the bond with his Anna.

He just had to figure out how.

Scratching the cat one last time, Frey sought the front door of the dwelling. His heart thudded heavily in his chest, but his claws itched to do something. He didn't have his dwelling and all the things he'd gathered for his future mate; he didn't have the day with his heartsong nor the chance to prove his prowess to her.

The least he could do was assure himself that her dwelling was safe.

And if it wasn't, he'd make it so.

Silently, he figured out the locking mechanism on the door and, with the cat watching on curiously, he opened the door.

A dark, silent hall greeted him with a long, narrow rug running over polished hardwood floors. A blank wall stood opposite Anna's door, and to the right was the end of a hallway, a small window set into the wall. Adorned with a window box of wilting plants, the window looked down at the next building over.

To the left, the narrow hallway marched along to a nondescript set of stairs. Another door along Anna's wall and two more set diagonally on the opposite wall were closed, gold symbols hanging above little holes covered in glass.

Stepping into the hallway, Frey drew a deep breath, taking in the smells. There were multiple humans behind each of the other doors, though their scents were muffled by time and the walls. No one had emerged from their dwellings in a while, likely asleep as his Anna was now.

Slowly, Frey edged outside, aiming to leave the front door ajar. Before he could close it enough, though, Captain slipped outside to join him.

Flashing his fangs in a groan, Frey gestured helplessly for the cat to return. Instead, Captain chirruped happily and went about sniffing down the hallway.

Grumbling, Frey crept along behind him, managing to find every creaky floorboard. He winced with each squeak and creak, and Captain hustled away each time he drew closer.

They'd made it nearly to the stairs before Frey lunged, scooping up the wayward feline. He pointed his claw in Captain's face. "Bad cat," he grumbled. Captain just licked his finger and purred.

Heart hammering now, Frey hastily retreated back to the apartment. Both of them safely inside, he reset the lock on the door.

Hands on his hips, he frowned down at Captain. For his part, the cat sat there grooming his nether bits.

With a huff, Frey resolved that that had been enough reconnaissance for one night. He'd endeavor to learn what he could about her nearest neighbors to deduce what level of threat they posed.

In the meantime, he began a thorough investigation of her dwelling, opening every drawer and cabinet, to see what he could see and learn what he could learn.

His heart lurched when his mate rose before the sun. He didn't have long, but he drank in the sight of her emerging from her bedchamber.

Clothed in a long, fluffy garment tied at her waist, she hid her hands in deep pockets as she gazed upon him from across the room. For a long moment, she remained in her doorway, silent and unsure.

"Good morning, *fy nghân.*"

Anna cleared her throat. "Good morning." She took a few hesitant steps further into the room, stopping as Captain wove between her feet with a serenade of happy chirps. "Good morning, Cappy," she said with much more enthusiasm.

She picked up the cat, hugging him to her and swaying. She would not quite meet his gaze when she said, "I'm sorry I left like that. I just . . . it's a lot."

Frey nodded slowly. "I understand."

Anna nodded, too. "I guess I should've told you—I have the next few days off work. So you don't have to worry when . . ."

One of the tight knots in his chest loosened. "I am pleased to hear it. You must be safe, my Anna. Always." He'd accept nothing less.

She didn't argue with his declaration, though her lips pursed ever so slightly. After a moment, Anna set Captain down and stuffed her hands back in the deep pockets of her garment.

"Do you want breakfast or . . .?"

"I don't believe there's time."

Her gaze flicked over his shoulder to behold the gathering day. It would only be another moment now.

"Oh." Her expression was somber when she turned her gaze back on him. "I'm sorry," she whispered.

"Do not be. I willingly give up the day if it means nights with you." As he said the words, he knew them to be true. The despondency still echoed inside him, but the sight of his mate, uncertain as she was, did give him heart.

Color bloomed across her cheeks at his words, and Frey took encouragement from the flustered way her gaze bounced around the room. His words pleased her.

I will not fail.

He would find a way to woo her. He would learn her world. He would prove himself a mate worth having.

Frey met every challenge, and winning his heartsong would be the most worthwhile of his life.

He didn't need to see it when the sun peeked over the strange buildings outside. His joints stiffened and his skin hardened. The air in his lungs compressed, driven out with a gasp.

Anna watched on with a deep sympathy, even taking a step toward him.

Frey stopped her, holding out a stiffening hand. He didn't know if being connected might mean she too turned to stone. He wouldn't take the risk.

Lips pulled into an unhappy line, Anna whispered, "I'll be here when you wake up."

The promise soothed him, allowing him to stop fighting the change.

With the last of his air, he made a promise of his own. "Until tonight, *fy nghân.*"

8

It was so weird to putter around her apartment into midmorning. Anna had sort of forgotten what weekend midmorning sunlight looked and felt like. Usually ensconced behind her desk, the brightness was a welcome change.

Well, sort of. She would've enjoyed it more if it hadn't turned her houseguest into a statue.

He stood near the windows, his look somber. Still, it was better than the day before, when he'd frozen mid-step with arms outreached for her. He was much more statuesque today, and it allowed Anna a little more peace of mind about all this. Although, it did mean drawing the blinds closed and adding privacy film to her shopping list.

As she sipped her second cup of coffee and absentmindedly watched the local news for the third cycle, she tried to swallow her guilt over the night before. Anna believed in dealing with things head on; no problem went away by sweeping it under the rug—it was just under the rug now.

Everything he'd said, though . . . it was just too much. Too outlandish. Even now, her mind rejected the thought of being anyone's soulmate and would've chalked up the very idea of early-medieval magical monsters as a side effect of her meds if one wasn't currently adorning her living room.

She'd chewed on what Frey had said late into the night, and this morning, her mind found the familiar ruts of disbelief and incredulity.

Maybe he was a fluke. An anomaly. Maybe she'd lost her marbles.

"Not helpful," she grumbled. She could sit here spinning her proverbial wheels some more or go out and *do* something.

One thing she'd decided on while hiding out last night was that if her houseguest was going to stay, he needed a crash course in modernity. Watching him stab last night's alfredo with the fork like it'd personally offended him had been something else. He obviously needed a few lessons in modern comforts, as well as technology.

She'd felt bad earlier, seeing him standing guard yet again at the window. Anna couldn't adjust her schedule to keep nocturnal hours, so she needed to teach him how to use the TV and laptop. Maybe she could find a solid world history series for him to watch. His claws and wings gave her pause, and she apologized preemptively to her little remote as she set it down on the coffee table to get up and dress. Yet, he hadn't broken a single thing since arriving. For his size, he was stunningly graceful.

And the guy needs a shirt. He hadn't been wearing one when cursed, and that bare chest was even more distracting now that it was on full display in her own home.

Decided, Anna marched into her bathroom, determined to get Frey ready for the modern world. If she'd landed somewhere unknown, having a few things of her own, everyday things she knew and understood, would definitely help center her. She could give him that.

Then, maybe she'd get more answers out of him, to questions she was dying to ask—like all about the druids he'd said made his kind, the Saxons he'd said he fought, and the landscape of early-medieval Wales he'd said was his home. Her history degree nearly vibrated with excitement.

Essentials first. Then onto the good stuff.

That started with a trip to a big box store. Even with her new job, Anna was on a budget, and if she was going to feed a person as big as Frey, she'd need box store quantities at box store prices.

It was the first time in months she'd been out and about on an actual weekend, and the crowds quickly wore down her patience. A headache threatened behind her left temple as she weaved between wailing children and people crowded around the sample tables, so Anna ducked into the quieter clothing and bedding section to steal a sip of water.

Taking a few calming breaths, she perused the men's clothing, looking for shirts that would cover Frey's wide chest. She held up t-shirts and flannels to estimate if they'd fit over that expanse of muscle. It was finally in a small corner of big and tall that she found anything that might fit him and survive putting cuts in to accommodate his wings.

Happy with a pack of t-shirts and a blue flannel that she definitely didn't imagine would suit his gray eyes, Anna wheeled her cart into the pants section. Jeans felt like too much trouble with his elongated, taloned feet. That meant dress pants were out, too.

And then she saw them.

Gray sweatpants.

A flush crept up Anna's neck.

It's just an internet thing. It can't actually be true, she told herself, even as she rifled through the stack to find a big enough pair.

Just to be safe and let herself off the hook, she found him a black pair, too.

Which will match his hair.

Dammit, she didn't need to be making outfits for him. He just needed clothes. And for her sake, she needed him to wear clothes.

Still, Anna wanted to get him things he'd like. She touched each of the fabrics and debated colors. It may have been a little thing, but she wanted him to enjoy his modern clothes.

Her budget wouldn't allow for much, but she could do this.

Anna hadn't had much chance or inclination to do things for others. Life so far had been about survival and meeting her own needs. She knew what it was to be in need and seek assistance. She'd signed up for every aid program she could in college and after, too. She wasn't above taking charity if it meant a full stomach and warm clothes.

Lots of people needed help, there wasn't any shame in it.

But . . . there was a bit of shame in being that friend who let someone else cover the bill and promised to pay them back but never did. Anna had lost more than one friend from becoming the girl who was never good for it. She hadn't been above shoplifting a few times, either. Nothing crazy, just a sandwich here, a power bar there. Well, there was one time she took a puffer jacket into the store bathrooms and roughed it up and walked out without paying. But it was damn cold that winter, and she'd been hungry those other times and . . . and . . .

You did what you had to. Yeah, she was a bit guilty over it, but she wasn't sorry. She was here because of those little indiscretions.

And look at her now—she was going to purchase everything in her cart, and most of it wasn't even for her. She was finally good for it.

Until recently, she hadn't been in much of a position to pay it forward. Hadn't been in much of a mood to, either. Why help out the world that just continually fucked her over?

But she wanted to help Frey. She recognized something in that forlorn gaze of his. Unbelievable as his story was of being soulmates, there was no denying how earnest he was. She wasn't stupid, she knew that even locked, if he'd wanted into her bedroom last night, he could have gotten in. He'd been a fairly polite houseguest so far, if bull-headed.

So yeah, she had a soft spot for Frey. She supposed she had for a long time. He'd been her favorite at the museum, so really, it shouldn't surprise her that she wanted to help him.

It's okay to have a soft spot, she reminded herself as she wended through the wide aisles. *It means you're a half-decent person.*

Her mother and several of her myriad of boyfriends had a much harsher take on life—take what you can and guard it. Sharing, helping others, means less for yourself.

Anna had never really believed it, but growing up, she'd had no choice.

Now, though, things could be different.

That soft spot had gotten her Captain, and he was something good. She'd found him one afternoon, mewling behind a dumpster and abandoned by his mama. He'd had a gunky eye and a limp but no fear. Anna had known she couldn't afford to treat and feed a cat; at the time, she could hardly afford to feed herself. But she hadn't been able to leave him at the clinic. What if they decided it was easier to put him to sleep than fix him? What if, like so many black cats, he didn't get adopted? She picked him up after a few days of treatment and added his care to her already eye-watering credit bill.

Maybe that soft spot was right about Frey, too. Somehow.

Not as a soulmate, of course. But maybe she could accept that this was the universe giving her a chance to help someone out. Helping him could be the next step in getting herself on the path of building a life and a self she could be proud of.

She liked the thought of that.

After splurging on a ride home, it took three trips to get everything she'd bought up to her top-floor apartment, but that wasn't what killed her mood. Nor was it her sore legs or the sweat slicking down her spine under her shirt.

As she huffed and puffed over a glass of water, Anna checked her phone.

A text message from her mother greeted her, sending her mood into a tailspin.

Hey baby howre you doing? Still at that new job?

The words sat there glaring at her, and Anna put the phone down to avoid them. She put away the groceries, put Frey's new clothes in the wash, and mopped the floor.

When she looked again, there was another message.

You there baby?

Her mom only called her *baby* when she wanted something.

It'd been a bit of a shock when, after turning twenty-one over seven years ago, Shannon had taken to playing nice with Anna. Sometimes. After that speech before going off to college about how Anna had ruined Shannon's life and dreams and tied her down blah blah, she'd thought they wouldn't speak ever again.

For a year, they hadn't.

Her freshman year of college, Anna spent every weekend, every holiday in the dorms. She didn't hear from nor contact her mother. After a year, she'd steeled herself to never having contact again.

Shannon had finally texted her happy birthday her sophomore year, and Anna . . . well, it was her mom. Some part of her hated it, but she'd texted back.

Since then, she'd seen Shannon a handful of times. Spent one awkward Thanksgiving with her and a boyfriend. Anna at least kept tabs on her mom's current address, and they exchanged pleasantries now and again.

The texts sitting on her phone now weren't pleasantries, though.

No, since Anna had entered the workforce, Shannon had seen another source of support.

Grinding her back teeth, Anna took up her phone and tapped out a quick reply.

Hi, mom. Yes doing fine. Still at the job.

She busied herself with more chores, cleaning out the litter box, putting the clothes in the dryer, starting dinner, before she let herself check the phone again.

Thats great to hear baby. They treating you well?

Yeah, they're real nice.

Good, they should be treating you right

They're good people.

Good

Im glad

Hey

Baby Im sorry

I hate asking

Ask what?

Anna knew what, but she always wanted the words.

I think Chaz skipped town

The rent is due tomorrow & Im a
little short

Im sorry baby

I hate asking

They both knew that wasn't true. If it was, Anna wouldn't keep a small fund just for these texts. Squirreling away a little money for her mom felt like a dirty secret; she didn't like thinking about it to herself, and she'd never admit it to her mom.

Shannon would berate her, claiming she was cruel to dole it out little by little rather than just giving it to her in her time of need. Except, that money would be gone in a blink and she'd always need more. Always. Anna could transfer everything she had, what little there was, and it wouldn't be enough.

Nothing ever was for Shannon. Her mom was out there chasing something—what, Anna didn't know. Maybe it was why she dated men in their fifties who still went by *Chaz*. Whatever her mom was after, it consumed everything around her. She didn't see or didn't care about what she broke to get it.

That's what Anna and the therapist she saw during college managed to work out, at least.

How much?

The therapist had had quite a bit to say about why Anna allowed Shannon to hang around in her life, most of which Anna hadn't wanted to hear then and didn't want to think about now.

She ground her teeth in annoyance as she waited for a number.

A few hundred

Anna rolled her eyes.

I can send $100

Thank you baby

Everything helps

I owe you

Sure.

Tapping through her apps, Anna went through the familiar motions of transferring her mom money while ignoring the litany of messages thanking her and saying to send only what she could. She knew they really meant *send as much as possible*, but Anna stuck to the $100.

Saying a quick goodbye, she laid her phone facedown on the dining table and scrubbed her hands over her face. An icky feeling clung to her skin, making her consider a shower.

She wanted to go back to that morning, the happiness of doing something nice for someone.

What she did for Shannon didn't feel nice. At least, Anna didn't feel nice.

When Captain came within grabbing distance, she snagged him from the floor to bury her face in his soft belly. He pawed at her head, but Anna just held him and listened to his reverberating purr.

With a little time, her soft spot stopped feeling so much like a bruise.

"Thank you, Cappy," she whispered before setting him on the floor.

She treated him to an early dinner before seeing how her own was getting on. She was setting the oven to temperature when the sun finally dipped below the horizon.

When a deep voice called her name from the living room, her heart gave a mysteriously happy kick.

Frey eased into wakefulness this time, letting the change happen. His skin prickled with the feel of the air, and his lungs filled with a steady breath. Unfurling his wings, he let them crack and snap, coming fully awake with a shake of his whole body.

Like throwing off water from a swim, he tossed away the last vestiges of his forced slumber.

His mate's dwelling was dim but occupied; the smells and sounds of cooking emanated from the kitchen, and the rooms had a warmth to them he associated with only her.

"Anna?" he called.

She stepped out from behind the wall separating the main living space from the kitchen. The cuffs of her thin sweater had been pushed nearly to her elbows, and fluffy socks clad her otherwise bare feet. Her hair had been piled atop her head, and large spectacles he'd never seen her wearing before perched on her nose.

The warmth he felt upon seeing her drew a smile to his lips. His heart gave a suspicious pang in his chest, and a rumbling purr began in earnest beneath his sternum. Frey closed the distance between them in a few strides, happy when she not only let him come but allowed him to ease a loose lock of hair behind her ear.

"Good evening, *fy nghân*. Have you had a fair day?"

The beginnings of a smile twitched across her lips. "I've had a productive day," she replied.

Frey didn't quite understand the difference, but it didn't matter, really.

"And did you miss me?"

A comely blush pinkened her cheeks, and those plush lips twisted to contain her bashful smile.

Frey hadn't been much of a flirt before; the partners he'd had were guardians—straightforward with their wants and desires with him and he to them. No need for coyness or games. But something inside wanted to play with his mate, to tease and coax and gentle. He was rewarded with that begrudging smile, even if she tried to hide it with a mock frown and turned back toward the kitchen.

He followed close behind, like a puppy chasing skirts, but he didn't let that wound his pride. A successful hunter was one who exercised adaptability and persistence.

And he liked watching the sway of her hips as she walked. That seam in her braies bisecting her ample backside made her stride damn near hypnotic.

"I did have you on my mind," she said.

Frey rumbled with pleasure. "Mysterious. And very flattering."

Although she'd given him her profile, he didn't miss that very female roll of her eyes.

"Dinner will be ready soon, but if . . ." She spun to face him, sliding easily on the floor in her socks. Her expression had gone pensive again, and Frey made himself be patient for what she would say. Clearing her throat, she continued, "I got you these today."

Skirting around him, she picked up a small pile of folded fabric from the dining table to hand to him.

The bottom of Frey's chest opened up, sucking his heart down to his feet.

His Anna had procured him clothing.

"*Cân fy nghalon . . .*" He held up the clothes in wonderment, astonished by their softness. They seemed thin and perhaps not practical for hunting and flying, but the tight stitching and softness spoke of their luxury. "You did not have to go to such an expense for me."

"Oh, ah . . ." Anna retreated to the kitchen to stir whatever was simmering over the small fire. "Don't worry about it, they aren't Gucci or anything. I just thought you'd like to have something of your own. I hope they fit, you can try them out in the bathroom. Or—" Her gaze cut nervously to him and then his wings, "or my room, there are mirrors in there. So you can see."

Frey wasn't sure what had invited her nervous chatter, but he wanted Anna to be at ease. He let an easy smile slide onto his lips and spread his wings wide.

"There is plenty of room right here. We can both see for ourselves the fruits of your gifts," he said, reaching for the ties of his braies.

The depth and violence of her blush was something to see, and Frey couldn't help a chuckle and lift of his brows before heading off through the dwelling. Nor another when he heard her guffaw at realizing he teased.

She'd said he could use her room and so he took the opportunity, stealing inside the one place he'd yet to explore. A bed took up almost half of it, a mattress piled with blankets and pillows laid atop a metal frame. A dresser with mismatched knobs and a trunk with a broken latch sat atop a faded but still striking rug. Thick curtains hung beside each of the windows, and two potted plants sat together on the windowsill.

It was a tidy space, nothing like the clutter of his nest back in his clanhome on the western cliffs near Caerdyf. After the death of his mother and sister, Frey lived in the family dwelling by himself but had been unable to part with anything. Over the years, he hadn't been able to part with much at all, and so things accumulated.

In Anna's bedchamber, everything seemed to have a space. There were a few things left untidied, though, like the thrown-back corner of her blankets, an undergarment laid out on the trunk, a scattering of small items across the dresser top. He found them all charming, like she couldn't quite contain herself. Most of all, the room smelled strongly of her, making it his favorite of the dwelling.

It took effort to ignore all the fine fabrics saturated in her scent. His claws itched to take the discarded undergarment, tantalizingly shaped like female breasts, and bring it to his nose.

He busied himself with her gifts instead, shucking his leathers to step into the gray braies she'd provided. They were just as soft as he'd hoped, skimming the contours of his lower legs but stretching across the muscles of his thighs. Frey slung them low on his hips, allowing his tail out from the waist of the garment.

Next was a sleeved shirt dyed many hues of blue with pleasing squares and lines in golds and greens. Another wave of gratitude overtook him; blue was the most precious, most expensive dye. His mate had gone to great trouble and expense for him, and he wouldn't forget it.

He was pleased to find two precise slits had already been made in the shirt, and when he pushed his arm into a sleeve, the first wing joint slid right through. With a few adjustments, the shirt laid upon his shoulders, leaving his wings free. The sleeves were a little tight around his upper arms, and though a row of buttons marched down the front, he doubted he could secure all of them with his claws and so decided to forgo it.

Twisting and bending, he was delighted with how soft and flexible the fabrics were, the clothes offering a pleasant caress with each movement.

Yes, these would do nicely. And perhaps in human clothes, his Anna would stop seeing him as a beast come to life. Perhaps, in clothes she'd chosen for him, she would see the male that wanted to be hers.

There was little light in the bedchamber, but Frey looked at himself in the mirror mounted above the dresser for a moment.

He knew what he looked like, of course. They'd had looking glasses and clear lakes to spy one's reflection in. Yet neither were as clear as the gleaming mirror here or in the washing chamber.

The face gazing back at him wasn't entirely one he knew. It was that of a young guardian, a male in his prime and strength. Frey had already lived far longer than his face. Or, if not lived, *existed* for longer than his face could tell. He felt older, and in these human clothes, he recognized himself even less.

Nonsense, he told himself. *It is just the novelty.*

And the suddenness of his new existence.

Just like wooing his mate, it would take time.

Good hunters adapt.

And speaking of his mate, he'd been away from her far too long.

Turning from the mirror, he snagged that undergarment off her trunk, unable to help himself. He buried his nose in the fabric, drawing in a long draught of her scent. It calmed his mind, and he couldn't help running the soft fabric in circles over his cheek, working a bit of her scent into his skin.

Guardians were much more sensory than humans, given bestial senses to better hunt and fight. It also meant a more visceral reaction and sense of one's mate, family, and kin. Already he knew he could find Anna's scent on the wind from leagues away. In the same way that her presence had called him from his stone sleep, their connection meant he would always be able to find her now.

With one last pull, he replaced the undergarment and made his way back into the kitchen.

Anna was spooning their meal into bowls but looked up when he stepped into the bright lights. Her brows shot up her forehead, and Frey wasn't above flexing his wings and puffing his chest for her, either.

Another blush overtook her face, and a sort of gurgling noise escaped her lips before she clapped a hand over them. Her eyes kept flicking downward, below his waist.

Frey glanced down at himself in the better light. Ah. The cut of the braies left little to the imagination about the size and shape of his cock.

He glanced up at her through his lashes, assessing. Perhaps this was a test, a show of his virility?

Anna spun back to the food, but the blush remained.

"They look great!" she said too loudly. "Do you like them?"

A smug smile curled his lips. The sight of him in these clothes, the hint of his cock, had affected her. A new scent began to permeate the air, even over the smells of the meal she'd made, one that only deepened his pleasure.

She feels something.

The scent of female interest was unmistakable.

If she'd been a woman of his kind, he wouldn't have been shy about articulating his intents and hopes.

But she's not.

He had to remember that.

Frey didn't want her fleeing from him like the night before. He had to be careful. Gentle. Gracious.

Still, when he went to pluck the bowls from her hands to bring to the table, he drew in a discreet lungful of her. His rumble of pleasure was less discreet, though he bent his head to the steaming food to hide it.

She followed him to the table, and he was grateful to sit and hide the other evidence of his pleasure. A garment that showed off his cock at ease would do little to conceal his cock at attention.

Perhaps the clothes were a test after all.

Frey ignored his cock's twitches of interest—although, he was more than a little relieved that his manhood still worked after centuries of disuse—and instead tucked into another fine meal from his mate.

He thought he recognized rice, though he'd never seen it before in his time, and only knew some of the vegetables. Beef was familiar, but the sweet, tangy sauce she'd soaked the meat and vegetables in were new quite tasty.

"It's teriyaki, with carrots and broccoli," she explained when he asked over the unfamiliar foods.

"And where is ter-ee-yakee from?" he asked, mouth stumbling over the strange sounds.

"From Japan. It's an island nation way across the Pacific Ocean." She looked up from her meal to blink at him. "That reminds me—I was thinking . . ." Anna set down her utensils, and Frey sat up straighter, preparing for whatever she might say next. She truly was a mysterious thing, keeping him guessing.

"I thought maybe I could teach you things about this time. I don't know what's going to happen, but it seems like you're going to stay." Another blush bloomed across her face. "I mean, if you want to . . ."

Carefully, Frey placed his hand on the table. It didn't quite touch hers, but it was there, offering the connection.

"I would stay with you, my Anna. For as long as you allow."

The moment of silence pierced his heart with panic. He didn't know what he would do if she demanded he leave. He had nowhere to go, no one else to rely upon. He hated this vulnerability, this absolute dependence on her, but he was determined it was only temporary, that given a little time, he would adapt, he'd learn her—

She nodded jerkily. "Good. Okay. Yeah, that's . . . good. Um." Moving the rice around in her bowl without eating any, she said to the table, "You can stay with me."

"You are a kind soul, my Anna. I swear your kindness won't be forgotten. I don't know or understand much of your world, but I hope that given time, I will learn to be a good mate to you."

Anna drew in a long breath before folding her hands in front of her and resting her chin on them. "I wanted to talk to you about that. I think this mate business is too much for me. I have another few days off from work, so I thought . . . we won't talk about me going to work, we won't talk about this mate bond. Instead, we'll give you a crash course in history and everything you need to know. Is that . . . doable?"

Frey considered. He would, of course, acquiesce, although he appreciated the illusion that he had any true choice. As his heartsong, he would give Anna anything he was able—and not just because a word from her and he would be alone in this new world. Still, that she asked and seemed genuinely desirous of his answer softened his grumblings at her conditions.

He didn't want her going back to her work. He didn't want to stay silent about their matehood.

And he didn't want her running from him.

Adapt. Compromise.

Truly, has a male ever compromised so much to win his mate?

Holding back his sigh, Frey nodded. "I agree. I should like to learn everything you have to teach me."

The smile she gave him was small but rocked the foundations of Frey's very soul nevertheless. His Anna wasn't given to easy smiles and flippant talk, so when her lips curved up with genuine relief and pleasure, Frey felt his own tingling in his claw and wing tips.

"You've got a lot to teach me, too," she said. And with an excitement he hadn't seen from her before, she leaned forward to say, "Tell me everything about sixth-century Wales."

"I will try, *fy nghân*, but what is Wales?"

It soothed some of the oldest wounds in his heart to speak of his home and time. Frey was delighted to find hours had passed and still she had more questions for him—how his kind made their homes, what he knew of the human druids, what the clan stories said about the invading Romans they were made to fight. They sat at her table so long, the plates were empty and then cleaned and put away, and a sachet of delectable treats she called cookies lay decimated between them.

Eventually, they drifted into the main living space, taking opposite ends of the cushioned bench she called a couch. As he spoke of his clan, of the Gorsedd and patrolling the sea near Caerdyf and fighting off Saxon raiders, Captain padded between them, sitting on Anna's lap for a while before climbing all over Frey, only to repeat this again.

Frey wished he too could lay his head in Anna's lap, but he had to be patient.

Her questions were many, and each pleased Frey a little more. The interest she showed was deep and genuine. She spoke of her love for history, how she had made it her main study at university.

"So you are a scholar," he crowed, shoulders thrown back with pride.

Anna smiled, amused. "Sort of. Lots of people go to college for lots of different subjects. I couldn't find anything I liked more, so I studied early-medieval history and loved every minute of it."

It was on the tip of his tongue to remark that even before her time at the place where he and his kin were kept, she'd been drawn to his own time and history. The connection was plain to him, and if the significant look she shot him over Captain's head was anything, it was plain to her, too.

Frey clenched his jaw and kept his expression mild.

He kept his vows.

After another moment, Anna continued, "We could watch a documentary on Welsh history if you'd like?"

Frey agreed, fascinated when she picked up a small object and the black surface on the far wall lit up with light. Words scrolled across the surface, followed by many boxes of color with more words.

"This is television?" he asked in wonder.

He'd heard of this, of television and movies and how they developed from the theater. A few of his kin had spent time in human theaters, had been able to glimpse the new arts the humans developed. He knew there was some sort of science to it, but didn't quite understand how the same thing that made the lights in the ceiling appear also made the television.

"Yeah. It's a pretty great invention." Turning to him, she winced and said, "My explanation of electricity and modern technological advancements won't be great, but should I start at the beginning?"

"No, I have heard of these technologies. Perhaps just a small explanation."

Her abbreviated explanation still left his head swimming, but he thought he understood the fundamentals. As she began manipulating the screen with the small device in her hand, Frey's eyes hurt trying to keep up. She explained what she did as she went, "In case you'd like to watch anything while I'm asleep. It'd be something to do."

She held out the device in her hand and began pointing to the small buttons on it and how they corresponded with the screen.

Rumbling, Frey covered her hand with his. "My Anna, you have the kindest of hearts, but I cannot read your language."

"Oh!" Her eyes bounced between the device, the television, and him, and she winced again. "I'm sorry, I completely forgot. Here . . ."

She moved closer to him on the couch, close enough that Frey only had to bend his head the slightest distance to take a long breath from the richness of her hair. She held the device, the *remote*, up, explaining a few important buttons and their symbols, like the green *power button*, but he was only half-listening, trying to keep himself and his unruly cock in check at her nearness.

"After that, press this one," she said, pointing to another button. She held her finger on it and brought the remote to her lips. "Find Welsh history documentaries." And after a moment, more boxes appeared on the screen. She turned back to him with a triumphant little grin that Frey felt everywhere.

"You say what you want to watch into the remote and it finds things. It's not perfect, you'd have to judge things off the thumbnail for now, but it's a start."

Drawn in by that smile, Frey matched it with his own as he leaned closer. "You are kind *and* clever, my Anna."

A blush, soft and comely this time, stained her cheeks, and Frey bit back his rumble of satisfaction.

With a few more presses on the remote, Anna set up her chosen *doc-*

umentary. He enjoyed the way she relaxed back into the couch, at ease as music swelled. It'd taken two nights, but finally his mate was comfortable in his presence.

With feinted ease and informality, Frey stretched his arms across the back of the couch as he too settled in, his hand coming to rest very near where her long dark hair spilled across the back of the cushion. Ever so gently, he ran his claws through the silken strands, careful not to tug or alert her. He bit back his rumble when the locks slid like silk across his skin.

And then his attention was stolen by the television. Images began to play of the sea and green, rolling hills, and a deep wistfulness arrowed straight through his heart. A male voice began to speak, and the images changed from landscapes to humans in clothes he recognized. Anna whispered explanations here and there, that the humans were reenactors and that not everything would be accurate or how he remembered.

Frey didn't mind. The documentary entranced him, and for the evening, he was content to learn what had happened to the world as he and his kin slept the stone sleep, his mate warm and comfortable beside him as he covertly toyed with her hair.

10

Anna wasn't quite sure if it was normal for someone to pick up on modern things as quickly as Frey did. It was one thing to have to wrestle with Excel or explain streaming to a grandparent; it was quite another to be a mythical being from the sixth century. Yet after just two nights, Frey was already a pro at the remote.

He navigated through the options after requesting videos on Anglo-Celtic mythology, barely needing her to read him the titles. Although he couldn't read modern English, he'd picked up on symbols quick enough and was an excellent judge of video thumbnails.

Anna didn't know if she should be impressed or terrified.

That first night, she'd gone to bed late with Frey set up with the remote and the TV volume on low. She'd woken up early to make sure she saw him before dawn, only to find that he'd managed to dive down a technology video rabbit hole and filled in some of his knowledge gaps on electricity, motors, and the internet.

The next night, he had her go around the apartment naming all the machines—*that's the stove, this is the microwave, and this is the fridge, it has to be kept closed*—as well as show him her ancient laptop and newer-ish cellphone. Over dinner, they'd discussed modern banking and the use of credit cards.

Anna was happy to answer, though she didn't understand how his head wasn't exploding with all the new information. He just gobbled it up and went right onto the next. She supposed she could understand; he was gorging on the new.

She wasn't surprised when he fell down the World War II rabbit hole his second night. He was unimpressed with her lack of knowledge about the merits of different fighter jets.

The horrors of the war brought up questions about more recent history—recent at least in the eyes of someone over a thousand years old—and Anna was saddened when his questions grew more somber. When told how many had been killed by the wars, Frey had gone silent for a long while.

She hadn't pushed him, and she was relieved when, upon waking up tonight, he'd been more interested in delving into what humans knew of his own history. It baffled him how humans had forgotten his kind and didn't like her suggestion of his resemblance to Judeo-Christian demons.

"We were created long before the conversion," he argued.

"Yes, but many people still saw you, even as statues," she rebutted. "All of you are so striking, it wouldn't surprise me that you stayed in the consciousness somehow."

"But we are not demonic. We were made to protect, to defend. Not scare or manipulate. Although . . ." His face went slick, frown easing into a smolder, "perhaps some of us were made to seduce."

Anna's face lit up like a neon sign—god, she *needed* to stop blushing around him! She'd never blushed this much, not when she'd lied to police officers and social workers about her mom being a responsible adult, not when she and that store clerk had made eye contact as they watched her steal some bananas, not even when her college boyfriend had screamed he loved her as he came.

The blushing was getting out of hand. It wasn't who she was.

So she threw the remote at Frey. To reassert dominance.

His smile turned smug as he clicked through video options, finally settling on one. Meanwhile, Anna hid behind her mug of tea and tried to will Captain over from the windows so she'd have something to focus on other than the big gray behemoth currently taking up her whole living room.

He'd rolled up the sleeves of the flannel and it wasn't okay.

He'd also never bothered to button it, so it was just all rippling muscles on display all night, which also wasn't okay.

For her state of mind.

For her sanity.

For her libido. And therefore state of mind.

Statues aren't sexy. Sure, they could be beautiful, moving, arresting. You had to be dead inside not to be moved by Michelangelo's *David* or *Pietà*. But you weren't supposed to *feel* things for statuary.

Just call me Pygmalion. Great, now she was thinking about his rippling chest *and* making art history jokes to herself. This was bad.

Maybe I should get some fig leaves to put over his bits. Even with pants on, *that* part of him bordered on obscene.

That impulse buy had come back to bite her in the ass.

Frey gracefully alighting to sit on the floor across the coffee table from her finally snapped her out of her spiral, and Anna nearly choked on her tea.

With deft claws, he pulled her one pack of cards from their cheap packet and laid them on the table. He'd asked over what kinds of games humans still played and was delighted to learn about card games. He'd promised to teach her to play *fidchell*, an ancient Celtic board game she'd learned about, if she could find a comparable board and pieces. In the meantime, he wanted to play a card game.

Setting down her mug, Anna took up the cards. She hadn't learned much from her mom's deadbeat boyfriends—except for a handful of party tricks.

She bit down on her smile as she made a show of shuffling the deck, starting with an overhand before riffling and cascading. An amused rumble echoed from across the coffee table, and Anna couldn't hold back her smile anymore.

Five cards landed in front of Frey in a crescent.

Replacing the deck between them, Anna put on her best poker face and took up her own cards. Leaning forward, she told him very seriously, "The game is Go Fish."

He leaned forward, too. "I must confess, I do not enjoy fishing."

"I hope you enjoy defeat, because I rule at Go Fish."

Unfortunately, though, after only two rounds, Frey took to the game as easily as he'd taken to the remote. She was again unsure whether she was impressed or terrified—and didn't know whether she should be offended he didn't let her win. It would've been the gentlemanly thing to do.

Instead, he seemed to take great pleasure in trouncing her.

"I take it back," he purred as she shuffled the deck again, trying hard not to pout about another loss.

"What?"

"I do enjoy fishing, when the fishing is good." And he waggled his thick brows at her.

Anna snorted with a laugh.

All in all, Frey thought perhaps things were progressing with his Anna. Not as fast as he'd hoped, of course. Five nights already and he'd yet to kiss her sweet lips or enfold her in his wings. Still, he took heart that she not only stayed in his company but seemed to enjoy it.

He bantered. He flirted. He triumphed at every game she taught him to prove his cunning. Frey didn't have the weapons to demonstrate his skills nor another guardian to wrestle with to demonstrate his strength, so he had to make do showing the sharpness of his mind and the attractiveness of his physical form where he could.

His ancestors might grimace at his methods, but they wouldn't fault him his cause. And besides, what guardian hadn't preened and showed off his muscles a little for his pretty mate?

Frey was content to spend another enjoyable evening in the company of his heartsong. Every smile, every laugh he earned from her felt like a triumph, and he didn't think he imagined her eyes lingering on him a little longer each time she looked.

Biting back the smugness on his lips, Frey cleaned up the cards as his Anna prepared for slumber. He enjoyed watching *videos*, had been relieved to find many that sated his curiosity and helped build his knowledge of her time, but it was always better while his mate joined him. Watching them quietly through the dark of night was better than staring out the window, but it was still lonely.

He'd much rather lay beside her and watch *her* all night. He knew he'd never tire of it, even if she snored or drooled, but he suspected it'd be another few nights at least before he'd be invited to stay in her bedchamber.

With a shy little wave, Anna bade him goodnight from her doorway, face freshly scrubbed and hair piled atop her head.

"Sleep well, *fy nghalon*," he purred.

Her lips twitched with a smile, and then she disappeared behind her bedchamber door.

The sounds of her preparing for sleep soon faded, and Frey resumed his video on Anglo-Saxon burial practices. He couldn't quite decide how he felt about so little of the invaders of his fair isle remaining. They were almost as much of a mystery to today's scholars as his own people, and they too had eventually been invaded and conquered.

Perhaps it all would've been a matter of time before his kin were destroyed.

Captain decided to make a nest of Frey's crossed legs, and so he and the cat lay upon the floor together, watching videos into the wee hours. The cat's little purrs and soft body were most welcome, and Frey took to holding him on his chest as he'd seen Anna do.

His eyes had begun to sting with fatigue, and he'd found his way onto videos about medieval sword recreation, when noises from the bedchamber perked his ears.

He'd listened to his mate sleeping enough to know that once she was asleep, she hardly moved. Now, though, he heard her rolling beneath the blankets and making frustrated little noises. Pausing the video, he listened carefully as she continued moving about, unsure if she'd woken.

Perhaps it is a nightmare.

Or perhaps . . . she's pleasuring herself.

The thought quickened Frey's blood through his veins, and his ears fixed harder to every noise escaping under her door. He listened for any little snippet that would tell him what she did, and as the minutes passed, his body hardened, muscles locking in preparation for . . .

Something.

Anything.

His cock began to ache and throb with the thought of her just steps away, warm and slick. His muscles bunched, considering going to the washroom and bring himself some relief—it certainly wouldn't be the first time.

The sweet agony went on for almost a half-hour before the bedchamber door cracked open.

Anna appeared, and for a moment, Frey's heart stopped.

His imagination, his lust, did not. They roared inside him, hoping, longing that she was about to call him inside with her. That their nights together meant something, had *finally* proven to her that he was everything she could want in—

A pained sound escaped Anna, and she clapped her hand over her eyes. She blindly but nimbly navigated into the washroom, and next Frey heard the sound of drawers opening.

Memories of that first night came to him, of watching her rummage through those same drawers.

Turning off the television, he placed Captain on the couch and carefully approached the washroom.

Anna had left the door open, allowing him to see as she manipulated a small cylinder in the unlit room. Her fingers were sure, the movements rote, but everything about this, her silence, the strangeness of it, had unease creeping up Frey's neck.

And then he saw it gleam in the low light from the main room—a needle.

He'd seen her do this before, but that didn't soften the shock and horror of watching his mate pull down the waist of her sleepwear and poise the needle over her soft skin.

"*No!*"

Frey lunged forward, instincts flaring. He snatched the cylinder with the needle from her hand, yanking it away from her exposed skin.

Anna yelped as he crushed the brittle cylinder to pieces in his fist.

Clear liquid gushed across his knuckles as he flung the remains into the sink.

"What the *fuck!*" Anna roared.

Frey reared back at her outrage, his own ire flaring. She glared up at him, the light from the main room glittering in her dark eyes. His lips pulled back over his fangs in a frustrated growl.

"You *will not* harm yourself!"

"It doesn't hurt much. And it's better than having this headache!" With a pointed finger and blunted claw, she poked the center of his chest over and over to punctuate her words. "You don't get to *fucking* tell me what to do. It's *my* fucking body. This is *medicine*. I *need* it."

"Harming yourself is unacceptable!"

"I'm not! And last I checked, watching a few videos doesn't make you a fucking doctor, Frey. So get *the fuck* out of my bathroom."

"I will not. This cannot be the only remedy."

"It is for me. This is how it is, okay?" And to his horror, tears rather than anger began to glitter in her eyes. She turned away from him to reach into a drawer and pull out another cylinder.

Throwing him an evil look over her shoulder, she retreated further into the washroom, lifted her garment, and stuck the needle to her skin.

His whole body clenched, and a growl of displeasure escaped his lips, but he held himself back. Instinct far more ancient than even him screamed to stop her—protecting a mate was vital, sacrosanct, even if it was from themselves. A mate who couldn't protect his heartsong wasn't worth the dirt beneath his talons.

A little *click* was overloud in the sucking silence between them. Anna removed the cylinder and threw it in the small wastebin.

After a moment, her shoulders slumped and she turned. Not all the way. Only giving him her profile, she said, "I get headaches, okay? Migraines. It's chronic and there isn't a lot I can do about them other than take that injection. I don't like it either, sticking yourself with a needle sucks. But it's better than suffering through a migraine."

Suffer. His mate *suffered.* A helpless rage seared across his soul. He'd had to sit and watch his sister wither in a loveless mating. He couldn't save her or their mother from perishing in battle. He hadn't been able to stop the fae in their attack. And now, he was helpless yet again.

He'd become the best, strongest warrior in his clan. He was undefeated in battles and brawls. He'd gathered everything he could to make a heartsong happy in his dwelling.

For what? All this he did and yet he couldn't ease her pain.

"Anna . . ." he groaned, his heart aching.

When she turned to look at him again, it was with a frown, her eyes shuttered. Whatever ground he may have gained over the past nights had been lost, and Frey brimmed with despair to realize it.

"It's the only thing that works. I don't have a ton of doses left and I can't get more until next month. Don't do that ever again."

It felt as though his chest caved in upon itself, his muscles and tendons and ribs snapping to crush his heart and lungs beneath. He could hardly draw breath enough through the agony to say, "My Anna . . . I didn't mean to hurt you. I just cannot stand seeing you do such a thing."

She pursed her lips and shrugged, arms winding around herself. "It sucks. I'm hoping there'll be a different treatment soon. But this is how it is. I deal with it, so you're going to have to, too."

Frey swallowed hard, swallowed the denial and argument and frustration. He didn't want to agree to that. He didn't want to see his mate in pain.

How could the world have come so far and yet his Anna still had to suffer so?

He hated it.

But if a small prick meant easing her pain . . .

Drawing a long breath, he relented. "I'm sorry, my Anna. I don't understand your pain nor its treatment. But I do know what it is to suffer. I have known pain and the bitterness of its persistence. I don't wish it upon anyone, especially not you."

She regarded him for a long while, those dark eyes roving over him for any sign of deceit or half-truth. She would find none.

Finally, she nodded. Shuffling forward, her gaze didn't make it higher than his chest as she said, "I'm sorry I yelled at you."

"Ahh, *fy nghalon,* you may shout at me all you wish, so long as I deserve it."

And because he needed it, and because he thought perhaps she needed it too, Frey carefully reached to run his claws through her hair. He held his breath, amazed and so grateful when she allowed him to cup her head. His claws were gentle, so very gentle, as they ran across her scalp, just the slightest scratch, as the pads of his fingers worked in small, soothing circles.

Her soft sigh puffed against his palm, and Frey's heart stuttered in his chest as he watched her lids flutter closed and she melted into his touch.

Goddess, how could I have forgotten so easily? She needs softness, gentleness.

Frey was a strong guardian, one of the strongest in his former clan. He was skilled with weapons and battle stratagem and had seen and won many fights. He was agile, quick, and brutal.

His Anna needed none of those things, and it terrified him.

Holding her head in his hand, feeling the delicate skin and curve of her ear terrified him.

She was so soft, so vulnerable—and could crush him with little effort. Again, terrifying.

He dared to step closer, and she allowed it. Dipping his head closer to hers, he whispered, "I will endeavor not to deserve it again."

A smile touched her lips, though her eyes remained closed. "That's a good plan."

Frey let the tension and terror of the last moments recede. They didn't leave him, but at least retreated to where he could focus solely on his mate.

If it'd been another night, another series of events that led them to standing so close, his claws twined in her hair, Frey would have closed the last distance between them. He would have finally had his first taste of her. He would be gentle at first, coax and tease her, before goading her tongue with his own. Their mouths would fuse together, tongues dancing in a heated display as old as the goddesses. He would bury both hands in that luscious mane of hers before running down her back to explore the curves of her backside and fit her more securely to him, where she'd no doubt feel his lust for her. They would lick and nip and suck until finally, they broke away for air, their breaths combined in a hot well of promise.

But that wasn't what Frey did.

She allowed him to touch her like this, and he wouldn't take more.

"You must rest now," he whispered to her, though he couldn't force his hand from her.

A sound of assent vibrated from deep in her throat. Frey's wings twitched when her eyes slowly opened, lids heavy. Her face was no longer stiff and scowling but relaxed.

"Goodnight," she said.

"Goodnight," he murmured, and let her go.

11

Anna woke to a medicine hangover and guilty conscience. Peeling back an eyelid, she humphed to find morning light spilling across the foot of her bed.

In her haze in going back to bed after taking the injection, the one clear thought she'd had was to make sure to get up early enough to apologize again to Frey—that thought hadn't manifested in setting her alarm, apparently. She hadn't meant to bark at him like that. Yeah, she was still pissed about the broken injector and would have to make sure her current stock lasted until she could renew next month, but he didn't understand all that. He couldn't know what she didn't tell him.

It was just . . . she didn't like talking about her migraines. They already took up so much of her life that having to explain them, describe what they did and how much they immobilized her, made her feel worse. She was allowing them to rule her life in so many ways.

In college, with the university insurance, they'd been better managed. A lot of her health had been. For a beautiful few years, Anna had actually lived. True, times had still been tough; there'd been nights she went to bed hungry and days where she couldn't focus in class over her empty, complaining stomach—but at least migraines hadn't been added to the mix for the most part. For those years, she'd had friends, she'd dated, she'd had *fun.*

Wading out into the adult world meant no more college insurance and her healthcare got much spottier. There were years she went completely uncovered and suffered through the headaches with generic medication. She'd waited in so many doctor's offices and urgent care lobbies. She'd spent years tackling medical debts and bouncing between coverages.

Friendships had fallen to the wayside. So had her love life. Her figure, always curvier, had grown when she couldn't afford or couldn't manage more than quick and cheap food.

Captain was the only thing she'd had the capacity to care for beyond nursing her headaches in years. She'd spent most of her twenties either with a headache or preparing to have a headache.

It's a crappy way to live, she ruminated.

Another reason why she'd be going back to her job with its stellar health plan tomorrow.

Groaning, Anna managed to get herself upright. Her mind fuzzier than a dryer lint trap, she shuffled out of her bedroom into a quiet apartment. Frey had taken up position in a discreet corner, not far from her door. That he'd stayed near had her heart fluttering in a way that felt . . . dangerous.

After a shower and thorough scrub, Anna dressed in her coziest loungewear and prepared for a day in. She wasn't much use to anyone with this kind of medicine hangover, and the best thing to do was sleep it off.

It was almost a crime to draw the curtains and block out a pristine, clear San Francisco day, but her sensitive eyes wanted darkness. That meant running to the grocery store was out, so Anna hunkered down, content to be a little feral for the day, and cuddled up on the couch with Captain.

Toggling through the TV's watch history brought a grin to her lips. Frey had already covered so many topics in his few nights with the internet. She found a documentary to watch and put it on for noise, hoping he might be able to hear even in his stone state.

Glancing at him over the back of the couch, Anna couldn't help wondering what going through so many centuries in stone must have been like.

I do know what it is to suffer.

She hadn't asked him many questions about his time as a statue, nor what it was like for him and his kind. Part of her didn't think she could stomach hearing about so much suffering. Another didn't want to burst the little bubble they'd made over the past few days.

Good to his word, he hadn't brought up her going to work or his belief that they were soulmates. What history they talked about had been his own living history or the far-flung dramas of world politics.

That she hadn't delved deeper seemed . . . wrong. She should ask him more. It wasn't a pleasant topic for him, she knew. And it would bring up harder questions about the situation of his kind remaining in the museum. Still, they were questions worth asking. She should know more about her mythical houseguest.

She should know more because he . . . he was her friend. Not just a houseguest anymore.

Somewhere in the past few days, Anna had grown used to the big, brooding gargoyle. She liked his curiosity and intensity, even liked his flirtatiousness, though she'd never admit it to him. Whenever he gave her that smoldering smile, her insides flipped and Anna felt *alive*. Like she was more than a body attached to a painful head.

She wasn't ready to think about what that all meant, but she could admit to herself that she enjoyed his company. She'd worried having him stay with her, after being on her own for so long, would begin to grate. Having roommates before was always a challenge, and Frey certainly came with a bevy of his own, yet Anna liked having him around.

She liked cooking for two. She liked their evenings of chatting and cards and history documentaries. She liked how much Frey and Captain got on.

Anna wouldn't have thought it a week ago, but she was enjoying her time with her statue-come-to-life.

And isn't that just insanity.

It'd certainly seem like it to anyone else.

Settling back into the cushions, Anna listened to the documentary with half an ear as she tapped through her laptop, on the dimmest setting, double checking her coming appointments and prescription renewals. She wanted a new plan with more robust treatment because life had to be lived and she wasn't really.

It just took a giant flying mythical creature with beautiful eyes and prettier pecs crashing into her life to make her realize it. Anna snorted with a laugh.

Not much got done that day, but then, there wasn't much to do. Anna didn't have friends or a significant other to go out and do things with. She couldn't run errands or do chores. So she dozed and ate and dozed some more.

It was after an early dinner, during another doze, that she felt herself moving.

Cracking open her eyes, she had to blink a few times before realizing she stared straight into a wall of warm gray chest.

Frey had gently picked her up bridal style, blanket and all, from the couch and was carefully carrying her.

She had only a moment to register the heat of his skin and the rich scent of him, like petrichor and pine, before the softness of her bed surrounded her.

He set her down as gently as he'd carried her, and when his arms slid out from under her, Anna's throat clogged with wanting to ask him to stay. His warmth drew her in, making her want to curl against that wide chest and hear the steady beat of his heart.

Don't go, something inside her begged. *Don't go.*

But she bit back the words and laid still, warm and comfortable and unsure what to do with the jumble of words and desires knotting inside her. She'd be lying if she said she wasn't a smidge terrified of a strong, hulking gargoyle carrying her around in her sleep and knowing he could do whatever he wanted to her with little effort—but mostly, she was curious. Anticipatory, even. To see what he'd do.

She tried to keep her breathing even, but she couldn't help holding it when she felt his warmth draw close again. The soft slide of his long hair brushed against her shoulder, and then warm lips pressed to her forehead in a tender kiss.

A needy pang wrenched at her heart.

Against her skin, he murmured, "*Mae fy nghalon yn eiddo i ti, fy nghân.*"

Anna's breath shuddered through her, but when she opened her eyes, she was alone in her dark room.

A slice of light cut across the floor from where he'd left her door cracked.

Burrowing under the blankets, she touched the place where he'd kissed her, swearing she could still feel the heat of his lips.

Frey's frustration was a familiar, sore ache as he took up his spot to stare out the window for yet another night. The mist and drizzle matched his mood, but his mate needed quiet.

He'd never forget the feeling of filling his arms with her, holding her to his chest, where she was safest. Her cheek had come to rest over his heart for a brief moment, and Frey would have given anything to prolong it, to lie down with her and hold her in his arms as she slept. If she would but let him in . . .

A more honorable male would have left, but he couldn't help stealing another small boon. Touching his lips to her skin, breathing in deeply of her scent—he'd nearly lost his head and fallen into bed beside her. She was so soft in sleep, all her sharper edges blunted. He would never forget the fan of her lashes nor the easy slope of her brow. They were precious to him, and Frey held onto them when he couldn't hold her, taking up his post at the window.

Captain soon joined him, and together they stood vigil over Anna's dwelling, watching as the night passed in a somnolent tide, flowing and ebbing as the moon arced overhead.

As the night wore on, though, that itching need to do something, to escape his confines overcame Frey. Careful to set Captain down and ensure he didn't escape again, Frey snuck out one of the front windows onto what Anna called the *fire escape.*

Spreading his wings, the delicate membranes trembled, the sensitive hairs along the undersides shivering at the feel of the wind. With only the barest squeak, he launched from the iron scaffolding into the sky, his wings filling with air and his heart a sense of rightness.

Getting to touch and care for his Anna, however small and briefly, sparked a current of electricity just under his skin. Staying inside that dwelling was perhaps the smart thing to do, but he vowed not to stray far. The invisible tether tied between himself and his heartsong wouldn't allow him far.

Frey kept the building in his sights, always ready to swoop back if he sensed danger.

He didn't. As he climbed higher, beyond the buildings and thin fog, it was only him, his thoughts, and the handful of bats and birds out on a nighttime flight.

As he looked out upon this modern world, he understood a little more of what he was seeing thanks to the videos. Some of the landmarks had names now, and he knew the body of water on the horizon was the Pacific Ocean. However, it did not bring him closer to this world.

The world had forgotten his kind, and that meant danger to him and his heartsong.

He didn't know yet what it meant for his still-slumbering kin. If it was possible to wake them, what kind of world would they awake to?

It doesn't matter, not truly. His kind deserved the chance to live again. They would make a place for themselves in this world, one way or another.

His ruminations were somber and prolonged, so much so that he had to physically shake himself to dispel them. Growling, Frey swooped down, looped, and banked, exercising his wings. Proving to the universe, the fates, the goddesses—whatever and whoever was watching that he was Frey of the Clawtip and he was here. He would not be defeated.

His chest heaved with effort by the time he landed on the fire escape, sweat pooling at his horn bases and hollow of his throat. He had just enough time to wipe himself down with a spare towel from the washroom, drying his wings of the predawn mist, before he felt it.

Weak dawn light had begun to filter through the foggy haze.

It wouldn't be long now.

The sound of Anna's door opening had him turning to behold his mate and bid her good morning.

Her attire gave him pause.

Gone were her comfortable sweaters and tight braies; instead, she'd clad herself in stiffer garments with many buttons and seams. He hadn't seen her wear such clothing since . . .

"Good morning, my Anna," he forced himself to say.

"Good morning," she said quietly. Her countenance was almost shy as she emerged fully from her bedchamber. "Thank you for carrying me to bed, that was very sweet."

"Your comfort is important. As is your safety," he replied with a pointed look at her clothing.

Anna cleared her throat. "I have to go back to work today. The break is over."

"*Fy nghân*," he sighed, "you know how I feel about this."

"Yes, you've been quite clear. And you know how I feel about it. I'm going." She held her hands up and approached him, until she was only a few handspans away. Looking at him almost beseechingly, she said, "I know you don't like it. But me not going in or quitting all of a sudden would look super suspicious."

"Damn what it looks like if it keeps you safe."

But Anna just shook her head. "These things are almost always an inside job, so I can't afford to look any *more* suspicious than I already do. I need this job, Frey. I need it for the healthcare and the money—I'm buying for both of us now."

From her tone, she didn't mean it to insult him, but the arrow of truth, that he was utterly dependent on his mate, struck him nonetheless.

Frey's lips thinned with displeasure and a sour shame.

Color bloomed across Anna's cheeks and she held her hands up again. "I don't mind. And besides, going back means I can keep an eye on things. Maybe I'll learn something to help the rest of your people."

The thought perhaps had merit, but that didn't mean Frey liked it. He wouldn't put his mate in danger for mere possibilities.

Still, that she wanted to help his kin at all mollified the worst of his bitterness.

He didn't say that he thought the best thing Anna could do for his kin was accept the mate bond. Whatever lay behind the curse and his partial freedom from it, their bond was at the heart of it. Nothing else explained his awakening after so many centuries, and having a link to this new modern world, a human mate, made sense for his kind, cut off from their own so long ago.

But he didn't say this. He'd promised.

Frey did open his mouth to argue about her leaving the dwelling again, but his jaw went stiff before words could form.

With a frustrated grumble, he managed to growl, "You must be safe."

"I will, I promise," she said, the words ringing in his ears as they too turned to stone.

It had to be enough.

Her promise and whatever connection he'd been able to form with her over the past days had to be enough.

The guilt in Anna's gut tried to work with the caffeine from her coffee to make her a nervous wreck by the time she made it into the museum an hour later, but she wouldn't let them.

She didn't have anything to feel guilty about.

Get safely to work? Check.

Put away my things in my very low-risk desk? Check.

Don't let on about the giant gargoyle taking up a considerable corner of my living room? Double check.

Settling in at her desk felt like slipping on a supportive pair of shoes. She found her grooves, sliding easily into routine to prepare for the day.

As more of a homebody, Anna always appreciated getting to be at home rather than work. Yet, coming in, having a routine, did offer a sense of normalcy and security. Going through the motions of the job was its own comfort; she was accomplishing something, earning her own keep. Establishing a routine over the past few months had even helped her migraines a bit—and she wasn't surprised that seriously deviating from it over the last week had incurred more headaches.

Completing her normal morning tasks gave her a sense of calm that'd been seriously lacking since a certain statue sprang to life.

Now that she was in and reestablished, though, she did have a few things to add to her routine. Namely, *find out what you can about the statues without looking suspicious.* That could prove tricky, but she had to start somewhere. She didn't know what else to do; Frey needed answers. He couldn't stay the only one of his kind awake, what kind of life would that be? She couldn't hide him forever.

What he and his kind could or would do after lifting the curse, she couldn't really fathom, either. And she wouldn't touch the inexplicable sadness she felt at imagining him leaving with his kind with a ten-foot pole.

Sipping on her coffee, Anna scrolled through the somewhat backlogged museum emails. She had her own organization email that received maybe two messages a day, since Carrie or Gavin were more likely to just come over and ask if they needed something, but Anna also manned the museum's main communique. They got the standard fare of solicitations, inquiries, and advertisements, along with a nice smattering of crackpots and doomsayers.

A bit of everything had piled up over the four-day closure, and Anna toggled through to see if anything caught her eye that needed immediate attention. Quite a few inquiries had been sent about the closure, which she flagged to respond to en masse, giving the Gwyneths' scripted excuse of cleaning and restoration. The scripted explanation was the one email sitting in her personal inbox that morning, and Anna's stomach knotted reading over the lie, especially as it was to staff, not just the public now.

> Hello, team! Gavin and I apologize again for the suddenness of the closure. It came to our attention that emergency restoration and cleaning was needed on several of the pieces, and to get that done, we needed to close. Please feel free to pass along our reasons and apologies to any guests who enquire. There are two new pieces on display in the main gallery while the others are restored.

> Thank you again for your commitment and hard work. We hope you enjoy the time off.
>
> –Carrie Gwyneth

It wasn't that Anna minded lying. She didn't, especially if it kept nosy people like cops or reporters, or worse, amateur internet sleuths looking to make a podcast, away. The crux of it was that she'd made promises to herself, and here she was, compounding this lie with another.

But how do you tell your bosses that one of their gargoyle statues sprang to life and has been living in your apartment?

You don't.

Unless they suspected it might happen.

Anna chewed on her straw, stomach knotting tighter. All the lies and Frey's dire warnings were getting to her. She just didn't see how the Gwyneths could know they owned a collection of cursed mythical creatures.

Then again, how could they not?

The thought drew Anna's gaze up, to the first corridor, where she could just spot one of the gargoyles from her desk. It was a dramatic piece, arms and wings flung wide. To her, it'd always looked upside down, like the figure should have been falling headfirst toward the ground.

They probably were when they were cursed.

Shuddering, she went back to the inbox.

Toward the bottom, with the oldest of the unanswered emails, was a name that sprang out at her. June Parkhurst. Quickly opening the message, she saw it was sent to the museum as well as Carrie's .org.

The message was succinct.

> Below you will find my intended schedule for the next few weeks while I complete the studies. Thank you for forwarding the details on the additional security measures. I look for-

> ward to working with you on this opportunity.
> June P.

Anna read the message twice, hunting for any hidden detail. It felt like the end of a thread between June and Carrie, but why then CC the museum's address?

Was she trying to let *Anna* know when she'd be in? As a warning? A threat?

After another chew on her straw, Anna hit reply. Not reply all. But she did add her own .org to the CC line as she typed out a quick response.

> Dr. Parkhurst,
>
> Thank you for your continued work. We highly value your expertise and look forward to working with you. Your schedule is perfectly fine. Please check in with Anna at the front desk when you arrive tomorrow to get your badge and fob.
>
> Until then,
> The Gwyneth Collection

Without overthinking it, Anna pressed send.

Maybe it was good that June was coming back. Anna could keep an eye on the art expert and have someone from the outside to ask some of her questions.

Alone in the lobby with a half-hour before opening time, Anna took out a small notebook and began jotting down what she already knew about the collection and its mysterious owners.

By lunch, more than a few curious visitors had filtered through the front doors to ask Anna about the extended closure. Some regulars came in too, namely the older man who read to the statues and the grad student who was drawing them, grumbling about the hiccup in their schedules.

Anna told the story enough times that the lie almost began to feel like the truth. "We're so sorry for the inconvenience. A few restorations and some basic cleaning needed to happen, and that was best accomplished with the museum closed. We hope you have a wonderful visit today and enjoy the new exhibits!"

The stream of museumgoers was steady enough that she didn't really notice one of the regulars until after he'd made his way through the circuit of the museum and back to the front again. She'd gotten halfway through her new spiel even before noticing it was him standing at her desk.

A middle-aged but well-kept man, his gray wool overcoat oozed money in its stiff, fine lines with a scarlet cashmere scarf tucked under the collar and lapels. His face was fine-boned, his blue eyes striking, almost dreamy beneath heavy lids. His skin was the type of tan that had known sun during his youth but maybe less of it now, and his lips were thin as they stretched into a polite smile.

The patron ran a hand over his parted, sandy blonde hair, perfectly coiffed with the expensive kind of pomade that didn't look like anything at all held the hair in place. He looked at her from across the desk politely, with a boyish kind of charm, though his eyes belied his age and more calculating mind.

He wants something, her instinct observed.

She'd seen this man before, had noticed him in his smart suits and coats. When she'd first observed him, she was struck by the impression of a slick 80s businessman he gave and always remembered him afterwards because of it.

The man let her finish before nodding. "I was surprised when the museum was closed. It's my favorite jaunt in the city."

Anna put on her best charming, what-can-you-do customer service smile. "It was a surprise to us, but the safety of the collection and our patrons comes first."

"Of course." He shuffled a little closer to the desk. "I admired the two new statues in the gallery. I didn't realize they weren't all on display before."

"Yes, the owners decided it would be good to rotate them, so the public can appreciate all of the beautiful statues."

"Can we expect more to come on display?"

Anna's smile grew brittle. *So many questions.*

"That's up to the owners, but it may happen in a few months."

The patron shifted his weight, one of his hands sliding into his overcoat pocket. A moment later, Anna felt an inexplicable tingle just under her chin.

"How many statues are there total in the museum's collection?" he asked through his neutral smile.

Anna's jaw worked a moment, the approximate number she'd heard from Carrie rushing to her lips, but she gritted her teeth against them.

"Over a hundred of the grotesques and double that in other statues and figurines," she answered, and the tingling stopped.

Please don't be a new migraine symptom.

"Most are on display already," she continued. "The owners love their pieces and enjoy the public coming to visit them."

Something like frustration flashed across the man's face, but it was gone again in a moment before another smile, again boyish, showed off his perfectly straight white teeth. Perhaps that may have worked on whatever suave businessmen this guy worked with, but Anna knew what she saw.

"Sorry for all the questions," he said, "this is just one of the most fascinating museums in the city. I'm Andrew Glendower."

When he reached out his hand to shake, Anna ignored it and smiled instead. "Oh, like the Welsh rebel?"

Glendower's smile spread wider, and he tucked his hand back in his pocket. "The very same. Though they changed the spelling on the boat over, of course." His eyes glittered with pleasure when he added, "You know your history, Miss Anna."

She fought the panic that wanted to leap into her throat at him knowing her name, but she reminded herself of the nametag pinned to her blouse. *He doesn't know anything, keep calm and carry on!*

"Well, I *do* work in a museum, Mr. Glendower."

"Still, most can be forgiven for not knowing a medieval Welsh hero."

"Sure, but not those of us who studied early-medieval British history."

"Did you," he said, though it wasn't a question.

Anna shut her mouth with a *click*, realizing she hadn't meant to give that away.

"I'm a professor of ancient and early-medieval pagan religious practices, in fact. Ancient Celtic paganism, to be precise."

Anna's brows rose. "Then no wonder you enjoy the collection. Many of the pieces are from ancient Celtic origin."

Glendower's smile grew again. "Yes, when I heard about this place, I couldn't resist."

She didn't hear Carrie coming, but Anna was grateful to break from the man's long stare when her boss came to stand beside her at the desk. Graceful as ever, Carrie placed herself in Glendower's full view, almost coming between him and Anna.

"Good afternoon," she said in that lyrical voice of hers, "I hope you're enjoying the collection."

"Immensely," said Glendower, and he reached out his hand again. "Professor Andrew Glendower."

Anna didn't miss how the corner of Carrie's mouth twitched, but ever polite, she reached out to shake the man's hand. It was her whole body that twitched when their palms contacted, and Anna swore the ends of Carrie's blonde hair lifted off her back.

Carrie quickly pulled her hand back to place on the desk, though her smile was big and warm enough to hide it. “Glendower,” she said, “you don’t hear Welsh names like that often anymore.”

“I’m proud of my heritage. *Fe godwn ni eto.*”

Carrie cocked her head as if she’d heard something strange. “How long has your family been in the States, professor?”

“Oh, a while yet. And yourself? That is a lovely accent I hear. Northern Welsh, if I’m not mistaken?”

“Something like that,” Carrie agreed without agreeing. “My husband and I have been here for a time, mostly to open the museum. We greatly enjoy it here.”

“You and your husband have a fine collection, Mrs. Gwyneth.”

Both Carrie and Anna stared at the man, sure that Carrie hadn’t given her name. But then, it wasn’t really a secret who the Gwyneths were. Their names and pictures were on the website. You had to dig for the pictures a little, but they were there, and more than one newspaper and magazine had done a story when the museum first opened.

“Thank you, we are quite proud of it.”

“I was just pestering your lovely docent here about it. I’ve never seen pieces like these.”

“They are quite rare. Quite special.”

“Indeed. Where, may I ask, did you find them all?”

“Europe, mostly,” said Carrie. “It took many years.”

Anna waited, like Glendower, for more, but when Carrie smiled and said nothing else, she was puzzled. She got not wanting to give the pushy patron any more information; even if they were a museum with art on public display, Carrie didn’t owe this guy shit. Still, Anna had expected something like *we inherited a lot of it and bought the rest.* Surely one of them had to have inherited the bulk of the collection—all of it couldn’t have been sourced and purchased in one lifetime.

Glendower asked a few more questions, all of which Carrie answered with the same polite vagueness she had the others. Eventually, the man bid them farewell, another pleasant smile on his face, and headed for the front door.

Carrie remained beside her even after they couldn't see the back of the retreating professor anymore.

"What a strange man," said Carrie eventually.

"Did you catch that he was an early medievalist professor? He's probably sniffing around looking for a research opportunity."

"Do you think so? Hmm."

When Carrie didn't elaborate, Anna couldn't help asking, "Do you know what it meant when he said *fe godwn ni eto?*"

She knew Carrie and Gavin both spoke Welsh, rare as it was these days. In fact, they seemed to speak several old Brittonic languages as well as the modern ones of Europe. Now that she thought about it, Gavin supposedly had been a professor himself. She wondered if he'd know Glendower. Early medieval studies with a focus on druids wasn't a large section of the academic population.

Carrie was quiet another moment before replying, "It means 'we will rise again.'"

Anna's stomach lurched in her gut. Seriously, who was that guy?

"He's been here before?" Carrie asked.

"Yeah, he's one of the regulars. He hasn't stopped to chat before, though."

"Hm. Let me know if he does, please."

"Of course."

That Carrie's feathers were ruffled just as much as hers only worried Anna more, her heart beginning to strum faster than a heavy metal guitarist.

It didn't help when Carrie said, "Oh, I came over for a reason, actually. Detective Ramirez got in touch yesterday to say he would be coming by the museum today or tomorrow for follow-up interviews." She made a sympathetic face. "I'm sorry you'll have to go through the story again."

"It's okay," Anna said through numb lips, "anything to help."

Carrie patted her on the shoulder before departing, but Anna barely felt it. Her stomach was in so many knots that the moment she was alone again in the lobby, she slapped down her *Be Right Back!* sign and booked it to the employee bathroom.

Shit shit shitshitshitshit!

Anna wetted a paper towel to hold to her burning cheeks and avoided looking at herself in the mirror. She didn't need to see her own face to know her anxiety was spiking. Her right eye twinged, and sparks of pain burst across her temples.

She took calming breaths, reminding herself that it would be okay. The detective would ask the same questions and she'd give the same answers. It would be fine.

Just so long as he didn't come to the apartment.

13

Frey woke to a darkening, cold apartment. Captain lounged across his shoulders, feet slung around his neck, and a thick purr rattled in his ear.

"At least you are here to greet me," Frey grumbled. It took merely a sniff to know Anna wasn't here.

A wave of protectiveness drew him toward the window, and his unease only grew when he saw no one on the street below. The night was still new, the sky not the full inky dark, but he knew Anna should have been home by now.

Scratching under Captain's chin with a claw, he remarked, "Where is your mistress, hmm? Is she often late? Why did she not say?"

The cat couldn't answer him, nor did he seem to share Frey's unease. Instead, Captain hopped from Frey's shoulder onto the couch, then the floor, to pad over to what Anna called his *feeding station*. His bowl stood empty, and it was past the time Anna usually fed him.

To dispel any ambiguity, Captain blinked at him and meowed. Loudly.

"All right, my friend, all right."

Frey got a little thrill turning on the lights to the kitchen, the spark of light, of electricity, still a novelty he enjoyed. In one of the cabinets, he found the tins of food Anna kept for Captain. Different pictures of different foods had been affixed to the tins, and he reached for one with what looked to be a fish filet.

Rumbling hungrily, he said, "I've always been partial to fish. You may have to share."

Another plaintive yowl accompanied the *pop* of the tin as Frey opened it with a claw. The metal lid peeled away easily, and he held it up to sniff what kind of fish would be put in a tin.

His eyes—and nose—were met with a fishy reek from a gray, tin-shaped blob that perhaps had once been meat.

Gagging, Frey unceremoniously dropped it into Captain's bowl, horrified when it kept its cylindrical shape. He managed to break it into smaller pieces with a spoon before Captain butted his hand out of the way and began to eat.

"You *enjoy* that travesty?"

The loud purring as Captain ate was Frey's answer.

Disgusted, Frey wandered back into the kitchen. The food Anna made was nothing like that. Opening cabinets, he eventually found a few things he recognized, and a search of the *refrigerator* revealed uncooked chicken parts.

Most excellent.

Frey was determined to find new opportunities to woo his cautious Anna. There were more ways than one to prove his worth, and until she allowed him into the bedchamber to prove his prowess in bringing her pleasure, he could at least cook her a meal.

Decided, Frey gathered the ingredients he knew and began.

By the time he heard the scrape of a key in the lock, dinner was almost ready, sizzling in a pan of fragrant butter and garlic cloves. Wiping his hands, Frey hurried to open the door.

Anna looked up at him in surprise from the other side of the threshold, her arms laden with colorful canvas bags.

"Oh!" she gasped when Frey took the bags from her and swept her inside with the crook of his wing. He shut the door and locked it with his tail.

Ushering her inside, he set the bags down on the counter before running his hands over Anna's arms.

"You are well, *fy nghân?* When you were not here, I worried."

Anna gave him a patient smile, and when he was satisfied she was unharmed and let his hands fall away, she shrugged out of her coat. Frey took it and hung it on its hook, Anna watching on with a bemused expression.

"I went grocery shopping since I hadn't yesterday. I'm sorry I forgot to say."

Frey bit back his agitation, instead poking through the bags she'd brought. Interesting, colorful things greeted him in boxes and thin film wrappers.

A happy chirrup sounded from below as Frey began unpacking the groceries, and Anna leaned down to pick up Captain. The loud purr again emanated from the cat, and Frey watched from the corner of his eye, with no small amount of jealousy, as Captain was given kisses and pets in greeting.

"I'm sorry I'm late, Cappy. I'll feed you right now."

"Don't believe his pitiful entreaties, he's been fed already."

Brows arched in surprise, Anna turned to observe the massacred remains of the gray blob strewn across the feeding station.

"Oh, that's great, thank you! I'm sure he appreciated getting dinner on time." Her smile was wide and genuine, and some of Frey's prickliness rubbed away.

Grinning back, he said, "He made a firm argument."

Chuckling, Anna hoisted the cat higher in her arms, cuddling him close, as Frey returned to their dinner.

She exclaimed when she saw him plating the meal. "You didn't have to make dinner! I brought enough stuff for a few days."

"Nonsense. It was no trouble."

Although she made a few more noises of protest, Frey eventually managed to herd his mate to the set table. She sat with a sort of stunned amazement adorning her face, watching on in astonishment as Frey laid out the chicken and seared potatoes.

Anna blinked at the steaming meal laid before her as if she couldn't quite believe what she was seeing. Frey sat down opposite her, threading his tail through the chairback and carefully folding his wings, awaiting her praise.

When she remained silent, he couldn't help prompting, "Is it satisfactory?"

Eyes still wide in wonder, Anna breathed, "It's . . . this is amazing, Frey. Thank you."

Pleasure suffused him. *I will win her over yet.*

"It pleases me to please you, my Anna. I want to do this and more for you, always. It is what mates do for each other."

Her face lost some of its light. "Frey . . ."

He held up his hands. "I know, *fy nghân,* I promised. But you didn't specify for how long we shouldn't speak of it, and it's been days. I merely wish to discuss it. Civilly. Over dinner."

Anna took up her utensils to begin cutting her meal into smaller bites. To keep himself busy awaiting her reply, Frey speared his own chicken and took a hearty bite to fill his mouth.

His patience was rewarded when she hummed with pleasure at her first bite. "It's good," she murmured around another mouthful.

He let her eat, the sight of her filling her belly with food he prepared sating Frey far more than the meal.

When her reply finally came, it was quiet and measured. "I suppose I just . . . I'm having a hard time wrapping my head around it, I guess. That there's even such a thing as this mate bond for starters, then that you and I are . . ."

Frey nodded. "I grant it would be surprising news if one wasn't raised with such knowledge. I know humans do not have such kinds of pairings. It is just part of the magick that gave my kind life. We have always known it and welcomed it."

"I can get behind that part. It happens with your people. But I have a harder time believing it can happen for a guardian and a human. For *us*."

Frey swallowed his next bite carefully, considering his words. He meant what he said, he wanted a civil conversation that would not end with Anna retreating. Still, it was hard to hold back all the declarations clamoring in his throat.

"I suppose I shall need your trust, my Anna. You will have to trust what I say is true, as you do not feel the same *knowing* being human. But that I'm even sitting here speaking to you is testament to what I say. I would not be here without you."

Anna took a long, deep breath. "It's . . . *a lot*."

"Yes. I work every day to earn such trust from you. It is not something I take lightly or for granted."

"I know you don't." A shadow appeared in her cheek as she chewed it. "Your people really *believe* in it."

"We trust that the goddesses will lead us to the right being, someone who will truly be our heart's song. It doesn't happen for every guardian, but we pray for it and celebrate when it does."

"But doesn't it bother you? Not having a choice?"

Frey frowned, not understanding. "It doesn't matter. You didn't choose to have your headaches, nor your hair color. I didn't choose the shape of my horns nor length of my tail. Having a heartsong is just as . . . innate. Part of who you are."

Anna pushed her food around her plate, not looking at him when she muttered, "I'd get rid of my headaches if I could, and I can change my hair color."

His nostrils flared with frustration. "But you understand what I mean."

"Yeah," Anna sighed, "I suppose. But it being intrinsic doesn't mean it's good. Lots of things can go wrong with something even innate to you. It can't be all rainbows and sunshine between every pair of mates. And what about same-sex pairs? If mating is about babies, what about them? Were they forced to be with someone they didn't want? And what—"

"Enough," Frey huffed.

Anna blinked at him, startled, but he wasn't sorry. He only regretted letting her go on so long.

"You are being willfully obtuse."

"I am not! It's a valid question."

"Plenty of guardians had partnerships that were 'same-sex,' as you say. There was no forcing pairs together. Some fell in love without ever feeling the pull of *knowing*. And . . ." He hated to admit it, hated thinking about his sister Seren and her unhappiness with her complicated mating before her untimely death. ". . . not all pairs were happy. We are all individuals. A successful pairing takes effort."

Anna sat back in her chair, arms crossing over her chest, and Frey felt a frisson of unease skitter down his spine. Her posture was all jutting elbows and arched brows, defiance and refusal.

"So mating isn't about love. You don't have to love your mate."

The words landed between them with all the grace and softness of the hammer striking the anvil.

Frey's heart sank.

"Not always. But it should always lead to that. Good mates care for one another. I—" He reached across the table and pulled one of her hands from the knot of her arms to hold in his. "I care for you, my Anna. I should like to love you, too."

Frey didn't know what reaction he expected—a feminine blush or even just a softening of her stiff shoulders, perhaps. Instead, Anna's mouth went tight and her gaze fell away, avoiding his. Beneath his own larger one, her hand was cold and unmoving.

Desperation and frustration were a heady, toxic sludge rising in his throat. Grasping her fingers, he said, "You are my heartsong, Anna.

There is no changing this. I swear to you that I will ever strive to be a good mate. Matehood *is* a choice. Those that work are by choice. I will always choose you, my Anna. I will always care for you and provide for you, for that's what it is to be a mate."

Frey was a proud male, but smart males knew when to bend. And when to beg.

"Please, *fy nghân*. Let me be your mate."

Every single one of Frey's words drew a tear to Anna's eyes that she fought to keep back. She blinked against the stinging burn of them gathering along her lashes, willing herself not to cry. She hated crying, and she certainly wouldn't be doing it in front of this handsome, eager gargoyle-man who was saying such beautiful, right things.

Too right.

Anna never trusted words. People said a lot of things. Sometimes they even believed what they said. But words were cheap, easy. There'd been a lot of them tonight about how this relationship between mates, by virtue of its very nature, was amazing and loving and wonderful.

The relationship between mother and child was supposed to be loving, too. Anna sure as shit never experienced it. Why would she suddenly get a soulmate-level partner who would be all those things?

What Frey promised was what she suspected her mom was always searching for, just in the form of a bad boy biker or dirty-talking cowboy type. The thing was, the Disney princess romance didn't really exist—especially not with the type of man Shannon Kincaid met. Men weren't really like that. *Love* wasn't really like that.

What Frey promised sounded nice, sure. Even with a partner who was a giant bat-winged cursed statue from the late Celtic period.

Don't lie, especially because it's him.

Right, she was trying to lie less.

Yes, having some sort of wild romance with this big brute of a man, who loved playing card games with her and singing old shanties off-key to make her laugh, might be nice. Wonderful. Amazing.

But would it last?

Would it even really be real?

No. She couldn't see how.

Pulling her hand out from under his, she tucked it beneath her other arm.

"You don't know me, Frey."

Another annoyed huff flared his nostrils. She was testing the guy's patience, she could tell, but so what. He was testing hers with all this romantic bullshit that made her heart ache. He had *no right* to make her want to cry over how lonely she was nor fill her heart with soppy hopes and dreams.

Eventually, he'd leave. Everyone did.

Whether with his people or just to get out of her apartment, he'd leave and not come back. Anna knew it, and it was time he started being honest with himself.

"I'm *trying* to know you, my Anna. I want to know everything. But you fight me at every turn."

His face was all frowns and scowls, his frustration apparent. Something in her sympathized; she knew she was being a brat, running hot and cold. The man had made her *dinner* and she wasn't acting very grateful. But she didn't know what to do with this mythical man and his mate spiel.

It'd be so easy to fall into his words. In that little weekend bubble they'd had, when they just hung out in the evenings, everything felt almost . . . perfect. Comfortable. Like they were . . . friends. Anna hadn't had friends in a long time. She craved it, though—but all this mate talk was too much, striking too close to all the most vulnerable, broken parts of her she hated looking at.

And if she could hardly bear to look at the worst of herself, how could she ever think anyone else would?

He didn't *know* her. He didn't see her. And if he ever did, he'd wish he hadn't.

Why couldn't this all have happened in a few years? She was just now getting on her feet, able to meet goals and start a better life. She was making progress, and while it was messy, it was something. And now everything was a jumbled mess.

Maybe if she'd met him in a few years, she'd feel on a better standing to truly consider what he was saying. Or at least let him have his mate bond ideas and still pursue something with him. Maybe future Anna would be ready for someone like Frey and everything he entailed.

But this Anna wasn't.

Pushing her chair back, she said, "Can we be done? I don't . . ."

Frey's wings drooped down to his shoulders, covering them in a leathery cloak. He hadn't done such a move since those first days, and to see him do it, almost like he was hiding himself away, hurt.

"Yes, my Anna. We can be done for the night."

She didn't miss his caveat, but she was too tired to stress more about it. Silently, she cleaned up the remains of their meal, ignoring his protests that he would tidy up.

Blinking back her frustrated tears as she scrubbed the dishes, Anna railed at herself for ruining such a nice gesture. The guy was trying to at least be a decent roommate. She was truly touched; nobody had made her dinner in ages.

The day had been so much between the weird patron and the even weirder vibe of the museum post-theft. She'd spent all afternoon stressing about when and where the detective would show up for follow-up interviews. The wind had been biting and the grocery store lines long. Everything had just conspired to make this a no good, very bad day.

Then Frey had made dinner. And fed Cappy.

By the time the dishes were washed and leftovers packed away, Anna had mustered the courage to face Frey long enough to say, "Thank you again for making dinner, that was really sweet."

His wings were still folded about his shoulders, secured by the two claws hooked together, and his expression had turned somber. He looked as tired as she felt.

"Always, my Anna. It is the least I can do after everything you've done for me."

She nodded, not knowing what else to do. "It's been a long day and I . . . I think I'm just going to go to bed. We'll watch something tomorrow, okay?"

"Yes."

"Okay. Good night."

And like the coward she was, she hustled into the bathroom to wash the day off and hopefully all the foolish little hopes that'd managed to sink their hooks into her heart.

Anna was grateful for a busy day at the museum, leading two different school trip tours and fielding enough visitor questions at the desk that she barely had time to take a sip of coffee or water, let alone think too much about her conversation with Frey the night before.

Still, busy as it was, she couldn't shake a despondent sort of listlessness that filled her. Like she was . . . sad about the whole thing.

Whenever she had a free moment, her mind invariably strayed back to their conversation and how she'd just . . . left it. Not her finest moment.

But what he's saying is crazy.

And yeah, she understood that in the scheme of things—fae, curses, magick, *gargoyles*—being someone's soulmate wasn't really even in the top three strangest things about all this. But there was still . . . she still had to wonder . . .

Why me?

Why now, why her, why Frey?

The questions spun uselessly in her mind, making her grateful for work to give her brain a break.

It was in the last hour of her shift, when the museum was mostly empty of guests but full of the vivid yellows and greens of late afternoon, that June Parkhurst arrived for her first official session with the statues.

Anna greeted her at the desk, nerves tangling in her chest as she gave June her museum credentials and fob to the employee side door. June watched on quietly, her beautiful face pensive. She'd pulled her red hair, haloed in gold in the afternoon light, into a loose chignon, pearl earrings dangling from her ears. With her brown cashmere turtleneck and tweed blazer, she oozed chic academic, and Anna, when she wasn't letting those wheels spin in her mind, practically drooled.

If she hadn't been so worried over what June may or may not have seen that night, Anna might've had a girl-crush on her. Or at least her wardrobe.

"It's nice to see you again," Anna said, leading the way deeper into the museum.

Before Frey, she might've been a smidge grumpy about having to stay a little late to babysit an academic, but today, Anna had her notebook ready to jot down any tidbit June said that could be useful. Or incriminating.

They made their way uninterrupted into the main gallery.

Even though Anna had made the trek a hundred times in the past few days, seeing the two new statues replacing Frey and the stolen gargoyle still made her heart jump. The place where Frey stood was *his* place, and it felt wrong to see another statue there. Searching for him was like muscle memory, and she was almost disappointed whenever she didn't find him there.

She hoped none of this showed on her face as she followed June to one of the statues. It was the one June had spent time over the first night, the one with the missing horn and arm. Restoration work had clearly already taken place at some point, but June's expert eye was going to help ensure nothing else happened to the piece.

Or something like that. Anna wasn't totally clear on what precisely the Gwyneths hoped June would accomplish—a bit of everything she supposed, restoration, research, and acquisition. And having a name like Dr. June Parkhurst associated with the museum certainly lent an air of authenticity and grandeur.

"How've you been? Since that night," Anna asked.

June looked at her carefully, those haunting eyes searching. "No lingering side effects, thankfully. And the shock has worn off. And yourself?"

"Just a headache, but nothing new there." She stopped herself before she began to babble as June set up a tripod for surveying equipment to begin taking measurements and notes. "I hope they catch the guys soon."

June made an unhappy noise. "Unfortunately, they seemed well-funded, so I doubt they will be. The best option is to wait and see if anyone puts out discreet inquiries, either looking to acquire or sell the pieces through back channels."

"But how would you find out about that? Whether people were asking around, I mean."

June's gaze didn't return to Anna, but she felt the art historian's full attention on her like a spotlight.

"You ask the right people the right questions. And, you know, the dark web."

"That's something that can be monitored?"

"Sure, but doing it from your personal computer will get you on a list. And the main problem is whether the thieves stole it to sell it, or were paid to steal it by the person who wanted it. If that's the case, it won't come up for sale."

Anna chewed her lip, not liking that at all. She sort of felt responsible for the stolen statue, like taking on Frey meant taking on his people. That was a *person* who'd been stolen, not just a statue.

"Who'd want a giant monster statue?" Anna asked with fake incredulity.

I definitely see the appeal. At least of a certain granite piece with swooping horns and an arrogant streak.

June snorted delicately, the first bit of real personality Anna had seen from the art historian. "Lots of people. These statues are amazing and so rare." A pensive frown stole over her fair brows, and she turned that troubled expression on Anna. "I'm not saying the Gwyneths deserved this or had it coming, but a collection like this was bound to be a target for thieves. This collection is . . . unique."

Anna recognized the squirrely look June got in her eyes; it'd been the same when they had their terse exchange in the bathroom.

"I've never seen anything like it," Anna agreed.

June shook her head but resumed preparing her camera for the high-res scans and photos she'd be taking of each piece.

"It's even more than that. This place is *special*." Her emphasis on the word sent a skitter down Anna's spine. She wasn't bold enough to acknowledge it or the bait June dangled, though.

When Anna said nothing, June went on, "There's something about this place . . . these statues. There's very little provenance for most of them, yet testing has proven over and over that they're legitimately from the sixth century. They're an enigma. Add to that that they're all owned by one couple? Who opens a museum to show them? Most art collectors own only a handful of rare pieces. Those from old families might have more, which they'll loan out in bits to galleries and museums. But to own all of these and display them? It's unprecedented."

"They certainly made a splash in the papers when the museum first opened," Anna said inanely.

It felt kind of wrong to be giving June nothing when the fishing was so obvious, but the wheels of Anna's mind were spinning again.

The museum and collection had always felt a bit strange, but Anna hadn't really questioned it after getting her first paycheck and new health insurance card. Rich people were eccentric. They didn't operate by the same rules.

What June was saying, though . . . this was more than just a rich couple flaunting their rare collection and making waves in the art world. Anna did a little due diligence before taking the job; both Carrie and Gavin had a bit of a paper trail back in the UK, as well as a few mentions about a long lineage from Wales. There hadn't been much information available, but then, if they were from one of those posh rich families that stayed out of the spotlight, it could've been easily suppressed or taken down. Still, it wasn't clear how the Gwyneths had acquired their wealth and therefore the collection.

Anna had to admit that this all added up to something that was at best fishy. She couldn't ignore it. Especially not since she knew there were living beings behind those frozen stone faces.

June fell quiet, probably realizing that Anna wasn't giving her anything, and focused fully on her work. As she began taking the photographs and scans, monitoring the rendering process on a laptop she'd brought, Anna slipped away to meander through the gallery with her thoughts.

Without fail, her feet brought her to the pedestal Frey had once stood upon. His replacement was another large male, this time carved from a grayish marble with veins of smoky black swirling across his chest and thighs. His arms and wings were thrown wide, as if he was protecting someone behind him.

His family, maybe? A wounded comrade?

The thoughts sobered her as she looked upon him and the many others of Frey's kind lining the gallery.

What are you all doing here?

This museum *was* strange. The whole situation was strange.

Fae magick, hissed through her mind. Anna thought it must be the magick binding his kind to the curse, but . . .

Could there really be some ancient magick here? She'd allow that many old objects held a certain power; so much history was imbued within them that they had their own gravity, pulling in the imagination and demanding veneration. Could so many objects like that, especially ones that had once been living beings cursed by the fae, brought together create their own kind of pull?

Something had always felt magical about this place. Anna had been attracted to it in a way that she didn't quite like thinking about. Just seeing the job application, her brain had had an itch, a sense that she should apply, she should *go there*.

She'd been drawn to the museum, to the collection.

To Frey.

Anna couldn't help a small blush—*damn all this blushing, he's not even here!* How many times had she found herself walking down the gallery to see him even when she didn't need to be in that part of the museum? How many times had she taken her lunch on one of the benches to sit and admire him?

Was there something drawing her here, to him?

The obvious answer was one she refused to accept.

Mate.

He'd said he could sense her even in his stone state, just because she was near. Because they were mates. He'd said he knew who she was before ever knowing her.

Maybe . . . I came here because . . .

No. No, that couldn't be it. She accepted that he believed in this mate bond. She accepted it happened for his people.

Anna didn't believe that meant she was Frey's mate. That they were meant to be together.

She was human.

She wasn't soulmate material.

There had to be another explanation.

Blush burning hotter, Anna shuffled a little closer to the new statue, a crazy idea coming to her.

She wasn't special, but what if . . .

Without thinking more, Anna reached out and placed a gentle hand on the new statue's leg. Cool stone met her touch, and she held her breath, looking up into the frozen face. Her heart pounded as she waited—for something to happen, for a shiver of life.

What did happen was a series of piercing, blinding bolts of light filling the gallery.

Anna yelped, clapping her hands over her eyes. Across the room, she heard the clatter of equipment fall to the floor as June covered her eyes against the sudden shocks of light.

For a long moment, nothing happened. There was no sound except the pounding of her heart and heave of her panicked breaths.

Then, the steady slap of feet quickly approaching.

"What happened?"

Gavin.

After another moment, Anna dared to peek out from behind her fingers. The light had faded, replaced by an imposing, frowning Gavin Gwyneth. He stood a few feet away, apparently having rushed from his office down one of the branch corridors. Face severe and stern, he took in Anna, still next the new statue, and June and her equipment.

"I-I'm so sorry," Anna rushed to explain, "I stumbled and caught myself on the statue. I shouldn't have touched it. I'm so sorry."

Eyes that were the palest blue Anna had ever seen slid from her to the statue and back again.

"You touched the statue. Nothing else happened?"

Anna swallowed hard. *Like springing to life?*

"No, nothing. I'm so sorry, I should've known better."

Sweat slicked down her back, and a wave of nausea washed down her body from throat to gut as Gavin stood on, cold gaze assessing.

"I see the new security measures work!" June called from across the gallery.

Gavin turned and gestured for Anna to follow him as he stalked toward June. She hurried dutifully behind, grateful to be away from the new statue. Anna made herself small and forgettable just in the periphery of Gavin's sight as he and June spoke.

"Dr. Parkhurst. That the needed security wasn't in place to begin with is a grave oversight on my part. I apologize again."

June shrugged, holding up a finger and waving it vaguely to indicate the room. That her hand shook gave away her nerves. "It's nice to know the new system works so well. I'm just sorry the thieves got here first."

Gavin nodded slowly. "A mistake that will not happen again." Anna didn't know how he managed to wrap a vow and a threat all into one, but she bit on her cheek to keep from shuddering at his words.

With one last look between them, his gaze lingering over Anna, Gavin bid them goodnight and headed back to his office.

Anna and June stood there silently, motionless, until he disappeared.

She was the first one to move, blowing out a breath to defuse the tension. "Damn, he's scary sometimes."

"Definitely from an aristocratic background."

They exchanged a bit more nervous banter before June resumed work and Anna left her to it, though she stayed far away from the other statues this time.

It was full dark by the time June completed what she wanted to for the evening, and Anna led her back to the front to finish up for the day. The darkness reminded her; Frey came to life at night, when she'd first touched him and now. Maybe the new statue hadn't woken because it hadn't been night.

But when she checked her phone's weather app, Anna realized the sun had gone down about two minutes before she touched the statue.

It should have worked.

Except that it hadn't.

Frey was the only one she'd awoken, and she didn't dare try on another.

15

"And then the lights came on, just *BAM*, blinding white light. No alarms, which is strange. I mean, I'm grateful, I'm sure that would've meant an immediate migraine, but most alarms have this horrible, shrill sound that repeats. And then Gavin was suddenly there and—" Anna grimaced, and Frey was grateful she took the moment to draw a breath during her frenzied explanation of the day's events.

With every word, Frey's concern only grew. His Anna had endangered herself and possibly drawn the ire of one of her employers.

And even worse, she'd been touching other guardians. Other *males*. To see if she could awaken them, too.

Because she doesn't believe me.

That truth sat like bad meat in his belly, sour and roiling. He'd known her reticence, of course. She'd made her uncertainty abundantly clear. Yet, Frey hadn't truly accepted that she disbelieved so very much. That she would try to *prove* he was wrong.

His heart ached with the knowledge, and he listened to the rest of her account with solemnity. His Anna became quite animated when telling a story, barely pausing for breath, hands flying as she emphasized certain words or points. Normally he enjoyed watching her speak, drawn in by the flutter of her hands and movement of her lips, but it was difficult to move past the troubling things she said—and his own intense jealousy.

Anna was *his* heartsong. His female to care for.

He wasn't at all surprised to hear that the male she'd touched hadn't awoken. Anna offered a tentative theory that it was the wrong time of day, but Frey knew better.

It was best the guardian hadn't awoken, for Frey didn't know what he'd do to another male touched by his mate—his soft, pretty, *unclaimed* mate.

That's not true. I'd have beaten him to a pulp.

Guardians were covetous of their mates, and likely the newly awoken male would've understood. Not the ideal way to wake from centuries of stone sleep.

Frey used the preparation of their nightly meal as an excuse to hide his face from Anna, lest she see the murderous thoughts playing out in his mind. By the time he plated the seared steak and roasted squash, herded Anna to the table, and seen her sat and cutting up her food, he'd gathered his thoughts enough to speak.

"You will not endanger yourself like that again."

Anna groaned. "I know I know I know, it was stupid. I just . . ." She popped a forkful of meat into her mouth and that groan turned into a moan of pure pleasure. "Oh, Frey, this is amazing."

"I have found the cooking tutorials," he said, waving her compliment away. Normally he'd have preened with her praise, but he wouldn't be distracted by her compliments nor the way his cock twitched with interest over the sounds she made.

"That place is unsafe," he said, enunciating each word.

"Technically, it's even more safe with all the new security." He knew her hedging by now, and rather than look at him, Anna studiously ate her meal.

"The new security is what worries me. From what you say, it sounds abnormal. One of many strange circumstances." How many would finally be enough to prove to her that something was going on in her museum?

"I know," she said again on a sigh. "Nothing is adding up. It's all *so* strange. But I just don't understand what it could be." She pointed her fork at him. "Don't say fae magick."

"But *it is* fae magick," he grumbled. "And the fae are *dangerous.*"

"So, what, my bosses are fae?"

His instinct was to declare that yes, it had to be the cruel creatures who'd cursed them now displaying them in their stone prison. But . . .

Jaw working, Frey admitted, "I don't know. It would be . . . unlikely. In my time, there were stories of the fae being trapped in another realm, only able to visit this one when the veil between realms is thinnest, on Beltane and Samhain. No one had known of a fae lingering in Albion in many ages."

"Okay, so then it's probably not the fae, even if their magick is still hanging around your kind."

From her bag, Anna pulled a small notebook. Flipping through the pages, she came to the end of her writings before saying, "I've been trying to take notes on what I've found out, but it isn't much. I'm working right now on a sort of inventory. How many statues, what they look like. Not sure what it'll be good for, but it's something."

A surge of conflict battled in Frey's chest. Pride and admiration and affection were a warm syrup in his blood. His Anna was brave and cared enough about him and his people's plight to try helping. Yet, outrage and protective instinct flared their jagged edges, agitated to know how much she truly was putting herself at risk.

Reaching a hand to place over hers and her notebook, Frey rumbled, "My Anna, I'm touched by your efforts, but you will stop this. You cannot put yourself in such danger."

"I'm being discreet," she protested.

A blush pinkened her cheeks at the unimpressed look he gave her. If today was any indication, she most certainly wasn't being discreet.

"Okay, today aside. I just . . . wanted to see what would happen. In case."

"In case I am not your mate," he accused.

Her blush deepened, and her gaze fell away.

Frey became almost as irritated with himself as he was with her, but he couldn't help the accusation. Nor the hurt from knowing he was right when she wouldn't meet his gaze.

"But nothing happened. Because you *are* my heartsong." His triumph was vicious and ugly; though he reveled in it, he was wise enough to keep it to himself.

"I'm . . . we're . . ." Anna sighed and ran her hands through her hair in a gesture of exasperation. "We're something, okay? There's obviously something going on that links you and me."

The mate bond! he wanted to shout, but clenched his jaw not to.

His Anna was a fierce but strange woman. He would take his victories where he could.

"Which is why I don't want you returning to that place," he insisted. "You are special to me, Anna. Something is going on in that museum, and until we understand more, it isn't safe for you."

"You're . . . special, too," she admitted in halting words. "But we can't find out anything if I'm not there. It's our only access to your people. And like I've said, until the investigation dies down, I'm under suspicion. It would look suspicious if I quit now. Especially after today." She muttered that last bit in an irritated huff.

"Perhaps, but it is a greater risk to walk into all the unknowns."

Looking conflicted herself, Anna said, "I really don't think my bosses have it out for me. Something is going on, but it doesn't feel . . . sinister? I guess?"

"The fae are clever and manipulative. You cannot let your guard down."

"I thought we agreed it wasn't the fae."

"We agreed on no such thing."

"But you—"

A heavy knock on the front door echoed through the dwelling. On the other side, a male voice called, "Anna Kincaid?"

Color drained from Anna's face at the sound, and Frey was up in a moment, marching for the door.

Anna was faster, darting in front of him to peer through the small hole.

She muffled her sound of distress in her sweater sleeve and turned on her toes into his body. Her hands splayed across his chest to catch herself, and for a moment Frey was too stunned by the feeling of her skin on his to do more than let her push him backwards.

Then there was another knock, more impatient than the last, and a growl worked up his throat.

Anna's hand made a slicing motion through the air.

"It's a cop," she hissed. Looking about, she nabbed his plate and utensils off the table, pushed them into his hands, and hustled him through the living room toward her bedchamber.

He stood his ground outside her door, not liking this turn of events at all.

Another knock. "Miss Kincaid, I need to speak with you."

"There's a *male* out there," Frey growled lowly. An affront. Who was this stupid man to interrupt their supper? To invade their dwelling?

"I *know*. No need to dilate those predator eyes at me." She gave another push, but Frey wouldn't budge. "It's the detective from before. I'll get rid of him. But you need to hide."

Frey needed to do no such thing. No man nor guardian in their right mind would come around making demands of another's mate in his time.

"I will not—"

"Frey." Anna frowned up at him, her expression grave. "He's looking for *you*."

Another growl rumbled in his chest, but through the instinct and outrage, he allowed himself to be sequestered into Anna's bedchamber.

Today was not the day to reveal that guardians hadn't quite been lost to time. And Frey knew enough of this modern world to know that making a law enforcement officer disappear would raise even more suspicion and therefore bring more danger to his mate's door.

So Frey bided his time.

And snatched up one of his mate's underthings to sniff to soothe the worst of his frustration.

Anna hurried across the apartment but made herself slow down and take a deep breath. She shouldn't seem flustered or out of breath when she greeted the detective.

Opening the door halfway, Anna found Detective Ramirez on the other side. He looked a little worse for wear; maybe it was late in his shift.

Well, sucks to be him. I didn't interrupt his dinner.

"Good evening, Miss Kincaid."

"Hello, detective."

"I just have a few questions for you regarding the situation at the Milton Building." His gaze assessed her in that way that was unique to law enforcement before he tried to see what he could see of her apartment over her shoulder. "Mind if I come in?"

"Do you have a warrant?" Old habits die hard.

Ramirez blinked at her, unamused. "No."

"Then I'd prefer to talk here." Give the cops an inch, they'll take a mile. That was the unofficial motto of her mom's myriad of boyfriends. Whether or not there was anything to hide, whether or not you were guilty of anything, no warrant no entry.

One of the detective's black brows arched slightly as he shifted to pull out his notebook.

"All right. You here alone?"

"Yes."

He tried to peer around her into the apartment again, squinting. "Thought I heard voices before."

"I was talking to my cat," she said. And because he was the best cat in the whole wide world, Captain chose that moment to butt up against her legs. She leaned down to pick him up and hold, putting something between her and the detective.

Ramirez looked from her to Captain and back again. "There was growling."

"He doesn't like men."

At least not human ones. He likes a certain gargoyle maybe even more than me.

The detective had an excellent poker face, Anna would give him that. After another moment, he moved on.

He asked her to go over her story again, and Anna told it just as she had before. Never get caught in lies. Stick to a story. It was kind of shitty that she knew all this and had had plenty of practice, but at least it was serving her and Frey now.

When Ramirez asked if there was anything else she remembered from that night she hadn't told him yet, Anna offered a few more details about the commandos that'd stormed the museum. The weird smell of the gas. How big the guns they'd had were.

All the while, she held Captain in her arms, grateful for his motorboat purrs. She made her eyes big and rounded her shoulders.

See, I'm just a little woman holding a cat. Harmless.

They stood on either side of the threshold for over fifteen minutes. The detective's questions were mostly routine, almost banal, but many were the same ones just worded differently, trying to trip her up. Anna stuck to her story, adding detail only when necessary.

Finally, when she thought maybe things were winding down, the detective did manage to catch her off guard.

"And what is your association with Timothy Moorlund?"

Anna blinked, not having heard that name in a while.

"Tim was my mom's boyfriend for a while. He lived with us for about a year."

All of her mom's partners managed to be shitty in their own ways, but not all were criminally inclined. Tim had been different. Small-time cons, check fraud, sticky fingers, that sort of thing. Nothing too crazy until he got greedy and shorted a partner out of their cut. Stupid. That'd been the second time the police had come knocking on her mom's door.

Her mom had many of her own flaws, but at least she tried to keep on the straight and narrow. Shannon hadn't been willing to wait for Tim to get out after being convicted to eighteen months in prison, but they also hadn't been able to afford their apartment without Tim's ill-gotten contributions. Moving had sucked, especially since it meant another change of schools.

"You haven't had any contact with him since?"

"Nope. And I wouldn't even if I knew how to." The vehemence in her voice wasn't fake, and she hoped the detective understood how little she ever wanted to do with Tim or any of the other shitheads her mom paraded through her life.

Anna tried not to chew her cheek as a few more notes went into that little leatherbound book.

A few more questions and the detective finally called it quits.

From a pocket he drew a no-nonsense business card with his name, contact information, and SFPD letterhead in blue ink.

"Call me if you remember anything else."

"Thanks. I will." She didn't let go of Captain to take it.

With a final nod, Ramirez turned to go, and Anna quickly shut and locked the door. She watched through the peephole to make sure the detective left.

She let another handful of moments go before she finally breathed again.

Well shit.

If he was bringing Tim up, Ramirez was definitely going through her records. Thankfully, the few things Anna had been caught for had happened when she was a minor. She never did anything more than some community service, and her file was supposed to be sealed. Still, if her name was somehow attached to Tim, the detective had obviously been able to find some things in her past.

Double shit.

Chewing her cheek, she turned back into the apartment, only to find Frey already a step outside her bedroom door, angrily chewing the last of his steak and inexplicably clutching one of her bras.

Deciding to ignore that, she stated the obvious. "He's gone."

Frey's nostrils flared. He tossed the bra back into Anna's room and then went about cleaning up the remains of their dinner, his movements jerky and agitated.

"I didn't like how he spoke to you."

"That's just their way. They try to trick information out of you."

Another huff and nostril flare. Anna was kind of touched by his annoyance on her behalf.

"I don't like it."

"Agreed."

She watched him for another moment as he took his frustration out on the dishes, working up the nerve to say what she had to say.

"Frey, this is why I have to go back. That cop is suspicious." While cops were trained and paid to be suspicious, Anna *knew* in her soul she hadn't seen the last of Detective Ramirez.

And while art theft was a difficult crime to investigate and solve (so many pieces had gone missing without a trace and were still missing to this day), this crime happened to rich people in a rich area. Gavin and Carrie would no doubt be keeping on the cops to deliver some answers. And Detective Ramirez and the SFPD would do their best to provide them. Money got things done.

It didn't help that the detective came right on the heels of her blunder today. God, that was stupid. Carrie had said the detective would be coming to do a follow-up, but what if Gavin had contacted him after what happened? What if Gavin and Carrie were suspicious of her now, too?

"Anna."

Startled, she looked up to see Frey standing before her, his expression softer, concerned. With a careful claw, he tipped up her chin then pushed her hair behind her ear.

"Don't let him trouble you."

"I just . . . don't like that he came to the apartment, you know?"

Frey nodded. "Yes. This is your dwelling, where you should feel safest."

A knot tangled in Anna's throat, and she fought back a sudden wave of tears. Detective Ramirez had rattled her, and she hated that.

Frey's chest rumbled again, but this time it was lower in tenor. A purr. He wrapped her up in his arms and wings and warmth. His claws burrowed through her hair, scraping gently against her scalp, and Anna melted.

Slowly, she wound her arms around his thick waist, hands barely meeting at the dip of his spine. A frisson of pleasure sparked across her skin everywhere they touched.

Warm lips pressed into her hair. "I will keep you safe, my Anna. I vow it on my life."

It was a wild thing to promise given he was stone half the time, but Anna's heart was lighter for it anyway. The words soaked into her as surely as his warmth, and for a minute, Anna let herself just *be* with him. Enveloped in his wings and scent, for the first time in a long time, she truly did feel safe.

16

It didn't last, of course. It never did.

And it wasn't just Anna's paranoia getting the better of her that made her feel unsafe. The next morning, she nearly got taken out by a speeding commuter as she crossed the street. Heart racing, she'd rushed for the sidewalk, turning to flip the driver the bird only to barely see the taillights as it disappeared over the next hill.

She then had computer issues three days in a row, all of which required the museum's tech guy Dave and then even Gavin to come out to investigate. She didn't mind picking up extra docent duties, using the time to take discreet pictures and notes about the collection, but it started to feel like anything she touched broke. Two mugs and a carton of half-and-half in the breakroom were all victims, as was every plastic spoon she picked up.

She almost felt cursed after the third day of bad luck.

And then reminded herself not to use that saying lightly anymore.

Through it all, she couldn't help noticing things she'd overlooked before. It wasn't just the type and number of statues in the museum that were unique. The collection also boasted incredibly rare codices and illuminated manuscripts. On closer examination, several had illustrated figures with wings and horns and tails. Perhaps at first glance demons or other fanciful creatures (there were also plenty of pages with knights fighting snails and cats doing farm work), but now that Anna *knew* about the gargoyles, it was hard to see the figures as anything else.

In fact, everywhere she looked, even in the pottery sherds and brooch designs, were motifs that possibly spoke to the gargoyles and their ancient origins.

It was . . . suspicious at best.

Now it wasn't just Frey and June in her head; she couldn't ignore that there was something seriously strange about the museum and its collection. Which meant there had to be something up with the owners. She didn't want to squint at Gavin or especially Carrie, who'd been so nice to her, but she couldn't help it.

All of it made work not the safe space she'd been starting to feel it was, and that bothered her. It was a bit of a haven away from Frey and his expectations and worse, the things he made her feel. Now, though, she dreaded what other realization she might have or what else she might find out about the collection or its owners.

She didn't want to go on unemployment and job hunt again. She didn't want to have a gap in pay and insurance. That meant doctor and pharmacy shuffles. It meant possibly running out of her meds.

So no, work wasn't a safe space, but it wasn't *un*safe, either. At least not enough so.

Unfortunately, home didn't feel safe now, either—but for entirely different reasons.

Somewhere through the days, Frey had changed tactics—and his hunky househusband routine was . . . working. Anna always came home to dinner steaming and ready. Although they were on a budget, Captain was eating gourmet too, fresh seared tilapia and peas or chicken and squash; his coat was downright glowing. Anna was a fairly neat person and didn't have a ton of things to clutter the apartment, but the place practically sparkled with how clean it was. Over her last faux weekend, she had time to read and do other small things she enjoyed during the days because everything was already taken care of.

At home, she was cared for. Doted on. The man rubbed her feet for an hour while she watched trashy TV! If she let him, Anna knew he'd happily carry her around and tuck her into bed, too.

Or join me.

No, bad libido. Bad.

But his chest, though.

Ah yes, that chest. Ever since getting that long, supportive hug after the detective came, Anna had been failing to keep the memory of his warm chest out of her mind. Given the chance, her brain was right back to it, thinking treacherous thoughts about how she'd fitted so . . . *perfectly* against him.

He was so, so dangerous to her yet she couldn't help indulging. When he wasn't being a butt about her going to work or pressing the mate issue, she adored spending time with him. She even found his arrogant streak strangely endearing; he'd clearly been hot stuff back in his time, and although he was making obvious efforts to modernize and gentle himself, there were times he couldn't hold back a preen or boast.

She couldn't help smiling to herself whenever he caught her looking at him; he'd puff his chest and his wings would lift. Anna almost expected him to strike a bodybuilder pose. But then, she couldn't argue that his showing off didn't work—she definitely checked him out whenever he preened or puffed or flexed.

It didn't help matters that the man never buttoned his shirts and his pants were always slung low to accommodate his tail. The number of times her gaze caught on that flat plane of muscle between belly button and *other bits* . . .

The sound of her own dreamy sigh startled her out of her thoughts.

God, if she wasn't careful, she'd have it bad. If she didn't already.

Would that be such a bad thing?

The denial wasn't as fast as it'd once been. And that worried her.

He'd made it clear he was an all-in kind of gargoyle, and she didn't want to play with his feelings or lead him on. Whatever more they might have could be amazing, but what if she hurt him?

What if he hurt her?

In Anna's experience, men rarely lived up to the hype. Not that there was anything normal about Frey. He wasn't even really a *man,* a human man at least. Nothing about him or the situation was normal. They couldn't really date. They couldn't even go out during the day. Still, whatever could happen would be serious.

And Anna . . . was terrified of that.

It scared her how easily a monstrous man from the sixth century had eased into her life. Sure, there had been growing pains those first days, and yeah there were moments she wanted to just be by herself in her own apartment. But those moments were far outweighed and outnumbered by the joy growing like a weed inside her each time she came home to him. To his smiles and flirting and curiosity. Even if it was just dinner and some TV before bed, her evenings felt *full.*

Sometimes the weight of loneliness weren't apparent until the burden had been eased a little.

She had Captain. She had things she enjoyed doing. But Frey drove out the worst of her loneliness. He had her looking forward to things again.

Did that all mean she could accept being someone's soulmate? Choosing to give his promises a chance and see what came of them?

She wasn't sure.

Because what if he regrets it? What if, after he's stuck with me as a mate, he gets buyer's remorse?

That she couldn't accept, and so all the rest went with it.

It didn't help that her traitorous heart (and lady bits) gave a discontented sigh of frustration. Her brain was rapidly becoming the only holdout against Frey's mate bond, and the rest of her (and probably Frey, too) was getting exasperated at the back and forth and hurry up and wait.

"Looking faraway today."

Anna jumped an inch off her seat, realizing she'd been lost to her thoughts again. She stared up dazedly at a familiar face smiling benignly at her from across the desk.

Andrew Glendower.

Nerves snapping like overstretched rubber bands, her attention focused on the suave professor. Today's coat and scarf ensemble was dove gray and robin's egg blue, respectively, and his hair was again perfectly parted and coiffed. She hadn't noticed before, but a signet ring on his pinky finger glittered in the fluorescent light. She only caught a glimpse but thought the face had been tooled to look like the Tree of Life.

"Hello again, professor."

He smiled at her recognition. "Good afternoon, Miss Anna. Long day at the office?"

"Absolutely humdrum," she agreed, plastering on her customer service smile with some effort.

Glendower made a noise of sympathy. "That's why I like to escape here." His sandy brows rose, and he wasn't quite able to hide the curiosity in his gaze when he asked, "Anything new I should stop and see?"

"Not this time, no."

"Hmm, shame. Well then, off I go to see the old friends." And with a polite nod, he headed off into the museum proper.

Anna chewed her cheek, watching him go from the corner of her eye.

When he'd disappeared, she pulled out her trusty notebook and flipped to the paragraph she'd written about the professor. She'd made notes on all the regulars, wondering if it was possibly not just her who'd been attracted to the museum.

Tree of Life signet ring, she added to the notes.

Finished, she looked up to find her coworker Suzie walking across the lobby. Calling her over, she had Suzie take over the front desk to free her to head for the Gwyneths' office. Carrie would want to know

Glendower was back.

Anna walked with purpose but not too fast, not wanting to catch Glendower up. She didn't spot him anywhere, though, as she followed the hallways deeper into the museum. She'd almost made it to the main gallery before the threshold to a small branch hallway appeared in the wall. You could easily miss it if you weren't looking for it, tucked behind one of the gargoyle statues.

Her steps were quiet as she went down the hall toward the office, but her own feet were the only thing she heard as she neared the open office door. She slowed, wondering if neither Gwyneth was in.

Stopping just before the door, Anna peeked around the doorframe.

She blinked, not quite understanding what she was seeing.

Both Gavin and Carrie were in there, obviously deep in conversation. Gavin sat in one of the overstuffed leather office chairs, Carrie to his left, hip leaning against the expansive executive desk. She gestured with a hand, emphasizing her point, and Gavin nodded along, eventually saying something.

At least, Anna thought he said something. His mouth moved.

But no noise met her ears.

She was close enough to hear if they were whispering; maybe not every word, but at least the murmuration of speech.

Anna tugged at her ear, wondering if they needed to pop.

She watched Carrie drum those perfectly pointed nails on the table. Nothing. No sound.

Anna's mouth fell open, a little gasp escaping her. This wasn't *normal.*

The sound was barely anything, and although she couldn't hear them, the Gwyneths apparently could hear her.

Carrie straightened immediately, and Gavin stood to join her. Both looked in her direction with an intensity that unnerved her down to the marrow. Their eyes were . . . wrong . . . liquid gold and mercury . . .

Anna's ears popped. Carrie's eyes were hazel again, and Gavin's a startling but human icy blue.

"Oh, Anna, apologies! We didn't mean to keep you waiting." Carrie smiled warmly, waving her inside the office.

It took her a second, but Anna forced her feet forward and a small smile on her face, even though she wanted to do anything other than enter that office. She'd heard of her coworkers catching their bosses canoodling before—the couple was still into each other after years of marriage and wasn't that cute and why couldn't she have caught them doing *that* rather than whatever . . . *this* was?

"It's fine, I just got here. I'll knock louder next time." Her voice sounded normal to her, even as she was screaming on the inside. *So strange! So weird! He's looking at me funny—get out of this office!*

"Is something wrong?" Gavin asked.

"No. At least, I don't think so. You," she nodded at Carrie, "just wanted me to let you know if Andrew Glendower came back. You know, the nosy professor from the other week?"

The smile slipped from Carrie's face. "Ah. I see." She and Gavin exchanged looks.

"Is he banned or something?"

"No, not at all," Carrie rushed to assure her. She made her way around the desk to usher Anna out of the office and back down the hall.

Carrie confided, "We're just cautious after what's happened, is all."

"Should we be keeping track of the regulars?"

"It's nothing for you to worry about, Anna. You've already done so much for us." Carrie gave her another one of those sweet smiles and then headed off into the main gallery.

Her words were probably meant to mollify and calm Anna, but they did the exact opposite. She hurried in the other direction, passing the front desk even when Suzie called out to her. Anna didn't stop until she was safely ensconced inside one of the employee bathroom stalls.

Her breaths came shakily and erratic, and Anna held her hands up to see how violently they trembled. Shoving them under her arms, she went through a few breathing exercises she knew until her pulse had come down from throbbing.

Okay, okay, so Gavin and Carrie are strange, too.

There was no denying it anymore.

But if they were strange, and the museum was strange, and the statues were strange . . .

They had to know. About the statues being living beings. Somehow, they had to know *something*. But why? Why open a museum and display them? Why keep them in a collection like this?

With all the other rare artifacts and codices, there was definitely a pattern. Everything was absolutely deliberate.

But why?

She didn't know. And that terrified her, too.

Her walk home was one of the fastest she ever did, her calves burning from the pace she set. She ignored them—she just wanted to get *home.*

Where it's safe.

The fog had never truly burned off that day, only lifted off the ground, and it gathered again along the pavement as the air cooled. The sun, mostly hidden behind the fog and tall buildings, completely disappeared as she turned onto her block.

She shouldn't have been hustling so hard through such thick fog; she could barely see anything over twenty feet in front of her. Even so . . . she could've sworn the same van circled the block three times. White vans were ubiquitous in the city, but after the second time, she glanced at the license plate. She was sure it was the same one the third time.

Looking for parking wasn't exactly rare or suspicious, but in the thick fog, after the day she'd had, Anna was practically running by the time she made it to her building.

She hadn't caught her breath by the time she opened her front door—and walked into an empty, silent apartment.

Her body didn't cope well with another shock, and pain throbbed at both temples as she hurried through the apartment, calling out his name.

"Frey? Frey!"

Captain joined her, purring merrily, unbothered by her panic. She picked him up, asking, "Where'd he go, Cappy?"

But he just licked his lips, fishy breath pungent, and then licked her cheek.

Anna checked his feeding station and found the remains of his dinner decorating the bowl. And when she investigated the kitchen, she found a roast and vegetables cooling in two covered ramekins. With Captain in tow, she checked her bedroom and bathroom, then the tiny coat closet, and then her bedroom again. Nothing.

Frey was gone.

Her insides twisted, and tears stung her eyes as she stood in the middle of her apartment, unsure what to do.

How could he just be gone?

That little bubble of anticipation, of coming home to see him, burst, leaving behind the kind of hopelessness that sucked all the energy out of her.

A tear escaped her lashes, and Anna hurried to wipe it away.

She told herself to move, to do something, but she didn't know what or how or . . .

Out of the corner of her eye, a dark figure swooped in the window. She turned just in time to hear the creak of the fire escape, and then one of the front windows was filled with the hulking figure of her gargoyle.

He'd unlatched the handle, pushed the window open, and gracefully extended one leg inside the apartment before Anna's brain came back online.

She rushed to him, holding the window open wide for him. Frey slid inside easily, folding his wings neatly behind him. He brought with him some of the fog, a sharp, cool smell that reminded her of mornings and mountains.

The smile he bestowed on her was wide and toothy, and he planted his fists on his hips. He looked happy, invigorated, and Anna could only look on, another tear slipping out.

His smile faltered. "Anna . . .?"

She threw her arms around his middle and buried her face in his chest. "You were gone!"

A rumble vibrated from that glorious chest, at first cool from the outdoors but immediately warmed against her cheek. His arms and wings came around her, and a hand gently stroked over her hair.

"Don't worry, my Anna. I just went for a short flight. The fog was thick and I couldn't resist the opportunity."

She could understand feeling cooped up—Frey had been trapped in the apartment since he'd woken up over three weeks ago. But still, she couldn't help the frustration from spilling out of her.

"Someone could still see you, Frey! There are cameras everywhere."

"I was careful. I'm always careful. It was only for a moment, and the fresh air does me good."

"Always careful," she repeated, and didn't miss how his wings bobbed, the gargoyle equivalent of *oh shit*. "You've gone out before?"

Frey's gaze drifted somewhere over her head, and his response was slow and reluctant. "Sometimes. When the night is dark enough."

"Frey!" She didn't mean to screech but—*what was he thinking?* "What if someone *sees you?*"

"No one sees me, Anna. My kind were meant for stealth. And I'm a strong flier, I hardly make a sound." There was that easy, confident arrogance again. It shouldn't have worked on her. It should have worried her.

But her nerves had had enough for today, and Anna's forehead gladly plopped back onto Frey's chest.

"You have to be careful, okay?" she muttered into his warm muscle.

"Always, *fy nghân.*" He resumed those soothing strokes on her hair, and Anna knew she should've been annoyed by how quickly it did soothe her, but she couldn't muster the effort to be. "Supper should be cool enough. Come eat."

She made a sound of agreement but couldn't force herself to move from their warm bubble. Standing there with him, wrapped up in him, was almost . . . perfect.

When she didn't move after another moment, she felt him bend down, putting his head closer to hers. "Are you well, my Anna?" His voice dropped to growl. "Did something happen at work?"

You bet something did.

The story jumped to her throat, but Anna bit back the words. She didn't want to hear about how work was unsafe. He'd gotten so worked up when she'd told him about touching the other statue. She knew he'd want to do something, and knowing now that he made little jaunts outside, she worried that something would be going to the museum *where there were definitely cameras.*

And . . . she didn't want to burst this bubble, too.

So . . .

"No," she lied.

Frey had known his little excursions would upset Anna, but that hadn't stopped him before nor after she found out. An unprepared warrior was a vulnerable one, and Frey refused to be either, not when his mate's safety was now his duty. At least when not stone. And she was home.

He grumbled in his stone state at the thought. Weeks now and he was still only a mate by halves. Only given the night. With a mate who didn't accept the bond.

And because in his stone state he had nothing better to do than think and worry, he wondered over how his bond with Anna would be progressing if he'd had access to his dwelling and everything he'd saved. Hobbled without his years of preparation, Frey had to make do with what he had—and that was his strength and resourcefulness.

He understood the dangers of exposing himself prematurely to a world that had forgotten his kind, but Anna was mistaken if she thought he wouldn't take on that risk if it meant better protecting her. He knew the layout of her building. All the best entry and exit points. The most and least defensible areas. He'd begun to recognize the other humans who lived in the area, as well as their vehicles.

His flights weren't long or very high, but they were his one taste of freedom. The biting wind and fog revitalized him, reminded him that while he may only be half-alive, it was more than he'd been in centuries.

So no, Frey didn't stop. He just got sneakier.

Still, over the next span of days, his Anna only seemed to grow more troubled. Her headaches came on almost every night, and while she put on a brave face to eat with him, their evenings were often cut short by him shooing her to bed to nurse her head. He worried over her discomfort, and there was nothing in this world or the one he'd known that brought him lower than watching his mate in pain and being unable to do anything about it.

So Frey patrolled. He improved his cooking skills. He watched videos on the cause of headaches in human women and their possible treatment. He stole into her bedchamber before she arrived home to check her mattress and pillows for supportiveness and then made suggestions based on his research.

And he watched and studied what he could of what the humans knew of the fae, for while he was grateful to at least have his half-life, it couldn't be borne. Not forever. His Anna needed all of him. He needed the day and to see what his mate looked like in the sunlight.

As the days passed, he couldn't stop a growing knot of dread forming in his chest. Anna had never been the most forthcoming, but when conversation moved toward the museum, she became monosyllabic.

That she was possibly withholding information from him stung. That it was information that could possibly endanger her stuck in his craw.

He was guardian enough to admit the hypocrisy of resenting having secrets kept from him when he kept his excursions clandestine, but that didn't soothe or comfort the growing frustration gnawing him from the inside out.

Frey kept these feelings from her, of course. They served no purpose but to drive them apart, yet they weren't easy to disregard or dismiss. With each passing night, Frey felt the bond stagnating, left to languish in unfulfillment.

He didn't know what to do, nor how to move forward.

His Anna wouldn't tell him what was wrong. He didn't know how to ask nor how to get a truthful answer from her. Frey saw the burdens she bore silently and railed against her in his mind, wishing to beg her to give them over to him. But she was silent, and so was he.

It wasn't until nearly a week had passed that, while in his stone sleep with nothing but time to ruminate and fuss over their situation, he finally came to a decision.

Frey had always been one to act. His Anna didn't like being pushed, but if he didn't find a way to help her, he'd crawl right out of his skin. So when the sun disappeared and the moon allowed him out of his prison, Frey set about rearranging the living room.

He had just enough time to do that and put leftovers in the oven to reheat before Anna returned for the evening.

Frey turned to behold her, hair a little mussed from the wind, buried under her layers of scarf and coat and hat to keep out the worst of the coming winter chill. He caught her smile under the layers as she began disrobing, and it gave him heart.

"How are you, my Anna? How is your head?"

"Nothing serious today," she said with a tired smile, allowing him to help her out of her coat. "So we're absolutely a go to watch the new doc episode."

"I'm glad to hear it, but before we do, there is something I'd like to teach you."

He led her into the living room, and he watched her take in how he'd pushed the furniture back toward the walls to make room for them on the carpet.

"Um . . . teach me what, exactly?"

"To defend yourself. Until we find a solution to this curse, I cannot be with you to protect you in the daylight. But I can prepare you."

It was another long moment before Anna responded. "You want to teach me self-defense moves?"

"Yes."

"I'm not sure . . ."

Folding his hands behind his back, he strolled casually for her, a flirtatious smile curling his mouth. "You'll get to hit me."

She blinked at him more, blush rising on her cheeks. Goddesses, he loved her blushes. She always blushed for him. A guardian could get lovesick with it.

"I don't want to hit you."

He didn't believe her for a moment, and his face expressed as much. "We could talk about your going out into danger instead. Or perhaps the mate bond?"

Her scowl was delicious.

"Okay, yeah, maybe a little bit." Throwing her hands up in the air, she marched for her bedchamber. "Just let me change."

More than a little smug, Frey did his best to hide his triumph when Anna returned in comfortable, stretchy clothing. He loved her comfortable, stretchy clothes, too. The leggings left little to the imagination about the contours of her legs, and she always looked softer in her knit sweaters.

Her expression was curious but open as she reemerged, coming to stand before him in the center of the living room.

"So . . ."

"First, we learn to take the proper stance."

He sank down into a stance, knees bent and weight on the balls of his feet. His wings unwound from his shoulders to hover at the ready.

Anna took all this in with a little smile that Frey felt all the way down to his talons.

"So we're not just doing the classic crotch-kick-and-run?"

"If you can strike a male enemy there with minimal risk, by all means. Strike hard, fast, and unforgiving." He adjusted his feet, turning his hips away from her when Anna's smile turned a little evil. "A male *enemy*. Leave my crotch, as you so eloquently call it, alone."

"Alone? Such mixed messages from you, Mr. Wants to Mate."

His lips twitched at her teasing. "Later. When you're ready. Now, take a stance, wench."

Frey's blood heated and rushed through him as he led his Anna through a few stances, showing her which was best to intimidate an incoming threat and which was good for defending the torso. They practiced kicks and throwing a punch. He thought she hurt her little fist more than his palm when she first struck him, but after adjusting her form, her next one did register.

"Good," he said with a wide grin, "that one almost tickled."

Anna huffed. "Har har. Not sure what good throwing a punch is gonna do against a person like you."

"Luckily for you, this would most likely be against a weak, spindly human male. Your strikes will have more impact."

Her lips twisted with humor. "Not all men are weak and spindly, you know. And those that are probably aren't going to attack me."

"Agree to disagree. Now, hit my palm, right in the center."

He held up his hands, cupped and ready for her fist.

Anna puffed out a breath, retook her stance, and put her shoulders into the strike, meeting his palms with a decent *smack*.

"Good. Again."

Set, stance, strike.

"Again."

Set, stance, strike—

Except he closed his hands around her fist when it met his flesh and tugged her forward, out of her stance and off balance. She stumbled forward with an *oof,* and he didn't let go of her hand.

So close, he could see the way her skin glistened with a sheen of sweat. Color pinkened her cheeks, and her eyes were bright as they blinked up at him. Her chest rose and fell quicker than usual, and he could just see her pulse drumming at her throat.

Her smell intoxicated him, heady and sweet and . . . something new. Deeper, richer, like the chocolate or coffee his Anna loved so much.

Frey dipped his head, getting into her space, and brushed his nose against hers.

Excitement. Arousal. That's what he scented from his Anna.

Thank the goddesses. And it was all the sweeter for its stubbornness. His patience was finally paying off, and he wanted to roar with triumph.

A slow smile spread across Frey's mouth, pleased and predatory. "I've gotten you in close. Now what do you do?"

Her lips parted, drawing his gaze immediately to their plush, rosy perfection. Human mouths and kissing had never truly fascinated him before, but now, Anna's mouth and her kiss were all he wanted. It took everything inside him, every morsel of patience and good sense, to keep from pouncing on her.

The tip of her tongue swiped across her lower lip, and Frey bit back a groan. He couldn't stop the twitch of excitement in his cock, though.

"Knee you in the crotch," she joked, though her voice had gone low and sultry. "Or go get a glass of water."

A purr rattled in his chest, and Frey stood perfectly still as Anna's gaze moved slowly over his face. If she moved closer, even just swayed forward, he'd swoop down and finally take what was his.

Do it, he begged her. *Reach for me. Give in.*

He didn't imagine her pupils blowing wide, nor how her fingertips made playful patterns against his palm. He waited, suspended in his anticipation, ready for the smallest sign . . .

After a moment, her hand slipped from his, and Frey let her go.

The blush returned, and Anna cleared her throat as she hustled from the living room to the kitchen.

Frey looked on in frustration. This time, though, it wasn't the kind with sharp edges and resentment boiling beneath. No, this was more like anticipation. Dangerous as it could be, hope sustained his battered patience.

He followed her into the kitchen.

Two glasses sat on the counter, Anna pouring water into each. She handed him one without quite meeting his gaze, and sipped from her own silently. Frey downed the water in a single gulp and replaced the glass to watch her.

His attention snagged yet again on her lips, how they bunched and moved, not letting a drop escape.

"Is my mouth particularly interesting tonight?"

"I'm always fascinated by your mouth, *fy nghân*."

"I guess human mouths are pretty different," she said, sidestepping his flirtation. But she didn't leave, instead set down her half-full glass, and so Frey dared a half-step closer.

"They are. Hardly intimidating. The druids that made my kind didn't even give us their own, but much more useful fangs." He flashed his, large and ready to take a bite out of her enemies—but for her, he'd be so, so gentle.

"My, what big teeth you have," she murmured.

He took that last half-step, hope and lust making his blood rush hot. With gentle fingers, he traced the column of her throat then used a knuckle to lift her chin. The pad of his thumb ran slowly over her velvety bottom lip, savoring its softness.

"It's *your* mouth I think about, *fy nghân*. I don't think you understand what you do to me."

Her blush deepened, but she didn't step away from him. No, she . . . leaned into his touch. Brushed her fingers against his forearm.

Frey's heart stuttered.

"Are you trying to talk your way into kissing?" she asked.

"Is it working?"

He watched her throat bob on a swallow, and he almost didn't hear nor believe it when she admitted on a quiet exhale, "Yes."

With her admission, the urgency and frustration he'd felt over the past weeks drained away. Left in their wake, a delicious heat licked up his spine. He still felt the urge to grab her and crush her to him, but he could go slow. Leaning an arm above her head on the cabinets, Frey bent down, indulging in the sensual vision his Anna made, watching him come for her.

Her pupils had blown wide again, and her chest rose and fell at a quick, hypnotic pace.

She didn't protest, didn't stop him.

When his lips finally, *finally* slid into place against hers, she lifted her head to meet him.

Shocks of pleasure sparked through Frey's body and soul, and another rumbling purr reverberated from his chest. Her taste flooded his mouth, sweet and rich, and he had to delve deeper, had to have *more*.

He heard her sharp inhale, and then her arms were around his middle.

It was all he needed.

Gathering her up in his arms, Frey held his mate tight.

Although it was him surrounding her, Anna enveloped him, subsuming him in everything she was. Her scent invaded his senses, and his mind blanked at the warmth of her. Her sweater and hair and skin were all so painfully soft under his rough hands, but he couldn't stop filling them with her. Every delicious slide of their mouths brought a little more of her taste to his tongue until finally he couldn't wait any longer.

Teasing her lips with his tongue, she opened for him on a sigh. He swept inside, exploring, conquering everything he could reach and feel. Little noises echoed from the back of her throat, goading him on as he chased down the sounds, determined to hear them again and hoard them. The little suckle of her lips and nips of her blunt human teeth nearly had Frey spiraling into a frenzy of need.

In a little show of bravery, her wicked tongue flicked against his long upper fang.

His cock throbbed behind the confines of his gray pants, and his wings itched to curl around her, surround her in everything he was.

Anna lifted her chin, gasping for a breath, and Frey almost roared with outrage.

He couldn't keep away, kissing her jaw, her neck, desperate to take as much as he could.

Her hands, once making delicious little scratches at his back beneath his unbuttoned shirt, moved to his front. Her splayed palms burned him, made his chest shudder.

Don't go, his heart begged, *don't go yet.*

He caught one last kiss, savoring how perfectly they fit together, the feel of her pressed to him everywhere.

Finally, he let her go.

At least . . . just a little.

Frey straightened, though he didn't release her from his arms. Pride swelled to see her lips swollen and pink from their kisses, and the sight nearly tempted him back.

But he knew he couldn't push too hard. So when she didn't initiate more, Frey swept her back into the living room. He made quick work of replacing the furniture, and in no time, he'd arranged them together on the couch.

His mate watched on with a precious sort of bewilderment—but she went along with it, so Frey indulged. By the time the documentary they'd been planning to watch all week had been queued, Frey sat with his wings flung wide and Anna tucked into his side. His hand rested easily in her lap, holding both of hers in a loose grip.

The documentary played, but Frey hardly paid attention. With his mate so close and warm and accepting, he pressed kisses to her temple and hair. He drew in her scent, committing it to memory. The richness of her had deepened even further, and Frey had to hope.

Soon. Please, let it be soon.

He knew now, after finally getting a taste of her, that he wanted *all* of Anna. He wanted *her* for his mate. And he didn't know how much longer he could wait.

18

What the actual fuck was that?

Anna had been asking herself that for days now without coming to much of an answer other than, *really nice.*

If she wasn't careful, she got all soft and soppy thinking about The Kiss with Frey. Who knew a medieval mythical being would be a good kisser—or that his fangs would get her so hot and bothered? And it wasn't just an isolated kiss, oh no.

Ever since The Kiss, it was like a switch had flipped for Frey. Like he had a green light. Like they were . . . together.

She came home to dinner ready as usual, but now there was more touching, more flirting. They'd migrated from sitting on opposite sides of the couch to sitting beside each other to flat out cuddling. Meaning they were horizontal with maximum contact.

Captain was all for it because it meant he could lay on both of them at the same time and get double the pets.

Frey was all for it if his wandering hands and rumbling purrs were anything to go by.

Anna was . . . well, her heart was all for it. She soaked up the attention and affection like a sponge. She was still sort of baffled by how they'd gotten there, when they'd moved from platonic roommates to cuddle buddies. And she wasn't complaining per se, but more . . . confused?

And worried. Mostly worried.

Clicking through the main museum email, Anna halfheartedly answered a few inquiries and shunted junk mail to the spam folder. It was about all she could do at the moment, as the computer had again decided to be uncooperative. Dave was currently taking his sweet time coming to fix it.

At the rate Anna was going, he'd stop taking her service requests.

She was starting to get a reputation among the docents. The computer didn't act up for anyone else. Just her. Yay.

Computer problems always had a way of souring her mood; Anna never liked having a problem she couldn't solve or at least deal with for the most part. Relying on Dave and being on Dave's schedule rankled. So did his attitude.

When the man of the hour finally showed up, he threw Anna a dirty look.

"What'd you do this time?"

"Nothing, as usual," she said, taking longer than necessary to vacate her chair so Dave could slump into it.

Ugh, he'll throw off the ergonomics again. I think he does it on purpose.

Dave just grunted his acknowledgement, signing her out of everything and typing in command prompts.

"I'm starting to think it has a bug."

Dave snorted. "Not likely."

Well, he *would* say that. It was his job to make sure the museum didn't pick up or retain any bugs. Anna wasn't so sure he was doing his job overly well.

Getting the message loud and clear that Dave didn't want her around while he worked, Anna put up the *Maintenance in Progress* sign and headed off to do a round of the museum.

The walk did her some good, and helping curious visitors took her mind off of certain hunky roommate-with-benefits.

Which was good, because her heart was getting away from her. She had to keep her head in the game because between Frey and her heart, it was the only rational one left.

It wasn't that Anna didn't want to maybe try things with him. She'd be a liar if she said she hadn't thought about having him put that boastful mouth to good use.

It was just . . . she hadn't *chosen* any of this. Not to waking him in the first place, not to being his supposed soulmate, not even really to start being more than roommates. It all just *happened.*

She'd spent a lot of her life being buffeted from place to place by other people or forces. Sometimes it was her mom breaking up with a boyfriend. Sometimes it was a change in finances. Sometimes it was her own body saying *nope, not today* with a migraine. Anna had worked hard to take some of that power back as an adult, and even though Frey and his cuddling were great amazing wonderful *wow*, that didn't mean she was just going to give in.

If her mother had taught her anything, it was that falling in love was amazing. Shannon was always falling in love. The butterflies, the flirting, all the firsts in a new romance. It was like a drug, addicting and consuming.

But like with all drugs, there were serious side effects.

Anna had been tugged around by the ear because of love too many times. Enough that she'd never let herself fall in love like that. Everything she'd learned about it had been second-hand, yet Anna had still seen and felt the utter misery of heartbreak. How it could rip apart your heart and life and leave you a shell.

So Anna didn't partake. The side effects of coming down off of love would be too much to bear.

Anna already had her share of things she'd never asked for. While Frey was definitely better than the rest, it didn't change that she hadn't chosen this. And really, neither had Frey.

Coming home now included a tangled knot of emotions. It lodged behind her sternum, at once nervous butterflies of anticipation and a sloshing wave of nausea. Sometimes, she found herself standing in front of her door, keys dangling from her fingers.

Go in before someone sees you lurking in front of your own apartment, she chided herself.

But she'd hesitate. Once she opened that door, she'd be home, with him, and it would be wonderful.

That night was no different.

She'd barely taken the key from the lock before the door swung open and Frey swept her inside. Then it was a spectacle of gargoyle and cat, both purring like motorboats, welcoming her home.

"How are you today, *cân fy nghalon?*" he asked between gentle kisses to her temples.

"Fine. Just a normal day." Which wasn't quite a lie. Not as much as other days when she said the same thing. She never really had a normal day, not after catching the Gwyneths having a conversation with no sound. Now, she noticed small things every day. And maybe it was a growing paranoia, but she swore things were going wrong or that she was being watched. Or followed. But all she told him was *Just a normal day.*

She didn't want the argument or the lecture. And she didn't want to ruin the cozy, romantic domesticity of coming home to Frey.

Dinner was delicious—he was a bit obsessed with the seared or broiled meat and seasoned vegetable combo, but it was always warm and hearty and oozing with effort. Even if it was burnt or too salty, Anna ate it with a smile.

They played card games and told stories and watched TV snuggled on the couch. She let him drape her like a blanket over him and always sighed happily when her cheek found that divot between his pectorals. It fit perfectly, and she listened to the drum of his heart all evening.

For all her worrying during the day, in the evenings, Anna couldn't help playing along. Once she was in it, she didn't want it to stop. Being with him was easy, and so was getting swept away in his fantasy. It was easy to forget all her vows and stipulations. It was easy to let herself be the center of his world.

Never much of a hugger, Anna hadn't realized how starving she was for physical touch until she had all she wanted and more. Some nights it was difficult to pull herself away and go to bed alone. The blankets weren't as warm as him, the bed not as comforting.

Spending the evenings being lavished with affection would soften anyone, and Anna was no different.

But when she woke up in the morning and watched him turn to stone, her heart hurt. When she left the apartment and breathed that first breath of cool foggy air, she came to her senses. With a mental slap, she could put her defenses back in place, her logic and reasoning and knowledge that this would never work, not really.

She needed the reminder—even if, day by day, it took a little longer to talk herself back into her senses.

It was easier, though, on bad days. Headache days. Days when crappy things happened.

Which, honestly, were happening a lot lately. Anna was used to headache days and just generally crappy days, too. Coffee burning her tongue. Missing the crosswalk light and having to wait through another interminable traffic cycle. The computer wigging out *again*.

But even for her, things seemed crappier than normal.

She twisted her ankle one day and had to limp through her shift. Her neurology appointment got pushed back a week. Every grocery store within walking distance ran out of Captain's kibble, which meant trying a new type, which he promptly vomited up, which meant a speech from Frey about why kibble wasn't food and Captain should get the chicken he made him for dinners for breakfast too, which meant Anna had to go back to the store for more chicken.

It was *a lot,* enough to send anyone running for the comfort of home. And Anna did—straight into the arms of her more than accommodating gargoyle. She let him cook, she let him cuddle, she let him end her crappy day on a better note.

All of it only added to the morning talking-to she gave herself on the walk to work, though. As the days wore on, she realized letting Frey do all this for her was a crutch.

Anna never liked being dependent. Just like love, it was a hard fall when all of it came crashing down.

But she didn't know how to stop. It was . . . addicting.

The realization had her actually groaning one afternoon, making a few coworkers look at her askance in the breakroom. She hid her burning face in her hands, trying to stop the world from spinning.

She wasn't just getting used to Frey, she was coming to need him. And that wasn't okay. Not for her. If her crappy childhood had taught her anything, it was that needing someone not only led to disappointment but crisis when they failed to show up.

Anna's phone vibrated in her pocket, drawing her out of the dark little hideaway of her hands. Rubbing her eyes, she pulled out her phone and almost groaned again. *Speak of the devil.*

Hey baby

Her mom.

Great. Just great. This week had been crap from start and now finish.

Hot on the heels of the first, another text came in.

You there baby?

Just wanted to let you know Im moving tomorrow

Wes & I are getting an apartment together! Woohoo!

You should come next Sat and meet him Ill text you the address

Who was Wes? What had happened with Chaz? Anna didn't have a clue. Didn't have a care, either.

She chewed on the lunch Frey had packed her (steamed carrots, leftover pot roast, and fried potatoes—how dare he), while her brain chewed on what to say. Was there really anything else other than—

Okay. I work on Saturdays so I can't come by.

...

OK

...

Baby

...

I really want you to meet Wes

Anna really didn't want to.

Hes really great

Anna really doubted it.

Angrily chewing a carrot, Anna typed:

I'm glad. I hope the move goes well.

You could take Saturday off

I don't have the time. Sorry.

OK

Anna's lips pursed, and she refused to acknowledge how her eyes stung. It wasn't really fair to be mad that her mom didn't try and then be mad when she did—but Anna had had this conversation one too many times. She didn't have the energy or patience to meet her mom's new flavor of the month, nor go through an awkward afternoon discovering how this one in particular sucked.

She didn't want to feel the dread of hating the new boyfriend, she didn't want to lie to her mom's face about how great he was, and she didn't want to have this sucking guilt over not meeting him.

At least she's not asking for money for the deposit.

Anna shoved her phone in her pocket and cleaned up the remains of her lunch. An old sore spot in her chest ached the rest of the day, and between that and being yelled at by a woman angry that one of the bathroom stalls was out of toilet paper, her day was unsalvageable.

Well, almost unsalvageable.

"What troubles you, my Anna?" asked Frey softly as they cuddled that night. His fingers sifted through her hair, claws rasping delicately on her scalp. “You’ve been quiet tonight.”

“Nothing,” she sighed, ducking her head to rest on his shoulder.

“Do you have a headache?”

“No, just tired. I promise.”

He grumbled his unhappy rumble, and Anna patted his thigh.

“I’m happy to be home.”

That turned the rumble around, and he curled one of those strangely beautiful wings around her. Anna had been amazed to realize the inside was lined in short, dense fur that was incredibly sensitive. Draped over her shoulders, it was like being covered in a blanket.

A warm kiss pressed against her forehead, and Anna sighed happily.

Not depending on it, she told herself. *Just enjoying it while it lasts.*

The next week, Anna sat in the lobby of her neurologist’s office, legs crossed and foot bouncing. She never liked medical offices, even though she was a frequent flier to them over the past few years. Hers was the last appointment of the day, which meant even though she was fifteen minutes early, the doctor was running over half an hour late.

By the time she was called back, got her weight, temperature, and blood pressure taken by the nurse, went over medical and treatment history with the neurologist, and made an MRI appointment, fifty minutes had passed. She was disheartened to be told her insurance may not cover the more expensive injection treatments, but the neurologist ordered them anyway to see what they could get. Anna chewed her cheek and told herself to be grateful that in the meantime, at least she had a new pill to try.

Even though it was full dark, she was exhausted, and over an hour late getting home, she made herself go to the pharmacy.

Sure, she was a little bummed that the neurologist couldn't wave a magick medical wand and make the headaches go away, or that the injections might not be possible, but she was still a bit heartened by the new medication.

Her little bubble of relief and accomplishment popped when she turned onto her street. A van she'd noticed two blocks back turned onto her street, too.

A cold, nauseating wash of panic drenched her, and Anna picked up her pace. Her thighs burned by the time she hurried into her apartment building. Hidden behind the mailboxes, she peeked out the front door and watched the van park down the street.

It was a bit late for commuters to be getting home but not terribly late.

Tell that to Frey.

Anna was still thinking about the van when she finally entered her apartment, and it took a moment to realize that there weren't kisses and soft touches waiting for her.

"Anna!"

A big gray mass came barreling toward her from the living room, and in the next second, she was swept into giant arms, crushed against a wide chest.

She might've enjoyed it any other night, but her panic was too fresh, too sharp. She squirmed away from him, heart racing and breaths coming fast. Clawing at her coat and scarf, she tried getting out of her confining layers but kept getting blocked by Frey's desperate hands.

He tried running his hands over her, searching for something.

"My Anna, *where have you been?*" he demanded, voice loud and as panicked as she felt.

"The neurologist's," she said, finally ducking out of his grip to get her layers off. She threw them over the back of a chair and hurried into the living room to look out the window.

There was the van, parked on the street with a slightly obstructed view of her building and window, but definitely visible. Her stomach churned as she watched, waiting to see if anything moved inside it. It was dark and she probably wouldn't have seen anything if it did, but she had to look.

"Anna." A big hand clasped her upper arm and pulled her away from the window. A glowering gargoyle took up her gaze, and another hand gripped her other arm. Frey's hold wasn't hard but it was firm. And unwelcome.

A different kind of panic bubbled up, and Anna squirmed again.

"Let me go," she said, but he didn't.

"You were gone so long and I—I had no sign of where you were! When you would return. I thought—" He bared his fangs in a grimace, and in her panic, her lizard brain shuddered at the sight of such a vivid predatory threat.

"I told you," she murmured, "I was at the doctor's. I finally had my appointment."

"You did *not* tell me. You said nothing about being late tonight."

"Oh." That was true, she hadn't said anything before tonight. She never really told anyone her plans and hadn't thought to tell him. "Sorry."

A hot huff hit her square on the forehead, and Frey's forbidding expression clearly stated how unimpressed he was with her half-apology.

"My mate, you must tell me these things. I worry over—"

"I don't have to do anything."

The words were a reflex, out before she could think, and landed between her and Frey with all the delicacy of a slap.

Frey went rigid, and Anna used the moment to finally break free of his hold. She never liked being grabbed or gripped or pulled.

"Look," she said, hurrying back into the kitchen to get the meds from her purse, "I'm sorry I forgot to tell you."

When he said nothing, Anna couldn't help glancing over her shoulder at him. The intensity of his stare took her breath away. He'd barely moved, just stood there, watching her, wings folded neatly over his shoulders.

Unnerved, Anna took the meds to her bathroom to sort into her weekly pill pack.

Finally, without a word, he plated dinner for her. Just for her. She sat and ate in silence as he did something else in the kitchen.

There was no conversation. There was no cuddling.

Anna went to bed soon after, dinner sitting unsettled in her stomach and a resigned sort of dread lodged in her throat.

Here it comes, she thought as she slipped under her covers.

She saw it coming, had prepared herself, but that didn't mean a few tears didn't escape for what might have been.

Sometimes she hated being right.

After another handful of workdays, Anna was sure there were too many strange vehicles in the neighborhood for it to be a coincidence. That van remained outside her building for another day but then was replaced by one of those hulking, souped up black SUVs that took up a parking space and a half. The van didn't reappear on her street, but she was sure she spotted vans just like it on her walk to and from work, and the SUV was always parked with a clear view of her fourth-floor window.

Bonus points for getting that privacy film.

Was it reasonable to think that someone new had moved in and that was their SUV? Sure. That's probably what she would've thought before a giant gargoyle swooped into her life. Instead, because she had illicit statuary in her apartment during the day, she got her phone out to pretend to be on it for the last leg of her walk home and took discreet pictures and videos.

She didn't know what SFPD surveillance vehicles were supposed to look like, but the paranoia sinking its claws into her whispered she was looking right at one. And did anyone other than law enforcement actually drive those shiny black SUVs?

It didn't help that Frey became his own little surveillance unit. He paced the apartment constantly, tail lashing behind him like an angry cat.

Between his sulking and her paranoia, the mood of the apartment took a nosedive. Even Captain seemed affected, burrowing under furniture to take his naps and avoid the passive aggressiveness.

They ate meals together. They sat together. But things were . . . different. Anna didn't know how to fix it or if it really should be fixed. Maybe it was better that they take this reminder that things just couldn't work between them, not that way. Did she miss coming home to his open arms and an evening of just being with him? Of course. But she'd lived without it before and she could do it again.

Even if living without it was less and less appealing.

Scowling at the SUV, Anna hurried into her apartment building, glad to be done with the day. A headache had been threatening since lunchtime and her new pills hadn't gotten rid of it. She needed a shot and a hot shower and her bed. Did she daydream a little about Frey's claws massaging her head in that way he did that somehow eased her headaches? Yeah, okay, she did. But a hot shower would be nice, too.

Anna shuffled into her apartment and put down her outside things. Captain came to rub against her legs. She picked him up for kisses and buried her face in his soft fur as he purred happily. When asked how his day was, he gave her a chirpy, chicken-flavored meow then licked her nose.

"You've definitely had your dinner." Looking around, the kitchen was lit and something was in the oven with about twenty minutes on a timer. "Where's Frey, hmm?"

Not seeing him, she carried Captain into the dark living room.

Backlit by the windows and the cloudy, sapphire blue sky, Frey stood on in silence, his back turned to her.

Her heart jumped into her throat to see him there, just barely illuminated by the weak moonlight filtering through the thin cloud cover. His profile was all sharp lines as he gazed out the window, a thunderous frown reflecting back in the glass.

"Frey, I'm home."

At first, he said nothing, only worsening the dread tugging on her insides.

When he finally did speak, his words drained the blood from her face.

"When were you going to tell me about the vehicles?"

"What?" she croaked.

His head slowly turned to stare at her, those intense eyes the color of starlight and just as cold. "Two large vehicles have been parked across the street for days now. Sometimes they are not there in the early evenings, but one is always back when you are."

A groan erupted from Anna, and she hugged Captain tighter.

Here it is. Here it comes. Here we go. Her mind whirred, and she had to swallow down the need to run. But the train wreck was barreling toward her and there was no getting off the tracks.

A thousand things to say jumped up her throat, but she couldn't get anything out.

As if sensing she meant to lie to him, Frey's upper lip curled. "Tell me," he demanded, in a tone he'd never used with her, that made her knees quake.

"I-I'm not sure, but . . . I think that van has followed me before. Like followed me from work back here. Which is why you shouldn't be hanging out in the window, it's not—"

Anna's ears rang with the ferocious roar Frey unleashed, and Captain yowled in fright and clawed her shoulder in his haste to jump and run. In a flurry of wings and black mane, Frey threw open a window and climbed outside.

"Wait!" she yelped, but he was too fast. That angry, lashing tail disappeared up the fire escape. Anna leaned out the window, watching in horror as Frey pulled himself up onto the roof.

"Frey!"

Her fear gave way to spitting anger, and Anna hauled herself back inside, pacing angrily. She kept her eyes trained on the SUV outside, just waiting for a SWAT team to come pouring out of it. Any minute now, a horde of police cars were going to light up the street outside and bust open her door. Detective Ramirez would arrest her with a smug little grin and she'd get taken to the precinct and be kept up for hours while they went round and round and round over her story and why there was a statue-shaped thing climbing over her building and—

Anna jumped when Frey landed on the fire escape.

Scrambling for the window, she waved frantically. "Get *inside!* Someone will *see you!*"

A growl rumbled through him, but he acquiesced, pulling himself back through the casement.

"What *the fuck* was that?" she demanded. "They could be watching the windows and you—"

"When were you going to tell me?" he roared. "You say you will be safe, you say you can take care of yourself. You're being *followed,* Anna!"

Gone was the sweet, hunky househusband routine—instead, Anna stared at an angry medieval warrior. His wings arched high above him and nose wrinkled like Captain's when he hissed. That tail whipped against the rug, and his fangs flashed with every angry demand.

"I mean—we don't know for sure. And it's probably the police staking out the apartment. I *told you,* they're watching me! They're suspicious. I have to go to work and be normal!"

"No! Enough! We have done it your way and you are in more danger."

"But it's okay that you go climbing over the building? Or go out flying? How is that not putting yourself at risk?"

Another snarl peeled his lip back from his fangs. "I need out of this dwelling sometimes. Of all people, I thought you could understand that."

Oh, so he can fight dirty. Fine.

"I *do,* but don't you think it's fucking hypocritical?"

"You aren't safe!" He stabbed a claw at the windows. "You go straight into danger at the museum! And now even your walking isn't safe!"

"And you think you're safe going out there? It'll take one camera, Frey. *One.* Then you'll be all over the news and everyone is going to be at that door trying to drag you into a lab somewhere. So don't stand there and tell me I'm taking unnecessary risks by going to work!"

"You're my mate!" He took two big steps toward her and Anna took two big steps back, making him halt. He snarled again. "I have to protect you, and I can't do that from here. When you leave."

"That's not my fucking problem, Frey. You need out of here sometimes? I get it. But I need this job. I won't let you keep me inside out of your fear. I've spent enough of my life sidelined. I won't let you do it to me, too."

A piercing hiss grated against her ears.

"I am not trying to sideline you. I'm trying to protect you!"

"From *what?*"

"From everything!" He came for her again, quicker this time, quicker than she could react to. He didn't reach for her, instead loomed over her, his energy frenetic and his face a tempest. "I am your mate. It's my duty to protect you. This world is dangerous, everything can be taken away in a moment. I'm finished allowing you to say it is otherwise."

Anna's jaw cracked with how hard she ground her teeth. "You don't *allow* anything. You don't get to tell me what to do."

"Clearly. You listen to nothing I say." And to her horror, a flash of desolation crossed his face. He turned it from her, giving only his profile, those arching horns casting long shadows across his eyes. "You refuse my protection. You keep secrets from me. You will not hear of being mates. You will not even try."

All the fire in her, all the anger and indignation, snuffed faster than a candle in a gale. The chill it left behind had her shivering, and Anna wrapped her arms around herself to keep from coming apart.

The trembling grew worse with each passing second, but she managed to croak, "Frey—"

But his claws swiped the air and he turned away from her.

"I'm done speaking, Anna. There's nothing left to say."

That's not true. There was so much to say. But Anna took his out anyway, as much as his dismissal stung, because everything that was left to say was far more terrifying than an angry gargoyle.

She fled into her bedroom, tears blinding her as she burrowed under the covers.

A questioning meow echoed from under her bed, and Captain jumped up to curl into her arms. He didn't usually sleep with her, and must've run into her room after being scared by Frey. Anna wished she could crawl under the bed and hide in the darkness, too. Maybe there, her terror would be less terrifying, her sadness less sharp.

Frey had scared her in every way possible tonight, shaken her to the core that she thought was stronger than this. Afraid of him and everything he meant, Anna knew they'd arrived at the point she dreaded. They were too different. He asked too much.

She couldn't be what he needed, and the sooner the both of them accepted it, the better.

The horrors of the night replayed in Frey's mind through the darkest hours. His anger over it all had cooled, forming a cold ingot of outrage in his chest. The anger still simmered, put a tremble in his fingertips every time he looked outside and saw that infernal vehicle parked there. But as the apartment went quiet with the lengthening night, Frey's plan formed.

I'm done speaking. That's what he'd told her. Because he was done using words to try convincing Anna.

He had asked her. He had *begged* her. Still she left him, day after day, walking straight into danger. Frey was done asking.

But he was not *done.*

His temper had gotten the better of him. Another guardian would've matched his flaring wings and flashing fangs with their own, but seeing them reflected in Anna's eyes, Frey had realized the difference in their sizes and forms. Although Anna's tongue was sharp, an acrid smell had filled the apartment. *Her fear.* The scent of it stuck in his nostrils, and with every breath he remembered how he'd frightened his mate.

Not only could he not protect her, now he scared her, too.

He'd thought she no longer saw his wings and horns and claws as frightening differences. He'd thought she was finally softening to him. Those evenings they'd shared had been the best of Frey's life, holding his mate close, being allowed to touch and caress her. *Learn* her.

He'd thought he'd gone slow enough. Hadn't pushed her.

Perhaps Anna needed to be pushed. *She's already angry with me anyway.*

So Frey waited until the small hours of the night, when the world was quietest, to silently ease Anna's bedchamber door open.

Inside, he found his mate asleep on her side, buried beneath her blankets. A black lump with two yellow eyes watched him enter. Captain made no sound, which Frey was grateful for, but the way the cat watched him warily had guilt nipping at him.

Frey ignored it. Guilt and consequences would be for tomorrow.

From the small table beside Anna's bed, Frey gingerly picked up her phone. He took it with him back out into the kitchen and placed it on the counter, as far from her bedroom as it could be. She used the phone for many things, including her alarm to wake for work.

That done, there was nothing left to do but wait.

In those hours anticipating the sun, Frey girded himself for her anger, even her rejection. Although his soul cried against it, although his kin and ancestors would've hissed with disappointment to see him, he could bear their disapproval and her anger.

What he couldn't stand was her being unsafe.

And so, when the sun finally rose, for the first time since Anna woke him, Frey welcomed the stone sleep.

20

Anna woke to a mild headache, a grumbling stomach, and Captain making biscuits on her cheek.

"Hmmnh?" she groaned, head and throat feeling fuzzy and thick.

"Mrr-ow," Captain replied.

"Oh." *Right.* She sucked in a deep breath, remembering last night.

Some of her indignation was still there, simmering just under the surface, but mostly she was just tired. Tired of waiting for the other shoe to drop. Tired of the headaches. Tired of the suspicion and paranoia and worry and . . . everything.

Letting out the breath in a deep sigh, Anna pulled herself out of bed and cringed. She was in yesterday's clothes still, and her stomach rumbled ferociously.

Right, she'd run away before eating anything.

It wasn't until she was halfway into a fresh shirt that she realized—

The sun was up.

A sound of distress stuck in her throat, she hurried through dressing. Her phone was missing too, but she was sure she'd had it in her pocket when she came in here? She always set her alarm?

Pulse pounding behind her right eye, Anna hurried out of her room.

"Frey, have you—?"

She came to a skidding halt in the living room.

Frey was already stone, and he'd positioned himself right in front of the front door, blocking her exit.

The reality of his big stone bulk trapping her inside took a moment to register. She staggered toward him, not quite believing it.

Something flashed on the counter, and she saw her phone, the alarm still going off.

He took my phone so I wouldn't get up in time.

He'd barricaded her inside the apartment so she couldn't leave for work.

Anna *screeched.*

She flew at him and pushed at his solid stone chest. Nothing happened.

She pushed again, pushed and shoved and kicked his shin but stopped when it only stubbed her toes. She smacked his chest and tried pushing him from the side. Nothing.

"You fucking asshole!"

She screeched again, hot, frustrated tears leaking down her cheeks.

How could he do this to me?

She had to go to work! She was already late! And she was supposed to be taking a long lunch to go get her MRI today!

He'd know that if you'd told him, whispered a traitorous little voice inside her.

Anna wasn't sure that would've made a difference. He was so fucking determined to keep her here with him. Well, she wasn't going to be some princess locked away in a tower by an evil beast. She was her own fucking person and how dare he try to stop her? She—*they* had bills! Life wasn't free!

Smacking him one more time, Anna balled up a dishcloth and threw it over his face. She wasn't sure how much he could "see" in his stone state, but now he'd enjoy just damp terrycloth.

She didn't know if he could "hear" either, but she still growled at him, "I'm going to work, asshole, and I'll get home whenever I fucking decide to."

Anna didn't think, just hurried through an abbreviated morning routine. She texted Carrie to let her know she'd overslept but would be in shortly. She fed Captain even though Frey had left out his morning meal of shredded chicken already.

And then, as she opened the window to shimmy up to the roof, she stuck her tongue out at her butthead roommate.

An acrobat Anna was not. It was harrowing climbing up the fire escape to the roof then using her keys to get in the door. She took the stairs down to ground level, really hoping no one, especially the SUV still parked across the street, saw her morning stunt.

By the time Anna got into work, she was huffing, puffing, and sweaty despite the chilly fog blanketing the city. She was over an hour late and apologized profusely to Carrie, who'd taken over the front desk.

"Please don't trouble yourself," Carrie said as she signed out of the computer, "we all have those mornings."

"It won't happen again," Anna rushed to assure her. She cringed having to remind her boss, "Today I'm taking a long lunch for an appointment."

"Yes, that's right. That will be fine, Suzie or Brian can cover the extra time."

"I can stay later if you need, do the last sweep, and—"

"Anna." Carrie placed a gentle hand on her shoulder. "It's all right. You're a wonderful employee and you've asked so little of us. You do what you need to do."

She nodded jerkily and bade Carrie good morning as her boss headed off into the museum. The compliments were hard to swallow, and Anna was too paranoid not to read into them. Either she'd stay late or take the time off. She didn't want to be indebted to the Gwyneths.

Later that afternoon, Anna walked back to the museum after her appointment, head throbbing. The shakeup in routine, with her tardiness and lunchtime appointment, plus her boiling anger with Frey and lackluster vending machine lunch meant that it was almost a full-blown migraine by the time she made it back to the Milton Building.

She wanted to get her day back on track, find a little comfort in routine and normalcy. Maybe spending the last few hours sitting still at the desk would take her headache down a few notches.

But, of course, the universe wasn't that kind.

"Hello, Miss Anna."

She looked up, startled to see Andrew Glendower holding the door open for her. She still had a few steps to get to the door and had meant to turn down the alleyway for the side door, but now that he was holding the heavy front door open, she had no choice but to hustle inside.

"Thank you," she said, feeling every footstep on the stone floor as she walked over to the front desk.

Glendower followed and watched with a small smile as she shed her jacket and scarf.

"Back from lunch?"

"Out for a walk," she replied, relieved to have the desk between them.

He pulled out a crisp, cream business card. "Whenever you have time to take another long lunch, let me take you out. Call me."

His smile widened as Anna gawked at the business card on the desk, and with a nod of that sandy blonde head, he left to walk through the museum.

In his wake, Anna stared at the little cream card with foiled gold lettering. She poked it with a fingernail, watching how the light caught and shifted over the Tree of Life insignia. It wasn't a university or organizational business card, either. It just included his title, name, and a phone number.

Weird.

Anna had just typed out an email telling Carrie that Glendower was in the museum again when another unfortunately familiar figure came striding through the front doors.

"Good afternoon, Detective Ramirez," she greeted with false sincerity.

"Hello, Miss Kincaid. How are you today?"

She and the detective exchanged pleasantries, neither of their hearts or interests in it. Finally, with the social niceties covered, Ramirez said, "I have an interview scheduled with Mrs. Gwyneth. Would you be able to show me to her office?"

He certainly already knew the way, but biting her cheek, Anna did her best to hold onto her accommodating smile. Putting out the *Be Back Soon!* sign, she ushered the detective further into the museum.

She could barely hear him over her pounding head, each pulse of pain like a mini thunderclap against her skull, but when he asked if she'd seen or heard anything of interest recently, Anna couldn't help thumbing the business card in her pocket.

When they reached the corridor to the Gwyneths' office, Anna turned to face the detective and handed over the card.

"There's a regular here, Professor Andrew Glendower. I hadn't really noticed him before the theft, but afterwards, he always stops by to talk."

Ramirez took the card, looking at it before Anna. She knew what this probably looked like, the iffy employee with a checkered past trying to shift the blame onto a squeaky-clean professor.

"Can you describe him for me?"

Anna did, a little heartened to see that Ramirez actually wrote down what she said.

"And has he given you any reason to be suspicious?"

Besides his smarmy vibe? "Nothing specific, I guess. Just . . . nobody hangs around and talks to me like that, you know? He asks weird questions."

Replacing the leather notebook in his pocket, Ramirez gave her another long look. "He's not the first middle-aged guy to hit on a younger woman."

Anna's stomach curdled. "It's not like that."

"All right."

Turning on her heel, she took the detective the rest of the way without a word. She knocked lightly on the door, announced Ramirez, and then left them to it. She'd said her piece. Had she really thought the detective would take her seriously?

Anna finished her shift without taking time off—mostly to stick it to the universe. Her righteous rebellion wasn't much of a comfort, though, and she watched her feet as she walked home, needing to concentrate on putting one in front of the other. The night was dark and foggy again, matching her mood.

She didn't care if someone was following her. She didn't care that Frey was going to have a hissy fit when she got back. She just wanted to take her shot and lay down.

Days like today had a way of wearing a person down. Unfortunately for her, she had more crappy days than good. At least . . . she had before Frey.

But now all of that was over. She was sure of it. After last night, it was obvious some ground rules needed to be set, including putting the breaks on whatever he thought was going to happen with his mate bond ideas. She didn't mind letting him stay, and he didn't have to do so much around the apartment, but he did need to butt out of her business.

She'd just turned onto her block and was trying out things she wanted to say to him in her head when the fog shifted.

Buffeted with a blast of air, Anna gasped.

Her head jerked up in time to behold a pair of giant wings spread wide and coming right at her.

Smooth as could be, Frey landed right in front of her. His feet had barely touched the sidewalk before he'd snatched her into his arms and jumped back into the air.

A high-pitched *eep* escaped her before Anna clamped her mouth shut. Her heart kicked painfully in her chest, and her head sloshed to the side as Frey gained height and then banked to the left.

Cold fog rushed past them, thick against her mouth, and she could hardly breathe as he flew and flew and flew. For a moment, they broke above the fog bank. Anna gasped, the night cold and clear around them, thousands of crystalline stars shining down and the moon a big pearl ringed in blue. Then the fog swallowed them again.

"Put me down!" she hissed. "Someone will *see!*"

He ignored her words, ignored her fists, full of his shirt and tugging. When she managed to kick his shin, he adjusted his hold so he had her under the back and legs.

She squirmed in his arms, not so much trying to get away (she wasn't that dumb) but to let him know she *wasn't happy about this.* Anna was considering biting him when his wings curled forward like big sails and he went from horizontal to vertical. His legs somehow found the ground through the fog, and they landed in a grassy area at a light jog.

It was a park, trees lining it several deep and a concrete pathway cutting through the middle, but she couldn't quite tell which one in the fog.

With the ground in sight, Anna really did start wriggling.

"Frey, put me *down.*"

"No," he growled.

She growled right back.

Fuck this. Fuck today. And fuck him, too!

She did her best impression of a fish, arching her back and kicking her legs, but his arms only clamped down tighter.

Her head falling off would've been a mercy with how hard it pounded from the altitude changes on top of everything else. Anna just wanted to lay still—no, she wanted to go home and get her shot. So she struggled in his arms, determined to break free.

"Let. Go. Of. Me!"

She gasped when his face got right in hers, his nose wrinkled in that way it did. Fangs flashing, he growled, "*Never.*"

A trickle of fear slithered down her spine, and her heart made a painful *tha-thump.* Tears threatened, and she shook her head even though it was agony. Shoving at his chest, Anna finally worked a leg free.

Finally, with a hearty, long-suffering growl, Frey let her go.

Anna stumbled away, catching herself after a few paces, and glared at him.

"Why must you always fight?" he demanded. "I'm the last one you should be fighting and yet it's me you fight hardest!"

"You're the only one who grabs me and flies to strange parks at night! What the *actual fuck,* Frey?"

"You left! Again! You knew all the dangers, knew how I felt about it, and you left!"

"Because I need the job!"

"There must be other jobs, ones that don't put you in danger."

"What the fuck do you know about getting a job? I need the money and—and you know what, I'm not having this argument again. You say I knew how you felt, well what about how I feel, Frey?"

"How do you feel, Anna?" He stalked toward her, all heaving chest and bright, angry eyes. "I would love to know how you feel, but you won't share it with me. You share nothing of yourself with me."

The accusation struck Anna square in the chest, but she refused to show it.

"How do I feel? Angry, Frey. I hate being manhandled and grabbed and taken somewhere I don't want to go. I want to be home right now, not in some random park in the cold."

"You would not listen to me. You were reckless and late and I had to make sure you were safe."

"I was *fine*. I can take care of myself, Frey. I've been doing it long before you."

His lip peeled back in a show of disgust. "Yes, I could tell. With your headaches hardly managed and your sad meals. *I* would take care of you, my Anna, if you'd only let me."

"I don't need to be taken care of." Which was good, because she never had been.

Frey snorted, the sound full of derision and frustration. "Fine. I *want* to take care of you. As a mate should. But you won't allow it. You insist on doing everything yourself, taking no help. You entrust me with nothing important. Never you."

She shook her head, wincing when a stab of pain lanced from her brow to the back of her head. The harshness to Frey's face faded as he watched while she rubbed a circle in her temple. He stepped toward her, expression softening, but she held her hand up to keep him back.

"I never asked for this. I didn't mean to wake you up. I don't know what happened, it just . . . happened."

"Because you are my heartsong," he said, voice gentler but still low and firm.

Anna sighed. "Frey, I'm not your soulmate. I'm just Anna. Nothing special. I'm not what you need me to be."

"You are you, Anna. That is enough."

"That's not true!" she cried, tears spilling across her fingers. "If it was, the curse would be broken."

A dissatisfied rumble emanated from his chest. Again Frey tried to approach and again Anna repelled him with a hand.

"Anna . . ."

"No. This has to stop, okay?" She rubbed circles into her head in time with her words, the tears coming faster than she could wipe them away. "Whatever this is, it has to stop. It's too much. It's—I can't, I can't."

"Anna," he groaned, the sound like she had her hand wrapped around his beating heart and squeezed the very life from it. "Anna, let me help. Let me be your mate."

"You've done enough today." She shook her head again and backed away blindly. "You want a mate, Frey. You don't want *me*."

Why would he? What was she? What did she offer?

Nothing.

"I want *you*. Anna." Big hands finally caught her by the shoulders, bringing her to a halt. She could hardly see him through the fog and tears, but she could feel his words when he said, "Tell me you don't want me. Tell me that, and I will leave you."

Her heart clenched more painfully than even her head.

I can't I can't I can't.

All she could do was what she always did. Run.

"I have to go," she said, breaking from his hold. She was probably already too far gone for even a shot, and if she stayed here any longer with him, she knew she'd break. "Just . . . just leave me alone, Frey."

And she stumbled away, finally catching the concrete path and following it out of the park. She could hardly hear anything above the pounding of her head, but when she looked over her shoulder, she saw only fog and the eerie outline of trees.

Numb with pain, she left him behind.

With her phone map, Anna managed to get to a populated street and call a cab. It didn't matter the cost, she had to get home.

She had to get back to her real life.

Even if, over the pain of her head and the absolute terror of knowing someone wanted to be with her, she'd left her heart with him there in that park.

Frey let her go. It went against every instinct, every belief. The weight of his kin's disappointment bore down on him until he could hardly breathe.

Still, he did not follow her.

Whatever bond had managed to build between them hung by a thread, and Frey stood on, waiting for the stone sleep to take him back. He almost wished for it.

But the fog continued to roll through the grassy land, illuminated eerily by evenly spaced lampposts. The thickness of it brushed against his skin with a damp chill, and Frey numbly wrapped his wings about his shoulders.

Just leave me alone, Frey.

Leave her alone. Leave his mate.

How could he do such a thing?

He couldn't—and yet, his soul shriveled at the thought of being somewhere he wasn't wanted. To know that his mate, his heartsong, did not *want* him.

Frey staggered into the trees unseeing. He hadn't realized that when the elders and the bards spoke of heartbreak, such a thing could hurt so badly. That he'd feel his very soul rending in two.

Amongst the trees, hidden by their great limbs and the interminable fog that rolled through this human city, Frey unleashed.

He *howled.*

With claws and fangs he swiped and struck at the trees and underbrush, scoring the bark and obliterating foliage. He bared his fangs and yowled, all his outrage, all his grief pouring into the sound.

He'd thought he was doing everything right. He gave her time. He gave her his patience. He gave her *him.* What little he had to give was all hers.

And she doesn't want it.

Guilt was a suffocating companion, clogging his throat. He and Anna were the only hope for his people in centuries. It was a heavy weight to bear, but he'd borne it for them. For what could be. And he'd failed. He'd failed his kin. He'd failed himself.

He'd failed his mate.

His stubborn, headstrong, fierce mate.

Frey roared again, wanting the pain out, gone, but whatever he shed with a swipe of his claws or snarl of his fangs, more flooded into the cavity left behind. Anna had left a hole the very size and shape of her inside him, and there would be no filling it.

He raged until there was nothing left but the devastation. He stood with shoulders slumped, panting, his human clothes askew and his hair tangled. His wings and tail shivered from the damp and effort, and his fingers had long since gone numb being grated against the thick tree bark.

What now? he thought. *What did he have left?*

He'd lost everything thrice now. Somehow, this time was worse than all the others.

Nothing could have prepared him for this modern world, nor what having a human mate would mean. He'd thought himself up to the challenge, that his strength and determination would be enough.

But would anything be? Would he ever be enough for Anna, for his clan?

Leave me alone.

He didn't think he could. But he didn't know what to do, how to make her see.

For the first time, Frey . . . lost a battle.

21

Anna regretted schlepping into work the next day. The migraine had indeed been too far gone for the shot, and although getting a few hours of sleep had helped a bit, she was now twenty-four hours in without much relief.

She could do little but squint at the computer and move emails around. Another coworker took pity on her and traded her desk duty for something further into the museum where the lights weren't so bright. By lunchtime, though, Anna's body just gave out.

Carrie was as understanding as ever, telling her, "Take care of yourself. And don't come back until you feel better!"

So Anna grabbed her things and steeled herself for the walk back to the apartment.

The day was cloudy but clear at ground-level. She thought maybe that van was back, and it gave an apprehensive tinge to her pain. She stuck to her route and walked as fast as she could.

A chilly, empty apartment greeted her. And Captain, of course.

"Hi, Cappy," she sighed. He meowed plaintively, but she didn't dare bend over and let the blood rush to her head.

Even though Frey would be a statue this time of day, not seeing him anywhere in the apartment brought another wave of heartache.

It'd been sharp, stealing her breath and keeping her on the verge of tears all last night. She'd concerned the cab driver who'd taken her home, the man asking several times if she was okay and if he could call someone for her.

"No, no one. I'm okay," she'd said. There was no one to call. She'd left the only one who cared behind in that park.

The driver's look of pity had been unbearable, and Anna fled from it as quickly as she had from Frey. Coming home to her dark apartment had been its own kind of agony. The dinner Frey had been preparing was still warm in the oven, the table set for two. Captain had been fed and a whole Tupperware of freshly cooked and shredded chicken sat in the fridge.

The apartment felt . . . devoid without him.

Heart heavy, she set about shutting the blinds and changing into comfy, stretchy clothes. She gave herself another shot and forced some oatmeal down her throat. Then with a full water bottle and heating pad, she laid down on the couch and turned the TV on for some noise.

Drifting on the ebb and flow of pain, Anna sipped her water and adjusted the heating pad over her face. Captain eventually settled on her hip, purring as she scratched behind his ears.

Daytime television eventually moved into afternoon variety shows then finally the evening news. From the little line of light she could see from under the heating pad, she knew when the sun slipped behind the buildings across the street.

He'll be waking up soon.

Wherever he was.

The thought gnawed at her. She'd just *left him there,* out in the middle of San Francisco. Sure, he could fly anywhere he wanted, but where could he really go? She was all he knew in the modern world.

Should've done more for him. She should've taken him . . . somewhere. Somehow. She'd never bothered with a car, but he might've enjoyed driving around. Maybe they could've gone out into the more rural areas; he could've flown around without worrying someone would see him. She could've gotten him a phone or something to keep in contact when she was still out in the evenings. She could've . . . she didn't know, done something *more,* but she hadn't.

She let him do things *for her*. She let them play house for a while. Yet she hadn't tried to do much for him, hadn't really taught or introduced him to anything after the TV. She'd let him cuddle her close and take care of her and offered him nothing in return.

Because that would mean letting him in.

And she just . . . couldn't do that, either.

So Anna did the only thing she knew to do. She kept her heart safe—but it broke anyway. And she'd no one to blame but herself.

For the first time in a long while, Frey followed the tendril of belonging back to his kin. It faded over distance, and even now, it was like looking across a fast-flowing river. Frey's mind found its way back to the collective of his kin, where they huddled together for safety and comfort, though he was too far to truly join them.

There was nothing to say. No one asked questions. They shivered in recognition at his familiar mind linking back to them.

They wanted to ask where he'd been. Why he'd been gone and why he was back now.

None did. Shrouded in his misery, devastation followed him like a shadow. He was a wraith, heartbroken and world-weary. His kin looked on with pity.

Frey didn't try to cross that river and join them. It was enough to stand on the bank and feel them, to have some sense of belonging in a world that made little sense anymore.

I tried, he wanted to tell them. *I tried.*

Anna had almost dozed off when what a reporter on the six o'clock news was saying caught her ear.

"A bit of a mystery out of McLaren Park this evening. Joggers reported finding a grove of trees shredded by what is likely a large animal. Claw marks were evident in the bark and the area is currently closed as officials . . . "

Heart jumping into her throat, Anna peeled back the heating pad to squint at the TV. The camera panned from the on-scene reporter to show a copse of trees and underbrush absolutely trashed. Huge gashes had been slashed into the trunks, four razor-sharp claw marks patterning every surface in that small area.

Anna's stomach clenched painfully, and she braved her phone as the reporter went on.

"Residents are urged to take caution. All signs point to a large black bear, though one hasn't yet been spotted in the area. Anyone with home surveillance footage is urged to call the San Francisco or San Mateo Sheriff's Office so they can begin tracking the animal's whereabouts."

She tapped every keyword combination her tired brain could think of into the search engine, trying to find any news about possible giant gargoyle sightings. To her relief, there was only today's story and one instance of someone asking about a giant bat flying around the city on a Reddit thread, and that was days ago.

Breathing a sigh of relief, Anna replaced the heating pad.

The scars left on those trees were burned into her retinas, though.

It had to be Frey.

That's exactly where they'd been the night before. Frey was definitely the size of a big black bear on its hind legs, if not bigger.

She shuddered to think of how angry he must be. How outraged to make such deep, horrid marks in those trees.

Her stomach churned unhappily, and her heart took to aching again.

She was still so angry with him for what he'd done, but there was no fire to it now. Everything else drowned under the weight of her migraine, and she hated that. She hated that her pain reduced her to yelling at him. Yeah, what he'd done was shitty, but he'd been right about some stuff, too.

Anna didn't let people in, not deep enough or long enough to hurt her. Rely on no one, trust no one. That's what she'd learned from life.

And isn't that just awful?

Was that really how she wanted to be?

She'd made herself promises about being honest, with herself and others. She was proud of the progress she'd made and being able to both support herself and take care of herself and Captain.

Frey wanted to take care of her, too.

Tears slipped out, soaking the heating pad.

Him wanting to take care of her didn't diminish how much she'd accomplished. And being honest, she loved how he was with her and Captain. Even with his gigantic gaps in knowledge and being, ya know, a mythical creature from sixth-century Wales, he was the type of partner most people would kill for. Playful, supportive, confident—he was the type she'd want, too, wings and all.

I've been looking a gift horse in the mouth.

But being supportive and attentive didn't mean that she could just trust where she hadn't before. She didn't know if he could *care* for her. For her heart.

You never gave him the chance to.

No risk, no reward—but also no repercussions.

And yet, Anna was living with all the repercussions, but had she really risked anything? Sort of. Not really. So was there no reward or was she just wrong?

The tears came harder, and Anna pulled off the heating pad, stifled by her own sobs.

Captain padded up her side, and his rough little tongue licked at what he could reach of her cheek.

Anna didn't like who she was in pain. Short-tempered, irritable, insensitive. Yeah, she knew she could cut herself some slack, that anyone with chronic pain understood you didn't start from go when you began the day already in pain. It was a struggle just surviving some days, and she couldn't be expected to be her best self.

But she also didn't like things about herself even when she wasn't in pain. She didn't like that she couldn't trust. She didn't like that at the first sign of something intimate or difficult, she fell back into her ruts. She didn't like that, rather than trying, she hid herself away.

Anna had told Frey she didn't want to be sidelined or sequestered by him. Wasn't she just doing it to herself, though? How was that any better?

It wasn't.

But what could she do about it now?

Scritching Captain, Anna sat up. After the dizziness dissipated, she hobbled to the windows. Opening the blinds revealed a cold, clear night sky. No stars were visible with all the city lights, but the moon hung full in the sky. Unlatching the window, she left it unlocked before staggering into her room.

It ate at her that she had no way to contact him. No way to ask him to come back. No way of finding out if he was okay.

She didn't know what she'd say to him or how she'd make this right, but he shouldn't be out there alone. Anna did know how much it sucked to be alone.

I'll go look for him, she promised herself as she climbed into bed. *Get rid of this headache, then go look for him.*

Frey woke in a strange place full of strange smells. It all came back to him slowly, finding a secluded place to take the stone sleep. He'd flown some distance the night before, passing over the bay and the large red bridge. In amongst the hills that faced the dramatic coastline, he'd found a quiet ridge to set down.

The tang of salt on the air was hauntingly familiar, and he turned his face into the last rays of the disappeared sun, soaking in its final warmth. Spreading his wings wide, Frey caught an updraft, following the coast north. Centuries ago, he and his kin had patrolled a western coast, testing the strength of their wings in the strong winds and racing the seabirds. It was a different coast, different seabirds, different *century,* but the familiarity of it soothed him. Frey felt . . . grounded as he soared.

The sea air and glittering stars watched as he cut across the night, a shadow that fell over the sparser human settlements. His hair tangled wildly in the wind, and his wings stretched and pumped. Muscles long tight and cramped from being kept to the confines of his mate's dwelling eased and loosened, and it was a pleasure to push himself to the point of ache.

It was almost a relief for something other than his chest to ache.

Frey tumbled between the wind and the waves for a long while, following a pod of whales and touching a toe to the glowing blue water that crashed against the shore. He filled his lungs with fresh air and twisted through complicated aerial maneuvers.

None of it filled the gashing hole inside him that longed for his mate.

A taste of freedom soothed but did not sate him.

He wanted his heartsong, whether or not she wanted him.

So Frey turned back, flying south. The lights of the great city shone for miles, a beacon calling him back to his Anna.

There was no fog for cover this night, so Frey flew high, in the colder air that was like a thousand little slices against his exposed skin.

It took him longer than usual to find his mate's building so high up. He descended in a tight spiral, arms and legs locked into a streamline shape. His final landing was silent, his claws catching on the roof of the building diagonal from Anna's apartment.

He stood in place, listening. When nothing moved nor raised an alarm, Frey crept toward the edge to survey the area.

The new perspective on the street offered a little more information—mostly that that large vehicle was still parked across from Anna's apartment. He growled at it, suspicion inciting his instinct to protect.

His glaring at the vehicle was interrupted when something moved in Anna's window. He watched as the blinds were drawn up and the window left unlatched. For a moment, he caught sight of his beautiful mate, framed in the window and bathed in moonlight. There was something ethereal, almost ghostly about her standing there, and Frey thought she looked sad.

Soon she disappeared from the window, and the apartment went completely dark.

Did . . . she leave it open for me?

His hopeful heart lurched.

Captain soon took up his post at the sill, grooming his paws. It was as if the cat too waited for Frey's return.

He ground his back teeth, the uncertainty agonizing.

Leave me alone, she'd said.

But why else would she leave her window open?

Hope was a painful thing, and Frey decided he didn't yet have the words to say to his Anna everything he thought and felt. She deserved those words, not said in anger. When he knew what he would say, and if she left her window open for him again, he would return to her.

Until then, he would watch over and protect her how he could.

Anna woke strung out from all her meds and still with a tension headache twinging at the base of her skull. Groaning, she fumbled for her phone and blindly opened it to call in sick.

This was why she always tried to have at least a few days stockpiled.

Carrie was understanding as always, insisting she seek further medical attention if the headache didn't go away soon. Anna always hoped it wouldn't come to that; even with health insurance, an emergency room visit was an ordeal she rarely wanted to go through. Besides, she wasn't sure she could even get herself there. At least it was her faux weekend tomorrow, giving her more time to rest.

Weak sunlight eked into her bedroom despite the blackout curtains, so Anna hauled herself up. A change of clothes and breakfast would be a good way to start the day.

But first . . .

She crept out of her bedroom, hope lodged like glass in her throat.

Captain greeted her, chirpy as ever. She knelt down to give him good morning scritches, asking, "Any gargoyle sightings last night?"

She peeked at the window and found it exactly as she'd left it. No statue stood in front of her door nor anywhere else in the apartment. Frey was still gone.

Disappointed and heartsick, Anna slumped into the kitchen to make a meager breakfast.

Why would he come back?

She wouldn't blame him if he didn't come back, but . . . she hoped he would. There were a lot of things she had to say. Even if just the thought of them terrified her.

22

The window was open again. Frey looked for it the moment his eyes could see, and his chest compressed with a heavy kind of hope. He hadn't quite found all the words for all the things he wanted to tell her, but the window called him home, to her.

I want you, any way I can have you, was where he'd start.

The night was dark with cloud cover, and Frey flew high to take advantage. Landing on the steel scaffolding of his mate's building, he took a long look about, assuring himself that nothing was amiss—nothing other than that infernal vehicle, at least—before pushing open the window.

He entered a dark, silent living room. That was, until a little shadow appeared from the darkness to meow fiercely at him.

"I know, my friend, I know," he said, scooping up Captain.

The cat's purring was loud and his claws little pinpricks as he kneaded them against the meat of Frey's neck. Captain's rough tongue scraped at his ear and cheek, and Frey was glad for the small but welcome greeting.

"Where is your mistress, hmm?"

Lick lick lick.

Frey took in the apartment, worried with what he found. Blankets thrown across the couch, heating pad left on the coffee table, bowls of half-finished, congealed oats.

He remembered how Anna had rubbed at her head the other night, one of the clear signs she was getting a headache. The items scattered about were even more indication, and Frey rumbled unhappily to find that his mate had been hurting.

Setting Captain down, he went about tidying the dwelling, replacing the bowls in the kitchen and folding the blankets into their basket. Then, there was nothing left to do but take the heating pad and brave his mate's bedchamber.

He found that even darker, her thick curtains drawn against any light that would steal inside. The lump she made in the blankets was small, her legs drawn up nearly to her chest, and for a moment Frey couldn't find her head.

"Anna?" he whispered, not wanting to wake her if she truly was asleep.

From under the pillows, Anna's head emerged, and she sat up, frowning through the darkness.

"Frey?" she said in a voice that was wobbly and small.

He crossed the room and knelt beside the bed, placing his hand gently on her leg. "I'm here, *fy nghalon.*"

At his words, her face crumpled. Anna fell forward, throwing her arms around his neck and burying her face in the crook of his shoulder. Her face quickly went hot and damp with tears, and Frey put down the heating pad so he could enfold his mate in his arms.

"I'm sorry," she sobbed, "I'm so sorry."

He purred for her, gutted by her tears. "No, my Anna, I am sorry. I shouldn't have pushed you. I let my fears get the better of me."

"Me too. Don't wanna be like that. I don't wanna be afraid." She sobbed the words into his skin, making him want to crawl out of it to soothe her.

He didn't miss how her words slurred, though. Reaching a hand up to her head, he gently massaged at the base of her skull. The groan of relief Anna gave only confirmed his suspicions, and she burrowed further into him.

"How long, *fy nghalon?*"

"About three days. Taken a lot of meds."

Frey grumbled, hating her pain.

"Nothing has helped?"

"Not really."

Her head lolled when he stood, and Frey gingerly felt along her skull and neck. "You're so tense here." He thought back to the videos he'd watched on the different types of headaches and their treatment. His Anna was resourceful and knew her body best, but Frey had to try making it better. He couldn't watch on as she suffered.

Pulling her gently to her feet, Frey encircled her in his wings. Her lids were heavy, eyes unseeing in the dark, but he heard her take and hold a sharp breath when she felt his face lean down to hers.

"Let me help you, Anna. Please."

The tiredness and pain pulled at her face, and he could see that right now, she had nothing left. She was at her wit's end—but she had him, a mate who would take care of her.

For that's what his Anna needed. Care. Tenderness. She wasn't a battle to win, nor a fortress to breach. He shouldn't be sharpening his blade against her hard exterior, nor trying to crack it with his brute strength. She wasn't a challenge nor a prize. Anna was a woman, one with a sharp tongue and stubborn mind and large heart. And she was his mate.

Mates deserved care and compassion. It was their due. In his haste and desperation to finally form and solidify their bond, he'd forgotten this important tenet.

Her voice wobbled again when she finally agreed. "O-Okay."

He kept his rumbling purr light, even though he wanted to roar with pride.

"May I carry you?"

"I can walk," she said, the hint of a grin touching her mouth.

"I know, but I should like to carry you."

A pause, then a whispered, "Okay."

Frey carefully lifted his precious mate into his arms to carry into the washroom.

He set her down on the fluffy rug in front of the bath and went about running the water. The light from the far window and the dim little nightlight beside her toothbrush were enough for him, so he didn't bother with the electric ones as he set out what she'd need and began pulling her sweater over her head.

"What are you doing?" she asked, her tone more curious than accusatory.

"Have you taken a bath to soothe the muscles?"

He'd absolutely never tell her, but he could smell the old sweat and pain on her skin, and her hair had crumpled at odd angles from sleep and the heating pad.

"I took showers."

"Let's try a bath."

"So bossy." He admired her attempt at humor as she took a half-step back to finish undressing.

She'd just hooked her fingers into her underthings when she stopped, tracing his form in the dark with a cautious look.

"How much can you see in the dark?"

"I will not look," he assured her. When Anna chose to show herself to him, he'd look his fill and more, but this wasn't about heat and passion, it was about taking care of her.

Frey didn't know if it was because she believed him or she was just that tired, but after another moment, Anna divested of her underthings. Keeping his word, he looked nowhere but her face as he helped her into the bath.

Her moan of pleasure resonated as she crouched then lay in the warm water. It swirled around her as she settled, and Frey laid down a soaked towel to cradle her head.

With a little maneuvering, he managed to sit down beside the tub, steam billowing around him. He helped Anna duck her head under the water to wet her hair and then replace it on the cushion. Ever so gently, he ran his claws through her hair and massaged at the base of her skull, taking its weight.

Anna's eyes slid closed and the line between her brows slowly eased. When the water was nearly to her chin, Frey turned off the faucet.

They sat in the steamy silence, the only sound for a long while the occasional droplet falling from his fingers as he gently worked her head, neck, and shoulders. It took a little time, but he finally felt the muscles begin to relax.

"Where did you go?" she asked so quietly he almost didn't hear.

Frey took a moment to answer, considering his words carefully. "I stayed in the park for a while and then flew north along the coast."

"Up into Marin?"

He made a noise of assent, but the name meant nothing to him. "I flew for a long while. It felt good to have the sea breeze in my wings again. But then I came back to you."

"You just got back?"

"No. I . . ." He didn't quite know why he flushed nor why the words tangled on his tongue. "I settled across the street last night. I didn't know if I was welcome."

She was quiet for a while, the only sign that she hadn't fallen asleep the movement of her fingers as they traced patterns on the surface of the water.

"You were here all this time."

It wasn't a question, but Frey answered her anyway. "Yes. You are my north star, Anna. My . . . my home."

Those brows drew together again, and Frey worried her headache was worsening. But then her hand, wrinkled and hot from the water, reached up to cup his jaw.

"You say things like that and all my arguments start sounding silly."

He wasn't sure what to do with her words, drowsy and muddled as she was, but he decided to take heart. Covering her hand with his, he pressed her palm into his skin, soaking up the feel of her touch.

They stayed like that until the water cooled, then he washed her limbs and back. Anna was warm and boneless when Frey finally helped her from the tub. He fetched clean clothes while she toweled off, and he helped her dress into loose, comfortable layers. Finally, he carried his mate back to her bed and set her amongst all the soft blankets.

The sight of her there, safe and comfortable, sated the fiercest of those protective instincts.

That she reached for him in the darkness and asked, "Will you stay with me?" sated the rest.

He'd never refuse her, but trying not to seem overeager, Frey eased onto her bed. He held still while it creaked, and when it didn't give under his bulk, he rolled to his side and drew Anna into his body.

The little contented sigh she made would stay with Frey until the goddesses sent him to the Otherworld.

"You're so warm," she said, words still slurred, but now from relaxation.

His chest rumbled with a purr for her, and he was more than content to lay with her like that, carding his claws through her damp hair. Her natural scent was stronger now with the previous days washed away, and he wanted to bury his nose in her hair and drink it down. He knew better than to jostle her, though, or press on her head beyond the gentle massaging he did with his fingertips.

Anna's breathing became easier, although he didn't think she slept. Laying with her like this brought all the stories, all the advice the elders had given about finding and taking a mate back to him. Frey hadn't listened to them as well as he should have, then or now.

In this moment, though, he thought he understood.

Whatever this took, whatever Anna needed, Frey would give it. Whatever compromises had to be made, whatever modernization he needed, he would adapt. It would take effort and time and patience, but their bond, *Anna,* was worth it.

Being Anna's mate was to be Anna's partner. Her support. Not just her sword but her shield, her sustenance, her home. She didn't just need the strength of his arm and wing but his heart and his compassion. She would test him, try him, and likely vex him again and again—but always would she be worth it.

Carefully, Frey drew her hands to his lips and kissed every fingertip.

"I understand now, my heartsong," he murmured to her. "I know now what I must do to be a mate worthy of you."

Her hand fumbled blindly in the dark, gracelessly finding and patting his mouth. "Shh," she chided, "you're great, Frey. You're more worthy than I deserve."

He wanted to hiss at her words but bit it back, knowing the sound would aggravate her head. "Don't say such things."

"It's true," she whispered back.

Her eyes remained shut tight, but Frey scented when fresh tears began to flow. A little sob burst past her lips, and he couldn't stop himself from gathering her even closer. He made soothing, shushing noises as his hands ran up and down her back.

"Don't cry, my Anna. Please," he begged.

"I haven't been fair to you. Everything has just been so much to deal with and I just—I did what I always do, and I hate that, I hate that I pushed you away and I'm sorry and—"

"Shh shh shh." He placed the gentlest of kisses on her brow and wiped her tears with the blanket. "I asked much from you without understanding everything I asked for."

"You're being too nice," she said, as if that was a bad thing. "You should be mad at me. I'm mad at me. And at you still, a little." She pulled her hands from his grip to cover her face as the tears came harder. Her voice was cracked and muffled, but he still heard her sob, "I'm just *tired.*"

"I know," he murmured, "I know you are. You should sleep."

"No, I—I'm tired of being this way. I'm tired of these fucking headaches. I hate what they do to me, and I hate that I can't make them better. And I worry . . ." Her voice warbled as she took a long, sniffling breath. "What if it's cosmic justice? What if I get them because I'm a bad person, or for everything I've done? I'm not a good person, Frey. I've stolen things. I've lied to people. I hold grudges. I'm not soulmate material."

"You are you, Anna. The good and the bad. Do you think I'm perfect?"

"No, but . . ."

Frey eased under the pillows with her, placing his face close to hers without quite touching. "I have killed before. I have looked at my kinsmen with jealousy and coveted what they had. I have been prideful and vain and hotheaded. Does this mean I'm unworthy of a mate?"

He'd asked himself this question before, in his heart of hearts, and it always left him cold with terror. What if it was true? What if he truly wasn't worthy, and that was why he had everything in his dwelling except what mattered—a mate, a family?

"No," she said.

"Then why are you less worthy? Why do you think you deserve less?"

"Good things don't happen to me, and having someone like you just land in my lap feels too good to be true."

His vanity was certainly pleased with her words, but he thought he understood her. His soul ached to know she thought herself undeserving of good things, when really, she deserved everything good he could give and more.

"Nothing about this has been easy. At least for now, I cannot go outside with you. I cannot do something as simple as stand beside you in the street." He still found it galling, that the stone sleep was his prison in the daylight and her modern world another at night. But he would make do because this all meant he had Anna. "It will not be easy, my Anna, but it will be good. This I vow to you. I will make our life so good."

He'd known how burdensome her headaches were, but now he understood. The pain weighed on her, and he could understand how that burden would be too heavy to bear sometimes. He'd known some in the clan who'd had pains they dealt with; old Hagar had lost his foot in battle and the wound often bothered him, and Carys had been born with malformed wings. Everyone had their burdens, and he thought his Anna admirable for weathering as best she could.

It was her strength that made him determined not to be a burden to her, too, and he told her as much. "I will share in your load, *fy nghân*. Not add to it."

She made an unhappy noise. "Frey, you've been amazing. I've never . . . no one's taken care of me like this before. I like having you around—at least when we're not arguing."

"Because I always win?" he teased, hiding his sharp relief at her words.

"You wish."

Carefully, Frey brushed Anna's hair back and ran his thumb over her cheek. He was always mesmerized by the softness of her. She could be prickly, most certainly, but there was another side to her, one that was soft and warm and so, so kind.

It terrified him to know that he could crush that delicate, beautiful part of her. And that she showed it to him at all. He would spend his life protecting it, for he wanted all of her sweetness and softness.

"Twice now I've lost everything precious to me." Soon he would tell her of his mother and sister, of their lives and their loss. He would tell her too of that horrible night when the fae stripped everything from him and his kin, when he'd thought it better to have died than suffer their curse. Now, painful as those had been, he could be grateful it'd brought him to his heartsong. "I spent my life gathering things to fill my dwelling and be ready for my mate. I've waited for you for a long time, *fy nghariad*. Even before the fae's curse. But I can be patient, my Anna. I can be whatever you need me to be, whether it is as your mate or not."

The breath she took was long, and it felt as though she stole it from his own lungs. She could have it, his air, his lungs, his heart, everything, if she'd only just—

"I don't think I can promise anything, but . . ." She licked her lips, and her fingertips found the curve of his jaw. "I want to try."

A rush of air, of relief and hope and determination, burst out of him, but he was gentle when he took her hands in his again and said, "That's all I ask. We will try. Together."

Her tears finally dried, Anna burrowed in close, her nose finding the hollow of his throat. She breathed in deeply there as Frey wrapped his arms and a wing around her.

"Together," she murmured into his skin, branding him with her promise.

Frey purred his happiness, and his chest went tight when she asked softly, "Would you tell me about everything you gathered?"

Stroking her hair, Frey told her of all the things he'd collected over the years, everything he'd gathered in preparation for a mate. The pretty shells and glass beads and soft furs. He spoke proudly of the large bed he'd made, ready to cuddle a mate close every night just as he was with her. He'd made strong nets and glazed pots and chairs of sturdy oak, and traded for fine cloth and pewter cups and gold brooches.

"'S beautiful," she mumbled, and he could tell she was close to sleep.

Frey lulled her with stories of his dwelling, of how he would have carried her across the threshold and shown her every single thing that was hers now, too.

Soon, Anna fell into sleep, and Frey held her tight.

His heartache was still there, but it was bittersweet. He'd lost his family, his kin, his dwelling. Speaking of everything that had been lost was never easy, but he realized that all those lost things had been gathered for a mate, a figment of his hopes.

What he had now was far more precious.

Anna was real, and she was *his*. He would fill the dwelling and their lives with everything she could want or need. He would rebuild. And this time, it would be not just for his mate but for *Anna*.

"*Mae fy nghalon yn eiddo i ti*," he whispered to her in the dark, giving her the words even if she didn't hear.

23

Anna woke tangled in blankets and wings and Frey's long hair. And without a headache.

In that split second between waking up and wakefulness, she worried he might have been a dream. That in her pained desperation and guilt, she'd conjured him up somehow. Feeling him lying beside her set soul at ease.

Then there was the profound relief of finally having a clear, pain-free head. She stretched her legs and spread her toes, feeling better than she had in . . . a long time, actually. Her heart was a bit lighter, her outlook a bit rosier. She was still mortified she'd stripped in front of Frey, but after being in pain so long, she hadn't had the capacity to care anymore.

And when she thought past her embarrassment, she remembered how sweet Frey had been. No feels were copped. He'd been a perfect gentleman and made her feel safe. Cherished. *Better.* She couldn't emphasize enough how much better she felt—in large part because of him.

The big, warm arm banded around her flexed, drawing her back into the curve of an even bigger, even warmer chest. A rumbling purr tickled at her back, and warm lips with the hint of fangs pressed to her temple.

"Good morning, *fy nghân*." The words reverberated in Anna's ear, making her smile.

She caressed the strong forearm fastened just beneath her breasts. "Good morning," she said, unable to help her blush.

"How do you feel?"

"A lot better."

Gingerly, just to make sure she didn't prove herself wrong, Anna rolled onto her other side to face Frey.

It was still very early morning, not even predawn light creeping inside. She could only really discern the outline of his profile, but she felt his attention fixed on her.

Waking up to him, getting to touch his warm chest and cuddle up close, was *amazing*. The soft coziness of sleep still hung around them, and Anna tucked herself into him and found that little place near the bottom of his throat. She couldn't help nuzzling and kissing him there.

"Thank you for taking care of me." Anna could do it herself, had done so many times before, even with bad bouts like this. Yet being taken care of, having someone there to help and comfort, was such an utter relief. She didn't have to be strong or brave, just focus on feeling better.

He made that rumble, the one that told her he was pleased, and his claws found her head again. Anna somehow both melted and arched in a contented, feline stretch at the delicious rasp of his fingers in her hair.

"No need to thank me." She felt his smile when he ducked in to brush her nose with his. "Though I wouldn't say no to a kiss."

Lord, she loved it when he was flirty.

Smiling, Anna asked, "You'd brave morning breath?"

"I'd brave anything for you, my Anna."

Well, that does it.

In the dark, she didn't quite meet his lips the first time, but soon they found each other. She'd gathered from a few things he'd said that he didn't have much experience kissing, but ho boy, what he lacked in experience he made up for in enthusiasm.

Soon all Anna could think and feel was the give and take of him, how he slipped so easily inside her mouth to touch and tease. Then the next moment he was coaxing her into following, chasing him down with her own swipes and nips. Her heart kicked in excitement every time she drew a pleased rumble from that big chest.

Their kisses were loud and messy and amazing. She buried her fingers in that thick mane, loving how his hair, thicker and slightly coarser than hers, slid against her palms. He shuddered when she teased her fingers along the base of his horns, and she shivered with delight when that rumble turned to a growl.

"Are these sensitive?"

"The bases are."

"You like it when I touch you here?"

With another of those wicked grins, he rolled them so he hovered above her in the soft, muzzy dark. A bolt of heat sizzled between her thighs to have him taking up her vision and pressing her into the bed.

"I like your touch everywhere," he said, before swooping in for another kiss that tilted her axis.

Some kissing shouldn't have been enough to completely shift her focus, rock her world, change her priorities—or maybe she just hadn't been kissed as thoroughly as Frey kissed her.

Whatever it was, the thrill of feeling better, the heady rush of feeling *good,* she rocked toward him when he came in for the next kiss, rolling their hips together.

Anna gasped at just how hot and hard he was already.

She'd lived with the guy for weeks, and in that time, he'd mostly been sporting the gray sweatpants, so Anna had some idea of what he was packing. At least, when he was at ease. Feeling him now, her cunt quivered in equal parts joy and terror at the idea of letting him sink inside.

The breath puffed out of her at the thought, but Anna didn't let herself dismiss it out of hand.

It wasn't the first time she'd thought about doing dirty things with and to Frey. She was a hot-blooded cishet woman. The visceral feel of his cock caught between them brought all those thoughts into stark reality.

Mistaking her gasp and silence, Frey said, "Just ignore it."

"Is it just morning wood?" She immediately wished the words back, wished it'd been something sexy that slid out of her mouth instead.

Anna could feel the brush of his lashes as he blinked at her. Then a snort of amusement huffed against her cheeks. "Is that what you call it now? Amusing. But no, my Anna, this is all for you. Whenever you're ready."

Frey leaned in for another kiss, and Anna let herself get swept away in the delicious glide of lips and tongues and fangs. But when he kissed her cheek then nipped at her jaw and down her neck, she braved asking, "What if I don't want to ignore it? What if . . . I want to touch you?"

Above her, he went completely still. She supposed she'd shocked him. Shocked herself a bit too, honestly.

There was no denying that she wanted to touch him, though. Wanted to fill her hands with all of him, finally discover what he liked, what made him groan and growl. Effervescent bubbles fizzed inside her, excitement and anticipation a heady mix with her happy mood at finally feeling human again.

Sometimes, after a long bout of headaches, when Anna finally felt better, it was like she'd touched a socket. Energized, she went out and did things like go to the library and farmer's market, or finally undertook that deep clean she'd been putting off, or read the book and watched the movie she'd been meaning to. Finally having the energy and the positivity to live a little felt so good.

Touching Frey would feel even better, she just knew it.

His breath finally rushed out of him in a hiss, blowing back her hair from her face.

"You can do anything you wish with me, *fy nghân.*"

"Anything?" She bit her lip in excitement, feeling the way he trembled under her hand. That he held himself back even though he shook, that he gave her the time and space and power, did something for her.

"Everything," he agreed.

She thought about teasing him a little more, but she was too greedy and impatient now.

"Lie back for me."

After another kiss, he obliged, rolling onto his side. Anna followed him, breath caught in her throat.

Nervousness nipped at the edges of her mind, but she pushed it and the litany of thoughts that wanted to run rampant away. She'd put her brain through enough; now it was time to just feel.

She started at that massive chest she was so enamored with, running her hands over him in long, appreciative arcs. Anna heard his sharp inhale when she thumbed the hard point of his flat nipple.

"Sensitive too?"

"Not as much as my horns."

"Hmm." She wormed one arm between them and cupped the side of his head so she could tease at the base of one horn. Her other arm slipped under his unbuttoned shirt to trace the thick mass that made up a wing base. "What about this?"

Frey wheezed. "Much more sensitive."

She strummed her fingers along his back, exploring every dip and ridge of muscle and bone. His skin was a little different than hers, a bit more like buttery leather, but it was soft and warm and just so him. He was a pleasure to touch, and he let her have her way, his hands set benignly on her hip and playing with her hair.

She felt him tense the further south she touched, and when she finally teased at the waistband of his low-slung sweats, along that plane of flat muscle just above his straining cock, Anna couldn't help an evil little grin.

"Not as good as this, though."

The breath he sucked in and then let out was noisy and full of overwrought patience.

"I don't know, you haven't touched me there yet."

Anna snorted a laugh. "Fair enough."

All she had to do was make the tiniest space in the elastic and his cock practically did the rest. Even hotter than she imagined, she could feel the heat he radiated before even taking hold of him.

The hand on her hip tightened its grip, but otherwise Frey held perfectly still.

At first her touch was tentative, exploratory. She traced his shape, the thick girth of the shaft and curve of the head. Her fingertip came away wet after teasing the slit, and she ran the pad of each finger over him before sliding down the shaft again.

Her cunt clenched at the feel and weight of him in her hand. There was a bit of relief to find that he was human-shaped, if inhumanly sized. His balls hung heavy behind the root of his cock, hairless and hot. She gathered them in her palm and squeezed ever so slightly.

With a huff, Frey's mouth took hers in a savage kiss, and Anna moaned with satisfaction. She pumped her hand in time to his invading tongue, a sense of feminine power burning her quicker than wildfire to hold such a big, powerful man in her hand like this.

When he let her go to take a breath, Anna asked, "Did you mean everything you said?" She pumped him again, root to tip, and added a little twist of her wrist at the end.

Fangs bared, he still didn't jerk his hips or tackle her to the bed or demand she hurry up.

"Yes," was all he said, voice gone gravelly and strained with how tight he held himself.

"Good," she murmured against his lips, "I did, too." And she kissed his fangs as a resonant groan filled her ears.

"If this is just your trying, I'm more than amenable."

Her lips twisted holding back a smug smirk, and she tried not to pat herself on the back too hard. "Yeah? You feel good?"

His grimace melted into a cocksure grin that Anna felt *everywhere*. Claws slid into her hair and tugged, arching her neck and holding her in place just so.

That horned head ducked, and then a hot tongue laved up the column of her throat. "Mmm," he hummed, "you are the sweetest pain, my Anna."

She shouldn't have found that so sexy, but right now, he could've read a vacuum manual and she'd have eaten up every word.

With her shirt rucked up under her tits after all their rolling around, she gasped when she held his cock to the exposed skin of her belly. The thick vein that snaked along the underside pulsed against her, and the head bobbed and leaked precum onto her skin.

She worked him with both hands, getting them nice and wet with his slick. She throbbed between her thighs, the beat keeping time to the pulse that pounded from his cock and chest. With his mouth working hers as surely as she worked his cock, Anna fell into the sensations, feeling her own orgasm growing inside.

She'd never been one to come quickly or without quite a bit of stimulation, so to feel one coming on had her movements growing greedy. She squeezed a little harder, pumped a little faster. As if sensing her need, Frey's hand slid from her hip to her butt, pulling her in tight to him and trapping his cock between them. He palmed her ass, kneading his fingers into the flesh.

Anna gasped, trying to form the words to tell him to take off his pants, when he went still in her hands.

His head snapped toward the window, and that purr she loved so much turned into a furious growl.

"Wha—?"

A loud groan burst from his lips, and Frey's hand closed around hers on his cock. He squeezed for a moment, face gone stark with need, but then he pulled her hands away.

"It's nearly dawn," he told her.

Anna's body screamed, her mind not quite understanding until she too looked at the window. Just under the hem of the blackout curtains was the faintest line of light.

With another groan, Frey climbed out of bed.

A plaintive noise escaped Anna's throat, and she followed him on her hands and knees. This couldn't be happening—they were just getting started and she *ached* for him and—

"Frey," she moaned.

He turned from where he'd come to stand in the corner of her room, just out of reach. His face etched in deep lines of hunger as he tucked himself away, the look he cast her took her breath away.

"I know, *fy nghariad.* Tonight."

Another protest clogged in her throat as she watched him turn to stone.

"No no no!"

When she reached him, only the faintest residual of his warmth remained. Her hands met cool stone, and Anna shivered at the contrast between it and her fevered skin.

His expression was still as harsh with longing, and his pants, stone now, retained a telling bulge. Curious and frustrated, she traced a finger over that rocky contour, wondering how much he truly did feel while a statue.

She sighed a deep and mournful sigh before kissing his cold chest.

Then an idea popped into her head.

Standing like that with him was a little comfort, but her body wouldn't be quiet. It'd been a long time since she'd felt even half this good—it'd be a shame to let it go to waste.

"This is for both of us," she whispered to him.

Rooting around in her dresser drawer, she found her trusty little bullet vibrator. A splurge a few years back after her last relationship fizzled out, it'd seen her through plenty of lonely and bored nights. She hadn't used it in a while; dealing with chronic pain often meant she didn't have the energy or inclination to pleasure herself.

Now, though, she thought she might come right out of her skin if she didn't do something.

Biting her cheek, Anna didn't let herself overthink as she shucked her sleep pants and got back on the bed. Frey watched on with that stone stare, and Anna imagined he could see everything, that even if he was awake, he wouldn't take his eyes off her.

Holding her breath, she parted her legs and peered at him from between her knees. He had full view of her; he'd see how slick and swollen she was, how *ready*.

Using two fingers, she opened herself to him, gasping at the cool air against her heated flesh.

"What do you think?" she whispered. "You think we'll fit?"

Clicking to her favorite setting, Anna teased the vibe over her clit and then down to her entrance, gathering her slick. The toy glided through her folds, making her moan, and the vibrations stimulated every nerve.

"I think we will."

It'd take a little time and effort, but it'd be so worth it.

Anna worked the vibe over herself in steady circles, finding a pace that had her squirming in the bed. She kept her legs open for him, and watching him stand there across the room made her clench and pulse. She imagined making him stand there if he was awake, just to watch. He would, he'd stand there until she said, all those big muscles shaking with the effort of holding himself back. He'd growl at her, tell her how pretty she was, how good she'd take his cock next, how her cunt and her tits and her mouth and her heart were *his*.

The vibe slid easily inside her, and Anna teased her clit with her fingers as the vibrations pulled her toward the peak. It wasn't the right angle to hit her g-spot, but everything she'd done with Frey, knowing he was there hopefully watching her, was more than enough.

The orgasm blew through her like a gale, whipping and shattering. She fell back on the bed, mouth open wide in a silent scream. She pulsed against her own hands, pleasure pulling her along in its current as her hips snapped. Chasing every scrap of pleasure, Anna came and came and came, a brutal orgasm that went on until she saw stars.

She came back to herself slowly, sprawled out on her bed. The vibe hummed inside her still, sending aftershocks of pleasure zipping up her spine.

Anna was messy, sweaty, and spent—and she felt the best she ever had.

Panting a little, she sat up slowly. Her gaze caught again on Frey, silent and stalwart in the corner.

A smile tugged at her lips, and her pussy pulsed again around the vibe.

The sheets already need changing. Might as well.

Throwing him a wink, she rolled onto her front, spread her legs, and propped herself up on elbows and knees. One hand snuck underneath her to work the vibe, and she moaned with the new angle.

"You wanna see a little more, big guy?"

24

Anna breezed through the apartment, almost wanting to sing. She played loud music and danced around with Captain, who wasn't too happy about being a dance partner or breakfast being late. She threw open the blinds to let in the late-morning sunshine, and if there'd been some birds to sing to, she would have.

She didn't even let the sight of the strange SUV sitting across the street dampen her mood. Though it did change her mind about going out today.

Although, she didn't need much convincing to stay in. Now that she was up, she was definitely still a tad woozy from the meds. Plus, she wanted to be near Frey.

Instead, she set herself up on the couch to do a little internet window shopping.

She spent the morning comparing pared down and refurbished smartphones, saving the tabs to show Frey later. She wanted to get his input on her idea and which phone he might like better. Getting him a way to keep in touch and an outlet to the modern world seemed like such a simple idea, she was a little embarrassed she hadn't thought of it before.

It took her a few minutes to actually transfer the bulk of the money from her emergency mom fund into her main account in preparation for the phone.

An aftertaste of guilt followed her around for a while, but when she realized it was Shannon's voice she heard in her head telling her that money was her mom's, Anna was able to put it from her mind.

In the afternoon, she finalized a one-day shipping order, only blushing a little bit that it included a bottle of lube. Anna was a realist and believed in having a plan.

The blush lasted her as the sun tracked across the sky, her body alight with a warm buzz at the thought of *more* with Frey. Sure, a lingering terror still lurked in her heart of hearts, and there would likely be a part of her that was always scared this was too good to be true—but the hope outweighed them both.

I want to try.

They would take work, the two of them, but that didn't mean it was work not worth doing.

So with dinner cooking and the afternoon shadows growing long, Anna cuddled with Captain and settled in to watch some trashy TV to wait out the remaining hour before Frey would finally wake up.

Frey pushed against his stone sleep, moving even before his limbs were entirely flesh and bone again. Memories of what Anna had done to herself as he had to stand there, unmoving, burned him from the inside out.

Ablaze with his need for her, Frey lunged for the bed, only to find it empty and the bedchamber dark and cool.

With a sensual purr vibrating from his chest, he stalked from the bedchamber in search of his mate. His cock bobbed inside the confines of his braies, the swollen cockhead pushing against the waistband. Each step was sweet agony, his skin sizzling and his heart hammering.

He stopped in his tracks when he finally beheld Anna, asleep on the couch.

The TV played one of her dramatic shows at a low volume, but at some point she'd fallen asleep curled up under a blanket. Captain lay on her hip, he too curled up into a cozy ball.

The scene they made was too precious, too serene for him to disturb.

Go at her pace, he reminded himself. It was advice made easier to swallow knowing now how talented and dexterous her fingers were.

Frey marched into the washroom and shut the door quietly behind him. Taking a familiar stance above the tub, he planted one hand on the wall and fisted his cock in the other. It wasn't the first time he'd tugged his cock in Anna's washroom to get himself under control, and knowing his heartsong, it likely wouldn't be his last.

Engorged and angry, his cock was almost too sensitive to touch. His hand was much rougher and more merciless than his mate's had been, but it was the memory of her soft hands, her nipping kisses, her teasing words that had him spurting into the tub within only a few tugging strokes.

Hissing through gritted teeth, Frey milked the spend from his cock, watching as it splattered against the pearly white ceramic.

When he finished, he was left panting and stooped, the force of his orgasm putting a wobble in his knees. After a few gulping breaths, he got himself and the tub cleaned up, watching as his spend swirled around then disappeared down the drain.

Next time will be inside her, he promised himself.

He was a little less urgent but no less predatory as he reentered the living room, wanting his mate.

The apartment smelled of savory things, and a glance into the kitchen showed something cooked in the oven with twenty minutes left. Plenty of time to greet his heartsong.

She and Captain made a perfect sight, curled up together, but Frey couldn't help himself. Scooping Captain up, he placed the cat gently on the back of the couch. He received a disgruntled blink before his feline friend yawned and went back to sleep.

Blanket and all, he picked Anna up next.

"Hhn?" The sleepy inquiry puffed against his ear as he sat himself down on the couch, Anna in his arms.

"Good evening, *fy nghalon,*" he purred.

Soft eyes under heavy lids took him in, and a warm smile spread across her face.

"Hi," she said, almost shyly.

Tucking her tight to his chest, Frey raised her chin with a knuckle. Her lips were just as sweet as he remembered, and within a mere handful of kisses, he was gone to the warmth and pull of her mouth. He could lose himself so easily in the softness, the chase and capture of her wicked tongue.

He swiped his along her bottom lip before pulling back, pride puffing his chest to see how rosy she'd gone.

"You, *fy nghariad bach drwg*, are quite the tease."

Her blush deepened, and she delicately cleared her throat. "Saw all that, did you?"

Frey grinned to hear the pleased note to her voice.

"Oh, yes. When you are near, my senses at least are alive. I saw everything." He pressed in close, running his nose along one side of hers and down the other. "Did you make yourself feel good?"

"Mmhmm," she hummed against his lips.

"Can I make you feel even better?"

Her mouth caught his in another kiss, and Frey forgot whatever else he'd meant to say. All he could think or feel or smell was Anna, her lips sucking on his, her hands tracing patterns on his chest, her thighs squeezing together in his lap. His hands dug greedily under the blanket, finding the generous curves of her backside. Frey kneaded his fingers deep, pulling her hips flush with his.

Soon, all he could do was chase the next sensation. He explored the contours of her back, running his fingers along her spine underneath her sweater. He savored every mewl and moan he could elicit, the sounds echoing in his ears as he sought the next.

For all her stubbornness and prickliness, his Anna was all softness now in his arms. He glided his hands across every warm, silken bit of her he could, desperate to feel more, to feel all of her. The rightness of holding his mate close, of exploring what made her shudder and quiver and gasp satisfied every instinct, ancient and male.

Anna smelled and tasted of home.

He'd just slipped his fingers beneath the waistband of her loose pants when the oven timer went off.

Frey grinned at her angry mewl when he pulled away and set her back on the couch.

"Dinner first," he said.

When she stuck her impetuous little tongue out at him, he chuckled. In return, she got a *click* of his fangs in a mock bite.

Her unimpressed snort pleased him as much as her lusty moans. He wanted all of his Anna, her happiness, her humor, and her stubbornness. Anna wouldn't be Anna without that spitting fire, and Frey loved her spirited nature, even if it vexed him just as often.

They ate their dinner of casserole on the couch. Frey hardly tasted it beyond the creamy tang of the sauce, too preoccupied with the way Anna's lips curled around her fork. After a while, he suspected she did it on purpose, to get a rise out of him.

She was certainly making particular parts of him rise.

Once their bowls were empty, Anna reached for her laptop and opened it to talk excitedly about what she'd found for him. He pulled her onto his lap once more, chin hooked over her shoulder as she toggled between screens to show him various phone devices.

She extolled the virtues of each option, but Frey was far more interested in her animated talk and expressive hands. When she asked him what he thought, Frey could only rumble happily and say, "Whatever you think best, *fy nghân.*"

Anna hmphed, that answer apparently insufficient. Pulling her own phone from her pocket, she tugged one of his hands out from under the blanket, where it'd been playing with the hem of her sweater, and had him hold it.

"How does that feel?"

Frey dutifully weighed the device in his hand and tapped the screen with his thumb as he'd seen her do. "Breakable."

"That's why you're not getting a new model. But you think you could use one?"

Handing back her phone, Frey answered honestly, "It is a generous gesture, my Anna, but I still cannot read your modern English."

"I thought about that. All of these phones are new enough that they have dictation abilities. So it could read you text messages from me and you could say your message back and it will write it out for you. I thought I could call or text when I leave work, to let you know I'm on my way. And if I forget to tell you ahead of time, I can message you if I'm going to be late. And . . . if you want, we can look into reading resources?"

Frey hugged her close, burying his nose in her hair. "You are the kindest, smartest human. I should like to learn to read your English." It wasn't just Anna who had adjustments to make; he too had things he needed to learn, not just for her but for himself. Her modern world was his too now, and their life wouldn't always be contained to her dwelling. He had to learn all he could for the day when his kind revealed themselves—but more, he had to learn so he could function in her world, even while on the periphery of it.

"I like the messages, too. To know you're safe." Frey knew a compromise when he heard it, and it touched him to see how much thought Anna had put into fulfilling both their needs.

She blew an annoyed breath when he still didn't have a preference of phone, just whatever worked. "Fine, then we'll get this one because it comes with a case."

Anna typed through a few more things on the laptop, fingers clicking, until she was satisfied.

"Okay, that should come in a few days."

"Most excellent. Thank you, *fy nghân*."

"I keep meaning to ask . . ." She folded the laptop on itself, gaze not quite rising above his chin. "What does that mean? *Fy nghân?*"

"It seems while I learn to read English, you shall learn to speak Welsh."

"You won't tell me?" She arched those brows in that way she did, imperious and teasing.

"*My song*," he rumbled. "That's what it means."

Her cheeks went rosy again, and pleasure trickled through his veins, sweet as syrup, to see her obvious delight in the pet name. His Anna being a proud woman, she of course tried to hide her pleasure, but Frey saw.

"You call me a lot of things."

"I do." He arched his own brows in an approximation of hers. "All sweet things."

"All sweet? That's hard to believe."

One side of his mouth kicked up in a grin. "It's true, for I enjoy your spines as much as your sweetness."

She absorbed his words with wide eyes, and Frey let her take her time, the words sitting between them. Admiration squeezed his chest tight when rather than protest, she gave him a small smile.

When she replaced the laptop on the table, Frey drew her high on his chest and laid down to recline on the couch. Anna spread over him like a blanket, her face tucked into the crook of his shoulder, and soon Captain came to curl up in the dip of her lower back.

Frey's heart swelled to the point of pain holding so much love in his arms. Their hands were soft and gentle as they spoke of easy nothings and difficult truths.

He described his strong, beautiful mother and sister. How they had taught him all he knew. How their family dwelling had been full of laughter and singing. How nothing had been the same since their passing. He didn't shy away from admitting his anger at Seren's mate, nor how he blamed the male for his part, or lack thereof, in the day she died.

He told her how lonely life was without family.

In halting words, she whispered to him of her life with her mother, the moving and the multiple mates. How sometimes she longed for what she'd never had. How she'd met her father only once and even then hadn't held much interest or hope, for he was no better than the other men her mother consorted with. She told him of her anger, her resentment, and her hurts. How her mother hadn't even loved her, not really, so how could she believe he would.

His heart ached for the girl Anna had been and the woman she'd become. That she'd even let him stay with her, let alone hold her close now, wasn't something to take lightly.

He told her of the night the fae attacked, how everything he'd ever known had been ripped apart in a spray of blood and lash of magick. He'd never felt anything like it, the magick first cajoled and then stripped from his very soul. The way his flesh had hardened, movement had ceased, and his mind had retreated into the dark collective with the others who were cursed.

There were years he sensed nothing. His mind remained dormant, darkness his one companion as his kind passed into myth and the world passed around them. He'd sensed when he was placed with a handful of his kin, and slowly, their numbers grew. It was a small comfort to be together, even if he knew only a few from their life before, and for centuries they endured together.

"I know what it is to lose everything. Twice now, my world has been taken from me." Lifting her face with a knuckle under her chin, Frey pressed one soft kiss to her perfect lips. "I cannot bear it again. It's why I am so insistent about your safety. You are everything to me, Anna."

Her throat worked on a swallow, and her eyes glistened with unshed tears. Slowly, she nodded. "I understand. I . . . I'll start looking into other jobs, okay? It won't happen immediately, but I'll look."

"Thank you." His breath rushed out of him in relief, ruffling her hair.

"But, Frey . . . if I leave the museum, we won't have any leads or way to get to your people. I don't want to leave them behind."

"Neither do I." His chest rumbled with grief, his heart torn between his kin and his mate. Yet, he knew, "Any guardian would understand making safe their heartsong. Any would do the same for their own."

The pain of such a choice played across Anna's face, and Frey loved her for it. That she cared at all for him and now for his kin as well was a gift.

"I don't know how else we're going to help them. I guess I could start researching your kind, though I may need to wait for a bit until the investigation is over. But honestly, probably the most helpful resources are in the museum already."

Another reason to find the place suspect. Why did her employers have not only his kin but tomes on their existence? He could only conclude that those who owned and displayed such artifacts took some sick pleasure in it.

Frey kept such suspicions to himself, though, for that's all they were. He would tell his Anna of them when he could put more of it into words. For now, he was more interested in the soft way she traced patterns across his chest.

Settling into the cushion of the couch, he splayed his wings wide and just enjoyed laying with his mate. Captain purred and Anna spoke softly of other ideas she'd had, of perhaps getting a car and going up the coast or somewhere remote so he could fly.

She filled the dwelling with ideas, and Frey could imagine it from her words. She spoke of the future, of ways that they could live. He ached with love for her, and more than anything, even more than the day and his kin, he wished for all the good things she spoke of and so much more to happen—for her. His Anna deserved everything he could give her, and it would be his life's pleasure providing it.

The hour was late and Anna's voice had gone raspy from overuse when Frey kissed her out of a doze and told her, "Time for sleep."

She grumbled and made a fuss, throwing mock scowls at him as she brushed her teeth, but within a few minutes, she was prepared for bed and he'd cleaned up the remnants of dinner.

When he reached for her, she put her hand in his and tugged him toward the bedchamber. "Will you stay with me until I fall asleep?"

Frey gently squeezed her hand. "I will stay all night, *fy nghalon*."

"And what's that one mean?" she asked as she turned down the bed.

Frey climbed in after her, setting his shoulders against the wall and headboard. Anna curled into his side, head pillowed on his chest, and his wing draped over her as a second blanket.

"*My heart,*" he whispered into her hair.

A lusty groan preceded a wet kiss to the center of his chest. Palms splayed on his abdomen, she lifted herself to look at him, her brows furrowed.

"You keep saying things like that, and I . . ."

Might love you, too.

The unsaid words remained unsaid, but Frey didn't despair. His mate was warm and safe in her bed, and even better, he was there with her. He could perish tomorrow a content male from that.

Anna dropped her head to press more kisses to his chest and neck, and while Frey could have let her go on all night like that, he pulled her face to his. "You need to sleep, my Anna—but first, will you let me make you feel good?"

A shy little smile lit her face. "You already make me feel good."

She got a pleased purr for that, but, "Then let me make you feel even better. Let me touch you?"

Her next breath was long and loud, and for a moment Frey thought she might back down.

He should've known better.

"You've been talking a big game," she blustered, even as she flipped onto her back. Her head settled in the crook of his shoulder, her hips and legs cradled between his. Laid atop him, his questing hands had perfect access to everywhere he wanted to touch and feel.

"Because everything I am is big."

Her snort of laughter turned into a moan when his hands delved under the waist of her loose pants and met warm skin. His claws caught the hem of her shirt and lifted. He went slow, waiting for her to stop him, and his heart thudded with every inch the fabric slid higher.

"And everything I am is yours." He growled the words into her skin as he revealed the rounded, rosy points of her nipples. Her heavy breasts stood proud in the soft darkness, and Frey's purr rattled viciously in his chest while taking each in a hand. The heat of them nearly burned his palms, and he held their weight, thumbing her nipples and indulging in the exquisite softness of her.

"*Ffyc,*" he growled.

"Mmm," she hummed, eyes slipping closed as he played with her, "what's that mean?"

"That you are the most beautiful, most perfect creature I've ever seen." He punctuated his words with gentle tugs to her nipples. "That I'd have waited another millennia for you." Hands so full of her, he plumped the generous flesh before raking his clawtips over the delicate undersides. "That I'm going to suck on these every day of my life until the Otherworld takes me."

Anna shivered in his arms, and one of her hands reached up to dig into his hair. Every time his purr gained in tempo, she arched and squirmed, drawing his attention to how she squeezed her thighs together.

Unable to let go of her perfect breasts completely, he kneaded one as his other hand strayed down the curve of her belly to her loose pants. His fingertips lingered over the waist, and he listened as Anna's breaths grew harsher.

Finally, his claws strayed over that warm center of her, and he could feel her wet heat even through the fabric.

Into her ear he rasped, "Off?"

She made a noise of assent, and in one determined move, he swept the fabric from her legs.

"Open for me."

Her thighs trembled as they parted. Frey hooked one with his knee, spreading her wide for his greedy fingers. Anna gasped when the pads of two fingers slid down her slit, and Frey hissed to feel just how hot and slick she was for him.

"Goddesses," he groaned. She would scorch him through, and he'd happily burn.

He spread her cunt wide, fingers gliding through her slick as he found and circled her clitoris. Anna threw her head back, arching nearly off his chest. He held her tight, thumbing her nipple as he teased her clitoris with the rough pad of one finger.

"Like this, *fy nghalon?*"

"Mmhmmmmm."

"Does it feel good?"

"Yes," she sighed.

"As good as your toy?" She arched again when his hand delved deeper, finding her entrance. He carefully pushed a finger inside, past the ring of muscle. Her cunt clenched around him, making his cock kick against his own braies, and he hissed to feel how tightly she gripped him.

"Did you imagine it was me, *fy nghalon?* When you used your toy, did you imagine it was my cock pushing deep inside you?"

"Yes!"

He nipped at the perfect curve of her neck, rumbling with pleasure when her nails scraped his scalp. She writhed as his fingers teased and played, making circles around her clitoris only to leave without pressing on the hood. She bathed his hand and her thighs in her own slick as he slid first one then two then three fingers deep into her greedy cunt.

Anna turned her head to press her hot mouth to his skin. "Frey," she pled, "I need—harder—please!"

Blood rushing, Frey couldn't deny her. His hands were merciless as they sought her pleasure, working her body with feverish purpose.

When the first flickers of her orgasm began to shudder through her, Frey pushed two fingers inside, needing to feel her come around him.

Her muscles gripped him and sucked him deeper, so tightly he nearly came with her.

But he couldn't look away from the glory of his mate in ecstasy. Head thrown back, breasts jutting, and hips working his hand, Anna chased down and took her pleasure. It was furious and shattering and Frey would remember it for all his days.

He prolonged her pleasure as long as he was able, petting and stroking and praising. He purred for her, and when her body went limp from the effort, he caught her up in his arms, ready to hold her.

Gently, he pulled away from her cunt, running his soaked fingers up her body. He painted one heaving breast in her slick before sucking his claws into his mouth and devouring her taste. She watched him with dazed eyes and heavy lids, her pulse fluttering at her throat.

Lips wet with her, he claimed her mouth in a savage kiss. He wanted to brand her taste into his memory, her heat into his skin.

She was boneless and soft when he set her down in the bed. He fetched a cloth to cleanse her, taking just a moment to finish off the angry cock throbbing between his legs. It took only a few moments, her taste still on his tongue, and then he rejoined his heartsong.

Once she was cleaned and redressed, he climbed back into the bed to hold her. She was asleep in moments as he purred for her, and to his surprise and pleasure, soon he too began to doze off in true sleep.

It'd been another life since Frey slept.

The first of many firsts he intended to have with his Anna.

25

If she didn't keep focused, Anna found herself staring off into space, daydreaming about last night. The water of the shower went lukewarm before she realized she'd just been staring at the tiles, remembering how Frey growled in her ear as his fingers worked her so deliciously. He shouldn't be that good right off the bat. It just wasn't fair.

After the microwave beeped at her when she didn't take her oatmeal out within a minute and reading the same sentence on her résumé ten times, Anna gave herself a physical and mental shake. It'd be hours before Frey woke up, and she had things to do. Otherwise, she might start groping a statue and she wasn't prepared for the questions she'd have for herself if it came to that.

Giving Captain a good scritch, Anna scrolled through her résumé, making updates and edits. Then, begrudgingly, she toggled to a job search engine and began looking. Nothing immediately jumped out at her; nothing was as close or paid as well or had as good of benefits—but she'd promised him, so she spent an hour looking and applied to two positions.

It was more than not wanting to interview again and possibly winding up with reduced benefits; there was something about searching for another job that felt almost . . . disloyal. Anna had never been attached to employers or companies before, and she didn't think there was a great reason to be now, given that the museum was some sort of weird magical prison, but it still felt wrong to be leaving the museum.

She didn't quite have the words to describe how or why she felt this way, certainly not enough to explain it to Frey. So, she applied for the positions that didn't sound too horrible and left it there for the day.

A quick check out the window showed that the big SUV was gone from across the street. Poking her head out the window, she didn't see it or the creepy van anywhere on the street.

Anna pulled on shoes and coat and grabbed her keys and purse within a minute. The pantry and fridge were in dire straits, and even Frey's culinary creativity wouldn't be able to pull off another dinner. So off to the grocery store she went.

The day was fairly clear and sunny, boosting Anna's already decent mood.

A good night's sleep and an incredible orgasm can do that for a girl.

Nope, she wasn't thinking about last night. Not in public, where everyone could see how her cheeks burned and her nipples hardened with the memory of Frey's fingers. Still, despite her best efforts, she stood inspecting the apples and bananas a little *too* long.

Even waiting at the pharmacy laden down with groceries didn't sour her mood. No, the only thing that managed that was catching a dark SUV out of the corner of her eye.

There were hundreds if not thousands of dark SUVs and white vans driving around SF, of course. It wasn't until she saw another one drive past while she ducked into a Greek bakery that she finally got a good look at the license plate. By now, she had the number of the one parked on her street memorized, and sure enough, same plates, same vehicle.

The sight tarnished her outing—not even fresh naan and baklava could turn it around.

Anna headed straight home after that, heart caught in her throat. She nearly ran up the stairs, out of breath by the time she made it to the top floor. Peering out the narrow window at the end of the hall, she could just see the black SUV pulling into its usual space.

Fucking shit!

Fumbling with her keys, Anna didn't notice the package sitting on her stoop until she'd nearly tripped over it. After putting down the grocery bags and petting Captain, she went back for her one-day delivery.

If she hadn't seen the SUV everywhere she'd been, her paranoia wouldn't have noticed something slightly off about the box. She swore the box had been double taped. Plus, one of the corners was damaged, the cardboard wrinkled and the very tip of the corner missing, leaving a small hole into the box.

Setting it on the counter, she retrieved some scissors to carefully open the package. She inspected the top flaps and yes, she was sure there were two layers of tape. Had the first been cut and the second added to hide it?

Anna chewed her cheek as she pulled out all the items. The lube was plastic-wrapped and vacuum-sealed, so it got set aside. The coffee seemed sealed too, but she still dumped all of it into a bowl and sifted through the fragrant grounds, looking for . . . something. Same went for the big bottles of acetaminophen, vitamins, and shampoo. Everything got poured into glass bowls and inspected.

Nothing seemed off.

But it *felt* off. Like she wasn't the first one to see the items after they'd been packed.

Anna's heart kicked sharply in her chest, the muscles in her neck tightening.

Stepping back, she took a deep breath.

It's okay. You've gotten damaged packages before. The delivery guy probably just tossed it from the top step rather than walk to your door. Deep breath.

Didn't the police need a warrant to go through mail? Opening it without one was super illegal. But could that mean they had enough probable cause to get a warrant? Fuck, what if they did and whatever they found in the box gave them reason to get another one for the apartment? What if they came during the day—she couldn't move or hide Frey.

"Shit shit shit!" Anna paced the apartment, hands on her head to contain the throbbing.

She couldn't just put clothes all over him and hide him! They'd look in all the closets. There was no way to hide a giant, hulking gargoyle in her apartment. And she didn't dare Google police warrants and mail inspection for fear they were or would track her search history.

Her feet carried her into her bedroom, where Frey stood in the corner. Had it really only been a few hours since he'd woken her with deep kisses and dirty promises? Waking up to him had been amazing, sharing soft words as they lay in that velveteen place between night and day. It made watching him withdraw and turn to stone with the sun even harder, like he took part of her with him.

Now, she counted down the minutes to sunset.

"What do we do?" she asked the statue, wishing with everything she had that he'd answer.

Of course, he remained stony and silent. It made Anna wish, for the first time, that she understood what he meant with his mate bond ideas. Was that the solution to all of this? Her touch had somehow broken part of the curse, but why hadn't being together been enough to fully break it? Was it because their kissing so far hadn't been true love's first kiss or something?

Well, she wasn't there yet but she was dangling precariously close to falling. Was that it, true love's kiss? Or was it a bit more X-rated than Disney—would sex finally break the curse?

With all his talk of Anna being his, of being his mate, the only one he could have kids with, she had to assume sex was a big part of the bond.

God, if so, she'd sex him so good.

Even if it didn't, she planned on using that lube and finally finding out what his cock felt like inside her.

Heart racing, Anna rested her forehead on Frey's stone chest, groaning.

She was now both freaked out *and* horny. And worried. And confused. And achy for him.

I'm spiraling.

Lifting her face to look at him, she kissed the point of his chin, as high as she could reach on her tiptoes. "Wake up soon, okay? I'm freaking out."

When he remained stone, Anna sighed and retreated from the room. She sank onto the couch, dejected, and pulled Captain in for a hug when he jumped in her lap.

"We'll hold down the fort," she whispered to him.

By now, Anna wasn't so startled being woken by the sensation of two big arms lifting her. Eyes not even opening from her doze, she turned her head, nose seeking that warm hollow at his throat, where his scent and pulse were strong.

His customary, "Good evening, *fy nghân,*" buzzed in her ear, and she couldn't help a smile.

"Hi, big guy." She really needed to think of a better pet name for him; his were all so beautiful. Maybe she really did need to learn Welsh.

"How was your day?"

Anna stiffened in his arms involuntarily. She made her muscles unlock, but Frey felt the change nevertheless.

"What is it?" His voice dropped to that low, threatening pitch he had, the one that made her lizard brain shiver and take notice of the big predator looming nearby.

Groaning, Anna rubbed the last of the sleep from her eyes and stood. She brought over the box to show him, explaining how the SUV had seemingly been wherever she was today and her suspicions about the package.

"I know it's crazy, but it *feels* wrong."

Frowning down at the box like it'd personally insulted him, Frey remained silent. Then, with a horrid rip, he tore the package into shreds with his claws. Cardboard pieces burst everywhere, raining down onto the carpet.

He stalked toward the window, tail lashing. Anna hurried to follow, ready to jump on him if he tried to climb out again. To her relief, he only flicked the blinds open to glare down at the street.

"I'm tired of their lurking and their threats. True warriors would face me."

"They aren't warriors. They're a police surveillance team." At least, she hoped it was the police. The ramifications of it being some other entity watching them was more than her brain could compute right now. *Who else would even be interested? Nobody knows about the "thefts."*

"It doesn't matter. They unsettle you. They have no right to hunt you so."

Anna tugged on his arm, and after another moment of stone-cold glaring, Frey let himself be led into the kitchen. She plated dinner for them, though her excitement over showing him gyros had long since popped like soap bubbles.

"They do this sometimes, to see if a suspect is doing anything suspicious. We just have to keep being not suspicious."

Frey's lip curled back, revealing those wicked fangs.

The sight made Anna shudder—with lust and with residual fear. It was hard to forget just how much damage fangs like that might do.

A grumbling noise echoed in Frey's chest, and his expression became troubled. Pulling her by the hip, he placed her in front of him.

"I need you to understand something, my Anna." He caged her in with his arms on either side of her, his head leaned down to align his gaze with hers. "For you, I will play and tease. I will never harm you. But my kind were made to protect. To kill. I don't care who those people are. If they threaten you, they are dead."

"We can't just go around killing people."

"I've never sought death and don't intend to start. But I will defend what's mine. Do you understand?"

The weight of his words, the truth of his power and potential for violence, settled on her shoulders. The flannel shirt she filled her hands with may be human and modern, but beneath, he was still all medieval gargoyle. Knowing such a being would protect her, would *kill* for her, was both terrifying and arousing.

Her heart fluttered with lust and trepidation both. Knowing she could point him at someone and have that person eliminated . . . a rush of power heated her blood. There was a responsibility that came with it, to ensure that Frey was safe in the modern world but that it was safe from him, too.

And it wasn't just his threat to the cops outside, either. She knew what he was truly saying—was truly asking.

"Yes, I understand." *I understand I'm yours.* She wasn't ready to say those words, but Frey nodded, seemingly satisfied with her assent.

With that settled, they tucked into their dinner. Frey waxed poetic about the gyros, which made Anna's heart happy. Still, even with the lighter topics and good food, an anxiety settled over the apartment. The glow from this morning had faded, and Anna desperately wished it back.

But burying her head in the sand hadn't exactly gotten her far. It was time to take stock of the situation and do what she could.

When dinner was finished and the kitchen cleaned, she pulled Frey into the living room. Staring up at him, she tried to hide her nerves. Hands delving under his shirt, she took comfort from the warm burn of his skin. It drew her in, and she pressed her cheek to his chest, listening to his heart.

A set of claws carded through her hair, and Anna blinked away a sudden sting of tears. Standing in the center of her apartment like this, with him, it was almost like . . . they were at the beginning of something. Like just one more step and she'd take the fall.

Anna was terrified of heights and of falling.

She was scared of a lot of things, honestly, including the big man she held in her arms and what he meant for her.

But she had to trust that when she fell, he'd catch her.

She had to trust.

Pulling in a deep breath full of his rich scent, Anna finally got up the courage to ask, "Do you think sex would break the curse?"

His purring abruptly cut off, and he was silent so long that she had no choice but to peer up at him and assess the damage.

If she didn't know better, she'd think from his face that he had a bit of gristle stuck in his throat.

His breath left him in a heaving rush, ruffling her hair. "*What?*" he croaked.

Anna shrugged, trying not to grimace with embarrassment. "I was thinking today about why the curse isn't fully broken, and I thought . . . with everything you've said about how your people feel for their soulmates . . . maybe sex would be the final step."

He blinked down at her owlishly, as if she'd started speaking a different language. He held himself so rigidly, she absolutely wasn't ready when he swooped down to claim her mouth in a savage, messy kiss. His tongue pressed against her lips, demanding entry, and Anna gasped. A rumbling growl reverberated between them, and just when it felt like he'd sucked the very air from her lungs, he lifted his head.

The way he looked at her now had her toes curling into the rug; those gray eyes flashed, pupils dilating like a predator that'd just spotted prey.

Jaw working, it sounded like every word was forced when he said, "The mate bond isn't solely about consummation. It's about intertwining lives, our very souls. It grows the more it is accepted. But," he stepped into her, hands dropping to her butt to pull her hips flush to his, "sex certainly helps."

A bolt of heat sizzled Anna from head to toe to see that wicked grin adorning his lips. She'd never have thought herself a horns girl, but everything about him did things to her. The way his tail alternated between lashing and curling around her calf. How his wings bobbed and fluttered with his emotions, and most especially how they wrapped around her, cocooning them together. The way those fangs that could rend flesh were so tender with her as they nipped playfully at her throat.

His hands moved restlessly at her backside, kneading her curves, and the heat of his cock nearly burned her even through their clothes. Anna's pulse thrummed in her throat, ready for him to sweep her into his arms and carry her off to bed.

Instead, he said, "When you are ready, I'm yours to command, my Anna."

"What if I'm ready now?"

His nostrils flared, hot gaze flicking down to watch her chest rise and fall with her quick, excited breaths.

"I don't want you to do it because you think you must," he said slowly, gaze rapturous as her nipples hardened and pressed against her sweater.

"Oh, my reasons are almost entirely selfish, don't worry."

His broad smile showed off his fangs, and Anna couldn't help matching it with her own.

"Are you eager to see just how fine your male is?"

"Hmm," she hummed as she pushed his shirt off his shoulders. "I know just how fine you are." Her touch was greedy and gratuitous following the shirt over his arms, feeling the firm swells of his biceps and the corded strength of his forearms. God, the man had beautiful forearms, and she suspected he knew it with how often he rolled up his sleeves.

"Excellent. Then let me show you just how well I can take care of my mate." His claws teased at the hem of her sweater before drawing it up over her head. The cool air kissed her skin, and Anna instinctively rolled her shoulders in and folded her arms over her belly.

She'd always been fairly confident in her sexuality, happy to get her pleasure, but her experience was confined to dim bedrooms. Something about standing in the middle of her lit living room in her bra and leggings felt infinitely more intimate than getting naked under the sheets.

Gently pulling her arms away from her middle, Frey kissed the back of each hand and drew her to the couch. He sat down, tail curled on the cushion and legs spread. The fabric of his sweatpants tented obscenely at his lap, and Anna gulped.

"We will go at your pace, heartsong. As fast or as slow, as much or as little as you want."

She nodded, and determined not to lose her nerve, she snagged the bottle of lube to show him.

He turned it about in his claws before looking up at her curiously.

With an infernal blush, she explained modern lubricant.

His gaze flicked back to the bottle before a grin cracked his mouth and he threw his head back and laughed merrily. His other hand shot out and pulled her by the hip down to him. Anna eased into his lap as he set the bottle on the end table, eyes glittering with mirth.

She tried not to pout too much as she straddled him, hands playing over that thick slab of muscle between his neck and shoulder.

"You've been planning this," he crowed.

"I thought it'd be smart to think ahead," she replied primly.

His grin was almost insufferably smug, but it was the way his eyes heated again and his hands filled with her backside to move her even closer that had her heart pitter-pattering.

"It pleases me to know you've thought about having me inside you. That you would be so determined to make it happen." He bestowed a nipping kiss, sucking on her bottom lip before he said, "Nothing will stop you from taking what's yours."

"Nothing," she agreed.

His smile grew fierce and proud, and Anna nearly squirmed to see him looking at her like that. Part of her preened, reveling in making him proud of her, wanting to do it again.

Frey leaned his head back onto the couch and Anna followed, her lips falling on his in a hungry kiss. He met her every stroke, willing to play and tease as she chased and coaxed his tongue. A growl broke the cadence of his purr as she traced a fang with her tongue, flicking the tip.

Her hands explored all the planes and contours that made Frey; the dense pack of muscle on his shoulders that formed the wing bases, the slabs of his pectorals that pulsed with his racing heart, the undulations of his abdomen and thick waist that shuddered with every teasing touch. When her fingertips strayed to his wings, she heard his sharp inhale and couldn't resist delving into the folds. She ran her hand with the grain of fine hair on the inside of the sensitive membrane.

A hiss slipped between his teeth, and his cock kicked against her belly from where it nestled between them. With a moan, Anna lowered her hips, chasing the hot friction.

Frey pressed wet, slow kisses to her neck, making Anna's back arch. He purred happily to have her tits in his face, fanning his warm breath over the tops.

"I remember something last night about sucking on these?"

His groan was resounding and gratifying. Frey's hands slid up her waist to her back, fingers plucking at the bra clasp.

"Show me," he rumbled.

Sitting back on his thighs, Anna held his gaze as she reached behind her and, with his hands covering hers to learn the movements, unclasped the hooks. The pads of his fingers were there immediately, pushing the fabric away. The silky bra slithered down her arms then went flying somewhere over his shoulder.

Those gray eyes fixed on her heavy breasts, nipples pebbling under his gaze. Another groan rumbled in his throat as he filled his hands with her, and Anna moaned, holding his wrists for balance as he kneaded and squeezed.

"*Harddach na'r môr a'r awyr,*" he breathed before burying his face between them.

Her whole body quivered as Frey made good on his promises. He lavished kisses across the tops of her tits, ran his nose down her sternum, and nipped at the sensitive undersides. Anna nearly jumped to feel his teeth set in some of her softest skin, but his tongue was quick to lave across her in soothing drags.

For all that he took his time, making ever tightening circles, Anna nearly squirmed out of her skin. He seemed in no rush to pay any attention to her nipples, which pouted for him and the promise of his hot mouth.

Under his hands, her hips began to rock, pressing ever closer to that cock that hid just out of sight. As he leisurely explored her, Anna delved below the waistband of the sweats and greedily claimed her prize.

Frey hissed against her skin as she tried closing her fist around his cock. It scorched her hand, his hammering pulse throbbing in her palm. She pumped him from root to tip and back again, tracing that thick vein that ran along the underside. Her other hand came down to help the first, neither quite closing around him, as she didn't want any part of him to feel left out.

A sudden hard suck on her nipple had Anna yelping.

"So greedy for me already?" He grinned up at her from his place between her breasts, eyes catching hers to be sure she watched as he rolled her nipple with the flat of his tongue.

"One of us had to get this show on the road," she panted.

A rumble of pleasure hummed between them, but then Anna was huffing in protest when he pulled her hands away from his cock. He set her on her feet in front of him, between his spread legs, eyes glittering as his claws teased at the waistband of her own leggings.

"Off?"

The memory of being asked the same thing last night had Anna flushing, and she only managed a jerky nod. He went slow, peeling away her leggings as if he meant to savor every inch he revealed. He helped her step out of them when the fabric pooled at her ankles, then his claws were slipping beneath her panties. Frey leaned in, pressing his lips to her mons and nuzzling her belly as the panties slid away.

Standing naked before him, fear clogged Anna's throat. It wasn't anything rational or reasonable, but the terror most women felt being so exposed.

Hands on her hips, Frey held her still and looked his fill. His eyes traveled over her almost torturously slow, and Anna couldn't help squirming—but he kept her there, making her accept and feel his adoration and need.

"You are a sight more beautiful than I ever could have dreamed, *cân fy nghalon*," he murmured against her stomach, then pressed every word into her skin with a reverent kiss.

He took a moment to shuck his own pants, setting them under him on the couch. Then he was back to slow, tender kisses up and down her torso, tongue swirling around her belly button and on her nipples. Anna ran her fingers through his long hair, goosebumps raising along her skin to feel how hotly he burned.

"What do you crave, my Anna? How do you wish to be touched?"

Throat working, she told him haltingly, "I like my tits played with. And my hair. I usually need a lot of stimulation to come. Like last night."

"Then that's what you'll receive, heartsong."

"What about you?" she asked as he pulled her back down into his lap. "And don't just say everything."

"Your hands on my cock may be the death of me, but I'd die happy. And my horns, tug on them. Show me where you want my tongue."

It was as much a dare as an answer, and Anna was too needy to hesitate. She filled her hands with his horns, making sure to circle her thumbs into the bases, and drew his head back to her breasts.

"You promised sucking, not teasing."

"That I did." His laugh rumbled through him, and then through Anna too when he caught her nipple with his mouth and sucked.

Anna's head fell back onto her shoulders, and she held onto his horns as he devoured her. Between tongue and teeth, he stroked and nipped and suckled at her, overwhelming her senses. His hand claimed her other breast, rolling her nipple between thumb and claw, and soon Anna's hips were rocking again. With every pass of his tongue or fingers over her nipples, a sizzle of heat burst against her clit, and she could almost imagine it was her cunt he petted and stroked.

She reached blindly for the lube. Frey's curious eyes watched as she opened the bottle, and he released her nipple with a wet *pop*.

"One day soon, we will have no need of that," he said with all the solemnity of a vow. Fingers slid from her hip down to her cunt, teasing through her folds to run in short, slick strokes across her clit. "Soon, you will become so slick with just the thought of my cock that we'll have no need of it. Soon, your body will know mine; you will know my shape and take me with ease."

"Until then," she breathed, squeezing a dollop into her palm, "we'll be responsible."

"Until then," he agreed.

Setting the bottle aside, Anna closed her hand around him again and pumped, spreading the lube up and down his shaft. Frey hissed, the slippery liquid heating with the friction of her movements. Her hand slid easily up and down, up and down, making his cock glisten.

"Let me feel you," he growled. "Soak me in your slick."

Trembling with need, Anna sat up a little on her knees, one of Frey's hands at her hip helping her balance. Cool air kissed between her spread thighs, and a needy sound escaped her to see how his fingers that had been stroking her glistened with her.

She eased over him, guiding his cock between her folds. They both hissed at the sensation of his thick cock gliding along her slit. Between the lube and how badly she ached, he easily slid in her wet heat and soon didn't need her hand to guide. His fingers found hers and pressed their joined hands to her clit, rolling it between them as his hips rolled beneath her.

Electricity sparked down Anna's spine, and she reached to balance herself against the meat of his shoulder. His gaze fixed on where their hips met in an undulating rhythm, and Anna watched him watch them. His hand at her hip squeezed, drawing her closer, urging her faster. His cockhead dragged against her deliciously with every stroke, and she could feel how soaked their thighs became as his pace gained speed.

Anna snapped her hips, pinning his cock between cunt and thigh. Frey growled, flashing his fangs at her.

"Inside. I need inside you, *fy nghân.*"

There was no play in his expression, no softness or escape. His big hands clutched at her, holding her steady as she reached between them to fit his cockhead at her entrance.

Anna's stomach swooped with terror and excitement, and she pressed down an inch.

Her mouth fell open as she dropped another, the head pushing past the initial ring of muscle. The lube and foreplay eased his way, but he was still much more than Anna had ever handled before. Her eyes almost watered from the pressure as she let gravity slowly work him inside.

Frey's hands twitched and spasmed on her hips, and his head fell back onto the couch. The ball of his throat bobbed, and his lips peeled back in something like a grimace.

"*Goddesses,*" he hissed. "*Dwi adref. Dwi adref.*"

If she wasn't so overwhelmed from being stuffed full of Frey, she might've been a bit smug about sexing the English out of him. But every inch was a marvel, and Anna's whole body throbbed like an exposed nerve as she sank down, down, down.

When he bottomed out, Anna gasped, what little air she had left leaving her in a rush. Frey groaned again, hands restless at her hips.

"Tell me you feel it, *fy nghalon.* Tell me it is good." His hips lifted in a small thrust, and they both groaned. "Tell me I can move and *fuck you.*"

"Gimme a minute," she panted.

She dared to peek at where they locked together, and her cunt clenched to see how wide he'd spread her. She'd swallowed him whole, her clit resting against the root.

Her heart stuttered in her chest, not quite believing.

A knuckle under chin had her raising her head, and then Frey's mouth was on her. Warm, drugging kisses pulled her back, into his current, and she let him take her away.

"*Fy enaid hoff cytûn prydferth. Fy enaid hoff cytûn rhyfeddol, prydferth.*"

Claws sifted through her hair, gently scraped down her back, kneaded her ass. Wings came around to pull her in tight, crushing her breasts against his chest and slightly changing the angle of his cock inside her. That broad head hit something tantalizing, and Anna quivered, hips rolling cautiously, chasing that feeling.

Between Frey's kisses and hands, she'd almost forgotten about the tight pinch of taking him. Instead, warmth seeped through her, sweet as syrup, and when his hands guided her hips into a gentle rhythm, she found there was no longer pain.

Her mind nearly went blank at the sensations, her world narrowing to the shallow thrusts of his cock. His hips rose to meet hers, pushing inside to tease that spot deep within her. He filled his big hands with her backside, spreading her cheeks and thighs even further, and Anna felt her excitement dripping into his lap.

She kissed his snarl, hands desperate on his chest. She could only move now, desperate and needy and so, so *full*. He reached inside to touch all of her, nothing escaped him, and with every delectable drag out and thrust back in, Anna was a little more lost.

And yet . . .

"Frey," she pleaded, not quite sure what she asked.

"I have you, *fy nghalon*. Hold onto me."

Her over-sensitized brain didn't understand how she could be clinging to him any more when, with a growl, he surged from the couch to stand.

Anna gasped, arms tightening around his neck. He gripped her with arms under her thighs and wings across her back, holding her aloft.

"Frey—"

"Do you feel me, my Anna?" He drew his hips back and then slammed them up at the same time he let her drop an inch, and Anna's mouth fell open in a silent cry. "Is this what you need? To take my cock without mercy?"

He thrust again, bouncing her on his cock, and all Anna could do was moan and hold on. She had no leverage like this, could only hold herself up as he worked her on his cock. It was brutal and demanding and merciless, just like he said, and it was *exactly* what she needed.

Her mind went quiet to all other thoughts—she rose and fell in his arms, caught every time. She moaned when his cock retreated, dragging nearly down to her entrance, and cried with relief when he thrust back inside. His hips pistoned beneath hers, pumping inside in a relentless pursuit.

Anna grabbed onto a horn and held on, the sounds of their bodies slapping together a crescendo that echoed through the apartment. A human man could never hold a woman of Anna's size up like this for the long minutes Frey spent giving her everything and more.

But he wasn't a human man. He was a gargoyle, a guardian. And he was *hers*.

"Frey!" she cried, head thrown back as her orgasm ripped through her.

Her cunt clenched tighter than a fist around him, drawing him impossibly deeper, and with a final thrust, his frenetic purr exploded into a howl of ecstasy. His big hands pinned their hips together, and Anna could do nothing but come and come and come.

She almost couldn't stand it, yet never wanted it to end. Unable to move, she could only gaze up at him, his face a rictus of savage pleasure.

"*Ti sydd a'm calon, fy nghân,*" he said, voice gone to a harsh rumble. "You have my heart."

Dwi adref, he'd told her. *I'm home.* It was how Frey felt, buried deep inside his heartsong. Even as they trembled in each other's arms with the aftermath of their lovemaking, even as he felt his spend slipping around where they were sealed together, he didn't want to pull away. Inside her was everywhere he wanted to be, everything he could ever want.

The bond he had with his Anna tugged inside him, as if a rope connected his heart with hers. Drawn taut, the bond pulled them ever closer together. Surrounded by her warmth and softness both stimulated and soothed, and for the first time in centuries, Frey had a sense of belonging that had died with his mother and sister.

When he was confident his wobbling knees wouldn't buckle, Frey carried his boneless, sated mate into the bathing chamber. Setting her on the stone counter, she shivered at the contact with her heated skin. Her head rested on his shoulder as he wetted a cloth and cleaned them both.

He took much longer with her, his movements lazy and gentle. Some primeval, instinctual part of him howled with pride to see the pearlescent gleam of their combined spend soaking her cunt. His fingers played in the slick before washing it entirely away, a part of him wishing to push his fingers and seed back inside her.

Later, he told himself. *There will be time.*

Still, it was long minutes before she was finally clean. When he finished, she reached for one of the cabinet drawers. His senses sharpened, thinking for a moment she sought one of her needles, but he was relieved to see she pulled out a different, smaller box.

Turning it in her hands, her expression grew shy, and she wouldn't quite meet his gaze when she said, "I'm on birth control. A medicine to prevent pregnancy. But this," she held up the box, "is an extra measure to make sure it doesn't happen."

Her hand cupped his face, as if to soften a blow. "I loved every second of that, okay? I want to do it again. I want to be with you, Frey. But I just . . . I can't have a kid right now."

Frey nodded slowly. "I understand." Matehood often meant younglings, but he was content with just having his Anna for now. When young came, he hoped to have a clan around them to help. Now wasn't the time to bring a youngling into the world, when he couldn't protect them, let alone his mate, during the day.

"I didn't even think about condoms."

His nose wrinkled in distaste. "I don't wish for them."

Lips quirking in amusement, she muttered, "Said every man ever."

He dipped his head, lips skimming hers without truly kissing. "I want to feel you, my Anna. I want you to burn me with your heat and squeeze me tight. Nothing should come between us."

"Frey . . ."

"I will be more careful with you, *fy nghân.* For now, no younglings—but when you are ready, I will sink inside you and not leave until you quicken with child. I will happily watch you grow our youngling, and I will carry you while you carry them."

"O-okay," she breathed. Then, after blinking quickly, "I mean, if and when that happens, we'll talk. For now, no babies."

"No younglings," he agreed. "And no condoms."

She narrowed her eyes at him. "Those two aren't usually mutually exclusive."

"I will be careful," he vowed. "I'll take care of you, my Anna."

The sound she made seemed unconvinced. So be it. He lived for proving himself to his Anna, for every part of herself she opened to him was more worth it than the last.

Anna finally nodded and in quick movements ripped open one of the sachets and took the small capsule.

Once she'd finished, Frey stepped between her legs, ready for more of her attention. His hands spanned her back, stroking over her impossibly soft skin. He could get drunk just on touching her, gorging on her textures.

"I would take you to bed," he whispered to her, "I want to hold you."

Anna's throat bobbed, and her eyes went curiously glassy. Her smile was small but heartfelt when she nodded. "I want that, too."

Rumbling happily, Frey carried her to bed, stopping only to snag the lubricant bottle from the table. He set her down in all her soft blankets, taking a moment to admire the sight she made, laid out like a sumptuous sacrifice to the goddesses. Rich hair spread across her pillows, limbs supple and relaxed, she looked up at him with sensuous, heavy-lidded eyes that called him down to her.

He crawled over her, dropping to his hands to run his nose and lips over her middle. Her belly jumped and her breasts quivered, enticing the predatory instinct in him to chase and claim. Careful of his horns, he licked a hot stripe up her body, worshiping the perfect handfuls of her breasts before working up her neck to her mouth.

He'd only meant to kiss her until she grew drowsy, but her mind seemed to turn away from sleep with every nibble and sucking drag. Her hips moved restlessly beneath him, and Frey rumbled contentedly.

"I'll take care of you, my Anna," he told her in whispers. Then there were no more words.

He took a bit of the lubricant, coating himself as he kissed her plush lips, savoring their give and softness and how she nipped at him when he pulled away.

It was slower this time, the urgency bleeding away to something richer. Frey pushed inside his heartsong, watching pridefully as his cock sank into her heat. He watched himself disappear, feeling how she welcomed him inside with a greedy grip. Her small hands fluttered over his chest, his horns, his back, trying to coax him faster, but he wasn't moved. He took her with a gentle rocking, hips moving in and back like the tide. He wouldn't be hurried, even as she dug her heels into his back and her blunted nails into his arms.

A desperate sound caught in her throat, and Frey kissed her there.

He only quickened his thrusts when he felt her fluttering around his cock, pulling him deeper. Frey's claws sank into the bedding as his hips thrust. His mate's sighs and moans filled his ears, and pressure drew taut at the small of his back.

Filling his mouth with her breast, he teased the nipple between teeth and tongue as he slammed one final time inside her before pulling out. An outraged noise ripped from her mouth, filling Frey's soul with a male satisfaction, but soon she was gasping when he pressed his cockhead to her clitoris.

Head thrown back, his mate came, and the sight of her elegant neck arching had him following her over the peak. Frey fell and fell and fell, caught in her gale.

This release was gentler but no less powerful than the one before, and Frey emptied of all his worries and fears. He painted his mate's belly and cunt with his spend, marking her with his very essence. He growled viciously to see it, spreading it across her skin even as she trembled with the aftershocks of release.

Oh, he would clean her up, take care of her like he promised, but for this moment, Frey devoured the sight of her, well-pleasured and covered in him.

Dwi adref.

Frey held her all night long, even dozing in the wee hours. The true sleep, laid out with his mate, fed his soul. So did waking up to her kisses.

Anna's lips and hands were greedy and fumbling as she reached for him in the dimness of predawn, but every touch was perfection. He lay there, holding her loosely in his arms, more than content to receive every kiss, every caress she wished to bestow.

A long while passed in that happy haze, so long that Frey didn't see how the light gathered in the room from the rising sun. When he next peeled an eye open to behold the room brighter than he'd ever seen it, hope, painful and new, pierced him surer than an arrowhead.

And with it, only a moment later, came the utter disappointment of feeling his limbs beginning to harden. Body already going stiff, he couldn't be as careful as he wished with Anna when he moved quickly out from under her and into the corner.

He heard her wail of surprise and sad cry of, "Frey!" before the stone sleep took him.

His shattered hope reflected in Anna's eyes, and he watched, able to see through his stone sleep, as she jumped up to hurry to him. Her hands searched him, as if she could find some part still alive and warm. But it was for naught, and Frey's heart rent in two seeing her crumple with grief.

His mate began her day with tears, and Frey hated every one.

The day slipped past in a dim blur, meaning his Anna left the dwelling for most of it. Frey tried to spend his time away from her wisely, reaching across the distance to the collective minds of his kin.

So far away, their thoughts were distant, but they recognized his presence. He couldn't quite speak with them, not like when he was in a room with them, but across the river of distance, he managed to communicate *mate bond*. He felt the shiver of their curiosity even across the distance, and he hoped somehow he would be able to reunite with them soon and perhaps learn something more.

He'd thought, driven as he was to have and claim a heartsong, that he'd known everything about their kind's mate bond, but perhaps there was something he missed. Perhaps it could even lead to the end of this wretched stone sleep.

Because Frey needed the day. He needed all of his Anna, and she needed all of him. If theirs was to be a true bond, it couldn't be done by halves.

He sensed Anna's presence before the stone sleep even began receding, and Frey's soul welcomed it as a balm to his restlessness. Pushing against the stone sleep, he urged his limbs into movement and his senses into wakefulness.

His eyes blinked open to see the last of the sun disappearing behind the trees. It was the first time he'd glimpsed the sun in centuries.

There wasn't time for such marvels, though, not with his mate rushing into his arms.

"You're awake!" she said, her voice breathy and relieved rather than happy.

His lips were too busy to form words, occupied by her questing mouth and tongue. Anna threw her arms around his neck and her legs around his waist, climbing up his body as if she wanted to meld them together.

More than amenable, Frey filled his arms and hands with her, feeling the warmth of her through her stiff clothes.

"You went to work?" he asked between frantic kisses.

"Yeah. Nothing weird today."

"Good."

He dropped her onto the bed, watching her bounce and gratified when amusement finally broke through the concerned slant of her brows. Frey meant to take his time peeling her out of her layers, but Anna had no patience, unbuttoning and unzipping in moments what he meant to take all evening.

Staring on, he meant again to ask how she was, why her heart beat so quickly, and why there was a frantic edge to her touch. He might've, too, except he was always distracted by the sweet sight of his naked mate, and her large breasts and feminine curves were too much of a temptation.

And then she sat on the edge of the bed, put her hands on his hips, and sucked his cock into her mouth.

"*Ffyc!*" Frey roared.

His hands dove into her hair, whether to pull her closer or push her away he didn't know—then her tongue swirled around the head and he stopped thinking altogether.

Anna hummed in approval, the sound vibrating all around his surprised, overjoyed cock. Barely half of him fit in her pretty mouth, but being a generous mate, she used her hands on what she couldn't suck and lick, stroking and teasing his root and gently weighing his bollocks in her palm.

Nearly choking on a wheeze, Frey watched, transfixed as his cockhead shuttled in and out of Anna's mouth, her tongue teasing over the slit and her plush lips wrapping around his girth. The sight was obscene, and Frey didn't want to blink for fear he'd miss it.

She worked him with enthusiasm, but there was still a franticness to her that Frey sensed even caught in the current of pleasure. It was difficult, but before she could work him to orgasm, he gritted his fangs and pulled out of her mouth. The sight of his cockhead pressed against her pouting lips nearly had him spilling.

"I'm flattered, *fy nghân,* truly. But I must know what troubles you.

Tell me, then I'm more than happy to leave you to your endeavor."

The pout didn't leave her face, and neither did the concern he spotted in the line between her brows.

Frey sifted his claws through her hair, waiting for her words. His cock throbbed, bobbing against her lips as if to tell her to ignore his daft mouth and continue her glorious attentions. He hung by a thread, but he gave her the moment she needed to compose her answer.

"I just—I thought that would work. Having sex. I thought it would break the curse."

Her gaze flitted away, but he caught the tears gathering there.

Purring for her, Frey pushed her back into the blankets and climbed into the bed with her. Laying at her side, he pressed soft kisses and traced gentle patterns into her skin, the small movements helping him get hold of himself, too.

"My Anna, it is as I said, the bond isn't just about consummating. Within my kin, sex often happened the first day of finding a heartsong. That doesn't mean the bond was fully formed. It's about connection, intertwining. We grow our bond every moment we are together."

The breath she took wobbled, and he silently begged her not to cry.

"I hoped we could hit fast-forward, I guess. I don't know what else to do."

"I don't know that there's anything else to do, *fy nghân.* So long as the bond is accepted, it will grow." It wasn't quite a lie he told her, for it was what he thought to be the truth. Mostly, what he said was his hope. He didn't know what would break the curse fully, only that it had to be tied to the mate bond.

His bond with Anna was nothing like he could have imagined—and it was more than his being a guardian and her human. So much stood against them that neither of them could have been faulted for hesitance or uncertainty. Through it all, the more he learned of his Anna, the more he wanted to know and the more he wanted this bond with *her*.

It would take time. Perhaps there was no way to break the curse, only encourage it to finally fade away.

"I just . . . don't want you to resent me," she whispered.

"Never. We are in this together, whatever may happen."

"Together," she repeated, and the word seemed to affect her. Her expression became less troubled, and the despondency he sensed in her a moment ago gave way to a fragile determination.

She wrapped her arms around his neck, pulling him down for another kiss. This one was slow, sensual, the kind that could convince a guardian to do anything.

"I was freaking out all day," she admitted, "trying to think of why this stupid curse won't just break. All I could come up with was maybe more sex would help."

A smile broke across his face, and his hand strayed down to catch and play with her soft breasts. "I'm certainly not saying it won't," he assured her. "I'd never say such a thing."

Her laughter set his soul alight, and Frey made a great show of kissing down the center of her body. Anna's fingers tangled in his hair, keeping it out of his face and so she could see as he swirled his tongue along her skin, down her belly, across her mons, into her wet heat.

Her appreciative moan set his cock to throbbing again, and as he knelt beside the bed so he could spread her legs wide and feast, he took it in one hand and squeezed the head mercilessly. For now, his mate was his sole focus.

"Show me," he rumbled.

Bottom lip caught between her teeth, Anna reached down to spread her cunt wide. He purred in pleasure to see her so pink and swollen and glistening. Swooping down, he laved his tongue from cunt to clitoris and swirled, making her hips buck off the bed. He held her down with an arm and settled into a rhythm that soon had her writhing.

He kept her on the edge of release for a long while with teasing circles and shallow thrusts. Her slick soaked his nose and mouth, but it was never enough. She gushed for him, but it only made him hungrier.

Frey only relented when her praises became threats, and even then, he started in on her clitoris with light swipes that barely touched the hood.

Now it was she who growled. "If you don't—"

Grinning madly, he wrapped his lips around her clitoris and sucked.

Anna yelped, body going rigid as she came. She was glorious in her release, hair wild, thighs trembling, pretty lips open wide just as they'd been sucking on him.

His cock gave another angry kick in his hand, and Frey knew he couldn't wait any longer.

The last of her release had hardly passed before he was dragging her to the edge of the bed. His movements lacked grace and patience, too far gone was he, but he did manage to get some of the lubricant in his hand before the bottle went clattering to the floor. Coating his cock messily in hard strokes, he snarled in pained pleasure to see how his mate's sultry eyes watched him under heavy lids.

"Are you going to fill me up now?" she crooned to him.

"Oh, my mate," he growled, throwing her legs over his shoulder and fitting his dripping cockhead to her entrance, "I'm going to stuff you full."

She opened her mouth to say something else, but all that came was a gasp of delight as he thrust inside. She was just as tight and hot as he remembered, and he fought for every inch. Sweat broke across his brow by the time he seated himself to the root, and his wings trembled from the force of his need for her.

The pressure at the small of his back drew tighter than a bowstring, and his bollocks had long since drawn up in anticipation. He meant to give her a moment to adjust, but his infernal minx of a mate smiled prettily up at him and cupped her breasts in her hands, pert nipples peeking between her fingers.

Hissing his pleasure, Frey drew back his hips and slammed inside. He was too far gone for a steady rhythm, and the room filled with the wet slap of their bodies meeting in a furious dance. Her breasts bounced in her hands as he pumped inside her again and again and again, chasing down his release.

It came with all the gentleness of a lightning bolt sizzling down his spine. Frey's fangs flashed as he roared and pulled her legs apart. He spilled in pearlescent ropes across her cunt and belly, lashing her with his spend. With the last of his coherence, he splayed his hand across her mons and pressed a thumb against her soaked clitoris.

Anna's cries rang in his ears for hours after, and Frey was more than content.

It took some time and some learning, but Frey was sure he spent a little less of each day in stone sleep. At first it was just a feeling from observations he made when he woke or solidified. The rooms were brighter, the sky different shades.

When the phone Anna had procured for him came and she taught him the basics, Frey tracked what time he was taken by and released from stone sleep. It was soon apparent that he no longer kept with the exact moments the sun rose and fell.

Yes, it was only a few minutes' difference, but they meant a handful of extra moments with his Anna.

And over the next week, as he lay beside his mate and cooked for her and laughed with her and made love to her, those minutes grew. They were small, but they were something. And even though such chipping away at the curse would take a long while, if this was how it was to be, he could be content with that.

For it meant, one day, he would have the day. One day, the curse would be no more and all of him would be Anna's.

27

During the afternoon lull, Anna discreetly pulled her phone out from under the desk and typed out a quick message.

Remember, going to be late tonight.

It was June Parkhurst's second-to-last visit to the museum. She'd almost finished up her surveys and photographs and would be handing in her findings soon to Carrie and Gavin. While Anna didn't love having to stay late, she would actually kind of miss seeing the art historian. Even though she'd never admitted to anything about that night, there was still a sense of camaraderie having gone through it with her. She liked the woman's dry humor and sensitive manner, too. June couldn't know that the statues were living beings, but she still treated them as if they were alive, with compassion and sensitivity.

A countdown had begun in Anna's head; if she was going to get any more information from June, whatever it may be, it needed to be soon.

In the meantime, Anna couldn't resist typing out a few more messages for her stony boyfriend.

What are we going to do tonight?

We could play cards

Watch a movie

Self-defense lessons

What if you fucked me against the front door?

Or the windows

What if we didn't use lube this time? What if you shoved deep inside me and didn't stop until I came?

What if I begged for it?

Her cheeks heated reading the messages back, and she squeezed her thighs together to try relieving some of the ache.

She hadn't exactly had sexting in mind when she got him the phone, but it was too delicious of an opportunity to waste. At first, she'd used the text messages and voicemails to let him know about her day, anything out of the ordinary, and if she'd be late. Even if he didn't receive the messages until he woke, it still gave her a sense of comfort to be communicating with him.

It hadn't taken her long to throw in a few flirty messages, too. The temptation was too much.

Sitting here at the front desk thinking about you. Aching for you.

They were in that sweet spot of new relationships, when everything was sweet and sexy and time together was never enough and time apart was too long. It was all soft caresses and deep kisses and whispers across pillows.

She knew the lovey dovey phase didn't last, but what she had now with Frey was better than all her past experiences and relationships combined times a hundred. Her heart sang when she walked in the front door to see him there. Her days went by interminably slow without him, though it made coming home to him and their evenings together that much sweeter. She was almost becoming nocturnal, not wanting to go to sleep and miss out on time with him. He was the responsible one, insisting she sleep.

It was amazing and Anna never wanted it to end—making that he turned to stone all the more difficult. She hated it. She hated that the damn curse wouldn't break. Frey told her not to worry, that he thought he was spending less time in stone sleep minute by minute. That one day the curse would lift.

Anna wasn't patient like that. She tried to take heart and believe as he believed, but she couldn't shake the worry that she was doing something wrong. Not enough.

So she tried to make the most of every second, to gorge on him and lavish him with affection.

She knew she couldn't force herself to be in love—Anna always hated being told what to do, even by herself—but with him, it didn't feel forced. When she let herself, falling for him was just so easy.

But what if my love isn't enough?

It had to be.

She'd never felt this way about someone before—like she couldn't get enough, couldn't be close enough or have enough of him. It terrified her still to have the depth and intensity of feelings for someone else; she knew that if it was all taken away, if Frey left her or was turned back to stone fully, it would devastate her. Yet, she couldn't stop. Didn't want to.

Anna had fallen for her flirty, surly gargoyle, and she wasn't a quitter. Those two things meant that whatever happened, she was determined to be with him. She couldn't give him up, not now, not with the promise of what could be.

What they already had was *so good*—and Anna wanted more.

She blushed thinking about the other night when, upon coming home, dinner was already cooking, filling the house with savory scents. She'd been a little late, needing to dash to the bank, but had messaged him to let him know.

> Thank you, heartsong. I wait with impatience for your return. We shall have chicken and roasted potatoes for dinner. But first I will be feasting on you.

Anna had had to slap a hand over her mouth to muffle her choked gasp and burning cheeks as she waited in line. She couldn't get home fast enough, already throbbing for him between her legs by the time she walked in the door. True to his word, he'd been all smiles and kisses, greeting her with warmth and greedy hands.

He'd swept her off her feet, placed her on the counter, shucked her dress pants, and feasted.

Anna's pussy clenched remembering the voracious way his tongue had swiped and swirled over her, spearing inside as if he meant to gobble her up. The bastard had stopped right before she came, addressing the dinging oven timer and boiling potatoes. She'd watched on in an aroused daze, arms trembling to hold herself up, as he put the potatoes in the oven and took the chicken out to rest.

His lips gleamed with her slick when he smiled wickedly at her. Anna had made desperate sounds as his lips teased hers and his fingers made quick work of her shirt and bra. When he had her naked, Anna expected him to pull out his cock or return to tonguing her, but instead he'd lifted her again and brought her to the couch.

A bit baffled but too horny not to just go along, she'd yelped in surprise when he spun her around and bent her over the back of the couch. She'd just gotten herself propped up on her arms when the hot bar of his cock slid between the cheeks of her ass. Anna moaned, forehead falling to the couch cushion, as Frey's hands kneaded and squeezed her backside. She heard the wheeze of the nearly empty lube bottle, and then his cock teased her entrance.

With her butt in the air like that, his hips aligned perfectly, and he slid easily inside on the first stroke. The second brought him deliciously deep, and the third saw him bottoming out. Already she was learning his shape, each time a little easier. Anna had come to relish the burn of taking him, how he shoved inside and made room for himself inside her.

His hands had been everywhere, caressing and stroking as his cock shuttled in and out in forceful but measured pumps. Her toes scrabbled on the floor for purchase, but he gave her no leverage, and as his pace picked up speed, he hooked her by the knees to place them on the back of the couch. He held her by the hips, pulling her back to meet every thrust, and Anna keened as she came.

The hot splatter of his cum on her backside made her shiver with aftershocks, and she'd almost told him to do it all again but come inside her. He was so good about pulling out, but Anna missed him.

After the couch acrobatics, Frey had picked her up—good, since she couldn't walk anyway—taken her to the bathroom to clean her up, and dressed her in cozy PJs. Then dinner was served and they cuddled on the couch watching history documentaries as they ate, Anna's brain a bit fuzzy on the details on how he managed all of it but too sated to care.

"Anna?"

She jumped in her ergonomic chair at the sound of her name. Clutching her phone guiltily to her chest, she peered up to see a curious June looking at her from across the front desk.

"Oh—hello! I'm sorry, I didn't see you come in."

June looked from her phone to her blushing face, and a small, knowing smile touched her pretty mouth. "No problem. We all get distracted."

Flustered, Anna made a show of gathering her things to follow June into the main gallery. They had something of a routine by now, and as June got herself set up, Anna typed out a few quick messages to Frey.

Maybe you should just be in an apron when I get home

Maybe I should suck on your cock under the table

What do you think?

It didn't do her blush any good, but damn, teasing him was addicting. The idea of him waking up to the flurry of messages, of having the automated voice read them out one at a time with each getting dirtier and dirtier got her all hot and bothered. Enough so that she almost wished to hurry this second-to-last visit by June along.

Taking a deep breath, Anna slipped her phone into her pocket and, once she'd given her lady bits a stern talking to, went to join June where she'd set up to take her scans and pictures on the far side of the gallery.

They looked up at the statue that had replaced Frey, and Anna's thoughts sobered. What was this gargoyle's name? Had Frey known him in their past life?

The thought saddened her. She'd kept her promise to Frey and had been applying for new jobs. She had a preliminary interview set up for next week at a medical office; not her preferred workspace, but her background in admin meant she could do it and the benefits were pretty good. Still, whenever she looked upon one of the statues, it was hard to imagine leaving.

What will happen to them?

Frey was the only one who'd come alive that they knew of, and even then, it was only at night. How would they help the others if she didn't have this job?

Chewing her cheek, her gaze flicked to June as the specialist did her thing. Engrossed in her work, June had that little divot between her brows that Anna had come to learn meant she was concentrating hard. The equipment didn't seem to be giving her any trouble, but still, Anna respected that she was focusing.

It wasn't until June took a step back from the scanning equipment and finished jotting down some notes that Anna made her move—even if she wasn't quite sure what the game plan was.

"We'll miss having you here. You're part of the team now."

June looked up, grinning. "The collection is absolutely fascinating. I'm sure next week won't be my last time in. There's enough here to keep any academic busy for their whole career."

Aware that the new security cameras were motion sensing, Anna tried to keep herself from twitching or swaying.

"I've definitely never heard of a collection like this."

June nodded. "To have so much on one kind of mythical creature—it's unprecedented. Especially for one that's more obscure."

"I've wondered if maybe these kinds of statues and the creatures they represent led to Judeo-Christian ideas about demons. There are so many similarities."

"I've definitely thought that, too. With the horns and tails and wings, it's hard not to see. Their timeline doesn't fit in nicely with earlier Judeo beliefs, but it certainly could have informed early-medieval Christianity in northern Europe."

"Could they be based on even earlier mythology, you think?" Despite all his growling about the fae any time they were mentioned, Frey had told her about how his kind were first carved to resemble them, humans, and the monstrous, ancient enemy of the fae, the Fomorians.

"I think that's likely. So little of the Celtic belief system was recorded, and what was comes from the Romans. Not the most unbiased source."

"None of the books here talk about those beliefs? Or do they not go back that far?"

June smiled patiently. "I'm a sculpture and statuary expert, so my knowledge on codices is a bit rusty. I think some of them are ancient copies of even older sources, though again, I think they're all Roman. Although . . ." Her gaze swept over the nearest gargoyle statue, "they certainly have a lot to say about how fierce of fighters the Britons were. Like they were demonic or otherworldly."

Anna's throat went dry. Clutching her clipboard to her chest, she asked, "What if the authors weren't being metaphorical?"

June went very still. "What do you mean?"

"What if . . . what if they," she nodded at the gargoyle nearest them, "aren't just *statues?*" *What if they are alive and being held captive, by a curse and the museum itself?*

"What else would they be?" asked a man's voice.

Anna jumped at the question, stomach plummeting to the floor when she beheld Gavin standing a few paces away.

How long has he been there?

He'd made no noise nor announced himself.

"Mr. Gwyneth, you're always so light on your feet," said June, her hand on her chest. She too looked like he'd scared the bejeezus out of her.

Gavin's gaze traveled from June back to Anna, and she gulped, trying to think of something to say over her hammering pulse.

Clearing her throat, she answered, "Votives or protective spirits. Demigods, maybe."

A frown creased his white-blonde brow. "And why would you think that?"

"Well . . ." Anna swirled her finger vaguely, indicating the gallery. "There are just so many with such similar features. Their characteristics follow patterns, like with the Egyptian gods. So maybe they're a pantheon, or even another kind of people."

She dared to peek at what June thought of her statement, and found the art historian's face gone stiff with pensiveness.

"Another kind," Gavin repeated, though he didn't seem to realize he spoke. The three of them stood there in silence, no one breathing a word until finally Gavin cleared his throat. "Forgive the intrusion. Carry on."

And just as quickly and silently as he'd arrived, Gavin swept from the gallery toward his office.

Anna looked back at June, who gave a mock shudder. "The man moves like a ghost."

She smiled stiffly in agreement but was too unnerved to say anything else. June returned to her work and Anna stood on silently, mind chewing over how and why Gavin had appeared suddenly. No alarm had been tripped, nothing had been touched or moved.

Are they watching us through the cameras? Was the conversation getting too close to the truth?

The thought made knots of Anna's insides, so much so that every minute that passed was an eternity waiting for June to finish so she could hurry home to Frey.

For her part, June was also quiet, and she completed her tasks quickly. Anna didn't miss how the redhead kept glancing her way, though.

When they arrived back at the front desk to collect their coats, June discreetly pulled a cream business card from her pocket. They were alone in the vast stone lobby, save for the cameras on either end.

"There's definitely something special about this collection and museum," she said, low enough so that only Anna could hear. "This is my personal cell phone number. When you're ready, I'd appreciate talking more."

Heart in her throat, Anna took the card and hurried to stuff it and her hand in her pocket. Carefully, she nodded.

"I think there's a lot to discuss."

Frey always had the most noble of intentions when teaching his Anna to defend herself. They had come into the habit of doing defensive training on Sundays, after his mate's final day of working for the week. With her continuing to work in the museum and the suspicious vehicles stalwart in their spots across the street, Frey hadn't wanted to give up on her lessons.

However, despite those good intentions of his, lately they had without fail ended up rolling across the living room floor with smacking kisses and wandering hands. Anna jokingly called it their *heavy petting cool down*. She could call it whatever she liked, so long as every session ended with his mouth on her skin and his hand between her thighs.

That very night, his tongue swirled over the steady pulse at her throat as his fingers traced her soft cunt through her leggings. He'd been showing her how to unbalance a bigger opponent and use their height and weight against them. Once he was on the ground, Anna had leapt on him, straddling his chest to finish him off, and that was that.

Yet even as his beautiful mate squirmed with need beneath him, he could sense her mind wasn't fully on his touches. She'd seemed distracted ever since arriving home, but rather than demanding to know what troubled her, Frey had tried coaxing her with food and good humor and finally touches meant to enflame her.

Still that troubled crease between her brows persisted, so Frey had to resort to more underhanded tactics.

With a final stroke of his tongue across the sensitive spot behind her ear and of his fingers across the swell of her clitoris, Frey lifted onto his elbows, denying her more attentions.

A frustrated growl burst from her swollen lips, and Frey couldn't help a smirk. She was starting to sound like a female guardian and getting just as fierce in her demands that he please her.

"Frey," she warned.

"I will spend the whole night petting your pretty cunt however you like, *fy nghân,* but first I would have you tell me what troubles you."

A big breath puffed from her flared nostrils, and her head slumped back onto the rug. He followed her down, kissing her cheek and purring for her.

"I was going to tell you, I'm just . . . trying to put it in the right words," she admitted.

"Just tell me. That's all that's needed."

Sighing, Anna finally explained the strange encounter with one of her employers that day.

"We were both weirded out about him suddenly appearing," Anna said, referring to the art historian she chaperoned. "I mean, he does that sometimes. And it was at the worst time, too. I don't know if she actually knows anything useful, but it felt like we were getting somewhere."

"Perhaps you should call her as she requested." He wasn't concerned about his own safety or another human knowing of his existence, but he did worry what it meant for Anna.

"Yeah, I'm going to. I just wanted to see what you thought. We should have a game plan, you know? Plan what we're going to say and how much we're willing to reveal."

He rumbled, pleased that she had thought to include him in her schemes. "We will think of something."

"Okay." Her fingers played over his cheek and jaw, then twisted in his long mane, but that pensive cast to her eyes hadn't yet completely faded, so Frey waited. "Frey, do you . . . could it be possible that not all the fae are gone? Could some be here?"

His rumble deepened with displeasure at the thought. "I don't think it likely, *fy nghân*, but anything is possible. None had been seen for millennia when they attacked us."

"You guys wouldn't really know, though." She grimaced with sympathy. "You were stone. Maybe they aren't as lost as they used to be."

"You think your employer is fae." He didn't mean to growl at her, but the idea of a fae close to his mate every day, without him there to protect her, scraped like dull claws down his soul.

Anna shook her head. "I don't know. I don't know what to think. There's something weird about both of them, but Gavin especially. They look human, but they say weird things and sound so old-fashioned. It's just a feeling, and it's crazy, but it'd explain why you sensed fae magick that first night."

"Anna . . ."

"I know, I know," she sighed, "new job. I'm working on it. But until then, is there any way to tell if they're fae?"

Frey struggled past his protective instincts, telling him to sequester her in the bedchamber and never let her out, to think on what he knew of the fae. It wasn't much, just whispers and old fairy tales told to younglings to make them mind.

"They were known to assume glamours, to appear as attractive as possible to humans. The only thing I can think is surprising or wounding them would force them to drop the glamour and reveal themselves." He rolled back atop Anna, frowning down at her. When she blinked innocently at him, he knew he was right to worry. "Not that you will. You won't risk yourself."

"I'm not going to attack my boss, you're right."

"Nor surprise him. If he is fae and you reveal him, he will eliminate the threat of his exposure."

"No attacking, no surprising."

"*Promise me.*"

"I promise." Pushing his hair back from his face, she tucked a lock behind his pointed ear and traced the tip with her fingers, eliciting a shiver of pleasure. He huffed at her for distracting him, and she smiled wide. "Now what about *your* promise?" she said, arching her brow at him just so.

"Which one?" he rumbled, dropping his face to skim his lips across hers.

One of her legs moved out from under him to spread wide.

"That thing about petting me as long as I want."

His rumble grew into a purr as he slid his hand down to resume his ministrations. His claws delved under the stretchy material of her leggings and past the soft fabric of her panties. Her cunt was warm and welcoming, his fingers sliding easily through her folds.

"I am a male who keeps my promises." And one who was wise enough to table discussions when they'd run their course.

Anna's hips began to rock in a gentle rhythm, her breaths coming quicker as she watched him with hooded eyes. The vision of loveliness she made nearly stopped his heart, and he thanked every ancestor and every goddess for the gift of her. When she smiled up at him, he couldn't resist taking her perfect lips, tasting her tongue and her moans.

"Harder," she rasped against his lips, "wanna come."

He spread her with two fingers and circled her clitoris with a third, making her gasp.

"As you say, *fy nghalon.*"

She choked on her moan, and Frey rumbled with satisfaction. There was nothing better than holding his mate in his arms and her pleasure in his hand. Anna was an enthusiastic, giving, and demanding lover, and Frey always sought to please her, to earn every gasp and mewl and kiss and be rewarded tenfold with her nips and caresses and wicked tongue. His chest swelled to see her nearing her release, and Frey chased it down, working her cunt with his fingers in successively quicker circles and thrusts. He wanted her pleasure and wouldn't be denied.

Two quick, heavy knocks rattled the front door.

"Delivery."

Frey's lips peeled back from his fangs, and a resounding, outraged growl burst from his throat as he snarled at the door and the human man behind it.

Anna's hands landed over his mouth, and she shushed him. With a groan, she squirmed out from under him. Frey only allowed it because he followed close behind, wanting to crush whatever creature was stupid enough to ruin their evening.

Before getting to the door, Anna poked the center of his chest and, with wide, warning eyes, motioned him to hide behind the wall that separated the living room and kitchen.

Another growl buzzed in his throat, and it was a long moment of silent stares between him and Anna, in which he demanded she be careful and she insisted he hide, before he ducked behind the wall.

He heard the rustle of Anna readjusting her clothing, and then the door cracked open.

If she hadn't seen him retreat into the living room, Anna would've sworn Frey loomed behind her as she opened the front door a few inches. On her stoop stood one of the biggest human men she'd ever seen.

Although scrawny compared to Frey, this guy definitely never skipped leg day. Or arm day. Or any day. His wide chest and bulging biceps looked almost comical in the brown delivery uniform. A brown cap hid a head with hair buzzed down to the scalp, and his chin nearly gleamed with how close a shave he'd gotten.

Definitely a military or law-enforcement type. And definitely not the regular delivery guy.

"Good evening," he said. "Just need a signature."

He held a decently large box under one beefy arm and a signature pad in the other hand. Anna hesitated, not wanting to open the door any more.

"I wasn't expecting anything."

The man blinked at her before angling the box so she could see the label. Sure enough, her name and address were printed there above the barcode.

"Are you Anna Kincaid?"

"Yes."

His brows lifted and he offered her the signature pad again. The only reason Anna finally opened the door just wide enough to lean out and jot a messy signature was the bored look in his eyes, the one every delivery person got near the end of their route and they just wanted to hurry up and get back to the depot and go home.

Replacing the little stylus, she caught the man's gaze flicking over her, taking in what he could of the apartment.

"That dog you got in there has one mean growl," he quipped as he handed over the box.

"Yup. And he's big and tends to bite men."

The man pulled a face, then touched the brim of his hat, bid her goodnight, and stomped back down the stairs.

What delivery guy tips his hat?

One that's an undercover cop.

Paranoia clogged her throat, and Anna quickly deposited the mysterious package onto the dining room table. Frey emerged to stand alongside her, and together they stared at the package.

Pulling out her phone, Anna quickly checked her email and confirmed that no, she didn't have any outstanding orders being shipped to her.

"I didn't order anything." She felt the need to whisper.

"What should we do?" he whispered back.

Chewing her cheek, Anna ran her finger over the label. It had her name and address printed correctly, and for all intents and purposes looked like an ordinary shipping label. However, a quick search of the return address yielded only a vacant property down in Carmel.

It smacked of surveillance, but did an art theft suspect really warrant all this espionage bullshit?

Anna picked up the box and gently shook it. Something rattled around inside, roughly half the size of the box. Without any stickers or branded tape, there were no other clues as to what was inside.

"I could drop it into the sea."

Tempting, but she didn't want to risk Frey leaving the apartment. This was probably one of those moves the cops did sometimes, trying to unnerve the suspect to get them to do something rash that they could then investigate. Anna wouldn't play into their game.

After peeling the label off the package to save the address, she deposited the box out on the stoop and shut the door. The lock sliding into place gave her a small measure of comfort. She'd throw the box away with the rest of the trash tomorrow.

"What do you think it is?" Frey asked, voice still low.

"I don't know. A trick, maybe. I don't want it inside the apartment."

"Agreed."

Anna's arms came around her, and she couldn't stop the prickle of tears. She hated crying, but this was all getting ridiculous. She didn't want to play games or keep looking over her shoulder. How long could their surveillance really keep going? How long until they believed she wasn't in on the heist?

She hated that they came to her home, reminding her that she was always under threat, always being watched.

Frey came to her and wrapped her up in his arms and wings, and Anna sank into the comfort. Drawing in a deep pull of his scent, her resolve firmed. They could get through this, together. They just had to lay low a little while longer.

There were one too many mysteries going on, and Anna wanted answers. For Frey and her peace of mind. If they were ever going to have a life, whatever that looked like with him being a gargoyle, they needed to be safe.

She hated it, but maybe on top of job hunting, she needed to start apartment hunting, too.

Despite having the world's best body pillow—who knew a big, bulky gargoyle would be such a good cuddler—Anna hadn't slept well the past few nights, and she was paying the price for it that afternoon. A headache crackled behind her right eyebrow. She'd managed it through the dreary morning rain, but now, with the clouds breaking apart, every time a visitor walked in, bright afternoon sunlight streamed inside and glared off the wet pavement straight into her eyes to stab her brain.

It didn't help either that no amount of massages, head rubs, or orgasms was able to soothe the unease growing inside her. Since getting that weird package, Anna had been on edge. Yeah, she knew those suspicious vehicles were still outside and sure Detective Ramirez had come to her apartment before, but none of that had made it inside her home. Her sanctuary. Where Frey was safe.

That they'd sent someone to her door to deliver a suspicious package made Anna's hackles rise. She'd bet money there was a listening device or something similar within whatever item was packed inside. Anna hadn't even opened the box before throwing it out, but just those brief moments it'd been in the apartment were too many.

Her home had been invaded. Violated. And Anna despised that.

Growing up, home had been wherever Shannon signed a lease or shacked up. The constant moving around had been exhausting, and once she was out on her own, Anna made it a point to try sticking in the same place for a while. Although it was expensive, she'd stuck to SF because it was what she knew; she understood how the city worked, its neighborhoods, its ebbs and flows. Her first apartment had been damp and crappy but it'd been hers. Getting the lease on her current place had felt like such a coup, and she'd been a good tenant for over five years. The space was small, the furniture secondhand, but everything was *hers*.

And someone was trying to infiltrate that space.

Not on my fucking watch.

She'd worked too damn hard for her little life. She wasn't about to let anyone, even the cops, ride rough-shod through it. Especially not now that it was Frey's home, too.

Indignation and righteousness weren't cures for headaches, though. The stress of it all was getting to her. She didn't want to leave her apartment. At least, not because she was forced out to retreat somewhere safer. When they moved, she wanted it to be her and Frey's decision, to find somewhere that worked for both of them.

As with most things, Anna didn't appreciate being rushed or pushed.

Those kinds of thoughts tumbled through her mind on the spin cycle, whirling back to her worry that something would happen. She couldn't quite put her finger on it, just a bleak paranoia that warned her a big, heavy shoe was about to drop.

Hating feeling unprepared, Anna didn't know what else to do other than hunker down, ride it out, and hope the surveillance ran out of funding.

It's not like the Mona Lisa got stolen. Again.

Anna muffled her grumbling in her hand, fingers pressing hard circles into her temple. Just a few more hours and then she'd go home, take a long bath, let Frey do that massage he did on her neck and head, and then when she was feeling better, suck on his fantastically fat cock until he couldn't remember his own name. *The perfect evening.*

A little heartened with the plan, Anna typed a quick message to Frey, letting him know exactly how the night would end with his cock in her mouth, and then braved the museum inbox.

The computer hadn't been helping her headache either, little glitches causing the screen to jump or fade and her eyes to strain keeping up. Anna rubbed her eyes, careful of her mascara, and tried to focus on an inquiry from a local magazine to run an article on the collection. She'd already read the same line twice when the screen winked into mismatched horizontal bars.

Her grumbling wasn't muffled this time. *Fucking Dave. Said he fixed it, but did he? Of course not. If he actually did a good job, he wouldn't have any work.*

Anna tried running the few command prompt scans she knew and had seen Dave do while working on the computer. Seriously, how did this not happen to everyone? Dave was probably starting to think she did it on purpose to lure him out from his office. *Ick.*

Not in the mood to call for reinforcements, Anna did the next thing she knew to do—turn it off and on again.

Her growl of frustration echoed in the empty stone lobby when the login page came up in the same stratified bars. Chewing her cheek, she fantasized about throwing the tower into the water feature before instead giving it a firm, authoritative whack. The monitor got the same treatment.

Something rattled inside the monitor.

Uh-oh.

Panic sucked the bottom out of her stomach. Great, now she'd gone and broken company property.

Feeling with desperate fingers, Anna ignored her throbbing head as she probed all around the monitor. When she didn't feel anything, she gave the monitor a gentler shake. Nothing. A harder shake, and there was the rattle again.

She traced slowly along the back of the monitor, running her nails down each vent hole. In the fourth gap, she felt something thin and metallic pressing against the plastic. Anna chipped more than one nail working the loose piece out from behind the plastic grate.

What fell into her hand wasn't like any computer part she expected to see.

A small cylindrical piece, it was about the diameter of a quarter. One green light glowed on the rim, and a small yellow wire looped from the metallic bottom half into a mesh top half.

It . . . looked like a teeny-tiny speaker.

But the front desk computer didn't have audio equipment. There was no need for it.

Glancing back at the computer, she saw the login screen had returned to normal, the layout looking exactly as it should. The cursor in the username text box blinked at her.

Her gaze fell back onto the little thing in her hand. Insides clenched with dread, Anna raised it to her face.

"So strange," she muttered.

A crackle burst from the little device, and she heard the faint feedback of her own voice, tinny and faraway, on the other end of whatever the device transmitted to.

A listening device.

That's what it was.

Fear gripped her in a cold fist, and Anna didn't think. Taking the device in her hands, she worked her nails between the two halves and ripped it apart. The soft crackle of feedback went dead as wires snapped.

Breaths coming in painful gulps, Anna dropped the broken thing onto the desk and backed away. Her hands shook, and she crossed her arms to keep herself from falling apart.

Holy shit.

A listening device had been put in the computer. One that somehow interfered with the computer.

The computer only acts up when I'm on desk.

It's only on when I'm here.

It's listening to me.

It knows when I'm here.

The truths hit her like hammer strokes, each more devastating than the last. Someone had been listening in on her working at the desk.

They bugged her work and had tried to bug her home, too.

Her lips went numb and her terror ignited into a cold, vicious outrage. *How dare they do this?* What evidence did they have to watch her every move?

She hadn't done anything!

How could it have gone this far? How could they have bugged the museum?

Not without the Gwyneths' knowledge and consent. There was no way.

The realization struck her harder than all the rest. The Gwyneths had to know. They had to suspect her, too. All this time, they were just keeping her close to keep an eye on her, to see if she slipped up.

Carrie had always been so kind, even after that night, but it must've been a ruse to lessen Anna's suspicion. And Gavin always showing up unannounced, he must've been trying to catch her saying something incriminating.

It'd all been a lie.

Enough, growled her cold outrage. *Fuck this.*

Grabbing the device, Anna flew through the museum, the stares of the few late-afternoon visitors following her. Tears burned her eyes, but she refused to cry. They didn't deserve any more of her tears or worries or consideration.

Anna didn't bother knocking on the open office door. Carrie sat in the plush leather chair, pen flowing elegantly over a stack of papers. She looked up in surprise to see Anna bursting in.

"Anna, is everything—"

The remains of the device landed on the desk between them with a tinkling clatter. Carrie stared at it, those hazel eyes wide with confusion.

She's good.

"I found this stuck into the front desk computer."

When Carrie only blinked up at her with concern, Anna ground her back teeth. They were doing this the hard way, apparently.

"A listening device."

Carrie's face paled. *Here we go.*

"I quit. Effective immediately."

The words surged inside her, giving her courage even as her hands trembled.

Carrie's mouth fell open. "Anna, I don't—"

"I hope the police had a good warrant because I've given them no probable cause. I've been a good employee. I had nothing to do with the heist, and I don't deserve this."

Anna spun on her heel and marched out of the office, her steps hurried to hide how her knees wobbled.

"Anna, wait!" Carrie called after her, but she didn't stop.

She rushed back to the front desk, stopping only to grab her purse and coat from the lockable compartment. There were a few things stored in her employee cubby in the breakroom, but she wasn't willing to stay longer for a hairbrush and second-favorite lip balm. She needed to get out.

From the corner of her eye, she saw Carrie hurrying for the front of the museum. They locked gazes across the vast space, and for a moment, from the shock on her pretty face and concern twisting her brows, Anna could almost believe Carrie genuinely hadn't known.

Shaking her head, Anna strode for the front door, ignoring Carrie's entreaties to wait.

Anna hurried up the street and ran to make the next light. Honks followed her for keeping up traffic as she hustled onto the other side long after the light turned. She looked over her shoulder to see Carrie outside the Milton Building, checking up and down the street.

Anna quickly turned and walked away, hoping traffic hid her retreat.

Her steps were fast, her heart pounding as she fished her phone from her pocket.

She still hadn't figured out exactly what she should say to June Parkhurst, but she'd programmed the art historian's number into her phone. Her stomach churned when the call went straight to voicemail, though it was a little relief to hear June's voice say to leave a name and number.

"June, hi, it's Anna Kincaid from the museum. I just quit. You're right, you're absolutely right, there's something strange going on. We need to talk. Call or text me anytime."

That done, next she dialed Frey's number.

It rang four times like it always did and went to voicemail. Even though she knew he wouldn't pick up, couldn't pick up, every unanswered ring made her heart lurch with panic. She waited impatiently for the tone and breathlessly launched into what she'd just done.

"I did it, I just had to quit, I couldn't stay there, I'm coming home early, I just need to be home and with you. I don't know how much they know but this can't be legal, it has to be harassment. We'll find a new place, we'll move somewhere better and if they keep coming at me, we'll get a lawyer and figure it out, but they can't just keep doing this, it has to stop sometime, and I just—" she gasped for breath, the words pouring out, "I couldn't take it anymore. We'll figure it out, okay? I'm telling myself that, too. We'll figure it out together. We'll find a way to help the others and we'll break this fucking curse and we'll do it on our terms, okay? No more of letting them do this, we gotta—"

Tires screeched, punching her eardrum, and Anna recoiled as sleek black metal rushed past her. The momentum of the vehicle sent her careening to the side, an SUV bouncing up onto the sidewalk just a few feet away.

Terror deeper and colder than she'd ever felt scraped through her as she watched doors fly open and men in tactical gear come pouring out before the SUV even came to a stop.

She'd only had the thought to turn, to *run,* when gloved hands reached for her, pulled at her coat, ripped her phone away. Anna opened her mouth to scream, but there was another hand. She bit on it, tasting leather, but it wouldn't let her go.

The commandos caged her in and hurried her toward the waiting SUV.

Never get taken to a second location.

Anna dug in her heels and struggled for all she was worth, but there were too many. They dragged her to the SUV and threw her inside.

The doors shut behind them with a resounding *clap,* and then it was dark.

30

The face staring placidly at her from the front passenger seat was all too familiar, but that didn't mean Anna believed it. Detective Ramirez would've been her first guess. Then maybe the buff delivery guy. Even Gavin Gwyneth himself.

Definitely not Andrew Glendower, in his crisp coat and silk scarf.

Anna could feel the car moving, the rumble of the engine and sway of the two big men, bracketing her on either side of the bucket seat she'd been shoved into, all registering somewhere in her brain. She thought maybe they were headed in a familiar direction, knew she should be paying attention to where they were taking her, but every time she tried to look out the windshield, her gaze snagged on that clean-shaven face.

He gave her a sort of wan smile and apologized for the suddenness of it all, as if she'd have appreciated a slower, more methodical kidnapping. "It wasn't meant to go like this, you understand," he went on, "we wanted absolute confirmation that the creature is with you before barging in, but then you found our little bug and, well, we had no other choice."

Anna gritted her back teeth, seething inside with a boiling rage and potent fear. Glendower, not the cops, had been the ones bugging her computer? *What the actual FUCK?*

Some of her rage must have shown on her face, though she tried hard to keep her expression neutral.

Glendower *tsked* and sighed, as if he'd done his best to reason with her. Turning to the guard next to her, he said, "Phone."

The man, a burly guy with an earpiece who could've passed for Secret Service, handed over the phone ripped away from Anna in the scuffle. She was more than a little proud to see the bite mark she'd left behind not just in his glove but the meat of his thumb, too.

Hemmed in like this, captured and held prisoner, she felt more than a little feral. Biting wasn't off the table.

Her head throbbed with a headache and fear, eyes straining to take in every detail—the characteristics of all the men, what Glendower said and did, where they drove to.

Glendower's signet ring glinted in the late-afternoon light as he poked at her phone screen. After a moment of trying, he sighed and asked, "The passcode?"

Anna said nothing.

Unimpressed, he said, "I applaud your bravery, but save it for now, Miss Anna. Let's get off to the right start."

Anna still said nothing.

The man on her right, slightly smaller than the other, huffed and in two quick movements drew and cocked a gun. The cold barrel dug into her temple. "Tell him what he wants," growled the guard.

She went very still, body gone stiff at the sight of the weapon. Her stomach churned, and the air in the SUV grew thick. The desire to tell him the passcode teased at her lips, but Anna bit her cheek and remained silent.

The guard pressed the gun harder to her head, making her eyes water. Her breaths came in panicked bursts, but she told herself they wouldn't do it. *If they wanted to kill you, they would've already. They need you for something.*

When menacing her didn't work, Glendower simply waved off the guard. "Enough of that." His gaze turned to her again, all veneer of pleasantry gone; a cold man stared at her, and she knew right then that her life meant nothing to him. Whatever he wanted, whatever his game was, Anna was a means to an end.

But she didn't intend to make it easy for him. Yeah, she was scared as fuck, but she was also so, *so angry*.

Her mouth stayed shut, though she hoped her murderous gaze was enough of a *fuck you*.

"I suppose it's time to show you a little of what you've gotten yourself into."

One finger of his free hand flicked up, and Anna's whole body shuddered when a cold sensation slithered up her chest. A phantom touch, it wound around her neck in silky coils, squeezing her throat.

She clawed and grasped with her bound hands at her own neck, but there was nothing to grab. Her fingers met only empty space as that cold sensation applied increasing pressure to her neck.

Through bulging eyes, she watched as Glendower's finger made slow circles. Circles that grew ever smaller.

"I'm interested in how much the creature has told you of his kind—and the ones who made them."

The invisible binds cut the air off from her lungs completely, and Anna gasped uselessly. She flailed in the seat, the men on either side watching on.

"Everyone sought to destroy us and our power. They thought they could slaughter us and take what was ours. But the old ways aren't dead, Miss Anna. *Fe godwn ni eto.*"

The pressure suddenly vanished, leaving Anna gasping and coughing. She sucked in air, tears streaming down her cheeks. Her throat burned, her vision wobbled, and it took everything in her not to buckle under the terror. That righteous anger faltered, and for one horrible moment, Anna teetered on the edge of bursting into tears.

"Magick cannot be killed, you see. Only forgotten. Not all of us have forgotten." His thin lips pulled back in an eerie, empty smile.

"Passcode, please."

Stay alive, instinct told her. *Live to fight another battle.*

Glaring at him from under her lashes, Anna croaked the four-digit passcode.

"Excellent. Thank you."

Glendower focused on her phone, tapping at the screen and ignoring her as she wheezed and struggled to fill her lungs. Harder was wrapping her brain around just getting choked with fucking *magick.*

The magick-wielding professor who apparently had his own little unit of shady mob-types spent a few minutes scrolling through her text messages, particularly those with Frey's phone. She'd named the thread inconspicuously as *BFF* (boyfriend Frey), but that didn't seem to fool Glendower.

His fair brows rose into a saucy arch as he read the thread, which was in large part steamy sexts mostly from her, but Anna refused to blush.

"Racy stuff," was his comment, throwing Anna a grin. He lowered the phone to look her over, his gaze assessing. "I had my doubts at first, but you are most certainly his heartsong. You woke him from the stone sleep."

Anna's heart thumped so loudly in her chest, everyone in the SUV had to have heard.

It nearly stopped when Glendower leaned toward her, his smile broad and too white, to say, "You touched him that night, didn't you? And it brought him to life."

She refused to acknowledge what he said, but something in her face must have satisfied him. He straightened back into his seat, his smug grin insufferable.

"I have a feeling you know plenty, Miss Anna, yet not nearly enough. I'm afraid you've been pulled into something far beyond your depth. Here's what's going to happen—at sundown, we'll call your guardian and let him know we're bringing you home. Then all of us will go to your apartment and have a civilized conversation."

Cold sweat trickled down Anna's neck. Who the hell was this man? How did they know Frey wouldn't be awake until the sun went down?

She dared to glance away from Glendower out the windshield. According to the clock and long shadows, evening was rapidly approaching. They could've been on her block by now but instead seemed to be driving aimlessly, though keeping near her neighborhood and to a safe, inconspicuous speed.

"I don't suppose you'd tell me his name?"

Don't suppose I would. The idea of being used to lure Frey out made her feel sick to her stomach, but on the heels of that, a violent and vicious desire to lash out at anyone who'd harm him.

Again the odd desire to tell him tickled her tongue, but she bit on it. *Magick.* Fucking magick. He was trying to influence her with it, had done it before when he came into the museum.

The Tree of Life ring, the Welsh name and phrases, magick. Was Glendower some sort of druid?

It didn't fit with the common conception of druids—though modern Druidry was far different from its ancient counterpart. What was known was far darker, though some suspected it was bad PR from the Romans. Whatever the druids knew and practiced, it'd been enough to forge Frey's kind—and nearly strangle her.

Fuck fuck fuck.

She pushed her aching head to go over escape scenarios, but nothing seemed plausible or hopeful. Every idea ended in recapture or worse, that cold magick slithering around her throat again.

The SUV lapsed into silence, which was somehow much worse than Glendower's monologuing. Her stomach clenched painfully every time the digital clock on the dash ticked another minute.

As the sky flushed with darker shades of blue and lilac, the guards got fidgety, weapons clicking in and out of holsters. She thought there were at least six of them crammed in there with her and Glendower, not including the driver.

By the time the sun disappeared, a frenetic excitement permeated the cramped cabin.

"Time to head over," Glendower told the driver.

As the SUV turned to drive the last few blocks to her apartment, Glendower held the phone in front of him, waiting. "We'll give him a few minutes to—"

Her phone buzzed, Frey's number and *BFF* taking up the screen.

"Ah, well, speak of the devil." Accepting the call, Glendower put it on speaker. "Is this the guardian?"

A thick pause greeted him, and Anna bit her cheek until it bled, wanting to cry out.

The phone buzzed again, not with a call but the rumble of Frey's furious growl on the other end.

"Who is this?" hissed down the line.

Tears she'd held back since getting snatched stung her eyes at hearing his voice. The need to call out to him choked her.

"A friend," said Glendower. "I'm here with Anna now. We'll be arriving at your home shortly. I'd like to speak with you about a few things."

"Where is Anna?" The words were hardly audible through Frey's bestial growl.

"Right here with me. I'm bringing her home to you."

"I would speak with her."

Glendower's icy gaze flicked up to Anna, and she felt that cold magick slither around her again. She recoiled into the seat, but the magick held her tight.

"Of course," said the professor, holding the phone nearer to her.

Anna leaned forward, the magick pressing threateningly around her throat.

"Black SUV!" she screamed.

The magick cinched tight, throwing her back into the seat.

"ANNA!"

Glendower huffed, pulling the phone away. "We'll be arriving in a moment in a black SUV, yes. We will come to you to—"

Something landed on the front of the SUV with all the speed and impact of a meteor.

The car came off its rear tires before slamming back down, the front completely crushed. Everyone inside careened to the left, the driver's head smacking sickeningly on the window with enough force to crack it.

The magick squeezing her let go, only for Anna to be squished between the two guards.

Tires squealed and metal screamed as the SUV came to a sudden and devastating stop.

The car alarm blared, and Glendower cursed, his head lolling to the side. With a wave of his hand, the car alarm and everything around them went fuzzy. The alarm died, and the buildings down the street hung in hazy lines.

Anna blinked, wondering if she had a concussion.

"Shit—*incoming!*"

Metal screeched, and the locked passenger door went flying off its hinges into the street. The new gaping hole in the car revealed a vicious, furious gargoyle looming over the SUV. A roar hit them next, the guards cussing and scrambling for weapons.

Frey grabbed the one on Anna's right, and the man went sailing over his shoulder, landing on the street with a resounding *crack*.

His gaze locked on Anna, and she reached for him with her bound hands. "Frey!"

"Anna—!"

Two bodies, one after the other, crashed into Frey, and he and the guards went staggering back out into the street. Anna yelped his name as the back doors opened and more men jumped from the SUV.

Left with only one guard, the unconscious driver, and Glendower, Anna threw herself at the hole.

Hands grabbed at her, and she wrestled with the guard on the bucket seat, kicking and flailing, fighting her way out of the car. She'd just managed to get her bound hands over the armrest of the far side, giving her leverage to pull herself away from the guard, when a cold pressure pushed her down in the seat.

"No!" she cried.

"Enough," said Glendower, his face pinched with frustration.

"You said you wanted to fucking *talk* to him!"

"Indeed." Looking out at the scene in the street, Glendower sighed. "Best laid plans and all that. Come along, Miss Anna, time to fix this mess."

He exited the SUV, and Anna was dragged by the guard out the other door and around the demolished front. Her legs didn't want to hold her up, and she stumbled along, head pounding trying to take everything in.

The guards were attempting to get at Frey, but he kept them back with his lashing tail and swiping wing claws. Two guards were already down, and Frey's claws dripped with blood. Her stomach nearly turned to see it, starkly red against his gray skin.

As long as it's not his own.

She knew of course that he'd been a warrior, a fighter. Those big muscles of his weren't just for show—but knowing and seeing were two different things. Frey moved quickly and brutally, every strike meant to inflict maximum damage. His wings and tail moved in unison with his arms and legs, every limb in movement to keep back all his attackers.

There was a brutal sort of beauty to it, even if the sight of him fighting made Anna's blood run cold.

"Frey, was it?" called Glendower.

The guards fanned out into a loose circle, keeping Frey hemmed in. Frey tore his gaze away to assess Glendower, and his lips pulled back in an angry snarl when he saw the guard holding Anna.

"Release her!"

"All in good time." The professor approached with his hands raised, as if he wasn't a threat.

"Frey, he's got magick!"

The guard holding her yanked her arm, and then the barrel of a gun dug into her side. "Shut up," he hissed.

Frey's growl grew louder, his shoulders bunching. He sneered as Glendower continued to slowly approach. "*Rydych chi'n dilyn yr hen ffyrdd?*"

"*Mae hud yn llifo yn fy ngwaed.*"

"*Derwydd.*"

"Yes. We are kin, *rhyfelwr.*"

Frey's nostrils flared in rage. "You would use magick against my mate? We are *not* kin."

"I mean neither of you harm. I admit, this isn't how I wanted introductions to go. Now, let's go inside like civilized people—it's quite a lot of work to glamour a whole block. We'll speak while we wait for another car."

"I will have my mate."

"Upstairs."

Frey snarled again as her guard pressed the gun up under her ribs, making Anna wince.

They stood at an impasse for a long moment, Glendower holding perfectly still and Frey coiling his muscles, ready to pounce. Anna locked her knees to keep herself upright even when she wanted to crumple—one movement from her and she worried Frey would retaliate and Glendower would magick him, too.

The silence was broken when a familiar white van trundled onto her street.

"Ah, excellent. They're here." Glendower waved a hand, and the van passed through the haze of glamour, coming to a stop behind the SUV. When the driver of the van rolled down his window, the professor said, "Keep the engine running. I'll call when it's time."

To Frey he said, "There are more men in that van. Let's not make this ugly. I only want to talk."

Muscles shaking with the effort of not attacking, Frey's nose wrinkled as he hissed at the professor. But when he turned his gaze to Anna, she gave him a small nod.

Divide and conquer, she figured. They both stood a better chance with fewer guards.

Finally, Frey grated, “Very well.”

He unfurled his wings and gave a mighty flap, sending all the guards stumbling backward. He leapt into the air and hovered above them, gaze trained on Anna.

Glendower waved at the guards to fall into formation around him and Anna. He wrapped a hand around her elbow and pulled her into motion.

“Shall we, my dear?”

“He’s going to rip you apart. You know that, right?” she felt the need to growl.

But Glendower only smiled. “I’m intrigued to see what he can do.”

31

Frey stepped through the open window into the apartment, not sure the walls could contain his rage. Captain chirped curiously at him, and Frey quickly bundled him into Anna's bedchamber.

The sound of the key turning in the lock raked up his spine, and Frey stood in the center of the apartment, waiting for them.

Men in black gear surged into the apartment, invading his and Anna's home. The insult disgusted him, and his lips peeled back to bare his fangs as Anna was brought in with the older man who'd done all the talking and wished to do more.

Her eyes were wide with fright, and she carried herself as if in pain. His rage only grew, as did his pride in her—she stood beside her captor bravely, her mouth set in grim but determined lines.

My beautiful, brave mate. Stay strong, and I will get to you.

With all of the humans inside, the front door was shut and locked.

The man stood starkly against the wall of his black-clad guards; a wool coat of light gray was unbuttoned, revealing a silky scarf and neckcloth. A waistcoat was buttoned beneath a suit jacket, and his trousers had a crisp pressed line down the center. Even to Frey's eyes, he looked old-fashioned.

The man breathed an audible sigh as everyone settled into their place. "That's better. This conversation warrants a bit of privacy. The world isn't ready to know about us yet, *fy ffrind,* but soon it won't matter." He handed Anna off to a guard, forcing Frey to split his attention between him and Anna.

Stepping forward, the man said with great circumstance, "I'm Andrew Glendower of the Silures Pritani. My line is as ancient as yours, and through it we have kept the old ways alive. I have studied the arcane arts, and just like our ancestors, I'm ready to stand side-by-side with guardians to defend what is ours."

A glint of light grew brighter in Glendower's eyes with every word he said, and though many of the words were familiar to Frey, calling to a time when his kind lived in clanhomes and fought alongside human warriors, they filled him only with dread.

The man knows too much of our history—and he has Anna.

Perhaps Frey would've been interested in what Glendower said if not for that fact. The man could be one of the very druids who carved his kind and he wouldn't care, so long as his Anna was in danger.

"And what is this to do with me and my mate?"

"*Everything.*" Drawing a little closer, Glendower smiled wide, all charm. "The fae destroyed so much that night. Those who weren't turned to stone were slaughtered."

"Don't presume to tell me of my own suffering, druid."

Glendower held up his hands. "Of course. I only meant that your kin weren't the only ones attacked that night. The hunt rode through the Pritani villages, killing many of our people. What was left, the English nearly exterminated. But there were some of us who survived, who kept the old ways. We remember what the guardians truly are—not statues, but the greatest creation of mankind. A fusion of magick and earth never seen before."

"You wish to wake the guardians."

"Yes. We will rise again," Glendower said, "to take back what's ours. Our land, our magick, our power. All of it has been stolen again and again. But now, with guardians, we'll finally take what's ours."

Anna sneered in disapproval. "You want super soldiers."

"I want these warriors to live again and have what is rightfully theirs."

"They couldn't stop the Saxons. What makes you think a few dozen guardians can do anything against a modern military force?"

"Excellent question. This requires a demonstration." Glendower held out a hand, and one of the guards placed a gun in his palm. Frey stepped forward, ready to defend Anna, but the gun pointed at him instead—and fired.

The gunfire crackled through the air, and the bullet hit Frey in the chest with such force, he stumbled back into the couch, the breath punched from his lungs. He heard Anna scream through his ringing ears.

Yet . . . though it stung, no blood gushed. Indeed, no wound had been made.

Into the stunned silence, Glendower said, "For starters, they're mostly bulletproof. Smaller caliber, at least. The guardians' skin retained some properties of the stones the rock-born were carved from."

Anna's mouth hung open in shock, and Frey himself was surprised, given what he knew of modern guns from the films he and Anna watched. He touched the place the bullet had ricocheted off, and though the flesh was sore and reddened, it was unbroken. He eyed the weapons strapped to the guards, considering. All had the smaller weapon Glendower had used but several also held larger firearms.

"Before you try anything, I'd like to make you an offer."

His gaze fell back on the druid, though his other senses were trained on Anna. It'd be only three leaping bounds to get to the guard holding her by the arm. He didn't worry about the human men or their weapons—even if he hadn't been somewhat immune to them. His Anna wasn't.

"Release my mate."

"In a moment. First . . ." From his inner coat pocket, Glendower presented a simple leather strap. Tooled with a modern buckle, it was a simple collar. "I'd like you to put this on."

He could smell the magick imbued within the collar from paces away. "It's magicked."

"Yes, I'm afraid it's necessary for now."

Frey howled in outrage. "I will not be the beast of someone who threatens my mate!"

"Without the collar, I can't give her over. But know, I won't hurt her. If the heartsong is lost, the curse can never be broken. Without her, you'd return to stone. So believe me, I understand how very precious your heartsong is."

Frey's stomach turned to hear another man talk of his Anna like that.

He didn't know if he could believe the claim, nor if he'd have any will to go on should he lose Anna. The curse was welcome to whatever was left of him if that happened. But he couldn't think like that, had to focus on getting his mate and fighting their way out.

"The collar is merely insurance—just as Miss Anna is. It's only needed until we trust each other, of course." Glendower dared another step forward, holding out the collar. "Come with me. I have a large property up in the hills—you'll be able to live freely. You and your heartsong will be cared for. And with the collar, there will be no more stone sleep."

His heart lurched in his chest, and a reluctant curiosity itched at his mind. "You can break the curse?"

Glendower's smile stiffened. "The collar is a workaround. It prevents you from attacking me, yes, but it's also imbued with enough magick to prevent the stone sleep." Again he presented Frey with the simple leather strap. "Help me free your kin and reclaim what our ancestors lost. We can do so much together."

Temptation sank its hooks into Frey, and he looked long at the collar. His warrior's soul cried out against putting on such a humiliating shackle, and he knew Glendower wasn't to be trusted. There would never be a time when the collar came off, for the druid would never want to give up whatever power the collar gave him over Frey.

But to have the day . . . to be with Anna always . . .

His gaze cut to hers, and he knew she saw everything, all of his thoughts and conflicts warring inside him. He saw the same longing in her own eyes, the idea of finally being able to truly begin something together.

The yearning was sharper than any knife and pierced him through the heart.

But his Anna was stronger. She shook her head in one curt move. "Don't," she said. "There's no reason to believe him."

Glendower frowned icily over his shoulder at her. "Miss Anna, that isn't helpful."

"Your mistake for thinking I would be. You snatch me off the street, point a gun at me, threaten us—why should we believe you?"

The man's lips thinned the more Anna spoke, and Frey growled a warning. Guns clicked and cocked, but his growl only gained in volume.

When Glendower turned back to Frey, his gaze had thawed into a considering stare. "Very well," he said, "I see we'll need proof." Pulling a handheld device from one of his pockets, Glendower said into it, "Please come up to the apartment, it's time for the reunion."

Frey's skin prickled with foreboding as he watched all the guards adjust their stances. There was only time to exchange a concerned look with Anna before something heavy and dark landed upon the fire escape.

In disbelief, Frey watched as another guardian stepped through the window.

"Dragan—" he choked on the name.

His clanmate looked back at him impassively, his gaze shuttered.

He was a large male, even for guardians. Dragan's line had been hewn from obsidian, and the black of his skin seemed to absorb the light of the room, broken only by faint gray striations. Conical spikes made a crown of horns from his brow back past his temples, and eyes so violet they were nearly black stared through Frey.

They had grown up together, though Dragan had been a few years his senior. They fought alongside each other when the clan went to battle with the Pritani. He'd shared a round of mead with the male and many other of their comrades at the Gorsedd, the very night the fae attacked.

"How—?" Had Dragan too found his heartsong?

Face still eerily devoid of expression, Dragan raised one hand and tapped at his neck. A leather collar had been strapped around his throat.

Frey hissed at the sight. "No."

"It's true, *brawd.* I have seen the sunlight."

"No heartsong required," chimed Glendower. "As you can see, a workaround until we figure out how to break the curse in full."

Frey looked upon his clanmate again and felt nothing but horror. The collar around Dragan's thick throat nearly sparked with the amount of magick coursing through it. The deadened eyes, how Glendower had so casually called and summoned him—Dragan was the druid's beast, no longer a guardian.

Seeing the disgust in Frey's face, Dragan said, "Andrew is kind to me. He'll take care of us, Frey."

"I don't believe you and your forced words." To Glendower he said, "I can never trust a man who steals and threatens my mate."

Glendower's mouth twisted, but before he could reply, static buzzed through the apartment, and a male voice on the handheld device confirmed that the new car that'd been sent for had arrived.

"Good, we'll be down shortly." Replacing the device in his pocket, Glendower again offered the collar. "It's time to go. Put this on and let's be done with it. There's no reason for things to get uglier."

"I will never submit to a man who kidnaps women and shackles guardians. You are an insult to the druids who came before you."

Glendower's left eye twitched, and a vein popped on his forehead. "Very well," he said, and reached an empty hand toward Anna.

For a moment nothing happened—or so Frey thought. Then a

horrid gurgle sputtered from Anna's mouth, and she clawed at her neck. Frey watched in horror as his Anna was strangled by magick, wisps of it rising like waves of heat off baked earth.

"NO!"

He exploded forward, his rage all-consuming.

Dragan's big body intercepted him, and the two went down, landing in a heap of wings and fists.

"Hold him!" Glendower shouted.

Men ringed the two guardians, trying to help subdue Frey, but he buffeted them with his wings and smacked them with his tail. It was Dragan who was the true threat, his eyes empty as he clawed and struck Frey's front.

They grappled across the living room, the couch screeching as it was shoved and kicked away. Dragan knocked Frey into two guards, sending them down to the ground, the coffee table splintering beneath them.

"Frey!" Anna called to him through the melee, the sound rasping in her abused throat.

He roared in Dragan's face. He didn't care that it was another guardian he fought nor about the promise of magick returned to his kind—*they have Anna!*

He slammed his fist into Dragan's empty obsidian face, knocking the bigger male off balance. They went rolling across the floor, breaking more furniture, and the guards scrambled.

The butt of a rifle hit him in the shoulders, but Frey could hardly feel it in his rage. It'd been centuries since his last battle, one that had ended in the devastation of his kind. He wasn't about to lose another fight, not when his Anna was in danger.

Frey rolled to his feet, slapping away a guard with his wings just in time to meet Dragan's next blow. He caught the male's fist and twisted until the wrist broke. His obsidian face snarled in rage and pain, the first true emotions he'd seen from his clanmate, and Dragan fell on him in a fury.

Claws swiped across Frey's chest, blood welling from the wounds, and Dragan's tail wrapped around his ankle and pulled, trying to unbalance him.

Frey bared his fangs and slammed his head into Dragan's, their horns grating against each other. They pushed and tossed like bulls, trying to throw the other off. Dragan boxed him with his wings and caught Frey's next strike, their hands locking into one large fist. Despite being broken, Dragan wielded his other hand, sinking the claws into Frey's arm.

Men rushed him from the side, hemming him in toward the wall. They overwhelmed him with their mass, two of them clinging to and weighing down his free arm while another grabbed at a wing, crushing the delicate membrane and straining the bones.

Dragan shoved, and Frey careened back into the wall, head bouncing off the plaster. He hissed at his clanmate, swiping his taloned feet at Dragan's thigh, but the big male kept coming.

From the corner of his eye, he saw Glendower approach carefully, the collar unbuckled and awaiting his throat.

I will not lose!

With a roar, Frey wrenched his arm to the side, smacking one of the men away with his fist caught with Dragan's. He freed his hand and filled it with the head of another and threw him across the room into a bookcase.

Dragan seized the opening, sinking his claws again into Frey, catching him on his exposed side. Blood spilled from the wound, the sting sharper than teeth.

"FREY!"

"Take the collar, *brawd*," Dragan growled. "End this."

In answer, Frey threw himself at Dragan, heaving the combined weight of his body and the men still clinging to him full force on the other guardian. They all went down in a heap of bodies onto the couch, which cracked and collapsed under the weight.

Frey got his feet under him and staggered upright.

Just Glendower stood between him and the one guard holding Anna.

He leapt straight for them, pumping his arms and wings, only to run into a wall of magick. Sent reeling, Frey just caught his balance with his wings. He charged again, needing to get to his mate, when a clawed fist wrapped around his ankle.

Glendower raised his hand again, his face rigid with fury.

"Enough! Just put on the goddamn—"

The front door exploded.

Frey staggered from the impact as splinters rained through the apartment.

"That was a bit much, my love," said a female voice.

All of them watched in shock as two more people entered the apartment. Both wore dark colors and body armor, their hair pulled back with ties. The woman was taller than Anna and curvaceous, her golden eyes assessing the scene with concern. The man was nearly as tall as Frey, with powerful shoulders and stark white-blonde hair.

They appeared human, but as the pair entered, the magick flowing from the male was more than palpable; it nearly choked him.

Fae.

Holy fucking shit! Gavin and Carrie Gwyneth had just blown open her door and waltzed right in.

As if the day couldn't get any crazier—getting kidnapped, strangled with magick, Frey deflecting bullets and fighting off a half-dozen guards *and* the obsidian statue stolen from the museum. Gavin and Carrie walked into the destroyed apartment, bold as can be, assessing the scene.

No cops ran in behind them—instead, all the pieces of her shattered front door shivered then zipped through the air, reforming into a solid, unbroken hunk of wood.

She couldn't help it, her jaw dropped.

To her left, Glendower went rigid. He turned to face Gavin and Carrie, giving Frey his back, as if the couple were the larger threat.

"I was wondering if you two would reveal yourselves."

Gavin's frown went from icy to frigid as he stared down the professor. "What are you?"

"Professor Andrew Glendower. I've already met your pretty *cariad*."

"I know who you are." Gavin advanced, his long legs moving so gracefully, he hardly seemed to touch the ground. "I asked what—for the druids of old would not have wielded magick as you do."

Glendower's smile was all teeth. "This coming from a thief and a murderer. The magick is of Albion, I am of Albion. *You,* however . . ." The professor raised his hands, and a wave of magick burst out, blasting Gavin back a step and making his and Carrie's hair flutter behind them. "Let them see who you truly are."

Like wax dripping from a hot candle, the space around Carrie and Gavin melted, revealing—*holy shit!*

Gavin was somehow even taller and broader, his hair a long fall of silver. His skin had gone a grayish-purple that shone an iridescent pink-green in the light from the kitchen. Long, pointed ears with silver hoops and mercury eyes screamed *not human!*

And Carrie . . . Anna's jaw dropped again.

Carrie was *pink*.

She was still a blonde bombshell with gold eyes, but now two little horns and pointed ears poked out from her curls, wings hung over her shoulders, and a thin tail whipped behind her.

She's a gargoyle, too. Her coloring was so different from Frey, but all the characteristics were there.

"Holy shit."

She hadn't meant to say it aloud, but the sound drew Carrie's attention. She looked over Anna and the guard holding her, a frown darkening her face.

"What have you done to Anna? She's an innocent."

"You know as well as I do that she's a heartsong."

"Yes." With a flourish, Carrie brandished her hands, now sporting wicked claws. "Which makes her *clan.*"

"Whatever your plan, it's over," said Gavin.

Glendower sneered. "Just like a fae to think Albion and humans are yours to command. You and your kind are a blight on the realms—you lost Faerie, you can't have Albion."

"I don't want Albion," Gavin growled, revealing his own set of fangs, "but I will defend it from the likes of you."

"I'm going to *save it.* From you, from everyone," Glendower hissed, all that poise and charm gone now. The man who glared at Gavin was dangerous, his eyes bright with belief and desperation.

Throwing his hands at Gavin, Glendower tossed another volley of magick, this one crackling through the air. Gavin grunted and threw up his own wave, the two clashing with such force that everyone else staggered at the impact.

Seizing the chance, Anna stomped on her guard's instep and pulled out of his grip.

He grabbed for her, but Anna whirled away, running for the other side of the room. She didn't have any plan, just get to a corner to protect her back. She felt the guard on her heels, the vibration of his boots as they smacked the floor. Heat sizzled through the apartment as waves of magick clashed across the dining room table.

She threw herself into the corner, turning just in time to see the guard barreling down on her. He reached for her arm, but Anna knocked it away with one of the moves Frey had shown her, shocked she remembered. The guard went for her again, and she managed to avoid getting grabbed until he overwhelmed her with his greater size and strength.

In close, Anna did what needed to be done—she kneed him right in the junk.

The guard wheezed but didn't go down. His hold loosened just enough for Anna to pull her arms out of his grip and shove him away.

A pink, clawed hand appeared on his shoulder, and Anna watched, stunned, as Carrie flipped the guard over her shoulder and onto the ground. She stepped on his neck with her bare, elongated foot until he went still, her beautiful face pulled back in a fierce hiss.

Frey and the other guardian tangled across the living room, the remaining guards trying to help get him down, and Glendower and Gavin were having some sort of magical duel—leaving her in the corner to stare in amazement at Carrie.

"Hello, my dear," she said with a smile, "sorry for being late. Evening traffic, you understand."

Anna didn't understand anything, no, but could only bob her head in a nod.

"This is all a terrible shock to you, I'm sure. We'll explain everything, but for now, please know that Gavin and I are your friends." Closing the distance between them, Carrie took Anna's hands in her own and squeezed. "We're clan."

The words were said with such intensity, such longing, but they didn't freak her out the way Glendower's had.

At least *she* hadn't tried to strangle her.

Anna opened her mouth to say . . . something, but what came out was, "Behind you!"

Carrie whirled in time to catch the guard coming at them. Despite being shorter than the man, she caught his arm and stopped his strike. Her left wing came up and sucker punched him in the jaw as effectively as a fist, the wing claw raking across his cheek. Her fist came next, striking him in the windpipe.

The guard stumbled backward sputtering, and Carrie had no mercy. She leapt, wings pumping, and threw him to the ground, where she got behind him and locked her arm around his neck. Her legs and wings kept him immobile as she choked the air from him. The man's face went red and then purple, and Anna had to look away when his tongue lolled violently between his overstretched lips.

Carrie counted down from five in a soft mutter once the man went limp and then let him go.

"I hate hand-to-hand combat," she said. "Swordplay is much neater."

She lifted her brows, as if expecting Anna to offer her opinion. All she could do was nod at the scene behind them.

"Quite right. Stay here in the corner, this will be over soon."

Anna did as she was told, huddling with her back to the corner, and watched as Carrie raced for the two grappling gargoyles and handful of guards left standing. She barreled into the human men, freeing up

Frey to knock the obsidian gargoyle off of him.

A magical duel was going on in her dining room, blue sparks flying across the table into the kitchen, and three gargoyles were brawling in her living room. Anna didn't know where to look, going dizzy trying to keep up with it all.

Her gargoyle won out, Anna unable to look away from him long. His every move was powerful, meant to inflict damage, but her heart still lodged in her throat as she watched him fight. The odds were turning, but the insidious thought still crept in—*what if I lose him?*

No. Can't think it. Won't happen.

That didn't stop her worry, nor make her heart descend back into her chest. Anna clutched her arms around herself, head drooping with its own weight. God, just standing upright was an effort, and tears stung at her eyes. *Not now, not yet. Hold it together a little longer. He needs you to stay safe.*

Frey leapt upon Dragan, and while the big male tried to buck him off, he went for the collar around the obsidian male's throat. He slashed and pulled, baring his fangs in frustration.

"Only he can take it off," Dragan grated.

The look Frey gave him was full of pity, and the obsidian gargoyle roared to see it. They went rolling across the floor again, smashing her coffee table into tiny splinters.

With a flap of her wings, Carrie bounded after the other two and landed on the obsidian male's back. She locked her arms around his shoulders and hung on as he bucked.

"We can help you, Dragan!"

"Not yet," the big male rumbled, trying to throw Carrie off.

Carrie growled with frustration before lifting her head and calling to Gavin, "I think we're done here, my love!"

Gavin's face was terrifying, stark lines carved in his statuesque features. His gaze swung over the destruction, and his nostrils flared in a huff.

His body exploded with blue flame, the magick licking across the walls and ceiling. The smell of ozone saturated the apartment, nearly choking Anna. The sparks around Glendower winked out, and the professor crumpled to the floor.

"I'm done playing, *mwydyn*. Leave with your life and be grateful."

Anna's knees almost buckled with terror, the raw power rolling off of Gavin burning the back of her tongue.

Glendower pushed to his feet, glaring. "How many years have you had, and you still know nothing? All those guardians in that museum and not one has come to life. I've done in a year what you couldn't do in centuries."

Gavin's lip peeled back, and Anna knew now what a mouse felt like just before a hawk ripped it apart.

"Get out."

The professor sneered, then righted his coat and began at a steady but limping gait toward the door. "This isn't over," he said before unlocking and opening the door.

"If you value your life, it will be."

Glowering, Glendower said, "Dragan. Let's go."

The obsidian gargoyle's hands dropped to his sides and he turned to follow the professor out, no expression on his face. Carrie slid off his back before he reached the door, watching on sadly as he disappeared with Glendower.

The ruined apartment fell silent with their departure.

Anna couldn't quite believe it.

The shaking started in her hands and feet then worked its way up her limbs.

"F-Frey?"

"Anna!"

In a moment, he was there, pulling her into his arms. Anna collapsed against his chest, comforted by his familiar strength. The shaking only grew worse, but Frey held her tight, held her together. She clutched him close, wishing she could just bury herself inside him, meld them together and never come out.

The tears started next, though she didn't truly cry. Fat, salty tears stung her cheeks and cracked lips, and hiccups clogged her throat.

"I—I thought—"

"I know, I know, *fy nghân*. I have you. I'm here."

Even from the shelter of his body and over the sobs that wracked her, Anna heard the wail of sirens growing louder.

"Oh no," she groaned.

"We need to leave."

She looked up with a gasp to see Gavin standing there, just a step away. Frey growled, baring his fangs and covering her with his wings.

"*Fae,*" he hissed.

"Indeed. I'm sorry to meet like this, but we must leave. I cannot manipulate all the human authorities and neighbors."

"We'll go *nowhere* with you!" Frey roared.

"Frey." Anna peeked out from behind a wing to see Carrie standing beside her husband. She looked up at Frey with a sad sort of awe. "He took no part in what happened, you can trust him. He's my heartsong."

"I know you, but . . ." Frey's brows hung low, his eyes almost haunted as he stared at Carrie. "It cannot be."

"I wasn't at the Gorsedd that night, so the curse didn't take me. Gavren and I have spent the years searching for you, protecting you."

The wailing sirens grew louder, drawing Carrie's attention to the windows. Blue and red lights flashed from the street.

"We'll explain everything, but please, come with us now. You'll be safe."

"We've been told that already tonight," Anna said.

Carrie gave her a sad smile. "No restraint required. You two are clan. I can't . . ." Her eyes glistened, and Gavin tucked her into his side as she wiped at a stray tear. "I can't tell you what it means to me to have clan. Please, allow us to explain. Let us show you."

Frey's rumble beneath her cheek was unhappy but not threatening. He looked down at her, holding her cheek in his palm. "It's up to you, my Anna."

"She did ask nicely."

Gavin nodded. "We'll go, then."

"What about . . .?" Anna nodded at the unconscious guards littered around her destroyed apartment. She didn't quite know if she meant the men or all her broken things.

Yeah, they were only things, but they were *hers*. This was her home. In a matter of minutes, everything she'd collected and earned throughout her was literally shattered. She could hardly look at it.

"Tomorrow's problem, I think," said Gavin, his expression softening as he looked upon Anna. "I can repair most of it."

She didn't think she could ever forget how his eyes had glowed and magick had burned around him, like he was some pagan god risen from the underworld, but that small bit of compassion in his gaze now went a long way.

Frey moved to pick her up, but Anna's stomach dropped when she realized—"Wait, where's Captain? We can't leave without him! Frey—" She heard the hysterical note in her voice, and clutched at her middle as it shook. The adrenaline crash had her stomach revolting and she didn't want to stay here any longer, but she couldn't bear the idea of leaving without Cappy.

"I know, I'll get him. He's in the bedchamber. Just stay here. Stay right here, I'll be right back." He pressed a fervent kiss to her forehead before rushing to her bedroom.

She watched on desperately, feeling herself cracking around the edges now that his arms weren't around her. A breath finally invaded her lungs when Frey emerged a moment later carrying a terrified Captain. The yellow of his eyes was almost hidden by his blown pupils.

Frey ducked into the bathroom and returned holding both Captain and a migraine injection. "For your head."

More tears burst out, and with a sob she said, "I love you so much, Frey."

A devastating smile overtook his mouth. "I have loved you for millennia, my Anna, and will love you longer still." He held out Captain, and she was able to unlock her arms to take him. Captain sank his claws into her shoulder, but she didn't care.

"Now, you hold Captain," Frey swept her into his arms, holding her bridal style and covering her and Cappy with a wing up to her chin like a blanket, "and I'll hold you."

Burying her face against him, she kissed the side of his neck, feeling his strong pulse thrum under her lips.

"This will feel strange the first time, but it's perfectly safe," Gavin assured them.

She peered at Gavin just in time to see a rip open in the middle of her apartment, splitting the very air. Within it, every color swirled and light bent in every direction.

Carrie gave them a reassuring smile. "Traveling through the rift is a bit uncomfortable, but it beats Bay traffic!" Turning on the ball of her foot, she accepted the hand Gavin offered and stepped through into the colors and light. They enveloped her, and it almost looked like she passed through a doorway into another room.

"Where does it lead?" asked Frey.

"To our house in Tiburon," answered Gavin.

"Will it hurt?" Frey's arms tightened around her at her question. She didn't think she could handle any more pain today, and the thought of Cappy in pain had more tears rolling down her face.

"No, I promise. It's just . . . different."

She breathed a big sigh through her nose. "Story of my life lately."

"Hold on tight," Frey told her, then stepped out of her apartment and through the portal.

Frey didn't enjoy the sensation of being ripped apart then put back together again in the space of two steps. His very cells vibrated with energy as he carried Anna through the portal to the other side, a kinetic energy that gathered and zipped through his viscera.

The other side of the portal was a sumptuous living space. His feet met shiny hardwood floor, and as he fully exited the rift, he turned to see a multitude of plush furniture taking up the spacious room.

It had familiar elements to Anna's dwelling—a TV, a couch, a coffee table. But where Anna's things were small and cozy, these pieces were almost grand, the sofa making three sides of a rectangle and the coffee table nearly as long as the dining table in Anna's dwelling. Soft blankets and pillows littered the sofa, and the TV spanned much of the wall it was mounted to over a handsome mantel and hearth. Glittering trinkets decorated the mantel, shimmering crystals and colorful glass and clusters of pinecones.

Yet, with its dark woods on the floor and ceiling, the space felt cavernous in a way that appealed to Frey. It reminded him of their clanhome by the sea and the pitched roofs of the Pritani halls.

Warm light spilled from several lamps and a cluster of tall candles on a side table under a set of diamond-patterned windows. Haloed in this light stood the female gargoyle, a woman he'd known in another life.

Frey heard the fae step through the portal, and the rift closed behind him. For a long moment, the three of them stood silently as Anna held very still in his arms.

The first to speak was Captain, voicing a curious chirp as he poked his little head out from under Frey's wing.

The female gargoyle smiled softly as she carefully approached.

Frey's heart seized in his chest. The light wasn't over-bright and she had aged in some ways, around the eyes and her wings had grown a little larger in the way they did when their kind aged. But he remembered her pink face with its golden striations, like rosy marble, and he most assuredly remembered her wings, small and malformed.

"Carys?"

Her smile widened, revealing her fangs, and she gently reached up to cup his face in her hand. Candlelight caught in the tears welling along her lashes as she gazed upon him, and a bittersweet ache lodged between his ribs.

"I can hardly believe it," she murmured, voice gone thick.

"You escaped that night?"

"I was never there. My mother . . ." An old pain creased her brows, and Frey remembered well how Carys's mother berated her.

Arda had been a bitter woman who took that unhappiness out on her youngest, smallest daughter. He was ashamed to admit it, but sometimes he'd look upon them and, even with Carys's bruises and defeated eyes, thought, *At least you have your mother*. It was an ugly feeling, and he was ashamed of it now; Arda hadn't been one of those cursed, which meant she was one of those slain. And . . . she hadn't been a kind mother.

The fae appeared beside Carys, tucking her into his side again. The movement was so fluid, so easy, it spoke to a couple familiar and comfortable in their bond.

"I raced to the glen, but I was too late." Her face grew sad, and while Frey harbored a small jealousy that she hadn't been cursed, he also couldn't imagine what being the last would've been like. Hellish.

Of all the guardians in their clan, Carys was the last one he expected to survive. When no one in their collective consciousness sensed her, it was assumed she, like her mother and sister, had perished by fae blade or beast. A small thing for a gargoyle, she'd been born with misshapen wings that made flight impossible. Soft where their kind was hard, Carys had studied under the Pritani druids rather than train as a warrior.

A few years younger than himself, Frey hadn't paid much attention to the little pink female. When the years passed and neither of them found a heartsong, he'd found himself looking a little more. Yet, he'd never hoped it was her. There was something delicate about her then, something utterly breakable that terrified him. *No, I need a strong, fiery mate,* he'd told himself.

In many ways, that's exactly what he'd gotten, too. His Anna was strong in her own ways, and he thanked all the ancestors for her. Looking at Carys now, though, he had a new admiration for her. If what she'd said was true, that the fae was her heartsong, then it meant they had been alive all this time. Not everyone could have weathered as she apparently had. He didn't . . . think he'd survive being left behind.

"We'll tell you our story, then we're anxious to hear yours. But first, some tea, I think," said the fae.

Wiping at her eyes, Carys nodded. "Tea would be lovely. Please, make yourselves comfortable."

"Thank you," said Frey, "but I wouldn't want to stain your fine things."

Anna gasped from his arms. "Ohmigod! Frey! You were wounded!" She squirmed as if to be let go, but Frey held her tight. Frowning at him, she protested, "We need to see to the cuts. You were bleeding!"

"I would rather you be seen to," he said, "your head and your neck . . ." The memory of witnessing his Anna be strangled with magick would haunt him the rest of his days, and the bruises already darkening her throat set him to rumbling unhappily.

Anna shook her head. "No, you're the one who's bleeding."

The fae held up his hands. "We can see to both of you." With a flick of his wrist, more lights came on. "If you will allow me to see . . ."

The rumble turned into a growl when the fae reached for Anna.

"I'll rip your throat out if you try to hurt her," he warned.

The fae's gaze flicked up to his, cool and assessing. "Likewise."

He held the fae's stare for a long moment. The quicksilver shine of his eyes was unnerving, as was the way raw magick saturated the space around him. But if he looked past that, what Frey found was another male protective of his own heartsong yet willing to help Anna.

"What are you called?" Frey asked.

After a moment of considering, the fae said, "Gavren will do fine."

"We've had many names through the centuries," said Carys. She held out a finger for Captain to sniff and then scratched his ears when he bopped her hand. "But to clan, I will always be Carys."

"So you're not Gavin and Carrie Gwyneth, huh?" said Anna.

"We are. But to you, we are just Carys and Gavren. Clanmates. So please, let my heartsong heal you. We have experience treating human patients."

"You did tell me you were doctors before," Anna said in good humor. "Though you never did say in *which* war."

One side of Carys's mouth kicked up in a rueful grin. "Too many, I'm afraid. You humans have a penchant for harming one another. Now, let Gavren see to you and I'll make that tea."

Twenty minutes later, Frey sat with Anna in his lap, each of them nursing a mug of milky tea. The scent of lavender and honey billowed from the steam, and the drink slipped down Frey's throat in a silky slide that soothed his very soul. Carys had laid out a plate of what she called biscuits that were hard and crumbly but went perfectly soft when dipped into the tea.

The magick that had healed them still tingled against his freshly knitted skin. His kind healed quickly already, but after explaining that he could coax the magick inherent in Frey to speed things up, Gavren had reached out with his own magick and, in a blink, the slashes and punctures had begun to close.

He'd decided to let the fae treat him first before touching his Anna. It was a little difficult since he refused to let Anna down, even as she protested that she could stand, but the fae had made the best of it and done his work without comment. Frey didn't wield magick the way Gavren or Glendower could, but there was still a well of it inside him, inside every guardian. That Gavren merely guided and augmented that source to heal him assuaged some of Frey's fears.

When it came to treating Anna, the fae made quick work of her neck but lingered over her head. "I can dull this headache but not get rid of the problem entirely. It's something inherent in how your brain is formed, and I haven't done enough reading to feel comfortable rooting around in there with magick. My specialty is in combat triage, but I'll do some research into neurology."

Frey and Anna had looked on with stunned appreciation, and she slumped in his arms with relief when the headache eased.

The four of them now sat around the large sofa, Carys and Gavren having stripped off their body armor and Frey divested of his ripped, bloodied shirt. They all sipped tea and watched as Captain explored the plush expanse. Despite his fright in the apartment, the cat seemed to be curious about their new surroundings, and Anna was content to let him roam when Carys and Gavren both let him climb over them and gave him affectionate pets.

Frey took a few bites of his biscuit and then gave Anna the rest, not content until she'd eaten three and drunk at least half of her tea. He worried that she'd missed dinner, but she insisted she wasn't hungry, after everything.

"Well," sighed Carys, setting down her mug, "I suppose we should start at the beginning."

"The night of the Gorsedd," Frey said, pulling Anna a little tighter to his chest in preparation for hearing about the horrible night.

"Even further back. Our story, Gavren's and mine, and the guardians', is intertwined with the fae."

Frey's lips thinned with displeasure, but he held his tongue when Anna patted his chest under his wing. So, setting aside his anger, he listened.

With solemnity, Gavren recounted the long history of his kind. How the seven realms were full of many beings and worlds, Faerie being one of them. Blessed by the goddess Danu, the fae were the only beings known to be able to cross between realms. They often visited Albion, the human realm closest to theirs, and many different human cultures revered them as gods.

But in a dark, watery realm waited the Fomorians, the ancient foe of the fae. Jealous of their powers and magick, the Fomorians broke free into Albion. The fae fought long, vicious wars over Albion, for it was the only realm standing between the Fomorians and Faerie.

Although generations of fae held them back, the Fomorians were relentless in their hunger. They toppled civilizations from the sea, flooded villages and temples, and ate away at the very fabric of Albion. Eventually, even the fae couldn't hold them back.

Consuming magick itself, the Fomorians grew stronger, bolder. Faerie was breached, and soon after, destroyed. The Faerie Queen Rhiannon couldn't stop it, but in an effort to save her people, she led them into the Underhill, the realm under all the others. A place of caves and roots and shadow, the fae sought sanctuary in its darkness.

Yet it was a trap of their own making. To defend against the pursuing Fomorians, Queen Rhiannon had used the magick of every fae to seal all the empty spaces of the Underhill, closing it off to all the other realms. Rhiannon's own sister, Lady Morrígan, sacrificed herself to the spell, and many believed her dead. The fae were safe from the Fomorians—and trapped inside the Underhill.

Over the years, the Underhill grew restless, wary of the intruders inside it and hungry for more magick to shore up its defenses. Fae were lost to the darkness, their magick consumed. Queen Rhiannon took to the eternal sleep to appease the Underhill and search for ways to break free. In her absence, her vain niece Titania ruled the remaining fae.

"It was her cruel mind that thought to take the magick used to create the guardians," explained Gavren.

"Our kind was created with blood, earth, and magick," said Carys. "Over the years visiting Albion, the fae imbued it with their magick. Titania believed that the magick was hers, that having it would somehow combat the Underhill. That night, she led a hunt."

"A royal fae like Titania can command vast power, enough to break free of the Underhill for a brief period during those rare times when the realms draw closer."

"Beltane," said Frey, the pieces beginning to come together.

Gavren nodded. "She was wrong, however. Magick isn't inert, it's always adapting. It'd been imbued so long, it wasn't fae anymore. It was of Albion, and therefore couldn't be reclaimed rightfully. So she stole it with a curse."

"Curses have rules, though. One of which being that the cursed must hear it. Not being at the Gorsedd that night, I wasn't affected," said Carys.

"If the fae are trapped in the Underhill, how did you two meet, then? And why aren't there Fomorians still on Earth?" asked Anna. Her brows were drawn low in a confused frown, and Frey rubbed the pad of one finger across the line between them, making her release the tension. No need to incur another headache.

"The Fomorians gorged on the magick of Faerie for a long while. They became slow, complacent. When humans sailed for the Green Isles, they were able to overpower the Fomorians by sheer numbers. Humans don't have magick, so there was nothing for the Fomorians to sustain themselves. Those that weren't slaughtered were driven back into their water realm, and the rip they'd made between the realms was sealed."

"How?"

"With magick and great stones, placed in a circle to secure the passage. I believe you call the place Stone Henge now."

"Holy fuck," Anna wheezed.

"As to how we met," continued Gavren, nonplussed, "it was by accident."

Carys returned his warm smile, and their hands found each other to hold. "There are weak points in the Underhill, where the fae inside can see out to other realms. I found Gavren looking up from the bottom of a well one day, and we got to talking. He found me after the attack at the Gorsedd and again when I camped at Llyn Tegid that summer."

"So you two met right around when the guardians were cursed? Wasn't that in, like, the sixth century? That would make you guys . . ."

"Ancient," Carys agreed. "We've lived many centuries now."

Anna cursed in wonder again under her breath, echoing Frey's own astonishment.

Gavren slipped his arm around his mate's shoulders, careful of her wings. "My people are long-lived, yes. We also have a mate fated for us, a *cariad,* chosen by the goddesses. I suspect it is a trait passed to the guardians as a residual in the magick used to give them life. Because she is my *cariad,* Carys was able to free me of the Underhill and tie her life to mine. She acts as an anchor to my magick, untethering it from the Underhill. I have a theory that this will be the key to breaking the curse."

"What do you mean?" asked Anna.

"The magick that gives the guardians life is trapped within the Underhill. If a *cariad,* a heartsong, is found to act as an anchor, I have hope that this will break the curse, at least for that individual."

"You both seem to be proof of it," chimed Carys, gracing them with another wide smile.

Anna shifted in his lap. "But it's not fully broken. The curse. He turns to stone during the day."

Carys's eyes went wide in surprise, and Gavren's frown deepened. "That's unfortunate. So all this time, you've returned to stone in the daylight?" he asked.

"Yes. Though as I've spent more time with Anna, I've woken earlier each night. It's only by a few minutes, but it may be slowly releasing me."

Carys and Gavren shared a look, a wealth of feeling passing between them. Frey didn't know if the fae were able to communicate in their mates' minds or if the two of them had been together so long that they could read even the smallest expressions in the other's face, but a whole conversation was had in the span of a few seconds.

"It could be that the curse didn't completely break because the anchor isn't fully in place. I have a theory, but I would hear how this all came about."

Taking the last sip of her tea, Anna explained about the night of the heist, how touching Frey had brought him to life. She described their first flight, as well as seeing him turn to stone the next morning. Frey didn't enjoy it but told of how it felt to fall back into the stone sleep with each day, and both Carys and Gavren's faces filled with sympathy.

Anna then told them of how Glendower had come into the museum often, asking strange questions. Frowns adorned Carys and her fae heartsong as they listened to the troubles and surveillance that had followed Anna over the past weeks.

"I thought it was all the cops," Anna said, "I thought you guys suspected I was in on the heist."

Carys's face fell. "We never thought that. We were horrified that it even happened in the first place. We underestimated Glendower—but we've never encountered another like him. The druids were destroyed."

"I'm sorry about the listening device, for accusing you." Anna blew out a breath. "I can't believe that was just this afternoon."

"I'm glad you found it and are safe now. Everything the man did disgusts me." She grew even pinker in her vehemence. "I followed you from the museum and saw when they grabbed you. I was horrified!"

"We've been looking into Glendower's past but haven't discovered much. He's independently wealthy and tenured at Stanford. He owns several properties in the state and in Wales. What his plans are, though, we have no idea. What he did today was a surprise."

"He must have felt like he had to move, since I found the bug and was quitting."

"Most likely," Gavren agreed gravely. "All we can do now is make safe the other guardians and monitor his activities."

"Poor Dragan," murmured Carys. She met Frey's gaze, and they shared a solemn moment of sadness for their captured clanmate.

"Not long after freeing Gavren, we returned to the Gorsedd glen and gathered those of you we could. Many had been taken. We've spent the centuries looking for you." She hurried through the words, as if what she said gave her pain.

Frey remembered sensing earth around him, as if his stone self had been toppled into the dirt for a time, but the majority of his confinement to the stone sleep had been spent in various shelters with other clanmates. It made the interminable time bearable, to be kept with kin.

"We sensed it, being together," he told her. "Thank you for keeping us safe."

"It's been my honor."

"We didn't know much, but we knew we were together. We were able to share what we learned. We heard the music you played us, felt the sunlight in our room."

Her eyes went wide. "You . . . could speak to each other?"

"In a sense. Inside, we're still sentient. Many have retreated deep inside the collective consciousness for comfort. We can sense one another, communicate."

"That's . . . I didn't know." Tears spilled from Carys's eyes. "I just wish we'd been able to do more. All these years—we've gathered many of you, but there are still some missing. A few have been destroyed. And now Dragan is taken. Yet the two of you are the only ones we know of who have woken. We've tried everything, I swear to you, we've *tried*."

Gavren gripped her hand tight as Carys began to weep. She turned into her mate's body for comfort, and Gavren held her tightly. For his part, Frey gripped his own mate tight, and they sat in silence, unwilling to interrupt Carys's grief.

When her tears slowed, Gavren fished a handkerchief from his pocket and wiped her tears.

"We've been waiting for you for centuries," he told Frey. "Why now, after all these years, we don't know or understand, but we're grateful."

"I want to do right by the clan," insisted Carys.

"You have," Frey hurried to tell her. "You've kept us safe, sheltered. You provided for us. And tonight, you came to our aid. I owe you a debt for saving my heartsong."

"You owe us nothing," said Gavren firmly. "Especially not when the two of you could be what finally breaks the curse. With what you've said, I believe the problem lies in Frey having an incomplete anchor to Albion. Perhaps this will grow naturally with the mate bond. Yet, I wonder if it couldn't be hastened."

Carys's brows arched. "The ritual?"

"Yes. My kind has a mating ritual, a ceremony with rites to tie our magicks together. This is what anchored me to Carys and freed me of the Underhill. I wonder if it would work for you."

"What would we have to do?" asked Anna.

Frey held very still under her, unable to determine her thoughts from her neutral tone. The idea of having a way to reclaim the day, to have all of his Anna, was just as tempting as Glendower's collar, if not more. Yet, he couldn't help worrying if Anna would hesitate or not wish to go through with such a ritual.

He knew she cared for him, had told him she *loved* him, but was that enough? Could he ask it of her if she was uncertain?

"It's a simple ritual. Just requires the right words and physical connection. Whenever you're ready, just repeat the incantation. It could take a moment for the magick to anchor." And Gavren slipped into a language far more ancient than any of them sitting there, reciting words that settled in Frey's bones and made his soul tremble.

Frey wasn't sure how he was supposed to remember a fae incantation, but when he thought of the words, they appeared in his mind, flowing from one to the next as easily as a summer stream flowed from the mountain.

"And what does it all mean?" Anna asked.

"That to each other you pledge your troth, your loyalty, your love. That you forsake all others and bind yourselves together. That they are your home and you are theirs."

"*Dwi adref*," Frey murmured.

Anna's eyes jumped up to him, and he smiled for her. "*Dwi adref*," he whispered in her ear before kissing her temple. "Whenever you're ready, *fy nghân*."

"I love you, Frey," she whispered back.

He wanted to soak in the words, but part of him worried that she said it rather than the incantation. They were both tired, he reminded himself, and too much had been asked of Anna already today. There would be time. They would have time.

"There is one last thing I must admit," said Gavren. "I hope the ritual works for you as it did for us. I want it for you and for my mate's people. I want it for my own as well. I have hope that as more guardians discover their mates and break the curse, that much more magick will be untethered from the Underhill."

"You want to break your people out," guessed Anna.

"Yes. Before escaping myself, Queen Rhiannon told me that her sister, Morrigan, hadn't died when we fled Faerie. She gave everything to the spell to keep out the Fomorians and had to take the eternal sleep, but she was outside the Underhill when she did. I must find her, and together, with the Underhill weakened, I hope to free my kind."

An echoing silence met Gavren's declaration, and Frey tried to swallow it. His soul raged against the idea of letting out the very monsters who cursed his people. Part of him took ugly pleasure in hearing of their suffering inside their own prison.

And yet . . . and yet.

The haunted way Gavren spoke of life in the Underhill called to the pieces still broken inside Frey from centuries of stone sleep. He knew what it was to wither, to watch his people fade away from despair.

He wished it on no one. Not even the fae.

"I will help how I can," he said, meeting Gavren's gaze. A promise. "It is the way of clan."

"Thank you," the fae said, simple and with feeling.

Captain jumped into Anna's lap and made himself comfortable. His happy purrs resounded through the living room as they all watched him knead Anna's chest.

"I reckon that's enough for one night. You both look exhausted. We have extra bedrooms in the house, but there's also a guesthouse on the property. We'd be delighted if you stayed there."

"We'd appreciate it," said Anna, "but I need to go back to my apartment."

"We'll go tomorrow," agreed Gavren, "and see what can be salvaged. We can move anything you want to keep through a rift easily."

"Oh, but . . ."

"I meant what I said, Anna," Carys said gently. "We want you to stay. There is plenty of room for both of you here."

"I appreciate the offer, but I can't exactly afford Tiburon rent."

Carys sat back in her seat, looking offended. "Who said anything about rent? You'll stay with us as clan. Family. We have the space and the means, we don't need your money."

Anna blinked. "But . . ."

Waving away her concerns, Carys said, "No, I won't hear of it. You'll stay with us as long as you like. The guesthouse has sat empty since we purchased this property."

"We've spent our years building a life for ourselves but also preparing," added Gavren. "We wanted to ensure our people had everything they needed to begin again."

"Which reminds me—I hope you'll stay on at the museum, but I also would love to have your help cataloging our collection."

"But . . . the museum is already cataloged?"

Carys grinned patiently. "The museum is a fraction of what we have. We've lived a long life, and I'm afraid some of our things have gotten away from me. I'd appreciate the help cataloging everything to assess what we have." Leaning forward, she said in a conspiratorial whisper, "Mostly I need someone to help me figure out spreadsheets. I can't make heads or tails of them."

"Yeah, I—" Anna blushed at how loud her voice went. "I could help you with that."

"And Frey, I can offer you a position at a new security firm I'm establishing," said Gavren. "It's in the beginning stages now, but I aim to use magick to enhance the digital security suite. For now, it would mostly be guarding the museum as I work out the details, but you'd be near your mate."

Frey's ears perked, but he couldn't help but point out, "And what would your human guests think of a guardian walking amongst the statues?"

"I'll need to experiment, but I believe I can make you something to glamour you. Carys and I use glamour to blend in with humans, but she is able to do it because she is my *cariad*. For you, we can attempt to make something that you control with your own magick."

It all was too much of a temptation. Not only could he spend his days with Anna, he could have a position, a purpose, and therefore the means to take care of his mate. That made Gavren's offer priceless.

He would ask more questions and learn more about what would be expected of him tomorrow—for now, he reached across the low table and clasped forearms with Gavren.

"I accept."

Carys clapped her hands and rose from the sofa. "Excellent. Now, time for bed. Let's get you two set up and comfortable. There will be time yet for more questions."

As they all stood, Frey steadying Anna as she swayed with fatigue, Carys paused in front of them, her face glowing with happiness.

"Welcome home."

34

Anna woke before dawn, groggy and in an unfamiliar bed. She blinked blearily into the inky blue darkness, running her hand along a silky-soft duvet as the events of yesterday slowly came back. Carys, Gavren, the attack, everything.

Holy guacamole.

There wasn't really anything better to say other than *mind blown.* It was one bombshell truth after another, and the only way Anna had been able to cope was to just nod along and tell herself she'd think about it later.

Well, it was later, and her brain was almost short-circuiting again with everything they'd learned. She still couldn't quite believe she'd been snatched off the street by a crazy, magick-wielding history professor, and rubbed her neck with the memory of that magick coiling around her throat. It'd be a while before the memory dulled, and she shuddered remembering the cold, tight press of it on her skin.

"*Cân fy nghalon,* go back to sleep." Warm lips kissed her hair, and a wing spread across her like a blanket. Frey's familiar scent surrounded her as he leaned over her, and Anna burrowed closer to his warmth.

She'd barely gotten one foot in front of the other as Carys led them through a lush courtyard to a quaint guesthouse. Anna hadn't seen much of it, so tired her eyes stung, and Frey was quick to whisk her off to bed once Carys bid them goodnight. Anna hadn't wanted to fall asleep, needing to talk things over with Frey and see what he thought of all this, but the moment he pulled back the covers, she'd been done for.

"Don't wanna sleep," she mumbled.

"It's still dark, and you've been through too much. I'm keeping watch. Rest."

Rooting around on the duvet, she found and clutched his hand, pulling him down to her. "Only if you lay with me."

"You make a compelling argument."

"I know. You wanna be big spoon or little spoon?"

"Big spoon."

The large bed dipped and the duvet rasped as he climbed in beside her. Captain sat up from where he'd been sleeping in the crook of Anna's bent knees, yawning wide as he waited for them to settle. Anna pulled Frey's arm around her and hugged it to her chest as the other slid under her head to support it. Comfy and cozy, Captain draped himself over Frey's flank.

The room settled back into a soft quiet. Anna traced patterns on Frey's forearm, her mind tumbling through the revelations faster than she could keep up with.

"The house went quiet soon after you fell asleep," Frey reported. "They seem to be sleeping, and I haven't noticed any other threats. But say the word and we'll leave, *fy nghân*."

"Where would we go?"

An anxious pause, and the tendons of his forearm tensed. "I'm not sure. But I'm in no mood to gamble with your safety."

"Do you want to leave?"

A heavy sigh fluttered her hair. "No. I knew Carys, before. She has always been unfailingly kind. Even in the stone sleep, we could all sense we were together in a safe place. That she took care of us for all this time . . ."

Anna rubbed soothingly along Frey's arm when his voice went

thick. "Yeah, I've always liked her. Even when I was suspicious, thinking it was them and the police behind the surveillance, I didn't want to believe she'd do that. And Gavren's always been intimidating, but I don't feel threatened by him."

"Strangely . . . neither do I. I'm not sure I can fully trust a fae, at least not yet, but I suppose time will tell."

"Did you . . . want to stay here? With them?"

"You must ask yourself that, my Anna. I go where you go."

"Yeah, but . . ." She blew out a breath. "Your opinion matters."

Frey pulled her in tight to his chest and kissed behind her ear. "You are my home. You are always where I'll be."

Blinking back tears, Anna kissed his broad, scarred knuckles. "I love my apartment, but . . . it doesn't feel safe anymore." She shivered remembering how trashed it'd been in the struggle, and even if Gavren could magick everything back together, Anna wasn't sure she'd ever be able to be comfortable there again.

Frey rumbled. "I understand. It was your home, a place you built yourself."

"Yeah. I know it's just stuff, but I worked hard to build that life."

"Your effort isn't diminished by starting anew. I know it's scary, but beginning again can be done. And I'll be with you through it all."

Anna's heart ached for him; he'd already lost so much. Her apartment was all he'd really known of the modern world, and having to lose his family, his home, his life twice over even before stepping foot in her apartment would've broken weaker souls.

She hadn't had any plans to move out of her apartment; the rent was doable, the location was excellent, and everything she'd worked for was contained in that little space. Maybe one day she'd move to a bigger place, but she hadn't truly ever considered it before Frey.

She hadn't thought of a lot of things before Frey.

He'd changed her life in so many ways, overwhelmingly for the better. She wanted a life with him, and if that meant starting fresh, in a place that worked for both of them, Anna knew she could do it. He was worth it.

"We can always find a place of our own if it gets weird being here," she said, to herself as much as Frey.

"Of course, *fy nghân.* You are resourceful, you'll find us the perfect place."

Anna laughed. "I mean, I'll do my best. I doubt I'll be able to beat out here, though. Tiburon is pretty darn nice, and it's really close to the coast. You should be able to fly without being seen."

"I like that. I like the possibility of having a position as well. I want to spoil you."

She blushed from her toes to her ears. Months with this guy and he still had her blushing like a tea kettle.

"You already do." Flipping to her other side, she pressed a kiss to his chin. "You're so good to me. I don't . . ."

Frey rumbled in warning, and he lifted her face with a knuckle under her chin. "You deserve everything and more, my Anna. It is my duty and my honor to provide, cherish, and *spoil* you, for I've asked much of you already and will ask more."

"You want to do the ritual."

"Yes. I want to be bound to you. I want the day."

Anna pulled in a long, fortifying breath. None of that was a surprise, of course. She'd felt how he went still under her when Gavren had first explained the ritual and how it'd bound him to Carys, freeing him of his prison. She wanted that for Frey, she did, but the idea sounded more permanent than marriage and even more serious than soulmates or heartsongs. It wasn't just promises and good intentions.

"You're unsure," Frey said, his voice carefully neutral.

"Yes and no." She couldn't help grinning when he made a face at her non-answer. "I'm just scared of big things, I guess. I never . . . I couldn't have imagined I'd find anyone like you."

"I should think not," he said with a grin, "since you humans have forgotten about my kind."

She stuck her tongue out at him. "You know what I mean."

"I know." He swooped in, capturing her lips in a slow, delicious kiss that made her breathing and heart rate pick up speed.

"I love you, my Anna. Not just as a heartsong but Anna. I am grateful every day that it's your touch that woke me, that it's to you I'm bound—ritual or no."

"I love you, too. More than I ever thought possible." Running her fingertips along his face, she pushed some of his thick mane behind the point of his ear.

God, she really did love him, so much it hurt. But then, growth usually came with some growing pains, and Frey had expanded her heart, her life. She'd had her reasons to avoid anything serious with him, but those reasons had long since gone silent. Did it mean she wasn't scared? Hell no. This was so big, and there was still the very real threat of Andrew Glendower out there. Who knew what his plans were or when he might reappear. And now she'd been pulled into a world of magick and fae and gargoyles—definitely not for the faint of heart.

And Anna wasn't. She wasn't faint of heart.

Because Frey was her heart.

He was surly, moody, flirty, and just as stubborn as her. Sure, it sometimes made her want to throttle him or throw her hands up in a huff, but she also loved it. He was too stubborn to give up on her.

Every day he showed her what it meant for her to be his heartsong. He took care of her, took care of Captain. He *cared*. When she was brave enough to let him in, let him care, it was . . . amazing. It took practice, and even now, laying with him in the soft darkness, part of her was reluctant to agree to the ritual.

That part deserved acknowledgement; it was borne of disappointments and struggles. Those would always be part of her. She wasn't always proud of the things she'd done, but she'd survived, and she was damn proud of that. It helped her believe, a little more every day, that she was someone who could be loved. Who deserved to be loved.

So no, it wasn't a quick and easy decision. Anna didn't know if she'd ever be someone spontaneous, someone who could jump into big things head first without much thought. And that was okay. It was okay to be scared—she just wouldn't let it define her anymore.

"Let's do it."

Frey's hand stopped where it'd been making circles on her back.

"Anna . . . we can wait. I want you to be sure."

"I'm sure, I promise. You're my person, Frey. I want to be with you."

With a rumbling groan, Frey's head fell to hers, taking her in a hungry, desperate kiss. Slipping her arms around his neck, Anna pulled him close, throwing a leg over his hip.

Gavren did say to have physical contact.

She wanted to fuse them together; if seeing him fight and get hurt had done anything, it was to confirm for her that he was more important than anything else. He was it. So she couldn't get close enough, needing to hold onto him with everything she was and could be.

"It may not even work," Frey said between kisses.

"It better work! I don't go reciting fae incantations for just anyone."

Smoothing her hair back from her face, Frey looked upon her in a way that was so soft, so full of love, it nearly melted her. She still wanted to shy away from such looks, but she made herself look back. Accepting what he offered, what he meant to her, would take practice, but it was worth it. He was sure of her, and she had to trust that he knew his own mind and heart—just as he had to trust that she knew hers, too.

The ball of his throat bobbed as he swallowed nervously. "Do you remember the words?"

"Weirdly, yes? I didn't think I would, but they've stuck in my mind. Like . . . magick."

One side of his mouth kicked up in a rueful grin. "Indeed." He kissed her again, and she could taste his nerves. They stood on the edge of a precipice—but Anna knew he'd catch her. Always.

"You're ready?" he whispered.

In answer, Anna began reciting the incantation, the words pouring from her lips like water. She didn't know what she said, but she understood. She chose Frey. She accepted him, loved him, and promised to do her best for him. She would care for him, make a home with him, build a life with him. She gave herself to him and accepted him in return.

Frey shuddered as the words settled around them as if they carried physical weight. Little sparks seemed to pass between them, and his voice rumbled through the thick air, repeating the incantation. The words sank inside her, filling her with an ancient promise—of family, clan, and home. That she would never be alone again.

Tears welled along her lashes and the hairs on her arms stood on end as he spoke the last words. Static crackled through the room, sending Captain bounding off the bed. Anna's skin tingled as something passed over her. Like the soft weight of a down comforter, it settled around her, a warm, comforting press. It kissed her lips before sinking into her skin.

Then, silence.

Anna and Frey lay there, holding each other as they shivered with the aftermath.

They didn't speak, for what could be said after such ancient words?

Slowly, dawn light began to gather in the sky. The room brightened in a colorless haze, and Anna gripped Frey's hands, her heart in her throat.

Please, let it have worked.

The two of them lay still, not wanting to be the first to look away at the brightening sky, but eventually Frey sighed. Giving her one last kiss, he pushed off the bed to stand before the sliding glass door that led out into the verdant courtyard.

Anna sat up, stomach knotting with nerves.

She told herself it'd worked. And even if it hadn't, they'd try again. The curse would be broken, she wouldn't accept otherwise.

The muscles of his wide back began to bunch with tension, and his hands balled into fists at his sides. Slipping from the bed, Anna padded across the room and threw her arms around his middle. She fit snugly between his wings, and she pressed her cheek to his back, hearing the drum of his heart. It thumped quickly, nervously, and she squeezed him tight.

It felt as though she held her breath for hours, but really it could only have been a few minutes. She couldn't seem to get air in her chest, so tightly clenched was it with anxiety.

The sun crested over the garden wall.

Frey tugged at her hands, trying to get her to release her arms.

"In case—"

"No," she said. "It'll work."

She knew when the sun fully rose by Frey's shudder. For one horrible moment, he went stiff, and she almost yelped in despair. Then he went slack in her arms, buckling. He caught himself with a hand on the door, and Anna hurried around to get her shoulder under his arm.

He looked out onto the courtyard garden with wonder.

Anna's face dripped happy tears before she even knew she cried.

"Good morning, sweetheart," she whispered.

Frey pulled his gaze away to look at her, the sweetest, most heart-wrenching smile breaking across his face. His eyes widened, the gray gone almost blue in the sunlight, and he touched her face with a trembling hand.

"Look at you," he murmured. "*Fy enaid hoff cytûn prydferth.*"

Frey's soul filled with sunshine as he beheld his Anna for the first time in daylight. *Goddesses, she is beautiful.* Strands of gold and red flickered in her hair, and freckles he'd never noticed before dotted her nose and cheeks.

He knew his Anna, had touched and tasted and explored every bit of her, and yet there was a whole new part now to discover—Anna in the sunlight. The artificial lights of her dwelling, although bright, didn't do her justice. His heart ached to see just what a vision she made, tears spilling down her beautiful smiling face.

He held her close, not quite believing yet that the sun warmed his skin. Any moment now, the stone sleep would creep across his body, stealing him away from his heartsong. And yet . . . and yet . . .

Anna reached for the door and slid the glass aside. "C'mon," she said, pulling him out into the morning.

The day shocked his senses. His eyes stung with how bright the sky glowed, and the chitter of birds and distant sounds of other houses of humans waking filled his ears. The grass beneath his feet was cool and dewy, the air perfumed with late-season blooms, lemon trees, and a salty tang from the nearby sea.

Tears slid down his own face, and for a long while, he stood there with his mate quietly, taking in the day. The garden grew busy with the activities of birds, butterflies, and bees, all flitting from the trees to the flowers. The air grew a little warmer as the sun climbed higher in the azure sky, and a breeze carried scents across the garden.

Heart so full it overran, Frey pulled his Anna close. He dropped his nose into her hair; she somehow smelled even warmer, even sweeter in the day, the sun bringing everything about her to vivid life.

Holding his whole world in his arms, he *felt* the bond. Oh, he'd always had the knowing, the surety that Anna was for him and he for her—but this was different. The same color but a different tone, perhaps. Lodged between his ribs, he felt exactly where he was bound to her. She filled up all the empty places inside him, claimed all that he was and would be, the good, the vulnerable, the ugly.

He may not have been able to wield magick like a fae or druid, but he sensed how his very soul reached out and tied itself to Anna's. Whatever the incantation did, however it coaxed the magick that gave him life from the Underhill and moored it to Anna, it worked.

I'm free.

The thought shocked him, and it came with an aftertaste of grief. He wouldn't rejoin his kin in the stone sleep, in the safe collective they kept for comfort. His mind was now separate from theirs, and he'd no longer feel their companionship.

It wouldn't be forever, he vowed. He would see to that.

He was blessed with his Anna, and he'd work to ensure his kin had that chance. They all deserved their freedom.

"How does it feel?" Anna asked, smiling up at him.

Jubilance surged through him, rousing his limbs from their stupor. He caught her up in his arms, spinning as he laughed and whooped. Anna laughed and yelped right back, throwing her arms around his neck as he jumped and howled and bounded through the garden.

With a running leap, he pumped his wings and threw them into the sky. He remained within the cover of the house and garden, but his soul roared with pleasure to feel the wind in his wings and have his arms full of his heartsong.

For a moment, it was just him and Anna, the wind catching their hair and sun warming their faces. Her smile was wide and just for him, and Frey couldn't help murmuring, "*Fy heulwen.*"

The sun in his sky, the warmth in his blood. She was his life, his sunshine, his heartsong.

"My Anna," he said, and he claimed her lips in a kiss, letting them float breezily to the ground. "It feels like home."

Epilogue

Four Months Later

Anna popped her siren-red lips in front of the mirror and gave herself a once over.

Happiness looks good on you.

And so did the slinky red number she'd picked out for date night. Never in a million years would she have thought to wear the body-hugging, strappy red dress, but something had come over her lately.

I wanna see his reaction to it. Okay, well, there was that. Frey never disappointed.

With extra room in the budget thanks to Carys and Gavren refusing to even hear the word *rent,* Anna had been able to splurge a bit on her wardrobe, and the red dress and strappy heels were one of the first things that called to her. She hadn't been brave enough to wear them out yet, but dinner at a swanky restaurant in SF felt like the perfect excuse.

Her little purse packed, Anna closed the door to their guesthouse/cottage/love nest and picked her way carefully across the courtyard to the main house. The late spring air hummed with vibrancy, just on the right side of warm. The sky above was streaked in lilac and peach, a pretty backdrop to the fairy lights Frey and Gavren had strung through the courtyard to help light her way.

They were always thinking of ways to make her life easier and safer, what with her dull human senses.

Living with a basically immortal, non-human couple the past few months had been . . . interesting. Carys and Gavren went above and beyond graciousness, and after the first month, the four of them had fallen into an easy coexistence, allowing them to be friends rather than hosts and guests.

The main thing Anna had to get her head around was how differently Carys and Gavren spent their time. Having lived for so long, with as much time as they had to do whatever they wanted, neither ever seemed overly hurried. If Carys wanted to read a book, she often sat in a comfy chair by a window and read the book. In full. If Gavren was working on one of his projects in the workroom he'd made out of the second garage, he often wouldn't emerge again until it was done. They didn't really need breaks and often forgot to take them with their minds focused elsewhere.

Despite this and being literally ancient, they didn't mind the new interruptions. In fact, they seemed to enjoy shifting to a more mortal schedule and often invited Anna and Frey for meals. The biggest adjustment was remembering that they couldn't run around naked in the courtyard playing sexy catch-me-if-you-can when Anna and Frey were home.

The first time the four of them ran into each other in the courtyard during one such romp, Carys had giggled as Frey slapped a hand over Anna's eyes. *"Ooh, I forgot. Inside we go, my love, before we embarrass the children,"* Carys had joked. After that, there'd been no more naked run-ins, though there were a few close calls.

Honestly, even though it mortified Anna in the moment, knowing that the two had been together for literally hundreds of years and were still hungry for each other melted Anna. *"Of course they are,"* Frey said when she mentioned it, his tone suggesting that she was silly to think otherwise, *"that's the way of guardians. We're always hungry for our heart-*

song." And that conversation led to their own sexy romp—as did most conversations, if she was being honest.

It was a bit wild, but after a while, they adapted fairly well to living together. Work at the museum helped, and whenever Carys and Gavren wanted to go in for the day, all four of them commuted via portal. She still wasn't used to the feeling of getting her molecules pulled apart and then put back together in the space of two seconds, but Carys was right, it was less painful than Bay Area traffic.

Opening one of the French doors, Anna stepped inside the main house. It smelled of sweetness and fruit; Carys must've been canning again. Preserving fruit and making jam was one of her current hobbies—one that she returned to and fell in love with every few decades or so, as she put it. The cottage's and all the museum docents' pantries were all stuffed with every kind of jam and preserve you could ever want.

Carys's blonde head was visible over the top of the plush sectional couch. As Anna approached, Captain's black head popped up from Carys's lap. After the first week, they'd stopped trying to contain Captain to the cottage and instead let him roam. Gavren assured her the property was warded and their animals knew to stay inside the boundary.

Anna had fretted at first, but when she saw how their two dogs minded, and heard about the hundreds of pets they'd kept during their lives, she conceded and let Captain live his best life. For the most part, he stuck to the cottage when she and Frey were home, but he also adored chasing butterflies and laying in sun puddles in the courtyard. She thought she was still his favorite person, but Carys was quickly gaining in the rankings. He loved to lay with her in the sun while she read since she didn't have to get up and move around much.

Hearing her coming, Carys looked up, too. "Ooh!" she exclaimed, turning so she could see Anna in her dress. "You look wonderful!"

"Thank you," Anna said with a blush.

"Go on, give us a twirl!"

She rolled her eyes but obliged. The dress didn't have much twirl, hugging her curves, but she spun on her heels to show off the fit.

"Your bum looks fabulous!"

Anna snorted in surprise. "Thank you?"

"Oh like you don't know." Carys winked. "You two don't stay out too late, though. I want you home by ten, young lady."

"Yes, Mama Carys." They shared a laugh over their ongoing joke, that Carys and Gavren were both easily old enough to be her parents many times over. Carys had a maternal quality about her, and more than once she'd fussed over both Anna and Frey, whether they were comfortable enough, eating enough, if they were happy and healthy and getting enough sunlight.

It was a new experience, to be fussed over and looked after, and it'd taken a while for Anna to warm up to it. At first it felt a bit invasive and overbearing, but given time, she came to enjoy the attention. Carys genuinely cared. She looked after her like a clanmate, and just as Anna came to appreciate what it meant to be Frey's heartsong, she now understood what it meant to be part of a guardian clan.

It didn't hurt either that working with Carys was downright fascinating. When Anna wasn't ogling all the amazing things Carys had collected over the centuries, she was listening raptly to anecdotes about this major event or that famous person. Anna had more than once asked Carys to describe their time in Renaissance Italy in painstaking detail and gobbled it all up.

The cataloging was moving along now that they had a system down, and there were definitely years of work to do. Once she had a good handle on it, she wanted to help Carys and Gavren document their long lives. It might never be shown to anyone else, but for posterity and their own memories, she thought it worthwhile. And she was greedy for more stories.

So yeah, life was good. So good, sometimes she had to center and remind herself it wasn't a dream, that she deserved good things, too.

There was still the threat of Glendower looming; they hadn't heard anything from him and he'd stopped frequenting the museum. They'd taken a little fieldtrip one weekend to scope out the property he owned in Carmel but found only a spacious, empty beach house. He'd gone to ground somewhere and taken Dragan with him.

Then there were her headaches. Gavren had been right, magick wasn't a silver bullet, and while he could ease her pain, he insisted she continue to seek treatment. He kept his promise, reading up on the literature on migraines and other chronic headaches, and gave her a list of things to ask her neurologist at each appointment. So far, the treatments were going well and she was managing her migraines much better.

Meaning she spent a whole lot less time nursing a headache—and that much more with her hunky gargoyle mate.

Speaking of which . . .

She found him at the front of the house chatting with Gavren. He looked devastating in pressed slacks that hugged his thick thighs and a button-up that molded to his glorious chest. He'd already rolled the sleeves up, revealing his corded forearms.

He knows how I feel about those.

She didn't know how every day with him just seemed to get better, but it did. Even bad days, when she had a migraine or they disagreed about something. Not everything was sunshine and rainbows, but it was *good*. Every morning she woke up in his arms grateful for him, and every night she fell asleep to the sound of his rumbling purr.

She'd harbored a small worry that being together so much might take some of the shine off their relationship. Frey and Gavren had worked for a whole week to create a metal pendant for Frey to wear, imbuing it with magick that he could use to glamour his appearance. It allowed him to fly without being noticed and walk amongst humans without issue—well, somewhat. People still saw how tall and striking he was, and she didn't blame anyone for doing a double-take when they saw him.

When Frey had first shown her the pendant and how it worked, swiping his thumb across the flat surface of the circle, she'd been downright floored to see him as a human. His features were the same but . . . not. His nose was the same shape, his eyes the same color, but he had a softer quality to him, something more distinctly human. Seeing him without fangs and horns and pointed ears had been so weird.

He'd gone all shy in her silence, quietly admitting he worried she'd like him better in this form. She was quick to assure him she preferred his real self. His human guise would take a while to get used to, but at least it meant he could have a more normal life and go out.

Using his glamour, he worked as a security guard at the museum. That meant spending a lot of their time together. Honestly, Anna loved it. There were days they weren't together that much, which was fine. They'd also found a few new hobbies they enjoyed on their own. But overall, she loved having her man nearby, loved sharing their lunches, even loved commuting on days Carys and Gavren didn't go in. He just made everything . . . better.

She knew her presence also made being amongst his kin a little easier on him. The first time he'd gone to the museum, they'd done so after hours, so he could walk through it at his own pace. Anna and Gavren had hung back, allowing the two gargoyles to walk through their kin. They shared words and memories about them, and Frey explained to Carys which guardians were mentally stronger and which were fading.

Using their combined magick, Gavren was formulating a spell that may allow Frey to again connect with his kin. They wanted to find some way to communicate with them, to give them hope and a means to alert that they'd sensed their heartsong.

All in all, every day was different, even if it followed routine. And Anna loved every minute of it with him. With his glamour and her headaches better managed, they had fun exploring SF, checking out different activities, and trying new things. It wasn't so bad getting out of her comfort zone with him, because he was like a big security blanket—plus, she loved seeing his reaction to things.

He absolutely loved chocolate but hated coffee, was viciously competitive at bumper cars, and amazing at finding the best shells when they beach combed. They'd strolled through the Monterey Bay Aquarium, the Santa Cruz Boardwalk, and Bodega Bay. They'd gone wine tasting in Napa and hiking in Yosemite.

He even made unenjoyable things bearable. After discussing it, they visited her mom's new place. Anna was surprised that, after a few months, her mom was still in the same place with the same guy. Wes wasn't her mom's usual boyfriend; he dressed for his age, held a steady job with the state, and liked to paddle board on the weekends. Shannon seemed to be doing . . . well? The afternoon hadn't exactly been comfortable, but Anna left feeling much better about it than she usually did. She genuinely wished her mom and Wes well, and her mom had mouthed *good job* to her over Frey's shoulder as he leaned down for a goodbye hug.

On that they could definitely agree.

Frey's gaze swung toward her the moment she appeared, and his wide, fanged smile made Anna's heart pitter-patter.

Gavren didn't seem to mind that Frey stopped talking mid-sentence, and instead threw her a wink as he slipped away.

Frey took her hands in his, holding them up so he could admire her. An appreciative purr rattled in his chest, and his gaze roved over her hungrily.

"You are beautiful, *fy nghân*."

"So are you," she said, admiring him right back.

With his pay from the security firm, Frey had modernized. He still wore the things she'd bought him in those first days, claiming they were his favorites. But he cleaned up real nice, too. Tooled silver caps for his horns so they wouldn't poke anything, and a set of small silver hoops for his pointed ears. Button-ups with slits cut in the back to accommodate his wings. Thin leather belts to emphasize his waist. And more than one new pair of gray sweatpants, just to get her hot and bothered.

The rest he spent on her, even though she insisted he didn't need to. She'd come to learn two important things—Frey was an avid gift-giver, and she needed to wield her power wisely. She only had to linger over something, show just a passing interest, and it was on her pillow, wrapped with a bow, by the next day.

He'd gone a bit crazy the first few months of getting his paychecks, and between that and what he'd said about his dwelling back in Wales, she'd deduced that Frey was a bit of a hoarder—or at least, a nester. He felt better when he could provide, and that meant gifts and home goods and every cozy blanket he came across. Anna eventually talked him into a joint savings account they could add to. *"For our future,"* she'd put it, and that resonated with him. Were there still gifts? Of course. But they were also saving up to build something together.

Pulling her close, Frey kissed behind her ear, where he rumbled, "I'm not sure I can stand other males seeing you in this, but I will enjoy their jealousy—but not nearly as much as I will peeling it off you later."

"Promise?"

"Oh, yes, *fy nghân,* it's a promise." He leaned down to claim a kiss, and before Anna knew it, she was balanced on her toes with her arms around his neck and his hands full of her backside.

"We're gonna be late. It took forever to get reservations," she managed to moan between kisses.

Frey bestowed one last lingering, devastating kiss before leaning back. He didn't release his hold though, fondling her peachy rear in the middle of the foyer without shame.

"Just so long as this place isn't one with tiny food." He'd been unimpressed with another high-end place they'd tried, where the portions were made for hamsters. They'd ended the night at a pizza place gorging on carby-cheesy goodness.

"Nope, they've got proper steaks, I checked the menu."

Anna went to wipe away the red lipstick transfer on his mouth, but he held her wrist.

"Leave it. Everyone will know you've staked your claim."

She still didn't quite understand why, but his need to show how he was hers never ceased to please her. Whether it was holding hands or carrying her purse or wearing coordinating colors, he always went out of his way to identify that they were together.

Finally letting her go, he tucked her hand into the crook of his arm and led her out into the attached garage.

Inside were the nondescript but luxury sedan Gavren drove, the hybrid compact SUV Carys drove, and Frey's biggest purchase: a behemoth of an SUV.

It turned out that the collection, as it should have been, was insured. Carys and Gavren were compensated for the "stolen" statues, but they'd been unsure what to do with the money, feeling it wasn't theirs to keep or spend. Anna suggested they put it aside for the guardians; so half had been invested for Dragan, for when they would hopefully free him, and the other was given to Frey.

He used the money to purchase his big blue behemoth. It was honestly one of the few vehicles that had fit him comfortably in the lot, and they'd managed to find an electric model that didn't guzzle gas. Because he didn't have legal paperwork, Frey had learned to drive with a combination of online classes and lessons from Gavren.

When Anna made a joke about driving with grandpa, Gavren had sniffed and said, *"Young lady, I've been driving since cars were invented."* Which only really proved her point.

Now, with a fancy fake ID and his own car, Frey drove them around a lot. He quite enjoyed it, and they spent many of their weekends cruising around California. Anna loved being a passenger princess. The SUV was spacious and comfortable, and she had the front passenger side all configured to her. She navigated and sight-saw with glee as Frey drove them around Tiburon or down the coast or into SF.

And she admitted, watching him drive, his wrist resting on the wheel, sunglasses shading his eyes, and his free hand wrapped around her thigh, always got her blood pumping.

Frey opened the door and helped her climb inside. He even held out the seatbelt and buckled her in, making sure to cop a feel the entire way.

Anna giggled and ran her fingers along the sharp edge of his jaw. "Dinner first," she reminded him.

Frey made a show of grumbling. "This better be good steak."

It was, in fact, good steak. Overpriced, but still good.

Anna was always happy to have date night at a local diner or family place, and they'd had plenty exploring exhibits or seeing films. Once in a while, though, it was nice to get dolled up and try a place she'd never in her wildest dreams thought about going to before.

And, okay, it was an excuse to see Frey dressed up, too.

The bistro was all warm colors, with deep booths of buttoned dark red suede, tables stained a rich mahogany, drapes of a sumptuous red velvet trimmed in yellow fringe, and vintage chandeliers dripping with crystals and golden light. It gave old art deco speakeasy, which Anna loved.

The booths and chairs were sturdy, a must for any dining gargoyle. Anna had reserved a corner booth, allowing them to sit next to each other rather than across. Frey wasn't a fan of sitting a table away, especially not while out and about where other people (men) could see them. Even sitting close together, he was always touching her somehow, holding her hand or putting his arm around her or leaning in for a kiss.

If he hadn't been so handsy himself, she might've been a little embarrassed over how much she reached for him, too. From her past relationships, Anna didn't consider herself a touchy-feely person, but she couldn't help but reach for him. The way he smiled to see it was its own reward, and his warmth beneath her fingers was always a comfort.

When he reached for her hand on the booth as they sat enjoying the final bites of their meal, she was ready, her fingers sliding into place between his.

"Most excellent," Frey sighed, leaning back against the booth with a contented pat to his stomach.

Anna hid a grin. She was going to get that catchphrase printed on a mug, T-shirt, everything for his birthday in summer.

He tugged on her hand, coaxing her to join him reclining in the booth, but Anna resisted. He looked at her curiously, but she only arched a brow.

It's now or never, she told herself, butterflies swirling in her stomach.

"Just going to run to the bathroom," she explained, slipping out of the booth with her purse.

"Fine," he huffed, "but hurry back. I'm ordering the chocolate cake."

She didn't know how he had room for a heavy chocolate lava cake after the dinner they just ate, but then again, Anna never said no to chocolate—and neither did Frey. They were perfect together.

"Get two forks this time," she told him.

A feline smirk was her only answer before she weaved through the bistro to the bathrooms at the back. He enjoyed getting only one fork and feeding her dessert. She enjoyed it, too—just not the sounds that came out of her in public when he did.

Inside the bathroom, Anna ducked into one of the stalls, pleased to find it was deep and dark and had an actual door. She wanted a little privacy for this part.

Blushing from her head to her toes, she hung her purse from the door hook and fished out the little toy she'd brought along. Anna had always been a fan of toys and had converted Frey, too. There were times when he just couldn't wait for her to be as ready as she needed to be, so they used toys to get her there. She'd branched out from her trusty bullet, and now had a new toy to try.

She was trying new things. Getting out of her comfort zone. Anna was *living* and having fun—because she knew, no matter what, that Frey would be there. He would catch her.

That's all she needed to know.

Frey grew more impatient with every moment his mate was out of his sight. It'd taken several outings before he was comfortable letting her use the facilities without following her. She'd been horrified when he tried the first time and promptly sent him back to their table.

In the months since the attack, Frey had slowly begun to trust that Glendower wasn't around every corner, just waiting to snatch Anna away. That he was able to go with her in the day helped. As did his training with Gavren.

In their time together, Frey had come to like and admire Gavren. The fae was selective in his words and often stern, but he was also patient with a quick wit. Frey enjoyed their training together, as well as their sparring and work on projects. And it pleased him to see how beloved Carys was by her fae heartsong; if nothing else, Frey could respect a man who treated his woman right.

Although he still couldn't wield magick like the fae, with Gavren's guidance, Frey was able to harness it in ways his people never knew. Controlling a glamour had opened up the human world to him, and he was eternally grateful to have not just the day with his Anna but a life as well. Grateful too that he could use his magick to prevent himself from breeding her—at least until she was ready.

He could also extend his senses with his magick, feel for dangers or threats. He'd avoided several potential car accidents thanks to that and even stopped an assault in progress while they were walking in SF one night. The heightened senses allowed him to feel secure that his mate was safe in the facilities.

But taking a long time.

He'd ordered their cake and taken a bite out of it by the time she returned.

Goddesses, he could watch her hips sway in that tight red dress for the rest of his life and die a happy man.

She slid gracefully back into the booth, and Frey lost no time pulling her across the soft fabric into his side.

"Let us eat, then back to the car. I need you alone," he rumbled into her ear.

A comely blush pinkened her cheeks, and batting her lashes at him, she pulled her phone from her purse and placed it on the table.

"Not too fast, though. I have something for us to try."

She pressed her breasts into his side, and Frey knew her games well enough to know when his Anna was feeling playful and needy. He lived for times like these. A grin teased his lips, and he looked down to where she tapped at her phone on the table—pausing to admire how the dress molded to her big breasts, of course. If the fabric had been darker and hidden the evidence, he might've sucked on them through the dress in the parking lot, but Anna had demurred and told him, *"After."*

He'd keep her to that.

Frey tried to pay attention to what she was telling him, he really did, but she was alluring to the point of distraction. He always found his heartsong beautiful, whether she was fresh out of a shower or taking her shoes off for the day or a grumbling lump who didn't want to get out of bed. Yet there was something to this date night; she always did her hair and wore a special outfit.

The red dress was undoubtedly his favorite.

He enjoyed anything they did together, though. His Anna was always finding things for them to do together, helping introduce him to the modern world. Every day, he was that much more confident in building their life; with the help of his clan, he was learning who he was in this world. And he had faith they'd do the same for the rest of his kin, too.

"Make sense?"

She blinked those big brown eyes at him expectantly. He rumbled and pulled her close to kiss her fragrant hair.

"I touch the screen," he replied, really all he remembered from her explanation.

"You touch the screen," she agreed. "Any way you want." She leaned her head back on his shoulder, gazing up at him with eyes gone sultry. Her breathing had deepened too, bringing his attention back to those pretty breasts.

It was only with passing interest that he tapped on her phone a few times.

Anna nearly jumped out of his arms, and he just caught a faint buzzing from under the table.

Her blush went almost violent, and Frey's heart nearly stopped.

He traced the pad of one finger in slow circles on the phone. Anna shivered against him, her red lips falling open.

"Oh wow," she breathed, "that's intense."

It all finally came to him. She'd left to put one of her toys in place, a toy he now controlled with touches to the phone.

A wicked grin spread wide across his face. It was like he was petting her cunt, right there in public. His Anna was often a shy thing about open displays of affection, so to know she'd planned this, had meant to drive him wild in this booth by playing with her—

His cock kicked against his trouser zipper.

"Mmm," he hummed, "*fy nghariad bach drwg*."

She smiled shakily, still shivering as he continued to draw little circles and figures along the phone screen. His Anna put on a brave face, taking up the one fork to cut a bite of cake. She managed to slide it into her mouth, those plush lips closing around the tines before the tip of her tongue pressed against them in a slow lick.

Frey tapped the phone three times in quick succession in retribution.

Anna startled, and he moved his hand from her hip to the curve of her belly. He could just feel the vibrations of the little toy, and ran his finger along the screen to experiment.

He played with her for the better part of a half-hour like that, seeing what motions drew which vibrations and reactions. When he knew she drew close to release, he'd set her phone aside to instead feed them cake. She made little moans of protest, hiding the noises behind her hand so the other diners wouldn't hear. But Frey heard, his blood nearly boiling by the time the cake was gone.

He sealed the last bite with a kiss, tasting the rich chocolate on her lips as he swirled his finger across the screen. Her fist clutched at his shirt, and he swallowed her needy little moans greedily, wanting to—

Their waiter cleared her throat.

He and Anna looked up sheepishly and accepted the check.

As Frey took care of the bill, Anna fished several paper bills from her purse. "Let's tip her well. That got a bit more R-rated than I'd meant."

"Really?" he purred into her ear. "What did you mean by doing something so wicked? Surely you meant for me to lay you out on this table and fuck you senseless."

She shuddered with lust in his arms. "Car. Let's get to the car."

"And what will we do there?"

The look she shot him would've been evil if he couldn't smell how thick her desire already ran. She'd practically be dripping on the short walk to the car, and a purr exploded from his chest to think of her slick running down her thighs.

Yet another dessert.

Their bill paid and waiter tipped handsomely, they made their way from the restaurant. Anna seemed steady on her feet now that she'd reclaimed her phone, but Frey settled his hand at the small of her back, a claim and a reminder.

The walk to the car was thankfully short and the parking lot fairly deserted. The cool evening air did nothing to ease Frey's burning skin as he opened the passenger door and helped his mate climb inside.

Rather than walk around to his own side, though, he crowded her on the seat, pulling her legs around him.

"Frey, someone will—"

"No one will see, *fy nghân.*" He'd tear their eyes out if they did.

Rucking up her dress, his hand delved between her thighs. The heat of her soft skin scorched him as he moved the soaked gusset of her panties away. *Ah, there you are.* He explored the toy with questing fingers, feeling how one node rested against her clitoris and the other part was buried deep inside her.

Anna braced herself on his shoulders, her face gone tight with need. Her lips rounded with surprise when he pulled the toy from her body and replaced it with his fingers. Two swirled inside her, sliding easily in her slick, while he ran his thumb over her clitoris.

"Frey!"

"Your toys are amusing, but you know your pleasure is *mine,*" he growled against her throat.

Anna keened and fell back across the center console, back bowing as her hips rolled and rolled and rolled through her orgasm. Frey let her milk his fingers, feeling how her muscles clenched and drew him deeper still, but had no mercy on her clitoris, working it beneath his thumb.

She was absolutely glorious in her pleasure, hair thrown back, breasts thrust skyward, thighs trembling with release. Her heels dug into his flanks and her nails into his forearms, making Frey hiss in vicious pleasure.

When she finally came down, her breathing heavy and her body still quaking, Frey pulled his fingers from her and replaced the toy inside. Anna moaned as she watched him lick his fingers clean.

"Holy shit," she muttered.

Frey grinned, his hunger for her a coiling, wild thing inside him. "I won't be having you home by ten."

Instead, he drove. Under a waxing moon, they drove through the city, the lights gleaming on the dark waters of the bay. He drove them north over the bridge, one hand on the wheel and the other gripped tightly on Anna's thigh.

The toy's battery had died a few miles ago, but Anna practically squirmed in her seat, and Frey was just as impatient. His cock throbbed angrily behind his zipper, greedy for his mate.

He drove north along the coast for a while until he found what he wanted—an empty lookout vista. Pulling into the dark lot, he parked in a far spot that overlooked the sea.

His gaze swung to Anna, catching her moonlit smile.

Goddesses, she's more beautiful than all the stars.

Frey pulled one of the levers on the side of his seat and fell back about a foot as Anna hiked up her dress and climbed over the center console. He helped her swing a leg over to straddle him and then filled his palms with his mate's supple flesh.

"*Ffyc*, you're too beautiful for words," he rumbled, hands running up and down her thighs.

With her dress gathered nearly to her waist, Frey could just spy her panties. Hooking them with a claw, he tore the flimsy fabric away and brought it to his nose. Her scent punched through him, making his mouth water.

"That's four on the panty count," she told him, though her tone was much too sultry to be scolding.

They'd made a deal between them—they kept count of how many of her panties he ripped and at six, he had to get her new ones. She'd joked a few days ago she should just sign up for a subscription service to make things easier.

"Your mistake for wearing them at all," he teased. His fingers found her soaking slit, and she gasped as he began to work three of them inside her.

"Did you like it? The toy?" she asked breathlessly as her hips began to rock.

"Ohh yes, *fy nghân.* I liked it very much. You've given me many ideas."

"Can't wait," she muttered as she attacked his belt. He knew she meant it, even if it was her who was now distracted.

He meant to say something smart, but then her fist closed around his cock and all the sound he made was a choked groan. Her hands were ruthless as they worked him, soft palms caressing the shaft and nails scraping gently at his bollocks. When she smoothed her thumb along the slit, he saw more stars than there were in the sky.

"Inside, Anna. Now."

"So bossy," she huffed, even as she notched his cockhead at her entrance.

Frey watched in rapture as he breached her. His cock had gone nearly purple with how badly it needed her, and quickly the length of his shaft disappeared inside her swollen pink cunt. Frey let out a low, resonant purr, his hands kneading at her hips.

Anna braced herself on his shoulders and fell the rest of the way down his cock.

With a moan, Frey's head fell back on the seat. Surrounded in her warmth, he was nothing but hers. Every breath was for her, every beat of his heart was for her. All he was and ever would be.

She began to move, and he couldn't lay still. His hips thrust up on her downstroke, earning him another gasp of pleasure. With his hands full of her hips, he moved her as he wanted, making her meet every pounding thrust. Their slick dripped from her, soaking her thighs and his lap. The cabin filled with the scent of sex and echoes of Anna's keening moans.

The sound pushed Frey beyond thought. He was only movement and need and pleasure. He sat up and sucked at the skin of her throat, tasting her sounds.

One hand frantically pulled at the strap of her dress then hooked on the neckline to pull it down. Her heavy breast spilled free of the cup and into his hungry mouth. He sucked and licked and gorged himself on her taste, rolling her nipple along his fang.

Her fingers tugged at his hair to the point of pain and found the sensitive rim of his horns. With just the press of her thumbs there, Frey broke.

He found her clitoris just in time, determined to take her with him. He thrust up inside her again, again, making them whole, making them one. He came inside his mate and never wanted to stop.

Anna's mouth spread wide in a silent scream, and her muscles clenched around him tighter than a fist. She went rigid in his arms, her pulse throbbing beneath his lips, and she clutched at his horns as she came and came and came.

He was lost to her.

Frey poured everything he was into his mate, his pleasure, his hopes, his love. He held everything in his arms, and his heart burst with gratitude for her, for the life they would live. Together.

With a final moan, she collapsed against his chest, body spent and trembling.

Frey carded his claws through her hair, cradling her head over the heart that beat for her. "I love you, my Anna."

She hummed happily and lifted up just enough to kiss the center of his chest. "I love you, too, heartsong."

June Parkhurst stared at her phone, considering what to write. She didn't want to come off as desperate or prying, but she also didn't want to let this go quite yet.

After leaving a very dramatic voicemail on June's phone months ago, Anna Kincaid from the museum had since called to tell her everything was just a misunderstanding. June had texted a few times after that and gotten nothing of value back.

Whatever happened, Anna had clammed up again.

And now, with her project nearly complete, soon June wouldn't have any real reason to be at the museum.

Grumbling, June set her phone back on the kitchen island. What else was there to say? How could she ask the questions she needed to without giving too much away?

"I don't think she's going to talk to me."

A considering rumble emanated from the shadows. The soft overhead light caught first on the great arching horns, then the massive swooping wings. Wide, powerful shoulders came next, and clawed hands came to rest on bulging biceps as he crossed his arms.

"I think it's time you take me there," said Alaric.

June sighed. She'd been putting it off because of the obvious risks, but with her only lead dried up, she had to admit, "Yeah, I guess you're right."

To be continued . . .

Glossary of (mostly Welsh) Phrases, Places, and People

Albion—ancient, often poetic name for Great Britain

Angles—Germanic tribe that invaded and settled eastern Britain in the 5th c.; their tribe and language is where we get "England" and "English"

Beltane—Celtic festival celebrated on May 1, the first day of summer

brawd—brother, friend

caer—castle, fort, fortress, especially of stone

Caerdyf—old spelling/name for Cardiff, modern capital of Wales

Caer Gwyn—Carys and Gavriel's home, translates roughly to "Castle of Magic"

cân fy nghalon—song of my heart

cariad—love, beloved, darling, sweetheart, lover

Cymru—Welsh name for Wales

Cymry—name of the Welsh people for themselves

derwydd—druid

druid—religious/spiritual leaders of Celtic society; soothsayers, healers, advisors

dwi adref—I'm home

Eryri—traditional name for the region of Snowdonia in Wales

fae/fairy/faerie—supernatural beings often associated with nature, the underworld, and magic; thought to be the original peoples of Britain and Ireland; called the Tuatha De Danann in Irish folklore

Fe godwn ni eto—we will rise again, popular Welsh motto for supporters of Welsh independence

ffyc—fuck

fidchell (Irish), *gwyddbwyll* (Welsh)—ancient Celtic strategic board game played between 2 opponents

Fomorians—monstrous beings from Irish folklore, believed to be the ancient enemies of the Tuatha De Danann; they were sometimes described as giants or sea raiders

fy enaid—my soul

fy enaid hoff cytûn prydferth—my beautiful soulmate

fy enaid hoff cytûn rhyfeddol, prydferth—my wonderful, beautiful soulmate

fy heulwen—my sunshine

fy nghalon—my heart

fy nghân—my song

fy nghariad—my love

fy nghariad bach drwg—my wicked little love

Gorsedd—a meeting or meeting place, usually a high mound; has also come to mean throne

harddach na'r môr a'r awyr—lovelier than the sea and sky

Llyn Tegid (Bala Lake)—a glacial lake in the Eryri (Snowdonia) region of Wales

mae fy nghalon yn eiddo i ti—my heart is yours

mae hud yn llifo yn fy ngwaed—magic flows in my blood

Morrígan—Celtic Irish goddess of battle, war, and fate; often depicted as a crow; portends doom and victory in battle

mwydyn—worm

Owain Glyndŵr—medieval Welsh prince and politician who led one of the last major rebellions against English rule in Wales; the last Welshman to hold the title Prince of Wales

Pritani—ancient name for the Celtic/Brittonic people of Great Britain

Rhiannon—magical female character of the *Pedair Cainc y Mabinogi*, the earliest collection of Welsh prose stories; associated with horses and may be derived from an older Celtic or Gallic horse goddess

rhyfelwr—warrior

rydych chi'n dilyn yr hen ffyrdd?—you follow the old ways?

Samhain—Celtic festival celebrated on October 31, last day of the harvest

Saxons—Germanic tribe that invaded and settled southeastern Britain in the 5th c.

Silures—one of several Celtic tribes that inhabited southern Wales before and during the Roman invasion

ti sydd â'm calon—you have my heart

Titania—one of several names attributed to the Fairy Queen, most famously by Shakespeare; the female ruler of the fae in medieval literature

Y ddraig goch ddyry cychwyn—the red dragon shall lead, Welsh motto that appeared on coinage in the 20th c.

Chapter Notes

Chapter 1

1. In architecture, there's a bit of a difference between gargoyles and grotesques, and we often conflate and mix them up. Gargoyles are a gothic architectural feature, often a bestial or animal figure, that includes a spout to carry rainwater off the roof and away from the building so it doesn't drip down the stone walls and infiltrate the masonry. Gargoyle derives from the French word *gargouille*, which in English is close to "throat." Grotesques are also a feature of gothic architecture and include fantastical and mythical creature statues that adorn buildings. These can be carved into the wall or free-standing, but they don't include the water spout aspect. They are often thought to have been carved and placed on buildings to ward off evil spirits.

2. Gorsedd is a Welsh word for "throne." It is believed it could be a meeting of sorts, where a ruler would reside at a higher place (like on a throne or hill). Today, the Gorsedd Cymru (The Gorsedd of Wales) is an organization of Welsh poets and literati that celebrate Welsh culture and promote other Celtic cultures and arts.

3. Albion is an old, often poetic name for Great Britain. Several Latin and Greek sources use the term to refer to Great Britain before the more recognizable Britannia came into use. In this series, Albion is used to refer both to the Celtic lands inhabited by Celtic cultures before and during Roman occupation, as well as the human realm (as opposed to Faerie, the realm of the fae).

Chapter 3

1. Pritani is a reconstructed name for the ethnic groups living in Celtic Britain before the Roman invasion. Through several linguistic grapevines, it may have come from an old Welsh word meaning "people of the forms," and perhaps informed the Latin term for the Picts (an Celtic ethnic group in what we now consider Scotland), often taken to mean "painted people." Pritani is thought to be linked the Roman term Britanni and Britannia.

Chapter 7

1. After a few generations, the gargoyles eventually moved from the human villages into their own communities, called clanhomes. About a dozen clans were spread across southern Wales at the time of the fae attack. The clans gathered together for celebrations such as a Gorsedd, as well as to go to battle with the Pritani against invaders. Frey's clanhome was situated in the sea cliffs near modern Cardiff.

Chapter 8

1. Black cats are often last to be adopted from rescues and shelters. There is still a bit of superstition around black cats (which is one reason many shelters won't adopt out black cats in the month of October—if you believe any of this superstition or have participated in black cat hate, sleep with one eye open, I'm coming for you). Others find black cats not as photogenic as other colors of cats. This is ridiculous. Love your fur baby for who they are. Don't get a pet for social media. Void monsters are perfect little kitties who deserve to be loved.

Chapter 9

1. Wales is the English term for the country. Through the etymologic grapevine of Latin, Proto-German, and Old English, we get Wales. The

term was originally used by the Anglo-Saxon conquerors of Britain to refer to the native Britons and soon came to encompass the western regions that now make up what we consider Wales. In Welsh, to the Welsh people, the country is called Cymru and its people are the Cymry.

2. Rice cultivation made its way to Europe in several waves, notably in the 3rd century BCE from the Middle East with the campaigns of Alexander the Great and with the Moors in the 10th century CE up the Iberian Peninsula. It was known about in Classical times but few, especially in Northern Europe, would have seen or eaten it. Grains were much more common.

Chapter 10

1. Because they often worked with wood, Celtic and Anglo-Saxon sites are tricky to find. Most archaeological sites from the time only offer some pottery sherds and the outline of the iconic Saxon roundhouse. By comparison, the Roman and Norman times that bookend the Anglo-Saxon period in Britain are much better documented thanks to the more numerous stone buildings and metal items. Earlier pagan Anglo-Saxon periods are almost as mysterious as Celtic culture, and much of what we know about them comes from outside sources like the Romans.

Chapter 12

1. Owain Glyndŵr (1354–1415) was a Welsh rebel, leader, and lawyer and the last Welsh Prince of Wales. After a land dispute with an English neighbor in 1400, Glyndŵr began a revolt to retake lands given to English lords. As a descendant of several royal Welsh lines, Glyndŵr was able to unite the regions of Wales into one independent country for a brief period. Henry IV of England launched a counter campaign and was eventually able to recapture Wales after several years of war. Glyndŵr waged a guerilla war for years and was never betrayed by the Welsh despite a large bounty being placed on

his head. He disappeared from the records and is believed to have died in 1415.

Chapter 15

1. Art theft is a fairly high-stakes crime, and much of the art is recovered as it's difficult to sell on. However, there are several instances of art being stolen and going missing. The most famous of these are the many pieces still missing after being stolen by the Nazis in World War II. Much of Europe's art was appropriated (stolen) to fill a proposed museum within the German motherland. Much of this art was recovered, famously in an Austrian salt mine, but there are still several famous pieces missing, such as Raphael's *Portrait of a Young Man.* No one knows if they survived the war or are now in private hands. More recently, in 1990, thirteen pieces were stolen from the Isabella Stewart Gardner Museum in Boston, and none of the pieces have been seen since.

Chapter 16

1. Medieval manuscripts are works of art. As important as the text written within the pages are the illustrations drawn in the margins. These drawings or doodles (called marginalia) are somewhat mysterious and often humorous. From the 13th to 15th centuries, some manuscripts include scenes of armored knights fighting snails. Why? We aren't totally sure! The marginalia don't always have anything at all to do with the subject matter of the texts. Other fun drawings include cats doing farmwork and lions playing a lute.

2. Many cultures throughout the world have a tree of life motif. It is closely related to the sacred tree motif and the tree of knowledge, such as the one to heaven in Genesis or Yggdrasil in Norse mythology. In the Celtic tradition, the tree of life motif is a popular design that symbolizes wisdom and strength and is often associated with oak trees.

Chapter 27

1. In Irish folklore, the Fomorians are the ancient enemies of the fae, or Tuatha De Danann. They are said to come from under the sea and are monstrous in form. They fought several wars against the fae before finally being defeated. In this series, the Fomorians were finally defeated not by the fae but waves of humans coming to reclaim the British Isles. The first gargoyles were carved to retain some of the Fomorians' monstrousness, and combine Fomorian, fae, and human features.

Chapter 29

1. One of the reasons the *Mona Lisa* is so famous is because she was actually stolen in the early 20th c. The painting had been in France since Leonardo da Vinci entered the service of Francis I of France 1516; the painting and several other works were gifted to the king upon Leonardo's death in 1519. The pieces eventually made their home in the Louvre, which was originally a royal palace. In 1908, Vincenzo Peruggia, an Italian expatriate, began work at the Louvre and, mistakenly believing the *Mona Lisa* was stolen from Italy during the Napoleonic Wars, he used his access to steal the painting in 1911. For 2 years the painting sat in his Parisian apartment. Finally, in 1913, he smuggled it back to Italy, where he tried to sell it on, believing he was doing a national service by returning the Leonardo to Italy. Art dealers recognized the piece and its significance and alerted authorities. The painting was returned to Paris after a tour of Italy. The *Mona Lisa* was already famous before the theft but it going missing became an international news story, and its eventual discovery and return caused a sensation and introduced a whole new audience to the *Mona Lisa* and work of Leonardo.

Chapter 33

1. A reminder that Gavren was the common name used for Gavriel by

his fellow fae. Gavriel is his true name, whispered to his mother at his birth by the goddess Danu. Fae jealously guard their true names, as to know it is to have power over them. Carys is the only being alive who knows Gavriel's true name.

2. Blink and you'll miss it, but yes, in this story, I'm implying that it's the Fomorians that caused the Bronze Age Collapse (c. 1,200–900 BCE). Many historians attribute part of the Bronze Age Collapse to a mysterious group known only as the Sea People. Ancient Egyptian, Hittite, and other Eastern Mediterranean sources speak of these sea raiders and their destructive attacks beginning in the 12th c. BCE. It is believed that these attacks exacerbated already strained economies and cultures, leading to widespread collapse. It is unknown who exactly the Sea Peoples were, though historians believe they weren't one ethnic group but different waves of opportunistic raiders from the Western Mediterranean, such as Sicily and Cyprus, or the Aegean. In this series, just for fun, I imagine it's the Fomorians, attacking from the sea as they're wont to do, but are finally beat back by the fae in one of their many wars. And yes, I also imagine the fae bopping around the ancient world and getting a kick out of humans considering them divine beings.

Epilogue

1. Toys are fun and a great option for solo and group play, but a word of caution! Toys with remote control options like the ones in the epilogue can be fun but they also aren't regulated and protected like other devices with Bluetooth/Wi-fi capabilities. There are many cases of these devices getting hacked! Information can get hacked and worse. So when buying and using these types of toys, be sure they're protected like you would any other internet device.

Author's Note

Hello! Thank you so much for reading *Heartsong!* I hope you enjoyed Anna and Frey's story. What a ride!

This was my first big foray into PNR and I had such a great time. The narrative styles I got to play with, with a more modern voice through Anna, was such fun! It was also so amazing to see Carys and Gavriel return and have their little moments throughout the story. They're very lucky to have Anna now, because let's face it, they're both pretty obviously not modern humans.

I knew from the beginning that Anna would be a challenging heroine. On the one hand, her suffering from migraines is extremely close to home. I too spent my 20s suffering with migraines and continue to struggle with them. I'm grateful more treatments are becoming available and more of us are getting the help we need. Everything Anna experiences and thinks about her migraines are thoughts and experiences I've had myself. Chronic pain isn't something anyone truly understands until they go through it themsevles. It's exhausting, emotionally, mentally, and physically. Waking up to a migraine, knowing you're going to suffer the rest of the day, is so disheartening. Most people mean well but they don't understand what it's like to deal with the pain on such a regular basis. Even medical professionals. We have to be our own advocates and seek the treatment we deserve. Because we don't have to live this way.

I also knew Anna would be a challenge because she's so different from me in many other ways. Her childhood was the exact opposite of mine. It took some time for her and I to understand each other. Her motivations are so different from mine, and it took time to understand that she wouldn't approach a situation the same way I would, nor have the same feelings about it. I absolutely love her for that.

And Frey. Oh, Frey. I was determined to write a hero who's a bit of a butthead. Less golden retriever, more akita. I love how arrogant and stubborn he is. He's a gargoyle who knows he's hot shit and he's not afraid to use that to his advantage. I hope you enjoyed him and his gray sweatpants.

I tried to do right by California and the Bay Area in this story. It felt important to locate it somewhere I knew, and I'm so grateful to Abigail for providing invaluable SF insight to make everything believable! I love my home state and am thrilled to place a story here.

On that note, the story will continue with June and Alaric! How did their story begin? Where did she find another gargoyle? Stay tuned!

In the meantime, my next release is *Ironling* in Summer 2024. Back to the Monstrous World we go!

Thank you so much for reading! If you enjoyed this story, I'd so appreciate it if you'd consider leaving a review. Reviews are so important in helping spread the word about a book and getting it in front of more eyeballs. Thanks again!

Come say hi on social media or check out my website, www.sewendelauthor.com, for more on my stories and to explore awesome merch!

Thanks so much!

Acknowledgements

I'd also like to take a moment to thank some of the people who made this book possible!

A huge thank you to Mita and Abigail, my writing besties and the best beta readers out there! They helped me get these characters where I wanted them to go and I'm always so grateful for their insights and guidance.

Thank you to Leah, my awesome PA, who helped me go from hobbyist to big girl author with my own website and everything.

Thank you to Magaidh, who was lovely enough to reach out with Welsh resources, and to Cymen for editing the Welsh language snippets that appear in this book. I feel so much better knowing professionals took a look!

I'm also so grateful to my amazing ARC team, y'all are amazing!

And I have to mention too the amazing artists who helped bring Anna and Frey to life. A huge thank you to Beth Gilbert, the stunningly talented artist who illustrated the cover. I also want to thank Carly, Flavia, Lucia, and more, you're all so amazing and I'm so grateful for the care you've taken with my book babies!

About the Author

S. E. is a California native who grew up with animals; her ginger tabby is her current writing partner and lets her know when it's time to take a break (by laying on her keyboard). She graduated from the University of California, Davis with a master's in creative writing and uses all her available time to build worlds, characters, and their stories. She enjoys animal rescue shows, almost everything in Trader Joe's, and all the beautiful landscapes of California.

Other Works

A Time of War and Demons (House of the Rising Sun, Book 1)

Aerie (Broken Wings Duet, Book 1), fantasy romance novel

Haven (Broken Wings Duet, Book 2), fantasy romance novel

Stone Hearts (War of the Underhill, Book 1), historical monster/fantasy romance novella

Halfling (Monstrous World, Book 1), monster/fantasy romance novel

Heartsong (War of the Underhill, Book 2), monster paranormal romance novel

Ironling (Monstrous World, Book 2), monster/fantasy romance novel, Summer 2024

Stay in Touch

If you'd like to stay in touch, come on over to socials and say hi! I'm around on most platforms as se.wendel.author, and I'm most active on Instagram. Come check it out to find out about what I'm working on, get some reading recommendations, and get spammed with pictures of my cat. What's not to love?

You can also check out all my books, commissioned art, and book merch shop on my author website! Lots of good stuff over there!